Una-Mary Parker
Drawing extensiv
social editor of *Ta*
social scene, writer and broadcaster Una-Mary Parker has crafted a dramatic and compulsive novel of suspense. Her previous international bestsellers, *Riches*, *Scandals*, *Temptations*, *Enticements*, *The Palace Affair*, *Forbidden Feelings*, *Only The Best*, *A Guilty Pleasure* and *False Promises*, are all available from Headline and have been extensively praised:

'A compulsive romantic thriller' *Sunday Express*

'Deliciously entertaining' *Sunday Telegraph*

'Scandal . . . saucy sex and suspense' *Daily Express*

'This novel has everything – intrigue, romance, ambition, lust' *Daily Mail*

'Blue-blood glitz at its best' *Prima*

'Will keep you glued to the page' *Daily Express*

'The characters ring true and the tension mounts nicely' *Sunday Express*

Also by Una-Mary Parker

Riches
Scandals
Temptations
Enticements
The Palace Affair
Forbidden Feelings
Only The Best
A Guilty Pleasure
False Promises

Taking Control

Una-Mary Parker

HEADLINE

First published in 1996
by HEADLINE BOOK PUBLISHING

First published in paperback in 1996
by HEADLINE BOOK PUBLISHING

10 9 8 7 6 5 4 3 2 1

ISBN 0 7472 5139 8

Typeset by Keyboard Services, Luton, Beds

Printed and bound in Great Britain by
Cox & Wyman Ltd, Reading, Berks

HEADLINE BOOK PUBLISHING
A division of Hodder Headline PLC
338 Euston Road
London NW1 3BH

Once again, this is for
Baba and Buffy
and their families
with all my love

PART ONE

June

One

It had happened on a night such as this, Sophie reflected as she stepped on to the terrace of La Madeleine. The garden was illuminated as it had been then, with concealed spotlights and little lanterns, but tonight she was more aware of those dark shady places that led to the olive grove and the blackness of the wych-elms and lime trees that enclosed the property like impenetrable walls than she was of the beauty of the garden. What had made her recall the dreadful happenings of that night with such disturbing clarity? She felt gripped once again with anxiety, tense and alert to every sound. A week ago she'd imagined herself safe, now she wondered if she'd ever feel safe again.

Of course it was very warm tonight, as it had been then, with only a gentle breeze wafting down from the hills of Grasse. There was also the heady perfume of the nicotiana which glowed like milky stars in the shadows of the mimosa trees – how it had filled the air with its heart-breaking sweetness that night! She shivered uneasily in spite of the balmy air and the warm stones beneath her bare feet. Going slowly down the terrace steps to the lower level where the large pool with its underwater lighting looked like a giant aquamarine set in the honey-coloured stones, Sophie stood in silhouette against the green glow, a tall slender figure in a softly patterned skirt and a peasant blouse, with her long dark hair pinned back.

She had loved this place, once. Now it had changed and the ghosts of the past lurked in every shadow with a thousand watchful eyes. Tomorrow she planned to face him and bring to an end the lies and the heartbreak, but would that erase what had happened?

It was the phone call, exactly a year ago, that had started it all. She'd arrived at La Madeleine the previous afternoon, flying over from London for a two-week holiday, her first since her divorce from Brock. The next morning she'd driven into Nice to stock up on provisions because her family were arriving the following afternoon. When she'd been married to Brock Duval he'd looked after the running of La Madeleine, the flat in London, the apartment in New York; every facet of their lives, in fact, during the twelve years of their marriage. Now it was up to her and she was relishing her new-found independence and freedom.

Brock had always treated her like a child, in his kind, benevolent way, thinking he was protecting her from the rough edge of life. In the end it was the one thing that had driven them apart. That, and his unwillingness to have children. It had been a painful time for both of them. Brock, twenty years older than Sophie, was acutely conscious that he had failed in marriage for the second time, while she felt a deep sense of disappointment and regret. She'd loved Brock passionately when she'd been twenty-one, insisting on marrying him although her mother had said it would never last. Her mother had been right. She still cared for Brock, but as a father figure now, which is perhaps what he'd been for her all along, although she hadn't realised it.

'The telephone, Madame,' Hortense, the housekeeper, had announced, breaking into Sophie's thoughts as she unloaded the shopping from the Renault.

'Who is it?' Visions of her mother and stepfather being delayed or her sister's small children suddenly going down with some illness immediately sprang to mind. She'd been looking forward to this family holiday, her first without Brock organising everything and everybody, and she hoped nothing was going to go wrong.

'The gentleman didn't say,' Hortense replied. She was as tall as Sophie, and as slim, but her skin was sallow and her dark hair dull. She and her husband, Henri, who tended the garden and the olive grove, had worked for the previous owners of the villa, and they lived nearby in a tiny stone house, built into the side of the hill.

'Thanks. Can you call Henri to help unload the car, please?' Sophie hurried indoors, taking a box of fragrant pineapples with her.

Hortense regarded the contents of the car. Crates of champagne and wine nestled under boxes of salad, meat, chickens and some very bright pink lobsters. She shrugged. Madame had shopped with as much extravagance as her ex-husband. Life up at the villa was obviously going to be as affluent as ever, even without the presence of Monsieur Duval and all his American dollars.

'Merde!' she swore as she lifted out a box of peaches and water melons. It was heavy. She would have to get her lazy husband to come and help.

In the sitting room the red tile floor gleamed with polish, testimony to Hortense's hard work. Sophie dropped on to one of the comfortable white linen-covered sofas and picked up the phone. 'Hello?' Her clear voice was crisp.

'Sophie? Is that you?'

'Who is that?' Her dark wing-shaped eyebrows drew together, puzzled. She pushed her long hair behind her ears. There was something oddly familiar about the voice.

'This is Tim speaking. Tim Calthorpe.'

There was a moment's stunned silence before she gave an astonished squeal. *'Tim!* My God, I don't believe it!' In that second, thirteen, nearly fourteen years vanished, and she was a student again, finishing her A-levels and longing to go out into the world to live a bit, live with a capital L. Tim was two years older and they were so in love she thought she would die when he announced he was emigrating to Australia. It had taken her months to be able even to think about him without crying, and although they wrote to each other, his letters became more remote and less frequent. Eighteen months later she met Brock and the memory of Tim was relegated to the years of her teens, alongside her favourite pop tunes, her first evening dress and her first car. Brock had been good at obliterating the past under a welter of expensive gifts and exotic travelling.

She could hear Tim laughing delightedly as she tried

to gather her thoughts. 'My God, Tim. After all these years. How did you know I was here? Where are you?'

'Ginny Howard told me you had a villa up in the mountains near Grasse, so I thought I'd give you a ring.'

Her bewilderment increased. 'But Ginny and Jonathan have a house in Monte Carlo.'

'That's right, Sophie. Well done.' She remembered how he used to tease her if she was slow on the uptake.

'But I don't understand . . .' Suddenly the truth dawned. 'Oh, you're not ringing me from Australia, then?'

Tim chuckled. 'I haven't been there for years.'

'You didn't stay?'

'I moved to Hong Kong after a couple of years. Got into business there for a while and then gradually drifted back to England. I hear you got yourself married and divorced.'

Listening to him, she saw him vividly in her mind's eye. Tall, well built and long legged, with the easy grace of an athlete. A narrow face, sexy more than handsome, and eyes that always looked as if he was keeping an amusing secret. At seventeen she'd found those eyes both thrilling and disturbing.

'Yes, I'm divorced; have been for several months now.' She still found it difficult to talk about it naturally, as if her divorce was somehow a shameful thing. 'How do you know Ginny and Jonathan?' she continued hurriedly.

'I met Jonathan in Hong Kong. They happened to mention you last night and when I told them we had known each other years ago, they said I should give you a ring.' He sounded chummy, as if he'd only seen her the previous week.

'So you're in Monte Carlo?'

'That's right. They've got a lovely place here, haven't they?'

Sophie felt stunned. After all these years. After the initial heartbreak when she thought she'd never love again, never be happy again, here was Tim telling her casually that he was only a few miles away.

Impulsively she said, 'Why not come to lunch the day after tomorrow? Bring Ginny and Jonathan, of course. My family will be here by then. We can have a party! It will be nice to see the Howards again.'

'And will it be nice to see me again, Sophie?' His tone was bantering, teasing, slightly flirtatious even. Her spirits lifted suddenly. It was nice to have a man to flirt with again; it seemed a long time since she and Brock had parted.

'It will be fabulous to see you again, Tim. Have you changed much?'

'I'm older, of course,' he said with mock solemnity. 'But I hear the years have been kind to you.'

Sophie burst out laughing. 'I'm only thirty-three, for God's sake.'

'And you've still got your own teeth?'

Sophie laughed. He'd always made her smile, and that was one of the things she'd missed most when he went away.

'Listen, Tim. Come at about noon. My mother and Alan will be here, and Audrey and Nicholas. Remember Nicholas? Audrey met him when she was still at Heathfield. He was the brother of her best friend.

They've got two little girls now of five and eight. You'll meet them all.'

'My God, the whole clan! Are you sure you can manage? That's an awful lot of people to have to lunch . . . Oh, but I forgot. Ginny says you're rolling in it now. A positive millionairess.'

'I don't know about that,' Sophie replied dismissively. References to her affluence embarrassed her. None of her peer group possessed the sort of riches that belonged to Brock and his contemporaries. 'I'm about to go back to work.'

'I want to hear all your news. I can't wait to see you again.' He sounded genuinely pleased at the prospect and for a fleeting moment she felt a tremor of hope for the future. It was only a pinprick of light, that flickered for a second in the darkness of her emotional emptiness but it was enough to make her feel that she might still, one day, have a rewarding love life.

'I'm looking forward to seeing you too,' she replied.

'We'll all be there. I'm longing for you to meet my wife, Carolyn. I think you'll really hit it off together.'

The next morning Sophie was up early, seeing to all the last-minute arrangements and enjoying herself as much as she'd done when she'd been a little girl, playing at houses. From the garden she gathered flowers to go in all the bedrooms, with bowls of fruit and bottles of Perrier. Fresh white linen was on every bed, and snowy Turkish towels were folded and placed in each room. Downstairs in the living room, she arranged stacks of magazines, a selection of the newest paperbacks she'd picked up at the airport, and games for her nieces. Nothing had been forgotten. Her family were going to have a wonderful holiday.

It was a glorious day with a brilliant blue sky and the garden looked at its best. Sophie wandered around for a while, inspecting the rosemary and lavender that grew in clumps on either side of the terraced steps, and dead-heading the rose bushes by the pool. Then she checked that all the white cane furniture was arranged in convivial groups, and that there were plenty of beach towels. She wanted everything to be perfect.

After a swim in water that was as warm and smooth as silk, she went and sat under the pergola that Brock had built on the side of the villa. It faced the terrace, high above the pool, and the vine that they had planted now grew like a lush canopy under which it was cool and shady. Here, Brock had placed a huge table of unpolished marble, and this was where they always ate; long leisurely luncheons followed by a siesta, or lantern-lit dinners to the sound of cicadas in the spinney of tall bamboos.

'Madame, can I get you anything?'

Sophie jumped, startled. Hortense had this unnerving habit of walking so quietly you never heard her coming. Like the bearer of bad news, she lurked in archways with a woeful expression, creeping up behind you like a sinister shadow.

Sophie looked at her watch. It was noon and her family would be arriving in three or four hours.

'I'd like some bread and cheese, and perhaps some pâté,' she replied. 'And a bottle of mineral water, please, Hortense.'

'*Certainement*, Madame.' She slithered away again, and Sophie watched her go, a tall black figure, like a perpetual widow. Idly, she wondered if Hortense would be offended if she offered her some of her cast-off clothes.

'Mummy!' Amelia tugged at Audrey's cotton skirt. They were waiting by the kerb, outside Nice airport, while Nicholas and her stepfather went off to collect the two Fiats they'd arranged to hire.

'Mummy!' The eight-year-old tried to attract her mother's attention again, but Audrey was hoping that if she pretended not to hear, her daughter would forget what she wanted to say and be distracted by something else. It was so hot she could hardly breathe and her T-shirt was sticking to her back. Her mother was sitting on one of the suitcases, in a wilting white muslin blouse that to Audrey's disgust revealed the white satin of her bra. If their holiday with Sophie was going to be as uncomfortable and irritating as this, she regretted not taking the children to Cornwall as usual. At least it was cool in Fowey. And it didn't require a two and a half hour flight in an overcrowded plane, being jostled by perfectly awful tourists.

'*Mummy!*' Amelia's voice had reached a high-pitched whine of impatience.

Audrey spun on her in fury. 'Will you be quiet, Amelia! Daddy and Grandpa will be back in a minute. Just wait, can't you?'

Rebecca, who was five, and had been opening and shutting one of the zips on a suitcase, looked up at her mother with surprise. She was a placid child, round faced with large blue eyes, like a girl in a Victorian painting, and sometimes Audrey had the uncomfortable feeling that Rebecca was much too mature for her years.

'Amelia might want to go to the toilet,' she pointed out.

'How often have I told you we don't call it the toilet,' Audrey said sharply. 'It's the loo.'

'I don't want to go, anyway,' Amelia cut in, 'Mummy, I want you to look at that lady standing over there. With a trolley and lots of cases. She's with that man who's wearing a straw hat.'

'What about her?' Audrey wished now they'd brought the au pair. If she was going to have to endure two weeks of childish prattle she'd go insane.

'Why don't you dress like her, Mummy? In smart white jeans and gold jewellery?' Amelia persisted. 'Like Daddy's friend that I saw him at the cinema with.'

The Fiats drew up at La Madeleine in a swirl of hot dust and tooting horns. Through the open windows Sophie could hear Amelia and Rebecca shrieking with excitement as she hurried from the poolside to greet them and there they all were, clambering out of the cars, and she was hugging and kissing everyone, and the children were jumping up and down, and then Henri appeared to take the cases indoors.

'It's so good to see you here,' Sophie exclaimed, taking her mother's arm and leading her forward. 'Let's go on to the terrace and have something to drink. That drive from Nice is hell, especially at this time of day.' She led the way, her brown legs covered by a brilliantly patterned wrap-around skirt she'd flung on over her bikini. Amelia and Rebecca, neat and rather old fashioned looking in the little cotton dresses Audrey always made them wear in the summer, were hopping down the steps of the terrace.

'Mind you don't fall!' Audrey shouted warningly. She looked very pale and strained, and her eyes sparked dangerously.

Nicholas, large, plump and gregarious, in an emerald-green golfing shirt, cream cotton trousers and yachting shoes, looked quickly round the garden, took off his glasses, placed them on the stone table, then bounded down the terrace with great lolloping leaps. The others watched, startled. Then there was an enormous splash that sent small tidal waves swelling from one end of the pool to the other, and he was waving at them all triumphantly from the middle of the pool.

'Daddy!' the little girls screamed with joy, running to the side of the pool, ready to jump in too as he spread his arms in welcome.

'No!' Audrey's voice rang out, louder than the others. 'Amelia! Rebecca! Don't even think of it. You'll ruin your clothes.'

'Oh, bugger their clothes,' Nicholas shouted back. 'Come on, girls! We're on holiday now.'

Audrey turned her back on them sharply, tight lipped. At that moment Hortense came on to the terrace with a large tray of cups and saucers.

'Ah, tea,' Alan observed in a soothing voice. 'How nice.'

They sat round the table under the shady vine while Hortense brought out plates of sandwiches and biscuits and a cake Sophie had bought at the local bakery. In the background, delighted shrieks and water skirmishes could be heard, but Audrey acted as if she was deaf to her family's high spirits as she picked at a sandwich and sipped her tea.

'I'd forgotten how beautiful it is here,' Sophie's mother remarked. 'You and Brock really did wonders with this garden, didn't you?' Jean had always been fond of her son-in-law, although she'd been against Sophie marrying him, but that was because she felt he was more a contemporary of hers than her daughter's.

'Brock stayed here for a weekend at the end of April,' Sophie said. 'He loves it here as much as I do.'

'I don't blame him,' Alan remarked wistfully. He gave a great sigh as he looked up at the vine that shielded them from the sun. 'This is my idea of paradise.'

'Your idea of paradise is anywhere where you don't have to do anything,' his wife remarked drily. 'You're a real beach bum.'

Alan smiled, his large blue eyes tranquil, his rounded face with its white beard benign. 'I think the term these days is a couch potato,' he said mildly.

'Well, we're all going to have to pull our weight now we're here. We can't expect Sophie to wait on us hand and foot for two weeks.'

'There's no need for any of you to do anything, Mummy.' Sophie leaned back with a luxurious stretch, hands behind her head. 'Hortense will be frightfully put out if we interfere. She likes to do breakfast, lunch and tea, and then she leaves supper ready for us to help ourselves to. I thought we'd have a barbecue tonight.'

Audrey wasn't listening. She was craning her neck round the thicket of bamboo to see what Nicholas and the girls were doing. Shrieks of merriment could be heard and Nicholas's hearty laugh was echoing around the garden. Audrey felt cold and a little sick. So her fears that Nicholas might be having an affair with his secretary weren't unfounded, after all. How dare he take that cheap little trollop to the cinema where his own daughter could see them together? Audrey's face flamed with anger and misery and she clenched her hands tightly until the nails hurt her palms. Denise was her name. She'd worked for Nicholas for only a year and she always wore white or cream. And lots of fake gilt Chanel jewellery. When Amelia had pointed out that woman at the airport, Audrey had immediately realised whom she was referring to.

'Audrey? Do you want some more tea?' With a start she realised Sophie had been talking to her.

'What? Oh, sorry. Yes, please.' She pushed the pretty pink and white hand-painted cup and saucer towards her sister.

'Are you all right?' Sophie asked in a low voice.

'Absolutely fine,' Audrey assured her with a defiant lift of the chin. She wasn't nearly as good looking as Sophie, and she'd always known it. Built on bigger and broader lines, the features of her face were more spread out, so that she lacked the neat symmetry of Sophie's face, with its small nose and chin, and the big child-like brown eyes.

'The girls have really grown, haven't they?' Sophie decided it would be wise to make casual conversation until her sister seemed more like herself.

'Yes.'

At that moment Amelia and Rebecca came running

up the terrace steps, grinning from ear to ear, rivulets of water streaming down their bodies to form little pools round their feet. Amelia deftly secured a chocolate biscuit for herself.

'Put that down at once!' Audrey commanded. 'You're to get dried and changed before you have any tea.'

Rebecca started tugging off her dress and knickers, her eyes, blue like Nicholas's, darting over the table to see what there was to eat.

Sophie rose, laughingly extending a hand to each child. 'Come with me. There's a downstairs shower and lots of towels. We'll get you nice and dry, while Mummy finds you something to change into.'

Then Nicholas lumbered up, beaming with bonhomie. 'Oh, I feel better now. That was great! Lead me to the shower room too, Sophie.'

Audrey eyed him coldly. 'For God's sake, take off those shoes before you go into the house, you'll make a terrible mess.'

'Yes, ma'am.' He chuckled good-humouredly. 'Watch out, girls, the boss is on the warpath.'

Audrey, left sitting with her mother and stepfather, looked white and hurt.

After the sun slipped behind the mountains and a violet darkness fell over La Madeleine, the atmosphere changed from prickliness to one of mellowness. Hot baths and a rest appeared to have restored the family's good humour, assisted by bottles of Moët et Chandon that Sophie had brought up from the cellar. Amelia and Rebecca were asleep in their room under the eaves, having been given supper by a doting Hortense, and the adults were able to relax and get into the holiday mood. Even Audrey, after a couple of glasses, was entering into the spirit of the occasion as she and Sophie cooked giant prawns on the barbecue and Alan and Nicholas made the salad in the kitchen, with a half full bottle of champagne to keep them going.

'Could you bring out the pâté and cheese as well?' Sophie called to them. 'You'll find it in the fridge, and there's lots of crusty bread in the basket on the table.'

'And don't forget the butter,' Jean reminded them. Somehow, while everyone else was busy, she always managed to avoid doing anything at all. She filled the gaps of inactivity with animated conversation, 'keeping the workers going' as she once described it. With a glass of champagne in one hand, a cigarette in the other, she sat, looking elegant, as she watched everyone else with detached interest and the occasional critical remark.

'I must say, this is like a stage setting, isn't it?' she observed. 'All those spotlit areas and little lanterns. Brock should have been a theatrical designer.'

Sophie pushed back strands of dark hair from her forehead. 'He wanted the garden to resemble an outdoor room, something one can only do in a warm climate like this.' She looked up at the moon, twinned in the swimming pool, and listened to the incessant noise of the cicadas. It was warm, the air languorous with the scent of orange and lemon trees, and she thought of the time when Brock had first brought her here. It was sad their marriage hadn't worked out and at moments like this she still missed him. Of one thing she was certain.

She'd done the right thing by asking for a divorce. The time had come for her to grow up and learn to stand on her own feet, and that was something she could never have done while married to Brock.

As if she knew what her daughter was thinking, Jean remarked, 'I'm glad you and Brock are still friends.'

'Oh, so am I,' Sophie replied. 'As a friend there's no one better.' She reached forward to turn over the prawns with a long pair of tongs and they sizzled appetisingly. 'Did I tell you we're having a lunch party tomorrow?'

Audrey looked at her with interest. 'Really? Is he nice?'

'Who?' Jean demanded. 'Have you got a new boy friend, darling?'

Sophie laughed, praying they wouldn't guess that for one mad moment she'd had similar hopes herself. 'Nothing like that. You two really are awful, all you can think about is finding me a new husband. No, these are old friends who have a house in Monte Carlo, Ginny and Jonathan Howard, and they're bringing over their house guests. Mum, do you remember Tim Calthorpe? Well, he and his wife are coming too,' she added so hurriedly that Audrey smiled maliciously. She remembered Tim Calthorpe, all right. She'd fancied him herself at one point, but he'd only had eyes for Sophie. At the time she'd been very jealous, but in the end neither of them had got him, she reflected with satisfaction.

Jean remembered him too. A self-satisfied young man, rather weak but brimming with sex appeal. She'd never liked him very much, never trusted him, really. And at the end she'd hated him for the way he went off to

Australia, announcing it only a few days before he departed, so Sophie had no time to prepare herself, no time to get used to the heartbreaking end to their romance.

'What's he doing in this part of the world?' she asked tartly. 'I thought he was supposed to be in Australia.'

Sophie looked startled by her mother's vehemence. 'He's living in England, apparently. He's over here for a holiday. He heard, by chance, that I was here too. It'll be fun to see him again.'

'I wonder what his wife is like?' Audrey remarked.

Jean shrugged, drew on her cigarette and looked up and down the long stone table. 'Is there any more champagne, darling?'

'There certainly is. Audrey, keep an eye on these prawns while I get us all something to drink, will you?' Sophie handed her the tongs. 'I'll fetch the men at the same time. They must have finished making the salad by now.'

'At least it keeps them out of mischief,' Audrey observed.

'Tell me something, Audrey,' Jean said, as soon as they were alone. 'Do you think Alan looks all right?'

Audrey was surprised by the question. She thought her mother had been about to ask her why she wasn't getting on with Nicholas.

'Alan looks fine to me. Why?'

Jean frowned, troubled. 'I get the feeling he isn't well. He says there's nothing wrong with him, but he's always tired these days. He seems to have lost his energy.'

'Well, he must be nearly seventy, isn't he?'

'So am I, darling, but I'm still able to do as much as ever.'

'Has he seen the doctor?'

'You know what he's like. Anyway, here they come. Don't mention what we've been talking about.' Jean raised her voice. 'What have you two been doing? Growing the lettuce?'

The men grinned at her with intoxicated high spirits.

Nicholas swooped over to Audrey, light on his feet like a heavyweight boxer. He planted a kiss on her cheek. 'How are you doing, pet?' He sniffed the air with exaggerated delight. 'God, those prawns smell good.'

Audrey, unbending a little, smiled back. Alan, plonking platters of cheese and fruit on the table, surveyed the scene with obvious pleasure.

'Fantastic, all this, isn't it, Jean?' he said, lowering his rotund body into the chair beside her. He patted her hand. 'This is the life, isn't it?'

'Talk about romantic,' Nicholas chipped in, taking the seat opposite. Then he seemed to have a sudden thought. 'I hope you've brought the pill with you, Aud. We don't want to increase the population as a result of this holiday, do we?' He laughed at his own wit.

Stony-faced, Audrey brought the dish of prawns to the table, their shells glistening and faintly charred by the flames. As she placed it in the middle, Nicholas gave her bottom a roughly affectionate spank.

'Cheer up, old girl,' he teased. 'We're here to have fun, you know.'

She turned on him, white faced and venomous looking. 'I thought you had enough of that with Denise,' she said icily. Then, without another word, she turned and ran sobbing into the villa.

Two

Audrey was down first the next morning, disturbed in the early hours by Amelia and Rebecca who appeared by her bedside, already dressed in their swimsuits.

'Oh, my God, what time is it?' she groaned. Her eyes felt so swollen and heavy she could hardly open them. Nicholas, asleep next to her, lay on his back, snoring gently.

'Can we go swimming, Mummy?' Amelia asked eagerly.

'Yes! We want to go swimming.' Rebecca always echoed her sister.

The travelling clock said six forty-five. Is this why she'd come on holiday, to France? Audrey asked herself. To be awoken at dawn by the children? To have no au pair to look after them because Nicholas had said it wouldn't be necessary. With Jean, Sophie and a housekeeper in residence, surely they could manage the girls between them. And on top of that she had to contend with the knowledge that Nicholas was cheating on her and try not to make a complete fool of herself in front of her family. Last night's outburst mustn't happen again.

Gritting her teeth, she climbed out of bed, cursing the

world into which she'd had the misfortune to be born. She hated her life these days. Every part of it. Not that she actually hated the children, but she wished right now she didn't have any. Ever since she'd begun to suspect that Nicholas was playing around, a bitterness had entered her life, souring everything. She envied Sophie more than she would admit even to herself. Her sister had everything, except a husband at this moment, but Audrey was sure she'd soon rectify that. She had a fantastic flat in the best part of London, she had this villa, and with huge wealth at her disposal, she was about to open her own antique shop. It simply wasn't fair, Audrey thought, as she led the children down the stairs and out into the garden, warning them not to wake up the entire household.

The day promised to be beautiful. The scent of lavender and rosemary permeated the fresh cool air, and down the terrace by the pool the cypress trees stood like dark sentinels against a pale dawn.

'Can we go swimming now, Mummy?' the girls chorused.

'I suppose so.' Audrey knew she sounded grudging but she couldn't help herself. In a terrible way she even resented the children's ability to be happy these days.

Hortense was already at work in the kitchen.

'You like coffee, Madame?' she asked. Today she was wearing a flowered ankle-length skirt and a deep blue shirt; some of Sophie's cast-offs, Audrey reckoned.

'I bring it on to the terrace for you,' Hortense continued, deftly filling the coffee pot. 'And you like a croissant, Madame? They are still warm and we have the apricot conserve.'

The gnawing ache in Audrey's stomach eased at the comforting thought of breakfast served on the terrace. 'Thank you. That would be very nice.' She tightened the sash of her Marks and Spencer dressing gown and went back into the garden where she could hear the shrieks of the children as they played in the water.

Alan was standing on the terrace, watching them benevolently. He was already dressed in cream cotton trousers and a sports shirt.

'You're up early, Alan. I hope the children didn't disturb you,' she said, seating herself at the stone table. 'Breakfast will be here in a minute.'

'No, my dear, they didn't wake me up. I've a problem sleeping these days. I wake in the early hours to go to the loo, and that's that. Might as well get up.' He took a place opposite her, and she thought he looked as bad as she felt.

'You shouldn't drink late at night, then you wouldn't have to get up,' Audrey observed.

Alan shrugged. 'It doesn't seem to make any difference. One of the penalties of getting old, I suppose.'

'Who's getting old?' Sophie stepped through the French windows, looking fresh in white trousers and T-shirt, her hair in a ponytail. Alan looked at her fondly.

'Not you, and that's for sure,' he remarked.

Sophie laughed. She was in high spirits. Entertaining was one of her favourite occupations and she was looking forward to the day ahead. She'd planned a lunch menu that included chilled melon, lobster mayonnaise, a variety of exotic salads, and then wild strawberries from the nearby hills, with *crème brûlée*.

'What time is everybody coming for lunch?' Audrey asked as she sipped hot, fragrant coffee from one of the large, thick, china cups that Sophie had bought locally.

'Around noon. I thought everyone would like a swim before lunch.' She looked up at the sky which arched blue and clear. 'It's going to be another scorcher.'

'Bliss,' observed Alan contentedly.

'Why are the English obsessed by the weather?' Audrey grumbled.

Jean and lastly Nicholas joined them, while Hortense brought out relays of fresh coffee and croissants and a basket of fresh nectarines.

'I never heard you get up this morning,' Nicholas remarked conversationally to Audrey. If he noticed her swollen eyes he said nothing.

'Someone had to keep an eye on the girls when they went swimming.' Her tone was martyred. 'I'm going to get dressed now.' She rose and without another word went into the villa. There was an awkward silence and then Jean spoke.

'What's wrong with her, Nicholas?' she whispered. 'She's been like this ever since we arrived yesterday. Isn't she well?'

Nicholas's smile was easy and relaxed. 'Oh, she's fine, Jean. Just a bit tired, I think. She'll be OK.'

Sophie looked at him closely, but his expression was bland and his blue eyes innocent. She wasn't fooled though. Something was wrong.

In spite of her nervous anticipation at seeing Tim again, Sophie swam and sunbathed before the sun became too strong, and then helped Hortense prepare lunch, setting the table with white linen, local pottery, a jug of wild flowers in the middle, and a round shallow basket of figs and peaches.

'It looks spectacular, darling,' said Jean, appearing as Sophie was doing the finishing touches. She had spent the morning attending to the care of her skin in the sun and was now wearing a chic blue linen dress and a large straw hat. 'I love those blue wine glasses. Where did you get them?'

'Brock picked them up in Paris, ages ago.'

'Tim Calthorpe *will* be impressed. Has he any idea how well you've done for yourself?'

'Oh, Ma, I do hate it when you talk like that. It sounds as if I only married Brock for his money,' Sophie protested.

'Everybody, probably with the exception of Tim alone, knows you married him because you were crazy about him,' Jean replied serenely. 'At the same time, it's very nice that you're so rich as a result.'

'*Ma!*' Sophie said warningly.

'All right, all right. I won't say another word.'

'Why don't you go and sit by the pool? I'm about to open some champagne.'

'What a civilised idea, darling.' Jean sauntered off to the pool.

By the time Sophie heard a car coming up the drive, all the family were by the pool, relaxing in the sun as they sipped their drinks. Putting down her glass, and with her heart pounding excitedly, she went to greet her guests.

Tim hadn't changed at all. In a heart-stopping moment, Sophie felt as if time had stood still. He looked older, of course, but that only made him more attractive, his features more clear cut now, and his eyes more knowing. He was grinning at her, his smile as sexy as ever, and just behind him, clambering out of the car, was a pretty, long-legged blonde whom Sophie took to be his wife. Remembering her manners, she greeted Ginny and Jonathan first.

'It's so good to see you again.'

Ginny was a capable-looking woman and only lived in Monte Carlo, which she loathed, for tax reasons because her husband had inherited several million pounds from an uncle. She greeted Sophie in her usual hearty way.

'Dear girl! It's great to see you. I hear you've got the whole family staying. I'm longing to see Aud again; it must be yonks!' She hitched her all-purpose bag onto her shoulder and strode off down the steps towards the sound of laughter on the lower terrace. Jonathan, bald and willowy, kissed Sophie on both cheeks before turning to introduce Carolyn Calthorpe.

'I don't think you two have met, have you? Such a coincidence, you and Tim knowing each other when you were young.'

Everyone laughed politely and Sophie looked more closely at Tim's wife. Her skin was as smooth and golden as a cosmetic advertisement, and her pale blue eyes were fringed with thick dark lashes.

'Hello,' she smiled shyly. 'I've heard so much about you from Tim. I've been longing to meet you.'

'It's great to meet you, too,' Sophie replied, taking to her at once. There was something fragile and vulnerable about the younger woman, giving her a childlike appeal. Her pale pink summer dress with its thin shoulder straps added to the pretty-little-girl look. Then Sophie turned towards Tim. He leaned forward to kiss her cheek, and she was at once aware of the warmth of his skin, and a fragrance that belonged to some distant past.

'I can't believe it's been all these years,' he exclaimed laughingly before she had time to say anything. 'You're just the same. Christ, how long has it been, Sophie?'

'Ages,' she replied, smiling up at him, thinking, all the usual clichés. Any minute now he'll tell me I haven't aged a day.

By the pool, Alan and Nicholas went around topping up everyone's glasses while Amelia and Rebecca offered platters of succulent black olives and sun-warmed pistachios. Audrey, in dark glasses and bright red lipstick was deep in conversation with Ginny, while Jean, preferring the company of men, soon ensconced herself between Tim and Jonathan.

'Where do you live?' Sophie heard Nicholas ask Carolyn as she stood, slightly awkward and isolated, pretending to look at the roses.

'In Wales. Tim is working at the moment for an insurance company in Cardiff.'

Jean's voice, once described as piercing enough to shatter glass, rose above all the others. 'You *must* come to dinner, Jonathan, when you're next in London. Is it *really* true that your house in Monte Carlo overlooks that vulgar pink palace?'

Amelia tugged at her father's arm. 'Why can't I have some champagne?' she whined in a voice not unlike her mother's.

Sophie decided it was time for lunch. Once they were

all seated at the long table in the soothing shade of the arbour, surely the atmosphere would become less fraught. She had planned the seating carefully, placing the little girls between their parents, men on either side of her mother, Tim on her right and Alan on her left, with Ginny next to Nicholas and Carolyn on the other side of Alan.

Hortense brought out fragrant cantaloupe melons and baskets of bread. Alan filled the glasses with the local vin du pays as everyone settled down for a long leisurely lunch that Sophie knew would last until late in the afternoon. Tim, looking around, was obviously impressed by the stylish simplicity of La Madeleine.

'Your ex-husband must be a multi-millionaire to have bought a place like this,' he observed. 'Is it yours now, or do you borrow it when you want to stay?'

'It was Brock's wedding present to me, so it's always been mine. Actually we both stay here, though no longer at the same time.'

Tim spooned the tender juicy flesh of his melon with relish. 'So what went wrong? Why did you split?'

'I wanted to remain in one place for a bit longer than five days at a time,' she replied with dry humour. 'Also, I wanted a family but Brock didn't as he's already got two grown-up children. We're still very good friends now the dust has settled but his career, which he adores, means he has to travel around all the time and I really needed to put down roots. After twelve years I'd had enough of living out of suitcases.'

'Do you have a house in London?'

'A flat.' She didn't tell him it was in Eaton Place.

'What was he like, Sophie?' Tim asked curiously,

dropping his voice intimately. 'Ginny told me he was much older than you.'

Sophie spoke carefully, her feelings towards Brock still loyal. 'Yes, he's twenty years older than me, but at the time that felt right. Since my father died, I really needed someone to lean on.' And you'd left me to go to Australia, she thought. Aloud she added, 'He's a very kind, very generous man. A large man with a heart to match. He was so incredibly understanding when I wanted a divorce that it broke my heart. Love, if you can't return it, can be a heavy burden and he was the first to realise that.'

Tim nodded but she wasn't sure whether he really understood. 'Is there someone else in your life now?'

Pushing her long dark hair back with both hands, she shook her head. 'Right now I'm so busy planning my new shop I've had no time to think about relationships. Anyway, I'm in no hurry to get involved again. This is the first time in my life that I've had the chance to be independent, and I rather like it.'

As she told him her plans for Gloria Antica, she glanced round the table, to make sure everyone was happy. As usual her mother's voice was the only one that could be clearly heard.

'I think *all* women should work,' Jean intoned as she lit a cigarette. 'It keeps them on their toes.'

'But you've never worked in your life, Mummy!' Audrey exclaimed, astonished.

'What's being a JP then? And vice-chairman of the local Heritage Association? And a senior executive of St John Ambulance?' Jean retorted.

Alan's mouth twitched almost imperceptibly. 'And

those are all very demanding jobs, too,' he said, deadpan.

Jean ignored him and rattled on about the importance of women having something outside the home to occupy their minds.

'Women who have children should stay at home,' Audrey observed sanctimoniously.

'Oh, I don't know,' Tim said unthinkingly. 'I believe women who work are much more interesting than women who tie themselves to the Aga.'

Audrey flushed and averted her face. Amelia, listening to the adult conversation with interest, spoke. 'Daddy's friend – you know, the one he goes to the cinema with – well, she works. In an office. Is she interesting, Daddy?'

'God! That was awful,' Sophie groaned, as she lingered over her coffee, talking to her mother. 'Trust children to spill the beans! It's a pity Audrey has found out Nicholas is having an affair. It might have blown over, otherwise.'

The others were relaxing by the pool, some to swim, others to doze in the shade of the wych-elms; Nicholas and Alan were strolling through the olive grove, Amelia and Rebecca were playing Snakes and Ladders.

'We don't know for certain that he is,' Jean pointed out, lighting another cigarette.

'Oh, come on, Ma. Did you see how embarrassed he looked? That's why Audrey rushed off in tears last night. I wonder what we should do?'

'There's nothing we can do and nothing we *should* do,' Jean replied firmly. 'This is something they must sort out for themselves. It's just very unfortunate that the children saw their father with this woman.'

'It's a disaster,' Sophie exclaimed, distressed. Then she rose. 'We'd better go down to the pool and join the others. I don't want Audrey thinking we've been talking about them. I told her I had to help Hortense clear away.' She seized a bowl of fruit and sped off down the worn stone steps.

Tim was lounging in the hammock, still nursing his glass of wine.

'This is the life,' he called to Sophie as soon as he saw her. 'Come and talk to me.'

Laughingly, she flopped onto the grass beside him. 'Like a peach?'

'Thanks.' He reached down to take the ripe fruit from her. 'Stay and talk to me, Sophie. We have such a lot of catching up to do. Listen, we mustn't lose touch again. I can't tell you how good it is to see you.'

'It's good to see you, too,' she replied.

'I hope we can be friends.'

She hesitated for a moment. It would be nice to be friends, with no emotional involvement, but was it possible? It was clear that Tim's attitude was brotherly now, and that whatever he'd felt for her all those years ago had long since gone. But what of her own feelings? For the first time since she'd split from Brock she was suddenly aware of being on her own. A single woman in a world designed for couples. Looking around the pool, she realised that even here, in her own home, everyone had someone: her mother had Alan, Audrey had Nicholas – well, for the moment anyway; Ginny had Jonathan, and of course there was Carolyn, Tim's wife, something which at one time she'd hoped would be her role in life. She glanced over to where Carolyn had joined Amelia and Rebecca in the game of Snakes and Ladders. She looked so young, little more than a girl herself, and Sophie could see why Tim was attracted to her. He always liked to be in control, she remembered, and Carolyn reminded her of herself when she'd been seventeen – gentle, malleable, totally in Tim's thrall.

'Yes, it would be nice to keep in touch,' she said lightly. 'I think Carolyn is lovely. I'd like to get to know her better.'

'Oh, Caro's great. We're very happy.' He wiped the peach juice from his chin with the back of his hand and chucked the deeply ridged stone into the nearby bushes. 'I'm very lucky.'

'Where did you meet?'

'Through mutual friends, at a dinner party. In London. It was soon after I returned from Hong Kong. When the bank she works for transferred her to one of their branches in Wales, I followed her.' He grinned sheepishly. 'We got married six months later.'

She looked up at him lying relaxed in the hammock, and in a flood of memories she could not control she recalled how his mouth had felt when he'd kissed her all those years ago; how strong his arms had been when he'd held her close; how hot and deep and wonderful his lovemaking. She looked away so he could not see her face, see how he stirred her again even after all this time. Memories were dangerous. They could conjure up the past and bring it hurling into the present so that it seemed only yesterday since they'd made love. The fair hairs on his forearms and the flatness of his stomach made her ache with sudden longing. Desire swept over her like a wave. She couldn't stand it a moment longer. Resolutely she jumped to her feet, slipping off the wrap-around skirt and top to reveal a kingfisher blue swimsuit.

'I'm going for a swim. It's so hot. This sun is a scorcher.' But the heat was inside her and the danger was Tim. She knew she must never see him alone in the future. Never allow him to come close, even as a friend. If he did, she would burn in the flame of her own desire.

'I'm coming in, too,' he shouted, following her to the edge of the pool. His voice echoed over her head, over the crystal-clear water as she dived in but she pretended not to hear.

PART TWO

August

Three

Walton Street had always been one of Sophie's favourite shopping areas. Originally a long row of early nineteenth-century terraced houses facing each other, the ground floors had long since been turned into small and intimate shops and restaurants. This was where the rich came to buy those little luxuries that make life so pleasant. Hand-painted toys and nursery furniture, flimsy lacy lingerie, gifts for everyone, and charming household trinkets.

Before she bought the premises for Gloria Antica, Sophie walked the length of the street several times, getting the feel of the other establishments but knowing instinctively that this was the place for her to be. The type of clients she wanted to attract already shopped here; they bought fresh crusty bread and cakes from the baker, had their sheets monogrammed at the linen shop, chose paintings at the art gallery and matched up wools for their needlework at the tapestry shop.

And halfway along on the left, Gloria Antica would soon be selling fine antique china and porcelain, together with a few small pieces of antique furniture. This was the culmination of years of planning and dreaming and she could hardly believe it was happening at last. Brock had invested in the shop as well as giving her a generous settlement, and this had enabled her in the past few months to buy in exquisite stock. She knew she could never repay the gratitude she felt. It was one thing to be financially cared for, although she'd been the one who had finally and reluctantly asked for a divorce. It was quite another to lavish several million pounds on her, which was hers for life, even if she remarried, as well as giving her La Madeleine and the flat in Eaton Place

'I want you to be happy,' Brock had said simply. 'And I can afford it, honey. It's only what you deserve for all the years of happiness you've given me.' Sophie had wept as if her heart would break when he'd said that. She was so fond of him and he'd always been so good to her. But she'd grown up and away from him in the past ten years. Sometimes she'd even seen Brock as her jailer, someone who prevented her making something of her own life while she stayed in the shadow of his.

As she turned the key in the lock of the shop door, she suddenly felt her spirits lifting with a tremendous surge of excitement. This was it! A shop of her own. Something that was hers and at last an outlet for the knowledge she'd gained working at Christie's before her marriage.

'I like the colour of the walls,' her mother remarked, following her into the shop. The official opening was in two days' time and Sophie had promised Jean a private preview before anyone else saw it.

'Do you? I wasn't sure at first.' Sophie regarded the crushed raspberry self-striped wallpaper, her head on one side.

'It sets off those pictures in their gilt frames very nicely.' Jean wandered to the back of the showroom, winding her way between small side tables, a couple of antique chairs and a pair of ormolu-mounted marquetry pedestals with marble tops.

'I chose it because I think it's warm and welcoming,' Sophie explained, adjusting the position of a pair of Louis XV Sèvres vases. She turned the price tag inwards. It said twenty thousand pounds. No point in frightening off customers when they first walked into the shop.

Jean looked around with approval, and started reaching inside her handbag.

Sophie shook her head. 'Not in here, please, Mum.'

'What? D'you mean you don't allow smoking?'

'Definitely no smoking – unless, of course, you're an American millionaire who's prepared to give me three hundred thousand pounds for those potpourri containers.'

Her mother looked aghast at the richly embellished gold and blue Louis XVI vases. They glistened under the concealed spotlights that shone down from the ceiling, and Jean drew back, clutching her handbag, as if too frightened to move.

'My God. Aren't you terrified someone will knock them over? You're surely not going to leave them on display for the press opening on Wednesday, are you?'

Sophie laughed. 'I'll put them in that glass-fronted cabinet for the party, along with anything else that is very valuable.'

'Let's go somewhere for a cup of coffee,' Jean urged, sidling towards the door.

'Is that because you're desperate for a cigarette or afraid of breaking something?' Sophie teased. 'I am fully insured, you know, and it may not be obvious but every inch of this place is wired up to an alarm that goes straight through to the police station.'

'I'd just like to talk to you, in a place where we can relax,' Jean said, shutting her handbag with a snap. Something in her tone of voice made Sophie look at her sharply.

'What's wrong, Mum? Problems between Audrey and Nicholas again?' When they'd left La Madeleine at the end of June, they'd seemed reconciled and quite happy. Two weeks in the sun seemed to have reignited their relationship, and there had been no more tactless remarks from Amelia about 'Daddy's friend'.

'Audrey's all right, as far as I know,' Jean replied, 'but you know how proud she is. We'd all be the last to know if anything was seriously wrong. No. I want to talk to you about Alan.'

As Sophie turned on the alarm again and locked up the shop, she wondered why on earth her mother wanted to discuss Alan. Surely *he* wasn't having an affair.

Over steaming cups of espresso, Jean leaned forward and talked in a low urgent voice. 'I'm sure he's ill, Sophie. He keeps going to the loo, sometimes every half-hour or so, and he looks tired all the time. I've tried to get him to go to the doctor but he absolutely refuses. Says he's fine. I don't know what to do. I'm certain there's something wrong.' Suddenly her eyes brimmed and she rummaged feverishly in her handbag. 'Don't tell me smoking isn't allowed in here either,' she said in desperation.

'There's an ashtray on the table. We must be in the smoking area.' Sophie pushed it towards her mother. 'I remember your telling me how you thought Alan looked when we were in France. I thought he seemed OK.'

Jean shook her head and wiped her cheeks with her fingertips. It was so unlike her to break down in front of anyone that Sophie felt a frisson of apprehension.

'Why don't you insist he sees a doctor, Mum?'

'You know what he's like. He doesn't believe in doctors.'

'Then get him to try alternative medicine.'

Jean gave a little snort. 'He calls anything like that witchcraft.' She looked out of the restaurant window into Brompton Road and envied the people who were hurrying by, apparently without a care in the world. She didn't want to worry Sophie unduly but she felt sick with misery. She cared for Alan much more than she'd ever cared for Sophie and Audrey's father, although she didn't think it would be right to admit that to them. Alan had made her happy for the past nineteen years and the thought of losing him scared her deeply. He was only sixty-seven. Not old at all by today's standards. And yet in the past few months he'd seemed like a very old man. She also knew he was trying to hide from her the fact that everything seemed an effort these days.

'Shall I try and talk to him, Mum?'

'Could you, darling? He might listen to you.'

'I doubt it, but I'll do my best. What's the alternative? Ask old Dr Thompson round for a drink and then spring it on Alan that he's come to examine him?'

'He would never forgive me.'

'He might, you know. Especially if it's something serious. He can't go on ignoring worrying symptoms for ever.'

'He puts everything down to getting old. Says we're in our sixties and we've got to expect things to go wrong.' Jean's voice wobbled dangerously, and she drew on her cigarette as if her own life depended on it. Sophie watched her closely.

'I'd say you're in more danger of dying first, with those dreadful cigarettes, than Alan is of being ill with something else.'

'I know. I know.' Jean took a final drag and then stubbed the cigarette out. 'I'll give up – if Alan is all right, but right now I *need* to smoke. But I have made a deal with God. I'll quit if he lets me keep Alan.'

'Oh, Mum.' Sophie reached over and placed her hand on top of her mother's. She'd never seen her in such a state. 'I'm sure it's nothing. Just a weak bladder, maybe. But we'll get him to see a doctor, no matter what.'

Sophie was up early in a fever of excitement. Today, at last, Gloria Antica was going to open. She'd invited the press and a couple of dozen friends to the champagne launch, and now as she dressed in her new navy blue suit with matching high-heeled shoes, and the gold earrings Brock had given her for her last birthday, she felt on a tremendous high. By seven o'clock she'd opened up, turned on the spotlights, and then wandered round and round the showroom, wondering what to do next. When her two new assistants arrived, she felt relieved.

She'd begun to imagine that no one would turn up and she'd be left to cope on her own. Frankie Bennett and Katie Williams both had degrees in fine art, and Katie had worked for three years in Sotheby's.

'Hi, girls!' They greeted each other with hugs and kisses. Sophie wanted there to be a team spirit in the shop, rather than herself as the boss and them as employees.

'Oh, doesn't it all look marvellous!' Katie crowed in delight. The previous evening florists had placed great arrangements of flowers on the matching pedestals and in the centre of the window. And on the pavement outside, neat box trees in dark green tubs stood on either side of the entrance.

'It does look good,' Sophie agreed. 'I hope the caterers arrive soon. The press, if any turn up, are due here in an hour,' she added nervously. Cards had gone out inviting guests to a champagne breakfast from nine o'clock until noon.

'Of course everyone will come,' Frankie said sturdily. Then she had a sudden thought. Her face lit up. 'We might even get our first sale this morning. Wouldn't that be terrific?' She was small, dark and half Italian; her almost black eyes sparkled with excitement. By contrast Katie, who was a natural blonde with hair as smooth and gold as spun silk, looked at them with serene blue eyes.

'I'm sure we will,' she said calmly. 'We've got such lovely things. I'd buy everything if I had the money.' Her gaze lingered longingly on a pair of Russian malachite vases, the gloriously green markings swirling in a natural pattern.

'I may have to if we don't make a success of Gloria Antica,' Sophie joked ruefully.

At that moment the staff from the Admiral Crichton catering company arrived with cases of chilled champagne, freshly squeezed orange juice, miniature croissants and brioche, and a large espresso machine for making fresh coffee. Sophie showed them into the working area behind the showroom.

'Look what's arrived,' Frankie exclaimed when Sophie came back. She was almost hidden behind a huge bunch of pink lilies, fuchsia, roses, amaryllis and scabious, arranged in a simple white vase.

'They're fantastic,' said Sophie, helping her to place the flowers on a table at the back of the shop. 'We're beginning to look more like a florist than an antique shop.'

'Who are they from?' Frankie was dying to know.

Sophie opened the tiny envelope that was tucked in the centre. For a moment she was silent, shocked although not surprised.

'They're from my ex-husband,' she said softly.

Frankie smiled. 'That's very nice of him.'

Sophie had never talked about her past life to the girls and now she only said briefly, 'He's a very nice man.' Then she slipped the card into her pocket. Brock was more than just nice, she reflected. He was a saint. 'Good luck, may all your dreams come true, my darling. I'll be one of your first customers on my trip to London next week. Love always, Brock.'

Deeply touched and feeling emotional, Sophie ordered one of the young waiters to open a bottle of champagne.

'Let's have a toast before anyone arrives,' she said, her voice shaky.

'Good idea,' Katie enthused.

'We'd better not overdo it, though,' Frankie laughed. 'We don't want to totter around offering free samples of our merchandise to the press!'

Sophie closed her eyes in mock horror. 'At twenty thousand pounds a throw? Don't! Now, let's drink to us!' She raised her glass. 'To Gloria Antica.'

'To Gloria Antica,' they chorused.

'To good sales figures,' Frankie added.

'You can say that again,' Sophie laughed. 'Stand by, girls. It's all about to happen. Here comes our first customer.'

From nine fifteen onwards, the shop was filled with a constant stream of journalists and friends, some staying only ten minutes with deadlines to catch, others remaining for up to an hour, gossiping and gawping at the selection of Meissen, Dresden, Chelsea and Rockingham china figurines, vases and plates, while enjoying glasses of Buck's Fizz.

Audrey arrived shortly before noon, with Ginny Howard. They were both in London for the day, Audrey from their home in Newbury, and Ginny over from Monte Carlo. They'd planned a shopping spree followed by lunch at Santini's after they'd 'done' Sophie's shop.

'It must have cost a fortune,' were Audrey's first words as she looked around, wide-eyed. 'It's all very swish,' she added almost grudgingly. 'Do you think you'll get any customers around here? Don't people usually shop in Bond Street for this sort of thing?'

'Let's hope not,' Sophie replied blithely, determined not to be riled. Audrey looked tired and strained again, all the benefit from the holiday in France gone. 'Have a glass of champers,' she urged. 'It will cheer you up.'

'I don't need cheering up. Is Mummy coming?'

'She can't today, she's sitting on the Bench. But she had a look around earlier this week. Excuse me, Audrey. The features editor of the *Financial Times* has just arrived. I must go and greet her.' Sophie slipped away, feeling guilty. Why did her sister always have this effect on her? It was as if she feared Audrey's sniping depression was catching.

At last the crowd started to thin out and she was able to have a quick look at the visitors' book. Almost everyone had turned up; the most important journalists had all signed in, and with a sigh of relief she knew the press coverage would be good.

A shadow fell across the open book at that moment and she was aware of someone standing beside her. Glancing up, she gave a gasp of surprise and her heart lurched.

'Hello. How's it going, Sophie?' It was Tim, and he was grinning down at her as familiarly as if he'd seen her the day before.

'Why don't you both go to Relate, Aud?' Ginny demanded, after they'd settled themselves at a corner table at Santini's and given their order for an aperitif. 'You can't go on like this.'

'Nicholas won't hear of it. He says I'm making a song and dance about nothing. When I try and talk to him about his ghastly secretary he walks out of the room. Refuses to even discuss it.' Audrey shook her head and her mouth drooped woefully. 'I'm at the end of my tether, Ginny.'

'Then you must go to Relate on your own,' Ginny retorted robustly. 'Ask their advice. You can't just sit in a heap waiting for him to leave you.'

'I'm hoping he'll grow tired of her, or she'll leave of her own accord to get another job.'

'Hmmm.' Ginny pursed her lips thoughtfully. 'It depends whether she really wants to hang on to Nicholas, or whether she's just after a few good fucks.'

Audrey winced at Ginny's language. 'I was wondering if I should go and talk to her. What do you think?'

Ginny spoke decisively. 'Terrible idea, Aud. She'll see it as your begging to have Nicholas back. That would put her in a strong position. Don't have anything to do with her.'

Their drinks arrived. Audrey took a gulp of hers and felt the sharp sparkling tingle of the first gin and tonic of the day hit her stomach with an icy glow. Ginny was right, of course, but it was tearing her apart to realise Nicholas no longer had more than the most scant interest in her, while he had to 'work late' most evenings, and had now taken to vanishing at the weekend to 'play golf', a sport he'd always previously said bored him to tears. Even the children were beginning to notice his absence.

'Has he ever done this before?'

Audrey looked shocked. 'Of course not!'

'Then you've been very lucky.' Ginny replied matter-of-factly. 'Jonathan has strayed several times since we married eighteen years ago. I don't pay any attention now. He always comes back.'

'Jonathan?' Audrey wondered if she'd heard right. She looked aghast and took another swig of her drink. 'Jonathan,' she repeated. 'Surely not.'

Ginny smiled good-humouredly. 'Even old Jono has moments of lust. I know he doesn't look the type, but get him in the sack and he fucks like a steam engine.'

Audrey finished her drink and signalled, rather weakly, for the waiter to bring her another. 'Really?' she said in a distant, embarrassed voice.

They ordered smoked salmon, *noisettes d'agneau poêlé à la bourguignonne*, and a bottle of 1987 Château Tannese Bordeaux.

'You're not planning anything serious this afternoon, are you, Aud? I'm staying in London tonight so it doesn't matter if I get pissed.'

'I thought I might go to Marks and Sparks to get some vests for the children.'

'Jesus, how boring. Let's go to the cinema. There are quite a few films I want to see.'

Audrey was rapidly beginning to feel out of her depth. She'd met Ginny and Jonathan through Brock, several years before, and she'd somehow been under the impression they were similar to herself and Nicholas, but now she was beginning to have her doubts.

'The cinema? In the afternoon?'

'Why not? It will help take your mind off Nicholas more than a stroll around M and S.'

Tim had phoned several times since the lunch party at La Madeleine, to say hello and to ask how her shop was coming along but this was the first time Sophie had seen him since then and the shock made her suddenly nervous.

'Hello. What are you doing here?' she demanded. His grin deepened, and he looked past her into the shop, taking in the chic atmosphere and fine antiques.

'You might sound more pleased to see me.' He pretended to look hurt. 'I know I had to come up to London anyway today but I have made a special effort to get here to congratulate you on the opening of Gloria Antica – even though you didn't send me an invitation.'

He'd always enjoyed teasing her but there had been times when she'd been unsure whether he was having fun at her expense, or being serious.

'I would have sent you and Carolyn an invitation if I'd thought there was any chance—'

'Oh, Sophie!' He burst out laughing, and then he hugged her, putting both his arms round her and holding her close in a brotherly gesture. She started laughing too, catching his mood as she'd always done.

'Well, have a glass of champagne now you are here,' she said. 'But first, you must sign the visitors' book.' She noticed that Frankie and Katie were giving Tim curious glances, and she brought them forward to introduce them.

Tim straightened up from writing in the visitors' book. 'So how do you like working for Sophie?' he asked. 'She's a real slave driver, you know. She'll have you working day and night.'

'We'd better put a camp bed in the back office then,' Frankie joked, clearly taken by Tim's good looks and easy manner.

He smiled and turned to Sophie. 'Now, I want a personally conducted tour of the shop.'

'I hope you've brought your cheque book with you,' she laughed as he linked his arm through hers. 'How about taking a little Fabergé trinket back to Carolyn?'

'How about my taking *two* little Fabergé do-dahs back to Caro?' He dragged her round the showroom among the last few visitors. Then he stopped in front of a display of china on a shelf. 'Those are rather jolly flower pots.' He pointed at an exquisite pair of jardinières which stood on their own little carved gilt stands. 'How much would they set me back?'

'Thirty-five thousand pounds. They're early Qianlong, and unique.'

Tim stroked the design of pale pink and yellow roses on a bluish-white background. 'On second thoughts I think they're rather over the top for Cardiff, don't you?'

'How about that then?' She indicated one of the ashtrays she'd hired along with the champagne glasses for the party, having decided she'd better allow smoking just for today, to keep on the right side of the many journalists who did.

'Now you're insulting me, and my lady wife,' he boomed, and looked helplessly at Frankie and Katie.

Being with Tim had always been fun and Sophie was reminded of the laughs they'd had all those years ago. Tim had a way of making even the most boring circumstances amusing.

'Haven't you anything inexpensive, Sophie?' he complained. 'I mean to say, look at this.' He flipped a price tag attached to a small tapestry cushion. 'Two hundred and fifty pounds!' His voice rose, quavering like an imperious old lady's. 'Daylight robbery, my dear. That's what I say, daylight robbery.'

'Be quiet, Tim,' Sophie beseeched.

People had stopped talking to watch and listen, and although they looked amused she knew there was a hint of truth behind his joking. Her stock was expensive because she only wanted to sell the best, but it had crossed her mind that she was pricing things rather high.

'What are you doing for lunch?' he asked, suddenly serious.

'I hadn't really thought,' she said lamely, thinking how nice it would be to sit down somewhere quiet for a while.

'Then come and have lunch with me. Oh, do, Sophie. I haven't seen you since we were all in France, and there's loads of catching up to do.' He glanced once again at Frankie and Katie who seemed mesmerised by him. 'You gorgeous girls can hold the fort for half an hour, can't you? Give the boss a chance to put up her feet?'

'All right, all right,' said Sophie, who was really enjoying herself for the first time in what felt like years. 'As you're only up for the day and I probably shan't see you again for ages, we'll go out for a quick lunch. I'll get my handbag.' She looked at her assistants. 'Will you be OK? I promise we shan't be long.'

They assured her they'd be fine. It was now nearly one o'clock, the last of the guests were departing and the caterers were clearing away.

'We'll bring you back a bun,' Tim called over his

shoulder as he and Sophie left the shop. Then he took her arm again. 'I didn't embarrass you, did I, darling?'

'You're as mad as ever,' Sophie grinned. And yet when he and Carolyn had lunched at La Madeleine, he'd been fairly quiet and conventional, she thought. Maybe his wife's presence quenched this part of his personality, the part she remembered so well and had loved so much. 'Where are we going, Tim? I really can't be long, you know. This is the opening day.'

'In which case, from my experience, you won't have any real customers, merely nosy people coming to have a good old gawp. Relax, darling. As you say, I don't know when I'll be up again, so let's make the most of it.'

Four

Whatever happened to those years in between? Sophie reflected as they lingered over their coffee at the end of lunch. She could never say they had been wasted because Brock had shown her the world. Weekends at his tiny apartment in New York or their flat in London had served as full stops in the pages of the story of their travels, pages rich with experience. He'd shown her the beauty of Thailand and the sophistication of Rome, the glamour of California and the ritziness of Paris. They had awakened to watch the Alps emerging through a swathe of pink mist at dawn, and they had sat on a beach at night by the light of a Caribbean moon, big as a glowing pumpkin. Hong Kong, Tokyo, Moscow, Madrid, Brussels, Mexico – like an incantation, the names of the capital cities rolled off her tongue, recalling a hundred visions and a thousand memories. And yet why did she feel, sitting in this little restaurant with Tim, that she had never really lived? Most people would envy the life she'd led with Brock and think her mad to have brought it to an end. But she was tired of the cosseting and the caring and never being responsible for anything.

'What's up, Sophie?' Tim was watching her closely.

Sophie gave a quick sigh. 'Nothing really. I was just wondering why I feel so ... so inexperienced. About life in general. I don't seem to have actually *done* anything until I opened my shop today.'

'It's a good start.'

'But it's only a start. I want to do more, much more.'

He raised his eyebrows. 'What sort of more? Have lots of affairs? Go all bohemian?'

'Idiot,' Sophie laughed.

'What you want is an adventure,' he said perceptively.

She looked at him. 'I suppose you're right,' she said slowly. 'I'd never thought of it like that.'

'So who do you know you can have an adventure with?' He looked at her with keen eyes, and as always they held secret laughter.

'No one,' she admitted, colouring. She hoped he didn't think she had any designs on him. The thought made her blush deepen. 'That's not the sort of adventure I want,' she continued hurriedly. 'I just want to live a bit ... you know, do ordinary things that everyone does. I can't tell you how sheltered I've been in the last few years.'

'At least it's kept you young. Mental age, what? Nineteen?'

'Shut up.' She grinned, remembering she'd been nineteen when he'd gone to Australia. Now if he'd stayed ... She reached for her handbag on the floor by her feet. 'I must get back to the shop, Tim. It's not fair on Katie and Frankie to abandon them like this on the first day. Anyway, I may be missing a good sale.'

'Being with Brock has certainly made you aware of business.'

'That's true. Tim, thank you for a delicious lunch. Give my love to Carolyn. Any chance of your both coming up to London soon?'

Tim paid for the lunch with his Access card as he spoke. 'It's not so easy for Caro to get away, but I'll be up again. I'm really looking for a job in London. I don't think I can stomach being in the depths of the country much longer. I'd like to get into advertising, actually. Anyway, I'll let you know the next time I'm up for an interview, and we'll do lunch again.'

'I'd like that.' Sophie kissed him lightly on the cheek as she said goodbye, and then she hurried back to Gloria Antica wondering whether it was the wine or Tim that was giving her such a lovely floating feeling. It was good to have a friend like him, she told herself, and it was silly to think she might get emotionally involved. He was married and that was that and there was no way she was going to be anybody's mistress. The words of her mother came back to her, advice given when she'd still been in her teens: 'If you can't get a man of your own, don't take someone else's,' Jean had pontificated. Sophie remembered it now. Anyway, she told herself fiercely, Tim belonged to the past, along with Brock. It was to the future she must look now.

'Damn! I must have left my shopping bag at Sophie's,' Audrey exclaimed in consternation as she and Ginny left Santini's.

'Does it matter? Can't you get it next time you're in town?' Ginny asked impatiently. Audrey looked as horror-struck as if she'd left state secrets lying about, and Ginny felt irritated. Why did Audrey have to make such a drama out of everything?

'No, I'll have to go back to Gloria Antica. My diary is in the bag, and some tights I bought earlier.' She looked distractedly up and down the street for a taxi.

'But what about the cinema? Surely you can phone Sophie and get her to post it on to you? And why do you need tights so urgently?'

'I can't do without my diary. It's got all the children's dates in it, when they've got tennis and swimming lessons, all that sort of thing. Ah! There's a taxi.' She raised her hand and waved frantically. 'I'll have to scrap the cinema this time, Ginny. I'm awfully sorry. You do understand, don't you? *Taxi!* Oh, thank God he's seen me.'

With detached amusement. Ginny watched Audrey scramble into the cab, gawky, ungraceful and flushed with anxiety.

'Goodbye, Ginny!' she shouted out of the open taxi window as it drew away from the kerb.

'If you ask me,' Ginny said to her husband later that evening, 'she might have less of a problem with Nicholas if she calmed down a bit and became more of a wife and less of a mother.'

Audrey arrived back at Gloria Antica at the same time as Sophie.

'Come for another look?' Sophie asked, paying off her cab.

'I left my shopping bag here. It's black leather. It's got my diary in it.' Audrey shoved three pounds into her taxi driver's hand and hurried for the shop entrance. 'I distinctly remember leaving it under a table in the corner. God, I hope it's still there.'

'I'm sure it will be. Was there something valuable in it?' Sophie looked at her sister curiously. She seemed more fussed than usual.

'I have to have my diary.' Audrey sounded defensive. 'Where have you been, anyway? I thought you'd be hard at work.'

Sophie grinned. 'Tim turned up and took me out to lunch.'

'Tim who?'

'How many Tims do we know, Audrey? Tim Calthorpe, of course. He's up in London for the day.'

'And you went out to lunch with him?' Audrey looked scandalised, pursing her lips prudishly.

'Of course. What did you expect me to do? We had a lovely chatty lunch, catching up on all our news. There's nothing wrong with that.'

Audrey was only half listening as she rushed over to retrieve her bag. Clutching it, she turned to face Sophie.

'And what about his wife?' she demanded shrilly. 'How do you suppose she likes being stuck in the country while he's running around town with a rich glamour girl?'

Sophie looked aghast. 'But he's not! I'm sure Carolyn wouldn't misunderstand our meeting for lunch. For God's sake, Audrey, you're making something out of nothing.'

'That's what the other woman always says,' she replied bitterly. 'They haven't got any money, according to what Ginny told me in France, and I bet he never takes *her* out to lunch.'

There was a pause as Sophie readjusted her supposition that they were comfortably off. 'I thought he had a good job in insurance and that Carolyn worked in a bank. He never gave me the impression they were hard up.'

'What difference would it have made? Except that you'd probably have paid the restaurant bill instead of letting him do it.' There was a sneering tone in her voice.

Sophie frowned. 'What's the matter, Audrey?' She faced her sister squarely, thankful there were no customers in the shop and that Katie and Frankie were in the back room. 'This isn't about my having a quick impromptu lunch with Tim, is it? Something's bugging you and I wish you wouldn't take it out on me.'

Audrey bit her lower lip and her shoulders sagged. She looked vacantly around the glittering little shop with tear-filled eyes. With a rush of sympathy, Sophie stepped forward and gave her a hug.

'It's Nicholas, isn't it?' she said softly.

'Yes.'

'Have you talked to him?'

'He won't talk. He just walks out of the room. He says talking to me is like being on the receiving end of a barrage of nagging.' Audrey's voice caught in a sob. 'Ginny thinks we should go to Relate.'

'I think she's right.'

'Unless I go to a divorce lawyer.'

'Oh, Audrey, you wouldn't, would you?'

A spark of anger shot into Audrey's eyes. 'If you can get a divorce from a perfectly reasonable, rich, kind man, why can't I get divorced for a two-timing rat?'

'I don't have any children,' Sophie countered swiftly.

Audrey was silent, swallowing hard as she reached for the diary at the bottom of her shopping bag. She wagged it like a long thin black finger in Sophie's face.

'I have it all down in here. Times, dates, weekends when Nick's been absent when he was supposed to be at home.'

Sophie backed away. 'Because he wasn't with you doesn't necessarily mean he was with his bit on the side.'

'Don't use that dreadful expression, Sophie. It's so common.'

If the situation hadn't been so serious Sophie would have laughed at her sister's snobbishness at a time like this.

'So, what are you going to do?' she asked instead.

Audrey stuffed the diary into her handbag. 'I'm going to have a showdown. I can't go on like this. I'm at the end of my tether.'

'I think you're right. You should sit him down and talk it through.'

'Who said I intended to have a showdown with *him*?' Audrey demanded, stomping out of the shop.

It was late when Sophie got back to Eaton Place that night. Letting herself into her first-floor flat, she turned on the lights, revealing a drawing room that was a glamorous landscape of mirrors and gilt, sparkling crystal, rich tapestries and white Thai silk draped and festooned at the two long balcony windows like whipped cream. Brock had engaged an interior designer to help Sophie put together some of the lovely bits of furniture and ornaments they'd bought on their travels, and now, looking around, she was glad. She'd been newly married at the time, with no experience of designing large important rooms, and the flat had remained unchanged ever since. Next to the drawing room, the bedroom glowed in subtle shades of pink, the kingsize bed sheltering under a canopy of rose-patterned chintz.

The phone rang as Sophie was changing into comfortable jeans and sweatshirt. She plumped herself on the bed and picked up the receiver.

'How did it go, honey?' The American accent was softly broad, and the voice richly timbred.

'Brock!' It was no surprise to her that he should ring her tonight. After all, if it hadn't been for him, there'd be no Gloria Antica. 'It was great,' she said enthusiastically. 'Thank you for the flowers. They're very swish.'

'Good. Listen, I'm coming to England sooner than I expected. On Friday, in fact. I'll be staying at the Connaught. Are you free for dinner that night? I could come by Gloria Antica and we could go on from there. I'll book a table at the Blue Elephant. There'll be a very nice German couple joining us...'

Dear old Brock, as controlling as ever, she thought. She could afford to be amused by it now, she was no longer his wife and could say no, but how it had maddened her in the past. Brock never made a suggestion without following it up with a definite proposal. Everything had to be done exactly his way, and he had to be the one who made all the decisions. In time she'd come to realise it was his own sense of insecurity that forced him to take command of every situation, no matter how trivial. He thought that if someone else was in charge he'd be forced into a position he hated and even feared, and while Sophie could understand this, she'd found it impossible to live with.

'Dinner on Friday would be lovely,' she told him. 'I'm longing for you to see the shop. It looks really stunning, and we actually sold a pair of Dutch Delft butter dishes this afternoon.'

'Good for you. By the way, I'm thinking of going to La Madeleine for a few days at the end of the month. You don't mind, do you? I could really do with a few days' rest.'

'Of course not. No probs,' she replied. 'The garden should be in full bloom by then. Shall I tell Hortense you'll be staying, or will you?'

'Whatever.' Brock got bored by the finer details. 'I'll see you on Friday. Six o'clock at the shop. 'Bye, my darling.' Brock hung up abruptly. Knowing him as well as she did, he'd be working through a long list of calls, ticking each one off as he finished.

When the phone rang a few minutes later Sophie thought it might be Brock again. That was another of his little habits, remembering there was something else he wanted to say. But it was Jean. She sounded distraught and at first Sophie couldn't make out what she was saying.

'What. Mum? Alan what?'

'He's collapsed! I'm waiting for the ambulance. Oh, I'm so terribly frightened, Sophie. He's in awful pain.'

Crushing waves of fear and apprehension turned Sophie cold. 'Is it his heart?' Oh, God! Please let him be all right, she prayed. Her stepfather had held a very special place in her heart since he'd married her mother, and although no one could replace her own beloved father, Alan had done everything he could to make her happy.

'It's not his heart,' Jean said. 'He's haemorrhaging. I don't know what's wrong ... Oh, I can hear the ambulance. I'll ring you back.' She hung up before Sophie had time to ask her which hospital they were taking him to. Shaken, she went to the kitchen to make herself a cup of coffee. There was nothing she could for the moment, except wait.

Nicholas didn't get home until nine o'clock that evening. Audrey, who had been hovering over grilled lamb chops in the kitchen for the past hour and a half, looked ready to explode with anger.

'You're late,' she snapped unnecessarily. 'I suppose I don't have to ask where you've been.'

'Give it a rest, Aud.' Nicholas sounded immensely weary. 'I went to have a drink with Kenneth; there's a problem with the builders we put on to the Aylesbury job. It had to be sorted out.' Kenneth was his partner in the architectural company they'd formed eleven years before, and while Audrey knew they sometimes went to the old pub near their offices in the centre of Newbury to have a drink after work, she also saw it as an excuse for him to stay out late.

'The dinner's ruined. I don't see why I should hang around all evening waiting for you to come home. Here.' She thrust a tea towel into his hands. 'It's in the oven. You can bloody well help yourself.' Then she turned and stalked out of the kitchen, her back rigid with self-righteousness.

Nicholas removed the scorched chops and vegetables and looked with distaste at the dried-up gravy that patterned the plate like an old bloodstain. He tipped the lot into the bin, removing his foot sharply from the lever so that the lid crashed back with a loud snap. Then he fetched some bread and a fine ripe Brie from the larder and, picking up that morning's newspaper, settled himself at the kitchen table. He knew that Audrey had cause for complaint, but for the life of him he couldn't bring himself to be a better husband. It was no good her going on about Relate, or her desire to 'talk'. Denise was a symptom of his basic unhappiness, not the cause. The awful, fundamental truth was that Audrey bored him out of his mind and no talking or counselling in the world was going to alter that.

When the phone rang a few minutes later, Audrey, upstairs preparing to have a bath, grabbed the instrument, daring it to be that bloody Denise woman with her cheap gold jewellery and cheaper scent that Nicholas sometimes still smelt of when he came home.

'Who is it?' she demanded in a defensive voice.

'It's me, Sophie.'

'Sophie? What's the matter? You sound odd.'

'Mum phoned me a minute ago. Alan's collapsed and they've taken him to hospital – I don't know which hospital yet, but it sounds bad.' Sophie's voice shook.

'Oh, God. That's all I need. What is it? Heart?'

'It doesn't sound like it.'

Audrey groaned as if in pain. 'Oh, why does this sort of thing happen to me?' she wailed.

'Actually, it's not happening to you, Aud. It's happening to Alan,' Sophie observed crisply.

'What?' Audrey paused just long enough for her sister's remark to sink in, then she said crossly, 'You know perfectly well what I mean. I've got enough on my plate without having the added worry of Alan. And Mum. She's going to need me if anything happens to him. It's all very well for you, but I've got the children and Nicholas to look after and this house. And I live miles away in the country. And I don't have unlimited funds to go up to London all the time. You're rich and you're free with no responsibilities. It's easy for you to say—'

'Audrey.'

'—and it always seems to be me . . . What?'

'You are, without doubt, the most self-centred person I've ever come across! What about poor Mum? Think about how she must be feeling. Alan is her life; she'll be devastated if anything happens to him. I've got to go now in case she rings back. I'm sorry to have spoilt your evening,' Sophie added sarcastically before hanging up.

When Nicholas came up to bed a couple of hours later, hoping to find Audrey asleep, he found her instead sitting on the edge of the bath. She looked as if she'd been crying her eyes out, and forgetting the phone had rung earlier in the evening, he said with ungracious irritation, 'What's the matter now?'

Audrey jumped to her feet and pushed past him, sharp elbows nudging him out of her way. 'What the hell do you care?' she raged.

A minute later he heard the door of the spare room slam. He shrugged. Life with Audrey really was becoming unbearable, and if it wasn't for his precious little girls, asleep at this moment down the passage, he'd walk out right now.

'It doesn't *have* to be cancer,' Sophie told her mother comfortingly. They were sitting in a small waiting room in St Mary's Hospital. Alan had been admitted two hours before and the doctors had decided to carry out an emergency operation.

'When the prostate gland blows up it usually means cancer,' Jean murmured in a flat voice. Shock had taken over and she was quite calm now. She took another sip of water from a paper cup, that being the only liquid beverage available at this time of night, and glanced at her wristwatch for the hundredth time. 'I wonder how much longer they will be.'

'Poor Mum.' Sophie squeezed her hand. 'At least you know he's in the best hands. This is a wonderful hospital.'

They sat on in the silent limbo of those who wait, while all around them the great hospital slumbered through the long still hours of the night. Sophie had not told her mother about Audrey's outburst, and now she felt guilty that her sister did not know which hospital Alan had been taken to.

'You can't ring her at this time of night,' Jean protested when Sophie mentioned it. 'It's three in the morning, you'll wake the whole household. Anyway, what could she do?'

Sophie remained silent. Jean and Audrey had never been close, and she feared an ill-chosen word from her sister could upset her mother even more.

'Why don't you stay with me while Alan's in hospital?'

she suggested. 'They're sure to keep him here for a few days.'

'He may never come home at all.' Jean's mouth quivered. Suddenly she looked old and defeated. 'What shall I do if that happens?' There was no answer to her deepest fears, and Sophie, the daughter nearer to her heart, knew it.

'Don't even think about it, Mum.' Then she straightened, stiff with apprehension, her heart beating fast. The doctor they had seen earlier was coming towards them, walking along the polished corridor neither quickly nor slowly but with a measured tread and a face blank of all emotion.

Heavy rain and grey mist shrouded Hyde Park in its bleak light as Sophie sat in the taxi that was taking her back to Eaton Place. Travelling around the world for the last few years had made her forget the Stygian gloom of a rainy day in England. Brief weekends en route to California or Hong Kong, Dubai or Mexico was all that she'd seen of London when she'd been married to Brock, and even then only from the back of a limousine as they drove to Mark's Club for lunch or Harry's Bar for dinner. This was real life, she told herself, looking out of the cab window at the dripping trees.

Letting herself into the flat, she hurried to the phone. Whatever Audrey had said, she at least owed it to her to tell her about Alan. It was Nicholas who answered the phone.

'You're up very early,' he remarked chattily. 'It's not even seven thirty. Is this your new regime now you've opened your shop, a working girl at last?' He sounded on good form. There was a moment's silence before Sophie spoke.

'Hasn't Audrey told you about Alan?'

'No. What about Alan?'

'He collapsed last night. They had to do an emergency operation to remove his prostate. Mummy and I have been at the hospital all night. I only got home a few minutes ago.'

'My God! I'd no idea. So that was why Audrey...'

'Do you mean she didn't tell you?'

'That doesn't matter. How is poor old Alan?'

'He's pulled through the operation, but he's got cancer. They think he's had it for some time.'

'Christ! That's a bummer. What are his chances?'

'Not brilliant. He's going to have chemotherapy, but after that who knows?' Sophie replied sadly.

'How's Jean taking it? God, she must be shattered,' Nicholas said in consternation. Now he understood why Audrey had been so upset last night and he'd... Shit! He really knew how to make a bad situation worse, didn't he?

'Mum's going to be staying with me for the next few days. I don't think she should be alone. Obviously she'll be visiting Alan a lot of the time, but at least she won't be by herself at night.'

'Good on you, Sophie. Well...' His voice drifted, wondering if he should go up to the spare room and awaken Audrey with the news or leave it to Sophie to tell her later. His sister-in-law solved his problem.

'Will you tell Audrey what's happened, Nicholas? I shall be at the shop in a couple of hours if she wants to speak to me.'

'As she's not speaking to me, I expect she'll want to talk to you. She has to talk to someone,' he added drily.

'Oh, dear, as bad as that?'

'Worse, if anything.'

'Look, I'll ring her later. I was a bit harsh with her on the phone last night. I think I owe her an apology.'

Nicholas made no comment.

Sophie said goodbye and hung up. Nicholas was one of her favourite people; a comfortable, jolly sort of man with a great sense of humour and a calming disposition. Except, it seemed, where Audrey was concerned. Sophie didn't want to get involved in her sister's marital problems, but she had a gut feeling that if Nicholas was straying, maybe he had cause.

Five

'How's the working girl?' It was a week later, and the third time Tim had phoned Sophie since they'd had lunch together.

'I'm fine,' she replied. She was sitting at her desk in the back room of Gloria Antica, and as she talked she doodled on her pad, great loops and circles that made her wonder what a psychiatrist would make of them.

'What about Alan? Is he any better?' Tim had been genuinely concerned when she'd told him about her stepfather. When he and Sophie had gone out together all those years ago he'd struck up a warm friendship with Alan, finding him a man of great understanding and compassion.

'He's coming out of hospital in a couple of days, thankfully. He's longing to get home,' Sophie replied.

'I bet. Listen, I'm coming up to London tomorrow. I've got interviews in the afternoon and another one the following morning. Can I pop into the hospital to see him?'

'He'd love that.'

'Good. I'll take him a bottle of Glenfiddich – I presume it's still his favourite tipple?'

Sophie laughed. 'I think one of the reasons he's so glad

to be getting home is so he can enjoy a good drink again, and that's definitely his favourite.'

'What are you doing for dinner tomorrow night?' It was asked casually, a brother to a sister, one colleague to another.

Sophie's heart gave a tiny flip. How often had he asked her that when she'd been seventeen, and how often had she said 'nothing' with all the rapture of careless youth. Now, for some reason, Audrey's words echoed in her head: 'How do you suppose his wife likes being stuck in the country while he runs around town with a rich glamour girl?' But Tim's tone had been utterly matter-of-fact; there was not a trace of intimacy or flirtatiousness in it and to have demurred would have sounded embarrassingly as if she thought he was harbouring ulterior motives.

'I'm not doing anything in particular,' she replied straightforwardly. 'And this time it's my shout, as they say in Australia.'

'No, I insist on taking you out,' he protested.

'Don't argue,' she said lightly. 'You're dealing with a high-powered businesswoman now, remember? Today we actually sold some Sèvres plates.'

'And I suppose, at your prices that will pay for the rent on the shop for a year.'

Sophie burst out laughing. 'Not quite, but almost!'

When he'd hung up she stayed at her desk thinking about him, remembering the things he'd told her about the years since he'd left England. After his initial enthusiasm for Australia had worn off, he'd decided to go to Hong Kong where the career prospects were better. But bad luck seemed to have dogged him; one of the companies who had employed him went into voluntary liquidation three months after he'd joined them. A series of other jobs had followed and then had come the offer of a highly paid post in a London insurance company.

'I thought I had it made,' he'd told her ruefully, 'and then the worst recession in living memory hit the UK and I was out on my ear.'

Things were improving now, though. His job in Cardiff was adequate but he had high hopes of getting a really good position in London soon. He'd always been exceptionally bright. Sophie had no doubt he'd make it big in due course; meanwhile he was only thirty-six, still a young man.

Audrey had thought about nothing else all week and now she had made up her mind. Things couldn't go on like this. Nicholas never seemed to be at home and when he was, he acted as if she wasn't there.

Dressing with care before setting out, she put on a navy blue skirt and a red jacket. Then she added the new gilt earrings Sophie had given her for Christmas. The effect was good. If Nicholas could see her now, she thought, he'd realise what he was missing.

Half an hour later she entered the Victorian house which had been converted into offices by Nicholas and his partner when they'd gone into business. Set back from the main road, near the centre of Newbury, the front garden had long since been turned into a parking space for the partners' cars. It was with a feeling of satisfaction that Audrey put her car in the space reserved for Nicholas. He wasn't in the office this afternoon; something she'd already ascertained. That was why she was here.

Audrey marched straight into his office on the first floor. At a desk in the corner a tall, very thin young woman with brightly dyed blonde hair looked up at her. They locked eyes and the girl tilted her chin up in a gesture of cool defiance.

'Good afternoon, Mrs Bevan. I'm afraid your husband's out at a meeting. Is there anything I can do for you?'

Audrey found her annoyingly perky and irritatingly over-confident. 'I'm perfectly aware my husband's not here,' she replied coldly. 'It's not my husband I've come to see.'

Denise O'Brien arched finely plucked eyebrows and her smile was insolent. 'So what can I do you for?'

Taking her time, Audrey went and sat behind Nicholas's desk. Her back was to the bay window now, her face in shadow. It gave her an advantage, she felt. While she could see Denise's expression clearly from this vantage point, she doubted the girl could see hers.

'I'll tell you what you can do for me,' she began. 'You can leave my husband alone for a start. In case you'd forgotten, he's a married man with children.'

Denise smirked. 'I'm hardly likely to forget that, Mrs Bevan. Surely it's up to him what he does. If he likes being with me, that's hardly my fault, is it?'

Audrey stiffened and flushed. This was going to be more difficult than she'd imagined. The girl didn't seem in the least in awe of her.

'You don't have to encourage him.'

'Are you suggesting your husband's a weak man?

That he can be easily seduced? If you are, you're greatly mistaken, Mrs Bevan. Nicky makes up his own mind about things.'

Audrey felt the sick bile of rage rise up in her throat. How dare this tart refer to her husband as 'Nicky'! How *dare* she presume to know him better than Audrey did herself.

She rose and, placing the flat of her hands on the desk, leaned forward, her eyes blazing. 'You're nothing but a common little slut!' she stormed. 'Get out of here! Take your things and go! Leave my husband alone, d'you hear? He's married to me. We've got two children and you're ruining everything! Now get the hell out of here.'

Denise O'Brien remained unperturbed, looking at Audrey with sullen eyes. 'It's not up to you to sack me,' she observed brazenly. 'Nicky employs me and I'll stay here as long as I want to, thank you very much.'

'Don't think you can get away with talking to me like this.' Audrey, who had never been good at standing up for herself or her rights, had a horrible feeling that Denise was getting the better of her. She was also afraid that Nicholas wouldn't get rid of Denise even if she begged him to.

'I didn't ask you to come here, Mrs Bevan. Nicky and I are in love; he's never felt like this before and I'm not going to desert him now. You can say what you like, but we're not giving each other up and that's final.'

It might have been the wife talking instead of the mistress. Audrey, her bravado gone, looked utterly crushed. This young woman was so *confident*, and she couldn't be a day over twenty-three, Audrey thought.

Suddenly she felt old and plain, and her red jacket seemed dowdy beside Denise's stylish blue mini-skirt and top. This girl had youth and, worst of all, very obvious sex appeal. Even Audrey could see that.

'I intend talking to my husband,' she said, mustering what shreds of dignity she had left. 'You're not going to get away with this. I'm not going to see my home broken up just so that you can enjoy having a grubby little affair with a married man.'

To Audrey's horror, Denise laughed. She actually laughed, a scornful sort of laughter, throwing back her head and looking at Audrey as if she despised her.

'I think you'll find, if it comes to a choice, that Nicky will stay with me. I give him what he wants, you see. I make him happy.'

For a moment, Audrey stood stock still, and then without another word she turned and walked out of the office, her head held high.

Once home again, she collapsed into great wrenching sobs, hiding away up in her bedroom so her cleaning woman wouldn't see her. She knew now she should never have gone to see Denise. It was the worst thing she could have done because the girl now despised her, and Nicholas was going to be terribly angry when he heard about it. But what was she supposed to do?

When Alan was discharged from St Mary's Hospital, Jean collected him and took him straight back to their Kensington flat.

'You can both stay with me, if you like,' Sophie had offered. Her mother looked as if she needed to be looked after herself, so haggard had she become.

'That's really sweet of you, darling,' Jean replied, touched, 'but I know Alan is desperate to get back to his own home and his own bed.'

'I can understand that, but will you be able to manage?' Jean had always been the helpless one, sitting with her cigarettes, giving orders, while Alan willingly and good-humouredly did many of the chores.

'It will do me good to try,' Jean replied wryly. 'Alan is going to need a lot of looking after, but I'm just so grateful to God that He's spared him this time that I'll willingly scrub floors if it will help.'

'Poor Mum. I notice you've stopped smoking.'

'Well, I promised, didn't I?'

'I'm sure he's going to be all right,' Sophie said comfortingly. 'The doctors are very pleased with the progress he's made. And he's had his first chemotherapy treatment hasn't he?'

'Poor lamb. He's going to hate going bald.' Jean shook her head sadly.

'Not if it saves his life, he isn't,' Sophie pointed out.

'Of course you're right. It's a day at a time from now on, and we've got to stop worrying about trivia and concentrate on what matters.'

With the flat to herself again, and Gloria Antica up and running, Sophie wanted to strike a new balance between work and socialising, making her life more structured and her days more focused. For the first time since she'd been twenty, she was able to wake up in the mornings and plan her days as she wished. And it was wonderful to be able to change her mind if she wanted to. When she'd been married to Brock there were times when she had no idea what was happening next, and was forced to wait for his instructions: see to the packing, we're leaving this morning; don't pack yet, we have to stay on another day. We're going here. We're not going there. Brock did it all with loving concern and even gentleness, but the fact remained he controlled every moment, so that she felt there was no destination point in her life, no sense of arrival. Time was spent *getting* there ... but where?

She enjoyed controlling her own destiny, but there was one problem. Since the divorce, many of their friends had sided with Brock and didn't want to have anything to do with her, although Brock had said very publicly that no one was to take sides. Of those who did remain friends, she found, for the first time in her life, that the other wives no longer wanted her to be around at the same time as their menfolk. They always suggested lunch, a gathering of married, divorced and widowed women, but never dinner. Some made lame excuses, such as they had a problem finding a single man to make up the numbers, but Sophie was not fooled.

'It's quite ridiculous,' she told her mother one day. 'Why should they feel threatened? They surely can't imagine I'm after their husbands.'

'You may not be, but a lot of newly divorced women are on the look-out for another man. There's something else, too, and the wives are quite aware of it.'

'What?'

'Divorced women are easy prey for wandering husbands.' Jean nodded knowingly.

'Why divorced women in particular?' Sophie asked.

Jean looked slightly embarrassed. 'Because they're missing regular sex. So along comes a man who offers it to them, no strings attached, nice and casual, and the divorced woman is so grateful she falls into bed without a word of protest.'

Sophie burst out laughing. 'Well, *this* divorced woman isn't like that.'

When she was alone again, Sophie thought deeply about what her mother had said. Since she'd been on her own, the one thing she did miss was sex. Brock had been wonderfully skilled in bed, and in the last few years his skill had made up for the lack of their original passion. She did want sex, but the difference between her and the women her mother had talked about was that she wasn't turned on by the idea of casual, meaningless sex. She needed to love and be loved in order to become aroused and she wanted a relationship that included a commitment.

Tonight she'd been invited to a drinks party; there'd be an opportunity to meet a lot of people. Sophie smiled to herself. Did she really want a relationship at the moment? The answer came to her swiftly and positively. Yes, she did. She wanted someone in her life again, with whom she could share her thoughts and desires, with whom she could drive into the country at weekends for a cosy lunch at an old inn, with whom she could try out new restaurants, drink champagne in bed with and enjoy the delights of La Madeleine.

Sophie looked in the mirror as she slipped into a black chiffon dress which revealed slim tanned shoulders and arms through the sheer fabric and wondered if she'd meet anyone tonight. It was unlikely because she'd already found what she wanted. The only trouble was Tim Calthorpe was now a married man.

* * *

The room was packed with people she'd known for years, mostly friends she'd made with Brock, who were also in banking. She was greeted with loud delight by the men, and a more reserved welcome by the women. Their attitude rather reminded her of Audrey and she recognised a certain spiteful jealousy in their remarks.

'So how's the little shop going? Have you sold anything yet?' asked one plump woman in a tight emerald-green dress and a cascade of pearls. She and her husband were old friends of Brock and had greatly disapproved of the divorce. Before Sophie could answer, the wife of another banker came up to her

'How are you getting on, my dear? Aren't you terribly lonely now that you're no longer with Brock? Do you ever get asked anywhere?'

Sophie was at a loss for words. She longed to be able to think up a quick, smart, witty reply, but her mind went blank. Nothing in her life had prepared her for the cut and thrust of the cocktail party where alcohol fuelled the vituperative manner of some of the women and the men saw her as a target with whom to flirt.

'I say, you're looking fantastic,' enthused the husband of the woman in green. Tall and jovial looking he towered over her, trying to peer down her cleavage. 'You look so marvellous, it must mean you're having an affair. Found someone new, have you?'

Sophie suddenly found her tongue. 'Why are men so conceited they imagine that only a man can make a woman look and feel good?' she demanded angrily.

'But you're positively glowing, Sophie,' he replied,

smiling inanely at her. 'You've got to be up to something.'

Sophie looked back at him, a ravishing figure in her black dress, with only a rope of large pearls round the base of her throat to relieve its simplicity. 'I could have just had a hot shower,' she retorted scathingly. 'Or it could be the satisfaction of running my own business. I can't imagine why you should think it has anything to do with there being a man in my life.' Then she turned and walked away, still feeling angry. What right had that jerk to imagine that only a man could bring a sparkle to a woman's eye and a glow to her cheeks? At that moment, a widower she'd known for several years came up to her. His name was Dominic Erroll, a gentle, amenable man, with horn-rimmed glasses and a kind manner.

'How lovely to see you again, Sophie,' he exclaimed, kissing her on both cheeks. 'I've read all about Gloria Antica. You are doing well, aren't you? Of course you're an expert on antique porcelain but what fun to have your own shop. I quite envy you. Tell me all about it.'

His interest was like a soothing balm to her ruffled feelings. Soon they were huddled in a corner, chattering about Meissen and Lowestoft, Tournai and Frankenthal wares, and comparing notes on which was their favourite china. It was the first time for ages that she'd met anyone, apart from the dealers, who shared her enthusiasm for porcelain and who knew almost as much about it as she did.

The other guests were beginning to go. She had not realised it was so late.

'Poor you,' whispered a spiky-looking little witch in

gold and purple lamé, 'being stuck with Dominic. We must meet for lunch one day, my dear.' She gave a conspiratorial wink.

'Oh, must we?' Sophie replied, not missing a beat.

Dominic, having bid goodbye to a couple he knew, turned back to Sophie. 'I wonder,' he asked, almost shyly, 'if you'd like to come out to have a bite of supper. We could go to...'

'I'd love that,' Sophie said firmly and loudly, so that purple lamé could hear.

Dominic took her to the Restaurant, an award-winning place run by Marco Pierre White, in the Hyde Park Hotel. The food was exquisite, the wine mellow and the ambience relaxed and gentle, like her host. They talked about other things besides porcelain and Sophie could honestly admit to herself that she was having a lovely evening, pleasant and friendly, easy-going and without any conflict. Much like the evenings she'd spent with Brock.

When Dominic dropped her off at her flat he saw her to the front door. 'It's been a great evening, Sophie.' There was a hint of gratitude in his voice. 'I've enjoyed your company so much.'

'Thank you for asking me, Dominic,' she replied with sincerity. 'I've enjoyed it too.'

His kiss, planted drily on her cheek near the corner of her mouth, was as exciting as a brush with a butterfly. Once in her flat, alone in her bed, she thought about Tim again. His kisses had never been like that.

Six

He turned up at Gloria Antica two days later, just before noon. Sophie, who was showing a customer a Derby vase embellished with porcelain flowers round the side and a small bird perched on the rim, looked up and was immediately aware of a hot flush creeping up her face from her neck. He smiled and winked at her and then started to examine some figurines as if he, too, was a customer.

'You can see the abundance of florets in delicate pinks and red, a typical example of Edmé Samson's work, and the tones of puce and blue are very true. In fakes these colours can be greyish...' Sophie was aware she was waffling but she was so conscious of Tim's presence her concentration had deserted her. He was wearing a grey suit, beautifully cut, and a pale blue shirt. As he stood, hand in pocket, examining a delicate Copenhagen porcelain teapot, the curve of his thigh showed through the fine cloth, sending her heart racing. Stop it! she told herself fiercely; it all ended thirteen years ago. He left you then, and if he's come back into your life now, it's only as a friend, a chum, an amusing companion to have a chat with when it suited him.

The customer decided to buy the vase, and Sophie gave it to Katie to wrap in cotton wool, bubble wrap, and finally insert it in one of the smart bags she'd designed, in a thick glossy red paper with the Gloria Antica logo on the side, while she wrote out a receipt. Her hands were shaking and her chest felt tight. What was he doing in London? He'd only been up the previous week when he'd been to see Alan in hospital, and then he'd taken her out to dinner afterwards.

At last the customer left, thanking her profusely for her help. Sophie turned to Tim, determined to keep it light.

'Hi, there!' she greeted him gaily. 'What brings you up here so soon again?'

'I've been recalled by one of the companies who interviewed me last week. I'm seeing them at three thirty,' he replied, grinning boyishly. 'Caro thinks it's a good sign. They don't usually want to see you again unless they're interested, do they?'

'That's great. Which company is it?'

'International Link. It's a telecommunications outfit and it's based in London. God, I hope I get it.' He clasped his hands together in mock prayer and cast his eyes to heaven. 'Think of it, Sophie. Thirty thousand a year, a company car, and lots of perks. Caro and I can get a nice flat in the centre of town; I've been long enough in the backwoods.'

Danger signals glowed in her brain while her emotions took flight in a great curve of hope. 'Sounds fantastic,' she agreed. 'Carolyn must be excited at the prospect.'

'Over the moon. We both are.'

Sophie looked up into his eyes, seeing still the secret laughter in their depths, and wondered how she was going to avoid seeing him if he came to London. He had got under her skin, into her head and through to her innermost heart in a way that scared her. How could she have let herself fall in love with him again?

'Are you ready for lunch?' he was saying. 'As it's such a gorgeous day, why don't we go to a restaurant where we can eat outside?'

'I can't be long,' she warned. 'What about that little place behind Harrods?'

Tim slipped his arm through Sophie's. 'Come on then. Let's go.'

Frankie and Katie watched them walk down the road together. Tim was talking and gesticulating, and Sophie was looking up at him, giggling.

'He's quite something, isn't he?' Frankie remarked.

'Well, Sophie seems to think so. It's romantic, isn't it? Meeting him again after all these years. She obviously still adores him.'

'First love and all that.' Frankie raised her eyebrows. 'I wonder if he'll leave his wife now he's found Sophie again.'

Katie shook her head sagely. 'No chance.'

'Why do you say that?'

'Because he's not in love with her. It stands out a mile.'

Frankie looked puzzled. 'How can you be so sure?'

Katie shrugged. 'I just am. I can tell you one thing, though. She's crazy about him. I wonder if he realises?'

They ate pasta, steaming hot and glazed with pesto, and

dusted with a drift of Parmesan cheese. With it they had olive bread and red wine and a side dish of green salad.

'It's hard to believe this is England,' Sophie commented as she put on her sunglasses. A brilliant sun beat down on them, dazzling on the white tablecloth, reflecting on the silver cutlery, bouncing off the pavement. 'I could almost imagine I was in France again.'

'What? In an Italian restaurant, eating Italian food?'

'You know very well what I mean, Tim,' she replied, grinning. 'It's the heat. Isn't it wonderful?'

'You should spend a summer in Australia, then you'd know what real heat is. Spend the day on Bondi Beach and it will cure you of ever wanting to sit in the sun again.' He looked rueful. 'When I first went there, I spent the day surfing and sunbathing, and then the next week in hospital. I could have achieved exactly the same effect, in my efforts to get a tan, by throwing a bucket of scalding water over myself.'

'Ouch! Sounds painful.'

'It was.'

'Why did you leave? You were so keen to go at the time.'

'I told you, job prospects were poor.' He spoke shortly as if he didn't want to discuss the matter. Sophie didn't press the point. She had really no wish to talk about Australia either.

'I hope I get this job I'm going after today,' he continued. 'I'm dying to get back to London. So is Caro. We both miss the theatre and the exhibitions and the whole buzz of city life. Who knows? We might even start a family.'

The pang of sheer jealousy that swept through Sophie

shocked her with its intensity. At that moment, she'd have gladly given up Gloria Antica, Eaton Place and La Madeleine to be in Carolyn's shoes; to be married to Tim, to be sharing the rest of her life with him, to be expecting his baby. It was all she'd really wanted, all those years ago. And it was what she wanted now, with a longing that was so acute she felt sick. She took a gulp of her wine, hoping he wouldn't notice, for surely desire was writ plainly on her face. Her hands shook and she made a play at looking at her wristwatch.

'Is that really the time? God, I must get back to the shop,' she exclaimed, forcing her voice to sound steady. 'Thank you for a lovely lunch, Tim. Good luck this afternoon.'

Tim looked bewildered as she gave him a polite peck on the cheek and hurried off down the road.

'I'll call you to let you know if I get it,' he shouted after her. She waved in answer and hurried on.

The afternoon was a slow agony of wanting; wanting to be with Tim, to feel his arms round her, his mouth crushing hers; to feel him inside her and his seed implanting itself deep within her, making her pregnant. Wanting to wake up with him in the mornings and go to sleep with him every night. Wanting to laugh and cry and talk and breathe the air he breathed, so that they became like one person. It was a ravenous hunger that consumed her now and she didn't know how to assuage it, but the worst part of it was that at the very centre of her hunger was a raging hatred for a blameless young woman who just happened to be in the position she so wanted to fill herself. Sophie had no idea she could hate so much. It stunned her and made her feel ashamed to realise she could bitterly resent the existence of another human being with such virulence. Tim had belonged to her, once. Now he belonged to someone else and it was something she had to accept, but how hard it was. How hard.

Alone in her grand flat that evening she made up her mind not to see Tim again. She'd resolved not to see him before, at La Madeleine. This time she must keep to it. How she would explain it, if he came to work in London, she didn't know, but it was imperative they didn't meet. At least not on their own. Maybe not even in a crowd. The pull of the past, of a passion torn up by the roots and cast aside, of a lost youth, and of a love not fully requited had somehow managed to come back and hit her with the force of a new obsessive passion. The years with Brock no longer existed or, if they did, remotely at the back of her mind with no more significance than her love for her father or her fondness for Alan. She felt nineteen again, swept along by the rapture of first love, with all its insecurities and bliss. She was also slipping down to the black depths of unfulfilment and she had to get away before it devoured her.

After a sleepless night, Sophie decided to fly to La Madeleine for a few days. Frankie and Katie could manage Gloria Antica, Alan was home again with Jean to look after him, there was no reason why she shouldn't slip away and be on her own for a little while. She needed the time and the space. La Madeleine had always provided the balm her sorely troubled spirit needed.

'If anyone asks where I've gone, don't tell them,' she

instructed her assistants, thinking that Tim might phone in the next couple of days if he'd got the job he wanted. 'Say I've gone to the country,' she added. 'Don't even mention France.'

The travel agent had arranged for there to be a self-drive car ready for her to collect at Nice airport. It was halfway through the tourist season, and crowds of holidaymakers were waiting to take possession of the cars they'd hired. She stood patiently in line, and tried to put Tim out of her mind. It didn't help that she'd dreamed about him the previous night.

Once on the road to Grasse, Sophie put her foot down, hoping to get ahead of the worst of the traffic, but it was nearly four o'clock when she finally drove through the entrance gates of the villa and waved to a surprised-looking Henri who was watering the garden with a powerful hose. She'd asked Frankie to call Hortense that morning to say she'd be staying for a few days but obviously Henri had been unaware of her impending arrival. He dropped the hose with a splat onto the lawn and lumbered over to help her with her luggage.

'How is everything?' she asked, her French fluent. While he mumbled some grumbling reply, his wife appeared, once again gowned in the familiar black.

'It is nice to see you, Madame. It is quite a surprise.' She looked ill at ease, and for a moment Sophie thought she was going to say something more but she seemed to change her mind and instead turned and walked back into the house.

Grabbing a bikini out of one of her cases before Henri

took it indoors, Sophie slipped into the ground-floor shower room and changed. She was dying for a swim. Dust from the road seemed to be clinging to her hair, sticking to her skin in a golden layer, and filling her throat. The August sun beat down like a furnace on the parched countryside, and there didn't seem to be a breath of air in the somnolent afternoon.

Running down the scorching terrace steps to the lower level, she dived into the aquamarine coolness of the pool and swam a width underwater, emerging on the other side gloriously refreshed. The water was sensuously silky, and for a while she floated on her back, her dark hair spread out like a fan, her eyes closed, a wondrous feeling of languor spreading through her limbs. How glad she was she'd come here. A few days of lazing under the almond trees and being looked after by Hortense would quickly restore her equilibrium. She would read to stop her thinking about Tim, but she would avoid listening to music; music could be dangerous, evoking emotions she must try to control. Tim is married now, she kept repeating to herself, but the longing for him remained. Perhaps she'd phone him this evening just to hear his voice. If Carolyn were to answer ... but she'd hang up quickly in any case. Tim must never know he'd reawakened her love for him; never realise that her hankering after him had developed into an obsession.

Sophie kept her eyes tightly shut, trying to blot out all images of him, but it seemed as if he filled her whole horizon, and the faint echo of an orgasm shot through her, leaving her strung out with an intensity of desire that made her feel quite sick. Tim ... Tim ... She whispered his name repeatedly while her hand slid up to her breasts, feeling the erect nipples, hard and small through the thin fabric of her bikini top, moving her hips to recapture that exquisite echo.

'So how's the little mermaid?' A man's voice, from the side of the pool, startled her. She thrashed in the water for a moment before turning to see who it was. Then she looked up. It was Brock. He was standing looking down at her, with his hands in the pockets of his casual cream cotton trousers, and he had a deeply amused smile on his benign face.

Turning scarlet, Sophie exploded with anger. 'What the hell are you doing here? I will not be spied on!' she yelled from the middle of the pool where she trod the water angrily, slim brown arms flailing around.

'I wasn't spying on you, my darling,' he responded mildly. 'You looked very pretty and ... er ... relaxed.' His mouth twitched at the corners. Her blush deepened. Brock knew her too damn well not to realise she'd been turned on by her own thoughts.

'But why are you here?' she asked furiously.

Brock wandered over to one of the white cane chairs and dropped into it, unbuttoning his open neck navy blue shirt as he did so. 'I did ask you if it would be OK for me to spend a few days here at this time,' he pointed out, taking off the shirt to reveal a broad barrel-shaped chest, the skin only lightly tanned, the hair white. 'You said it would be fine, that you'd be busy with the shop.'

Sophie's expression was appalled. 'Oh, God! I completely forgot. I am sorry, Brock. I decided to come here on impulse, it had completely slipped my mind that you'd be here too.' She swam to the pool steps as if to climb out.

'Stay in the pool, sweetheart. I'm coming in to join you.' He stripped off his trousers and underpants and dived in, naked. She could see his bulky form swim smoothly to the bottom, and then he swam underwater, rising with a plop, like a champagne cork popping out of the bottle, just beside her. He was smiling broadly, and reaching forward kissed her wetly on the cheek.

'Good to see you, my darling. A nice surprise,' he commented affably.

Sophie tried to hide her vexation. She'd so longed to be on her own, and she realised why she felt resentful at Brock's appearance. She'd really wanted to be alone so that she could think about Tim undisturbed. She'd been fooling herself when she'd said that a few days at La Madeleine would help her forget all about him and would put their whole relationship into perspective. She'd really come here in order to wallow, alone with her secret obsessive fantasy, imagining herself back with Tim, reliving the torrid days and nights of their affair. And now here was Brock with his bonhomie to spoil it all. She felt as cross and frustrated as when her mother and Alan had hung around when she'd first met Tim, staying up half the night rather than let them be alone.

'When did you arrive, Brock?' she inquired politely as he swam strongly up and down the pool.

'A couple of hours ago.'

'What? This afternoon? Why on earth didn't Hortense tell Frankie when she phoned to say I was on my way.'

He hoisted himself out of the pool onto the stone

surround, his arms and shoulders strong. 'You know what the French are like. They probably thought we were planning a dirty weekend.'

Sophie snorted at the absurdity of the idea. 'How ridiculous. Don't worry, Brock. I'll check into a hotel. I'm sure I can get a room at Le Moulin de Mougins; I'll get on to Roger Verge right away.'

'Are you crazy, sweetheart?' His expression was a mixture of astonishment and hurt. 'Surely we can both stay here for a few days? Do you really hate me so much that you can no longer bear to be under the same roof as me?'

Sophie coloured again, ashamed of her graceless behaviour. 'Of course not, Brock. That's not what I meant. I just don't want to be in your way. I know you've come here for a rest.'

'And why have you come here, darling?' he asked softly.

'The same reason; to have a few days' peace and quiet,' she replied lightly, averting her face. 'The shop's going brilliantly, and with Katie and Frankie to look after everything, I thought I'd get away for a break.'

'Then there's no problem, is there? If Hortense hasn't already made up two beds, we can ask her to, can't we?'

Sophie nodded, thinking how strange it was going to be, staying at La Madeleine with Brock, now they were divorced.

It was ten days since Audrey had gone to see Denise O'Brien, and in that time she and Nicholas had not exchanged a word except in front of Amelia and Rebecca.

He'd come back from the office that evening looking thunderous and she didn't have to ask if Denise had said anything. It was written in the angry angle of his shoulders and the jutting line of his jaw. Ignoring her presence, he went out almost immediately again and had been out every evening since, coming back so late that she was already asleep, or at least pretending to be, by the time he slid into the large bed beside her. Sleeping at the furthest edge, he said not a word, night or morning, and her attempts at conversation were met with total indifference, followed by Nicholas turning and walking out of the room.

'For a jolly man like Nicholas, that's quite an act he's putting on,' Jean observed when Audrey told her how she was being treated. 'He's such a gregarious man, I'm sure he won't be able to keep it up for much longer,' she added.

'You've no idea what it's like to live with,' Audrey complained. She was phoning her mother on an almost daily basis since she'd fallen out with Nicholas, and Jean, absorbed in looking after Alan, was beginning to lose her patience.

'Well, you'd better sort it out, and the sooner the better,' Jean replied tartly. 'Tell him you're sorry you went to see that girl.'

'Mummy, I *can't*!' she wailed. 'I did it to try and save our marriage, to get her to give him up.'

'And it was a very silly thing to do, too. Why should she listen to you? She has everything to gain by hanging on to him, and now she'll look upon it as a challenge. A wife must never go and beg the mistress to leave. It's rotten psychology.'

'Well, it's no good my asking *him* to get rid of her. He'd never listen to me.'

'Right now he won't, but give it time, Audrey. Play him at his own game. Ignore him, too.' Jean sounded brisk and impatient.

Audrey burst into tears. 'But it's so lonely ... having no one to talk to. I can't bear it. I feel so excluded from life. What have I done to deserve this? It simply isn't fair.'

'Haven't I always told you life *isn't* fair?'

'But all I want is to be happily married. It isn't much to ask.' Her voice had taken on the whining note that had irritated her mother even when she was a child.

'Why don't you go away for a few days? Let Nicholas simmer on his own,' Jean suggested.

'How can I leave the children? Where can I go?' Audrey blew her nose loudly, and Jean could just imagine her, sitting in a heap by the phone, wearing one of those long droopy cardigans she so favoured.

'Stop making excuses, Aud! You're being really hopeless. Your Mrs Thingemby can look after Amelia and Rebecca, and Nicholas can take them to school. Why don't you go and stay with Patricia what's-her-name? That fat girl you went to school with? She's got a nice house in London, hasn't she? Go and stay with her.'

'I suppose I could go to Pat's.' Audrey sounded doubtful.

'And get a make-over while you're in town,' Jean said candidly.

'A what?'

'You know. A make-over. Go to a beauty salon or

something and get made over. A new hairstyle. New make-up. Some smart new clothes, in a different style, perhaps.'

'What's wrong with my clothes?' Audrey demanded suspiciously.

Jean didn't hesitate. 'They're dowdy, dear. If you're going to win Nicholas back, you've got to beat his secretary at her own game.'

'I don't think I know how,' Audrey wailed in despair.

'Then find out; and find out fast, dear.'

Hortense, smiling slyly, served dinner to Sophie and Brock on the terrace, just as she'd done when they'd been married. Tonight, as if in celebration, she'd made large bowls of *moules marinières*, the shells like polished pewter in the lantern light, the fragrance delicate and spicy. Then she served a dish of saffron rice with oyster mushrooms, asparagus tips and garlic, blended in a creamy sauce, with which they drank a rich fruity Valvigneyre Syrah, a Côtes-du-Rhône wine Brock particularly liked.

'I'm glad I didn't come here to lose weight,' Sophie said as she loosened the waistband of her skirt. Barefoot, and with her dark hair flowing loose around her shoulders, she had the wild rose beauty of a gypsy tonight, but there was something restless in her face, and a hungry look in her eyes. Brock, watching her, did not press her for an explanation. He knew her better than anyone, and he knew she had to be allowed time and space before she would say what was on her mind. It had been the same before she'd asked for the divorce. For a year he'd watched her work out everything, in silent agony, before she said anything to him. To have intruded on her private world then would have been emotional rape as far as she was concerned, and Brock knew it. Always intensely private about her feelings, she was inclined to close up like a clam if anyone probed, and then she shut everyone out.

'Don't forget Hortense has also made *pots au chocolat* to follow,' he said, by way of making conversation. 'And I spied a beautifully ripe Brie in the kitchen.'

'Don't!' Sophie clasped her stomach in mock pain and leaned back in her chair. 'I always forget how well she cooks and I come here, intent on eating only salads and fruit, and then end up stuffing myself like a pig.'

Brock laughed. 'And I come here because of the food. The woman's a genius in the kitchen. We must make sure she always stays here. Perhaps we should give her more money.'

Sophie nodded. 'And a bonus at Christmas.'

'More wine, my darling?'

'Yes, please.' She sipped her drink thoughtfully, considering the generation gap and how it showed at times. Tim never called anyone 'my darling' and he never had, yet Brock always used that term of endearment. Tim had called her 'Pet' in the old days and sometimes 'Sausage'. A smile flickered fleetingly across her face at the memory, and then a look of pain replaced it, and she got up and wandered to the edge of the terrace, gazing down the garden at the rectangle of aquamarine light below. The hammock Tim had lazed in when he'd come to lunch still hung from the tall oak, and she recalled that as he'd lain there that day, she'd realised he still had the power to attract her deeply. Swiftly she finished her wine and, returning to the marble dining table, refilled her glass to the brim.

'How about a swim when we've digested this feast?' Brock suggested.

'Maybe.' Sophie shrugged. She raised her face to look up at the night sky, and a million stars shone down, melting and disintegrating as her eyes brimmed with tears. She dashed them away swiftly, and then with exaggerated casualness sauntered down to the pool. Brock remained on the terrace, enjoying his wine and cheese, glad that Sophie was also staying at the villa although she was a thousand miles away from him. He'd never stopped loving her and he never would, but they'd been right to divorce. Bluebells and autumn leaves were never meant to go together and he'd been a selfish fool to try and make it work. At least they were still friends, and he hoped that, with care, it would always be so.

It was midnight, and the little lanterns that edged the paths and hung from the trees like winking glow-worms were on the wane. Above, a full moon stridently dominated the darkness, while the cicadas kept up their high-pitched drone in the shrubbery. Sophie, lying on cushions along the side of the pool, reclining in silhouette from where Brock sat, sipped wine and dreamed, and conversed inconsequentially.

'You're happy with Gloria Antica, aren't you, my darling?' Brock observed quietly, watching her.

'It's what I always wanted,' Sophie reflected, turning to gaze at him. The wine made her feel languorous. It was almost too much effort to complete a sentence. 'And it's all mine...'

'I'm glad you're happy.'

She didn't answer, but closed her eyes in momentary anguish, thinking of Tim. Tim with his wife; kissing her, making love to her, impregnating her with his fine strong body. She rolled onto her side, burying her face in her arms, her hands clenched into small fists as she fought to rid herself of the picture her mind had created. I shall die if I don't have him, she thought desperately. I want him so badly. A sob escaped her lips and a moment later she felt a warm hand on her shoulder. Startled, she rolled on to her back again, looking up into the kindly familiar face of Brock.

Without saying a word he leaned forward and kissed her gently on the lips. His breath, as usual, smelled sweetly of peppermint, and almost automatically, from habit, Sophie returned his kiss, reaching up to wind her arms round his neck. Then, taking her in his arms, he pulled her close, kissing her closed eyes, and her cheek, and the warm curve of her neck. In response she stroked his back, slid her hands down to his buttocks, retracing the familiar territory of a landscape she knew as well as she knew her own body. With his weight pressing her into the ground, she spread her legs and held him close. She was ready for love, aroused and full and ripe and wanton, needing to be filled, desperate to be satisfied.

'Oh, yes ... please,' she moaned, her eyes tightly closed as she clung to Brock. He was kissing her now, passionately and hungrily, and then he entered her, deeply and greedily ... and the blond hair on his arms glinted in the sunlight, and the laughing eyes held a magic secret, and his tall, slim young body was probing her, possessing her, and she was all his. For ever. In a flash, the exquisite heat rose to a peak, burst into searing flames, driving her over the edge so that she thought she would die from the ecstasy of the moment, and then she cried out blindly, 'Oh, God, Tim! I love you so much.'

They breakfasted separately the next morning, Brock under the shade of the vine-covered pergola, Sophie in her room. She felt dreadful. A splitting headache from all the wine she'd drunk the previous night, together with her shame and embarrassment at what had happened, had made her decide to leave La Madeleine as soon as she'd dressed and packed. There was no way she could face Brock and his anger again. When he'd realised it was not him but someone else she'd really been making love to, he'd turned on her in a rage, bellowing that she was selfish and cruel. Shocked, because never once in all the years they'd been married had he talked to her like that, she burst into stormy sobs, realising that alcohol and imagination had combined to delude her into confusing reality with fantasy. So much so that never before had she experienced such a powerful orgasm. And while Brock was flattering himself that he was the cause, she had gone and blurted out Tim's name. One thing was certain, though. If last night's experience was anything to go by, how much more wonderful the reality would be.

Sighing deeply, Sophie put on white jeans, a cool white cotton top, and stuffing the rest of her clothes into a case, crept out onto the landing and listened. There was not a sound. Tiptoeing to the top of the steep wooden staircase, she stole down to the empty living room and looked around. Through the windows she could see Brock's back as he sat at the marble-topped table, on which were a jug of orange juice, a basket of croissants, and a pot of coffee. At one point he raised his hand to smooth down his windswept white hair and then he started to rise from his chair. Sophie didn't wait. She shot into the hall and swept through the kitchen to the back door. Hortense, who was preparing vegetables in the sink, looked up startled, exclaiming 'Madame!' in a loud voice.

Sophie shook her head, put one finger urgently to her lips. Then she fled into the back courtyard of the villa where she'd left her car the previous afternoon. Throwing her case into the back she jumped in and started the engine. Her one desire was to get away as soon as possible. How could she have let Brock make love to her now they were divorced? And how could she have possibly deceived herself into believing it was Tim who had held her in his arms?

Pressing her foot hard on the accelerator, she shot down the drive. She glanced in the rearview mirror. Brock was standing on the terrace, his arms hanging helplessly by his sides. And in that moment, before the curve in the drive made her lose sight of him, she caught a quick glance of his face. His expression was one of profound sadness.

The village was already busy, and there was a queue of people at the bakery. A small group of children were playing on the dusty tree-edged central square, watched by a couple of old women in black, their grey hair drawn back from their sallow faces, their eyes like bleary oysters.

Sophie drove on, heading for an ancient olive mill which was now a famous inn and *pension*. It was run by a French couple and their reputation as restaurateurs had spread throughout Europe. Sitting in her car, heading twenty kilometres west of La Madeleine, she hardly noticed the beauty of the countryside with its rows of neat poplars and picturesque villages cleaving to the rocky hillsides as she sped along. Her only thought was to put as much distance as she could between herself and Brock.

When she drove into the cobbled courtyard of Le Moulin de Mougins, her heart sank to see how crowded the place was. She'd been mad to think they'd have a room available in August. Nevertheless, she parked the car and hurried into the reception area. The last time she'd been here it had been with Brock.

'Oh, I am so sorry, Madame Duval,' the receptionist exclaimed, throwing up her hands in dramatic despair when Sophie asked for a room, 'but we are absolutely full. There is not a corner, nothing.'

'I was afraid that would be the case,' Sophie replied. 'Never mind. I'll go on to Nice, although I expect all the hotels are booked up there too.'

'Shall I phone the Negresco for you, Madame? Why don't you relax with a nice cup of coffee in the garden and I will see what I can do.'

'That's really kind. Thank you.' Gratefully, Sophie strolled through the restaurant with its pink brick arches and massed arrangements of white lilies, and out into the garden. Small tables and chairs were arranged around the courtyard. She chose one under the shade of a mimosa tree and instantly wished Tim could share the beauty of the place with her. Tim. Tim. She drummed her fingers on the white linen tablecloth and wished she could rid herself of this obsession. She felt desperate, in the grip of something she couldn't control. Until the day he'd phoned her at La Madeleine, she'd been so happy; well, happy*ish*. Contented, certainly. She'd been free, rich, about to realise a lifelong ambition by opening her own shop and, for the first time in her life, in charge of her destiny. Then Tim had appeared and all she'd done from then on was hanker after him as if she was a lovesick girl of seventeen again. Sighing, she turned at the sound of approaching footsteps.

It was Brock.

'Why are you running away from me?' he asked in a puzzled voice.

Sophie flushed. 'Why do you think?'

Stepping forward, he sat down in the chair facing her. 'I apologise for what I said last night, Sophie. It was very wrong of me to talk to you like that and I deeply regret it.'

She remained silent, not knowing what to say.

'I know we're divorced,' he continued, 'but I do still love you, you know. It was stupid of me, but for one brief moment I thought you still loved me.' Brock paused, frowning as if in pain. 'Last night you were so ... so responsive. Stupid of me to think it was for me. Then, when I realised there was someone else ... well, my disappointment was so great I'm afraid I just lashed out.' He shook his head. 'Of course you must have someone else in your life, a beautiful young woman like you. I was a fool to think otherwise. Has Tim been back in your life for long?'

Sophie shook her head.

'May I ask, was it because of Tim that you wanted a divorce?'

'No!' she exclaimed, surprised. 'You know it wasn't. I didn't seen him until he rang me when I was at La Madeleine in June. He was staying with Ginny and Jonathan Howard.' For some reason she couldn't bring herself to tell Brock that Tim was married although she didn't know why. Perhaps because she didn't want Brock to think she was having an affair with a married man. Or maybe she didn't want him to know she *wasn't* having an affair but was suffering from an unrequited obsession.

'Then why don't you come home ... I mean to La Madeleine?' he asked gently. 'I promise you there will be no repeat of last night.'

'No, I'm going to Nice,' she told him firmly. 'It's your turn to stay at the villa, and it wouldn't be fair for me to be there too. Especially after last night,' she added in a quiet voice.

'Where is Tim now?'

'In ... er ... in Wales.'

Brock raised white bushy eyebrows but said nothing. No doubt, she reflected wryly, Ginny would tell him in time that Tim was married, but at least she wouldn't be facing him when he learned of it.

At that moment, the receptionist appeared, beaming as if something wonderful had happened.

'The Negresco have a suite available, Madame, Monsieur. Shall I confirm you will be taking it?'

Brock remained silent as he looked at Sophie.

'Yes,' she said without hesitation. 'Could you tell

them I'll be arriving in about an hour, please? And I'd like it for four days. Thank you.' Her smile was confident.

The receptionist looked inquiringly at Brock but he remained silent, his eyes never leaving Sophie's face.

'Very well, Madame Duval.' She walked briskly away, her shoulders hunched as if in a permanent shrug.

Brock rose. 'I'll be off then. Have a nice rest in Nice, my darling, and I hope you'll forgive me for last night.'

Sophie smiled ruefully up at him. 'It's you who should be forgiving me. I'm sorry for what happened. I wouldn't have hurt you for the world. You do know that, Brock, don't you?'

He nodded. 'Let's just blame the wine, shall we? And forget it ever happened. After all, we want to stay friends, don't we?'

'We most certainly do.'

As he walked away she watched his back and wondered at how, in the bright light of day, he attracted her not at all and yet last night, in the lantern-lit garden, while her mind had dwelt on Tim, he'd been able to transport her to paradise.

PART THREE

December

Seven

Audrey regarded her reflection critically in the mirror that hung on the back wall of Gloria Antica. There was a definite improvement in her appearance, she thought with satisfaction. Her friend, Patricia, though no beauty herself, had a sharp eye when it came to seeing how other women could improve themselves and Audrey had taken to following her advice slavishly. There was only one problem. Nicholas hadn't even noticed her expensive haircut and blonde highlights, or the fresh new tones of her make-up. And if he'd wondered about the sharp suits she'd bought herself, he'd made no mention of it.

'Don't you think I look much better?' she asked Sophie who was rearranging a group of 1760 Bow porcelain figurines on a small table in the shop window.

Sophie looked up absently. 'Yeah. Great.' It was obvious her thoughts were miles away.

Her sister snorted irritably. 'I wish you'd pay attention when I'm here, Sophie. God knows, I don't come up to London that often, but you're so *distrait*, there's no point in my coming to see you these days. What's the matter with you? You look dreadful.' She was unable to conceal a certain secret satisfaction in the fact that for once she actually looked better than Sophie.

'I'm fine.'

'You've lost a lot of weight. You don't want to get too thin, you know. It can be very ageing.'

'I'm not too thin. I've only lost a few pounds.'

'Have you been dieting? Patricia says it's pointless to diet because one only puts it all on again. I'm glad I'm a perfect size twelve. It's the best size for buying clothes. You look as if you're down to size ten.' Audrey's voice had a discontented querulous tone, as if she was spoiling for a fight.

Sophie shrugged, aware that she'd lost weight. The trouble was she felt slightly sick and strung out most of the time and didn't feel like eating. Food nauseated her while hunger of a different kind kept her running on adrenaline during the day and awake most of the night. Tim was still in Wales, having failed to get a job in London, but it made no difference. She'd only seen him once in the past two months and she'd no idea when she'd see him again but that didn't stop her thinking about him. Or wanting him.

'I think this shade of blue suits me, don't you?' Audrey was still at the mirror, patting and smoothing and prinking. She turned her head from side to side. 'These are a good pair of earrings, too. I can't bear the cheap stuff that woman wears.'

Sophie dragged herself guiltily back to the present. It was true that Audrey seldom came to London, and the least she could do was show a little interest.

'They're lovely earrings,' she said encouragingly. 'Nicholas doesn't know what he's missing.'

Audrey spun round. 'Exactly,' she said gratefully. 'What am I going to do, Sophie? I've done everything I can think of to get Nicholas back, but nothing seems to work. We're talking again, thank God, but that's all.'

'Are you sleeping together again?'

Audrey flushed darkly. 'Not really,' she said stiffly.

Sophie tried to suppress a smile. 'What does that mean? Either you are or you aren't.' Her sister had always been very embarrassed at the mention of sex.

'That doesn't come into it.'

'Audrey! That's what it's all about. Don't you enjoy it?'

Audrey's blush deepened. 'Of course,'

'And you and Nicholas are compatible in bed?' As Audrey was about to turn on her furiously, Sophie put out her hand and gripped her sister's wrist. 'Now, don't get in a bate. I'm only trying to help, and as you refuse to go to a marriage guidance counsellor, someone's got to do something. Nicholas is a very nice, kind, caring man, and you don't want to lose him, do you?'

'Of course I don't.'

'So instead of worrying about the colour of your hair, you should be working out *why* it's all gone wrong. What's his secretary providing him with that he doesn't get at home? Apart from the attraction of forbidden fruit and all that, of course.'

Audrey looked stubborn. 'He gets everything he needs at home. I'm a good cook. I keep the house immaculate. I care for the children. And I don't consider myself unattractive.'

Sophie caught her gaze and held it. 'And are you a riot under the covers?'

'Oh, how can you be so vulgar?' Audrey exclaimed,

looking away. 'You always did have sex on the brain. Let me tell you something, there's a lot more to marriage than sex.'

'I know that, and I realise that if sex is good then it's not a problem. It's part of the whole scene, like eating and laughing and sharing things together but if the sex isn't good, then it mushrooms out of all proportion, overshadowing everything else and ruining a relationship. That's when the problems start.'

'Since when have you been an expert on the subject? You're four years younger than me, and you've been married since you were twenty-one. What do you know about it?'

'I've watched a lot of marriages go wrong,' Sophie said quietly. 'Amongst Brock's contemporaries there was hardly one who hadn't been through the divorce courts.'

Audrey gave the back of her hair a final pat and turned reluctantly away from gazing at herself in the mirror.

'Are you suggesting I divorce Nicholas?'

'I'm suggesting you try and analyse the problem. Only you can do that, Audrey. No one else knows exactly what goes on in a marriage. Ask yourself: why does Nicholas feel it necessary to play around with his secretary when he's got a perfectly good wife at home?'

The silence of the elegant little shop was broken only by the soft ticking of an ornate gilt clock. Then Sophie heard a small sob and saw that Audrey had her hand over her mouth, as if to force back her emotions.

'Oh, Aud,' she said sympathetically, putting her arm round her sister. Sophie knew how she felt, more than Audrey realised. There was nothing worse than loving someone and not having that love returned. And if she felt jealous of a wife she hardly knew, how must Audrey feel about Denise O'Brien?

Sophie decided to spend the evening quietly; she'd been out every night and now it was Friday and she was exhausted. Running Gloria Antica itself wasn't hard work, and she loved going to antique sales to see what she could find, but there were times when the business side drove her mad. Brock had originally recommended she use his firm of accountants to do the books but she was still required to keep detailed daily records of every single transaction. Apart from a normal sales ledger, she had to keep a stock book in which she kept a detailed description of every item she bought, including where she'd purchased it and for how much, plus buyer's premium. She also had to keep every auction catalogue filed carefully for the next seven years, as a record of purchase. Added to this were the normal accounts required when running a shop, VAT records to be kept, PAYE and National Insurance payments to be worked out on Frankie and Katie's salaries, and her own profit margins. It was exacting and laborious work and the one part of Gloria Antica that she really didn't enjoy.

Running a hot bath, into which she lavished her favourite gardenia bath oil, she turned down her bed with its mound of snowy pillows, switched on the television in the corner and poured herself a glass of wine.

It wasn't often she pampered herself these days. When she'd travelled with Brock, they'd been relentlessly fussed over by assiduous hotel staff who would hardly let her pour a glass of water for herself. A valet, assigned to look after them in their suite, pressed clothes, served dinner, poured wine, arranged flowers, took messages and, as Sophie once remarked crossly, did everything except sleep with them. Tonight, though, she felt like a touch of luxury. There was cold lobster in the fridge and some fresh raspberries chilling in a glass bowl sitting on crushed ice. After her bath she'd have supper on a tray, in bed, with all the latest magazines to read. It would have been perfect if Tim had been here. For a moment she let herself indulge in the notion of Tim in the bath with her, and then between the cool smooth sheets ... '*No!*' She said it aloud. Stop it! Stop fantasising. Stop thinking of him in bed with Carolyn. Stop visualising them sharing all the little things that are so precious between lovers.

Sophie started almost guiltily when the phone suddenly rang at her bedside, as if the caller might guess what she'd been thinking.

'Hello?' She hoped it wasn't Audrey with some further tale of woe. Then she chided herself for being uncharitable.

'Hello, Sophie.'

Was it telepathy that had made Tim think of her at this moment? Just when she'd been thinking of him? Were they still linked in some way by the past?

Her heart was hammering so loudly in her ears it was like hearing heavy rain on a tin roof.

'How are you, Tim?' she asked with just the right amount of lightness.

Then he told her. She found herself reeling with disbelief as a terrible thought swept through her mind.

Had it happened because she'd wished it so? Was it possible she possessed powers beyond understanding? But not this. Surely not something like this.

Audrey stood in the doorway of the living room and looked over to where Nicholas was writing at his desk. A stack of unpaid bills lay before him and he sighed heavily as he wrote out cheque after cheque.

'Are you coming to bed soon, Nick?' she asked in a small voice.

He looked up and saw his wife in a white chiffon and lace garment which he supposed was called a negligee but which had been designed for a voluptuous woman. On Audrey's rather angular frame it hung in limp folds, revealing the flatness of her chest rather than enhancing what should have been ripe breasts. It struck him, in fact, that she cut a rather pathetic figure. There was nothing remotely sensual about Audrey, but then there never had been. She'd had other qualities that had attracted him when they'd married, a physical aloofness that was a challenge to a man, promising hidden fires beneath the glacial surface. Alas, that smouldering heat seemed to have cooled after Amelia and Rebecca had been born, and now he found her plain cold, through and through.

'I'll be along in a while,' Nicholas said absently as he sealed an envelope addressed to British Telecom. 'Don't wait up for me. I've got all these bills to see to.'

He thought of Denise. Always hot and hungry for sex. Always wet and ready and longing for it. She could do things to him that Audrey probably didn't even know about, and certainly wouldn't want to do. He could just imagine her saying, 'How disgusting!' if he were to suggest something a little different. In her mind the missionary position was the only position, and oral sex meant 'talking dirty'. Most of the time her hands never even moved below the level of his shoulders. She'd seemed to enjoy herself at first, and he'd realised she was inexperienced, but the last few years had been about as fulfilling for him as making love to a marble statue.

Audrey moved across the room on silent feet and stood beside him, looking down at him with pleading eyes.

'I thought it would be nice to have ... er ... an early night.'

Nicholas felt suddenly angry. Why did she have to mince around the subject as if she was ashamed?

'What you mean,' he said, lumbering to his feet, his Fair Isle jumper making him look bulkier than ever, 'is why don't we go to bed now and have a jolly good fuck.'

The colour drained from her face. 'There's no need to talk like that.'

He regarded her squarely. 'It's because we never talk like that and you always act as if you had a pickle up your bum that our marriage is in trouble,' he bellowed.

'Hush! The children will hear you.' She looked anxiously in the direction of the living room door.

'Maybe they will! Maybe it would be a good thing if they did. When they grow up it might prevent them being as frigid as their mother.'

'Oh, my God, Tim. I'm so sorry.' The words were spoken automatically. It was the sort of thing one said under such circumstances but Sophie felt stunned, unable to take in what Tim had told her. 'When did it happen?'

His voice was hoarse as if he'd been crying for a long time. 'Last Tuesday week. Thank God she was killed outright. I couldn't have borne it if she'd suffered.'

'I never saw it announced. I'd have sent flowers, I'd have written to you, Tim, if I'd known.' Sophie couldn't keep the bewildered shock out of her voice. 'When was the funeral?'

'On the Friday. It was just a family affair, my mother, and Caro's parents. They came over from Ireland, where they live. It was just a small service at the Cardiff crematorium.' He sighed heavily. 'I simply couldn't face anything else.'

'Oh, Tim.' She'd never felt so sorry for anyone in her life. 'I don't know what to say.' It was true. And coupled to her sorrow for him were her own feelings of appalled guilt. Only five minutes ago she'd been wishing with all her heart that he was both single and hers. She had been fantasising about him in bed! Oh, God. Her cheeks flamed with remorse and self-reproach. For some reason, she felt as responsible for his wife's death as if she'd been driving the car that had knocked Carolyn down and killed her.

'What will you do, Tim?' Her concern was maternal now. Tim had metamorphosised from a desirable man into a heartbroken boy, and her love for him grew and swelled into a protective emotion, filled with warmth and compassion.

'I can't think, right now.' It sounded as if he was weeping.

'Oh, Tim...'

'I don't know how I'm going to manage without her. She was my life, Sophie.'

'I know, love.' If she hadn't already guessed that, she knew it now.

'It hasn't really sunk in yet. I can't believe . . . believe I'll never see her again.'

Sophie felt cold and shivery as she huddled on her bed, gripping the phone, while Tim continued to talk.

'We were planning a holiday, you know. I was going to ask you if we could borrow La Madeleine for a few days . . .' His voice drifted off, immensely tired. 'I don't want to stay in this cottage. Not now. Not without Caro.'

'Why don't you go to the villa now?' Sophie suggested, glad to be able to offer something. 'I can call Hortense—'

'No, thanks. It's sweet of you, but I don't want to be on my own right now, and the villa is isolated, isn't it?'

'Do you want to come to London?' Sophie asked. Only her own guilt would make an invitation to stay in the spare room of her flat appear unseemly.

'I can't afford to, Sophie,' he replied candidly. 'I've chucked in my job. I can't face anyone at the moment but funds are going to run out soon. To be honest, I don't know what the hell to do.'

'But why don't you stay here? You could have your own suite and come and go as you like. At least it wouldn't be as lonely as being on your own in the country.'

'I couldn't do that, Sophie, though it's very sweet of you to suggest it.'

'Why not?'

'There are a million reasons. I can't impose myself on you. I'll be fine. Thanks all the same.'

'Tim, of course you must come and stay. Don't be silly. It'll be no sweat. This is a huge flat and I've got a daily. What's the problem? You won't even have to see me if you don't want to. At least it's in London, though, where there's lots of distractions and that's what you need.' She suddenly realised she was becoming as controlling as Brock. Is that what great wealth did to a person?

'Oh, I don't know, Sophie.' He sounded despairing. 'I don't think I know what to do any more.' He sounded so utterly lost and desolate that it broke her heart. It was obvious he had no idea how to come to terms with his grief.

'You're not alone in your house, are you, Tim?'

'Yes. My mother has had to go back to York. St Agnes doesn't break up for another two weeks.' Mrs Calthorpe, Sophie remembered, was a widow who taught English at a girls' boarding school.

'Then you must definitely come up to London,' she insisted. 'There's no way you can stay there on your own.' She didn't add that Christmas was in three weeks' time. How the hell was he going to get through the season of universal jollification on his own, when his wife had just been killed?

Eight

Sophie made sure it was a low-key affair. With Alan still recuperating from his operation, this wasn't difficult.

'Let's have a quiet Christmas at the flat,' she suggested to her mother when she phoned her one morning from her little office at Gloria Antica. Tim had arrived the week before and seemed disinclined to see anyone or go anywhere. 'I can do lunch and in the evening we can have a light supper and watch a film or something.'

'It sounds wonderful,' Jean agreed, thankful that she was not expected to do anything except turn up on the day looking elegant. 'It will suit Alan perfectly. He still gets very tired and the doctor says he's got to take it easy.'

'Then that's settled. What about Audrey? Shall I invite her and the family too?'

'Then we certainly shan't have a quiet Christmas,' Jean observed drily.

'But I don't want to hurt her feelings. You know how touchy she can get.'

'Sophie, what have you done on previous Christmases?'

'What do you mean? Brock and I were always in the States or Canada for Christmas.'

'Exactly. Don't you see? You've never entertained them at Christmas in the past so why start now? Anyway, I'm sure Amelia and Rebecca prefer to stay in their own home. Children usually hate being away at a time like that.'

'Well, I hope she won't mind. Maybe I'll invite them for New Year's Eve, although on second thoughts I doubt if Tim will feel like celebrating that,' Sophie remarked thoughtfully.

'How is he getting on?'

'I think he's still in shock. He's very quiet.'

'You can hardly expect him to be his usual breezy self, my dear. He's had a shattering blow. How long is he going to be staying with you?'

'For as long as he wants.'

There was silence on the line and Sophie could imagine her mother drawing herself up stiffly, a look of cool disapproval on her face.

'Is that a good idea, Sophie?'

'I think it's a very good idea. The poor man is inconsolable. It's the least I can do to help him get over this tragedy.' Sophie felt amazed that after all these years and all that had happened, her mother still did not really like Tim.

'And in great comfort, too,' Jean murmured.

'What do you mean?'

'You know perfectly well what I mean, Sophie. Of course I'm sorry for him, but I don't think it's right that you should take him in, house him and feed him, and not put any deadline on how long you expect him to stay. Remember, the longer you let things drift, the more difficult it will be for you to ask him to leave when you want him to.'

'Mum!' Sophie exclaimed in astonishment. 'He's only been here ten days. How can you talk like that? Have you any idea how shattered he is? Remember how you felt when you thought Alan might die? Tim needs all the friends he's got at a time like this, and I like having him here.'

'Yes. I'm sure you do, my dear.'

Jean's remarks annoyed and disturbed Sophie. As she sat at her desk going through her stock book and marking out the Ludwigsburg chinoiserie group of figurines she'd sold for a good profit that morning, she thought about her mother's remarks. The trouble was, she felt deeply confused. Before Carolyn's death she'd have given everything she possessed for Tim to be free and in love with her once more. Now, seeing him so heartbroken made her wish with equal passion that the accident hadn't happened. She had the feeling that he'd been so traumatised and hurt, he'd be unable to love anyone again, at least not for a very long time. Meanwhile, where did that leave her? By inviting him to stay and by looking after him, she'd put herself firmly in the category of best friend-cum-sister. It also struck her that maybe men rarely fell in love with the same woman twice. She belonged to his youth; Carolyn belonged to the matured man who had loved her, married her, and held her dear and now always would. The dead did not grow old and crabbed. Carolyn would be twenty-four for the rest of eternity, blonde, fragile, child-like, her blue eyes smiling gently as they'd done that day at La Madeleine.

Sophie had hardly known her, had resented her existence, had wished she was not married to Tim. But now that she was dead, her heart ached at the waste of such a young life and the pain that loss was incurring.

Sophie unwrapped the white tissue paper and drew out a little navy blue cardboard box. Tim sat watching her, a sad smile on his face. It was Christmas morning, and they were having coffee and warm croissants on a tray in the drawing room where she'd set up a large but simple blue pine tree the previous day, decorated with silver stars and angel's hair.

'I hope it will be useful,' he said.

Intrigued, she found the box contained a blue velvet pouch and from this she drew a two-inch long solid silver paperclip, shaped like a Grecian column. 'Oh, Tim! It's beautiful,' she exclaimed, delighted. She had not expected anything so stylish, and her cheeks flushed pink with pleasure. 'Thank you very much, Tim.'

'I'm glad you like it.'

They sat in awkward silence for a moment. Then Sophie spoke. 'I've got a present for you, too. It's under the tree.' She had agonised for days over what to get him. It mustn't be anything overtly expensive or lavish because that would embarrass him, yet it couldn't be anything tacky or he'd think she was mean. In the end she'd settled for a black leather wallet. It was good quality but not over the top.

'This is really just what I needed, Sophie,' he said with sincerity when he opened it. 'You've been so good to me, and now this lovely wallet. I'm very grateful, you know. I realise I'm not a bundle of laughs at the moment, but with your help I'm beginning to feel a bit less fraught.'

She grinned. 'That's what it's all about, isn't it?' she replied lightly.

That evening, Brock phoned her. She took the call in the bedroom, as Tim, Jean and Alan sat in the drawing room watching television.

'I wanted to wish you a very happy Christmas, my darling,' he said immediately. 'Do you have your family with you?'

'Mum and Alan are here,' Sophie replied brightly, unable to bring herself to mention Tim. She still squirmed with embarrassment when she remembered how she'd blurted out his name. 'What are you doing?'

'I'm in New York, overwhelmed with hospitality from all our friends, and everyone here sends you their love.'

Sophie could just imagine it. Eager hostesses in their sixties arranging endless lunch and dinner parties for Brock because he was rich, charming and once again single. How often she'd sat, bored out of her mind, through those geriatrically glittering functions when she'd been married to him, and how thankful she felt now that she was no longer part of that scene.

'Give them all my love, too,' she said politely, feeling like a well-mannered little girl.

'My present to you won't have arrived yet,' he continued equably, and she could imagine him as he lounged on a velvet sofa with his cigar and a glass of brandy. 'I had it dispatched by Federal Express two days ago, but with Christmas you know how it is.'

'You shouldn't be sending me Christmas presents, Brock,' she pointed out. 'I haven't sent you anything.'

'But I like to give you presents, my darling. I shall go on giving you little presents for the rest of my life.'

'But you've been generous enough, Brock. I can't go on accepting things from you as if we were still married.'

He sounded genuinely amazed. 'Why not, sweetheart?'

'Because—'

'We're still good friends, aren't we? In spite of everything? Can't a good friend send you a little trinket from time to time, my darling?'

'For God's sake, stop treating me like a child!' she burst out, exasperated. 'This has been the problem between us for years now. The reason I had to get away. I wish you'd find yourself someone else, Brock. I really do.'

There was a hurt silence on the line and then she heard him sigh gustily.

'Whether I do or not, you'll always have a special place in my heart, Sophie. And I'll go on sending you presents until you have someone in your life who objects. I don't suppose Tim minds, does he? He shouldn't be jealous of an old man like me.'

How could she be ungracious in the face of such benevolence? And yet Sophie knew that very sweetness was a weapon in itself.

'My life is my own,' she replied stiffly, glad that he couldn't see her blushing at the mention of Tim. Thankful, too, that Tim, grieving for his dead wife, hadn't overheard him. Swiftly wishing Brock a happy

New Year, she replaced the receiver and went back to the drawing room.

'Who was that, dear?' Jean asked possessively. She liked to know exactly what her daughter was up to, at all times.

'Brock. Wishing you all a happy Christmas,' Sophie replied shortly.

Her mother looked at her curiously. 'That was very nice of him. I've got a feeling you two might get together again one day, you know. He still loves you.'

As Tim looked up sharply, Jean's smile became mischievous. Sophie reddened with annoyance.

'Oh, Ma, what nonsense you talk!'

'Your mother's an old romantic,' Alan observed soothingly. 'I say, can I have a little more of that delicious port?'

'Do you think Brock really does still hanker after you?' Tim asked. Alan and Jean had left half an hour ago, and Sophie had made some fresh coffee, as neither she nor Tim felt inclined to go to bed.

'Of course not,' Sophie scoffed, tucking her feet under her as she snuggled down on the sofa. 'He's just a very kind and thoughtful person. All he did was phone to wish us all a happy Christmas.' She didn't say anything about a present winging its way across the Atlantic.

Tim looked surprised. 'He knows I'm staying here, does he?'

She shook her head. 'No.'

'How come?'

'Well, why should I mention it? I'm not married to the man any more,' she added irritably.

'So he doesn't know we've met up again, after all these years?'

'No . . . at least he may do, I'm not sure,' she replied vaguely. If Brock were to phone her while Tim was alone in the flat, it could be very embarrassing.

'Hadn't you better tell him what's happened?' Tim said as if he knew what she was thinking. 'Supposing I answered the phone and it was him? He might think we were having an affair or something ridiculous like that.'

Sophie's face paled at his tone. 'I don't suppose he'd think that,' she said painfully, 'but I will tell him, next time I speak to him. Not that it's any of his business.'

'Were you ever unfaithful to him, Sophie?' Tim asked curiously.

She looked straight into his eyes. 'Never,' she replied truthfully.

'Were you never tempted? There must have been times when you fancied someone a bit younger, surely.'

'I didn't often get to meet anyone who was younger,' she replied with a wry grin. 'But honestly, I don't believe in cheating when you're married. Why get married in the first place if you're going to play around?'

'I never cheated on Caro,' he said softly, 'but that was because I loved her so much. I didn't want anyone else.'

Sophie remained silent, her fingers tearing the silk fringe of the sofa cushion she was leaning against into fine tangled shreds.

'It would be nice if I found someone else, one day, but I

doubt it will happen,' he continued sadly. 'Certainly not for a very, very long time.' He turned to look at her. 'Do you think you'll ever fall in love again?'

She looked away, fastening her gaze on a landscape painting which Brock had bought as an investment that hung above the mantelpiece. 'Who can tell?' she replied, frustration and misery welling up inside.

Tim rose slowly, hands in trouser pockets as he stretched and yawned. 'Thanks for a great Christmas, Sophie. You've worked miracles getting me through today. I wasn't sure how I was going to survive, but it's been lovely.'

She rose too, longing to put her arms round him and comfort him, but all too aware he still belonged to Carolyn.

'At least it's been nice and quiet,' she said, wishing she could think of something less boring to say. It was the sort of remark Alan would make.

'Yeah.' Then he sauntered out of the room and went to his own quarters without another word.

Audrey was in a fever of excitement.

'I'm so glad they've asked us,' she exclaimed, waving the white card that had arrived by the morning's post. 'I've been dying to get invited to a party at Milton Manor. I believe Susie and Quentin Burchfield entertain on a grand scale. Oh, God, it will be fun.'

Nicholas, about to leave for work, realised she was talking to him. He hadn't seen her look so animated for ages. These days she went around like a martyr, unsmiling, bitter-eyed and sullen.

'Oh. How nice. When is it?' He paused in the kitchen

doorway, a portfolio of drawings for a barn conversion tucked under his arm.

'New Year's Eve.' She read the invitation again with shining eyes. '"Dinner 8.30 p.m. Carriages 2.30 a.m. Black tie."'

'What? In five days' time? They haven't given us much notice, have they? Perhaps they've had some refusals.'

Audrey flushed with annoyance. 'How like you to try and spoil it. I expect they've been so busy over Christmas they've got behind sending out the invitations. I'll reply right away and drop it through their letter box.'

'I still think we're probably an afterthought,' Nicholas grumbled. He didn't mean to spoil her fun, but it annoyed him that she was quite happy to go with him to a party given by a couple of jumped-up *nouveau riche* vulgarians, yet she'd all but ignored him over the whole of Christmas.

But Audrey wasn't listening. She was wondering whether she should wear her long red silk dress with the cut-away back and long sleeves, or her black velvet evening dress. Or should she buy something new? The thought was tempting. She might even nip up to London and get Patricia to help her choose something – something sexy. Yes! That was what she wanted. A dress that would make the men look at her and even, perhaps, make Nicholas sit up and take notice.

As she skimmed through the housework, thankful that Amelia and Rebecca had gone to play with some friends, her mind was a whirl of excitement. To get to know the Burchfields better had been an ambition of hers ever since they'd moved into the area. They seemed such a glamorous couple as they whizzed up and down the muddy country lanes in their respective sports cars, hers scarlet, his deep blue. Audrey was convinced they were fascinating, sophisticated and amusing. Now if she were to get really friendly with them ... Visions of herself being invited over for tennis, a swim, cocktails before lunch, formal dinner parties – the sort of life style Denise O'Brien would never be invited to participate in – floated before her eyes.

A few minutes later she was on the phone to Patricia.

'Are you doing anything tomorrow?' she asked without preamble. 'I want you to help me choose a drop-dead evening dress for a *very* special New Year's Eve party.'

Sophie's efforts to try and ignore New Year's Eve for Tim's sake were proving difficult. Friends kept phoning all week inviting her to parties. She refused, saying she was already doing something, but it was obvious that everyone, with the exception of themselves, was gearing themselves up for the big night.

'Why don't you go out?' he said at last. 'I'll be perfectly happy having an early night.'

Sophie smiled. They'd had nothing but early nights since he'd come to stay, their only diversion being to watch television.

'Don't you remember how I hate New Year's Eve, Tim? I always get depressed and weep. Remember that year we went to a party at some artist's studio? And you were cross because I said we should have booked a minicab to get us home because there'd be no taxis around. And in the end we had to walk from Islington to Chelsea.'

He grinned. 'Yeah. I was rather beastly to you, wasn't I? I think you cried all the way home.'

Sophie's laughter filled the room. 'No wonder I hate going to New Year's Eve parties. Honestly, Tim, I'd like to stay here and I'll cook us something special. Do you still like lobster?'

'Is the Pope Catholic?' For the first time his eyes held a hint of their old sparkle.

'That's settled then. Champagne, lobster, and an early night. We'll pretend it's mid-June or something,' she added gaily.

'What about your family?'

'My mother and Alan always see in the New Year on their own, it's a tradition. As for Audrey, she's already phoned me three times to tell me she's going to a swanky party given by some neighbours. Let's hope it brings about a reconciliation with Nicholas, that's all I can say.'

'He's still got his lady friend then?'

'According to Audrey, she's just found a receipt in one of his pockets for a piece of jewellery. She thinks it must have been for Christmas.'

Tim grimaced. 'Ouch! That's a bit rough, isn't it?'

Sophie nodded, her expression serious. 'I just wish I felt more sympathetic towards Audrey. I know Nicholas is behaving badly, and I really disapprove of cheating husbands, but somehow I've got this feeling it's Audrey's fault. She's such a moaner. She nags and grumbles about everything. I know she's my sister and I feel awful talking about her like this, but honestly, I'm not surprised Nicholas has looked elsewhere. I think he just wants a bit of light relief, and I don't blame him.'

'Marriage is a funny thing,' he said thoughtfully. 'It's always the little things that cause the trouble. Boredom is a real killer. More couples get divorced because they're bored than for almost any other reason.' Tim looked at her closely. 'Were you terribly in love with Brock at the beginning?'

'Yes. I was besotted, but looking back I'm sure it was partly because...' She drew in her breath sharply and started to blush. She hadn't meant to get into this and now her slip of the tongue made her grow hot with embarrassment.

'Because of what?'

'Oh, nothing, really. It was because I was too young, I expect,' she stammered.

'No. You were going to say something else,' Tim persisted. 'You met him shortly after I left for Australia, didn't you?'

'Something like that.' She sounded vague.

'So what happened that made you fall in love with a man old enough to be your father? I know you well enough to know it wasn't for his money.'

Sophie looked indignant. 'You're dead right. It most certainly wasn't for his money!'

There was a long silence before he spoke again.

'Was it because I went away, Sophie?' he asked softly.

She looked down, unable to meet his gaze. 'It might have been,' she said, unable to lie to him. 'But it was a long time ago,' she added hastily.

To her surprise he reached out and laid his hand on hers. 'I had to get away, you know. My mother was smothering me. I was twelve when my father died and right away she began to depend on me as if I was some sort of surrogate husband.'

'I never knew that.'

Tim sighed. 'I know it was awful for her, but being an only child, it was pretty hellish for me, too. Then this chance to go to Australia came along, and ... well, I'm sorry, Sophie, I probably treated both you and my mother pretty badly, but I just had to get away before I was devoured by the whole situation.'

'Did your mother take it badly?' she asked, curious. She'd never met Mrs Calthorpe but she imagined her to be frail.

'I think it was the best thing for her, really. She took up teaching again and now she's fine.'

Sophie wondered how long he was going to keep his hand on hers. Pleasurable tingles were going up her arm and suffusing her body, but she knew he was unaware of her feelings. His whole attitude was one of brotherly understanding.

'You didn't marry Brock on the rebound, did you?' His voice was soft, considerate.

Startled, she looked up and he was staring into her eyes with a fixed expression, and she knew she couldn't lie to him.

Slowly, she nodded, biting her lower lip as if in pain. 'You left so suddenly,' she blurted out. 'I had no warning. One day we were together and the next you'd gone, for ever. It was such a shock.'

'I know. I'm sorry, Sophie. I didn't really have any

time to tell you what was happening. I had to make a snap decision and I just grabbed the chance. Selfish of me, I know, and I regret hurting you and my mother, but I was desperate to get away. I had no idea you'd rush into marriage. You were still so young.'

'When Brock came along, he really took me out of myself, Tim. He swept me off my feet, almost literally. In no time at all we were flying around the world to amazing places I'd only heard about in geography class. It was a wonderful marriage for a while, and I've no regrets,' she added sturdily.

He squeezed her hand before letting it go. 'I'm glad, Sophie. Well . . .' He paused for a moment. 'We're both on our own again, aren't we? Strange how things work out. I wonder if either you or I will ever find anyone else?' It was the sort of question that did not require an answer and she looked away so he would not see that, for her, nothing had changed.

'We don't want to arrive late,' Audrey fussed as she checked her appearance one more time in the hall mirror. The turquoise taffeta dress she'd bought, with a matching jewel-encrusted jacket, set off her figure to perfection. She'd had her hair professionally done that afternoon, and as a final touch she'd bought herself a pair of crystal chandelier earrings which glittered like tiny icicles.

Nicholas gave up the attempt to button his dinner jacket. He'd put on weight but he didn't care. Life was too short to worry about one's waistline. 'We don't want to be the first, either,' he remarked, polishing his glasses. 'What do we know about these people? What sort of a party is it going to be, anyway?' He was showing the first signs of being fed up before he even got there.

'Very grand, I should think. Catering vans have been driving up the lane all day and a florist arrived at lunchtime. I expect everyone who is anyone in the county will be there tonight.' Excitement had made Audrey almost forget about Denise O'Brien.

'I suppose you want to take the car?'

Her geniality vanished. 'What do you expect me to do, walk?' She extended a satin-shod foot as if to exhibit the absurdity of his question.

'But it's only a hundred yards up the lane and there won't be room for everyone to park their cars in the drive.'

'Then you'll just have to drop me off and bring the car back here.' She shook her head like an enraged bantam. 'You needn't think I'm going to go trailing up the lane, getting covered in mud and frozen to the bone, just because you don't want to get the car out. My hair will get blown all over the place and I'll arrive looking like a wreck!'

'OK, OK.' He was trying to keep from losing his temper, but he'd much rather have spent the evening at home. He loathed large parties, his trouser waistband was uncomfortably tight, and he didn't even know the Burchfields. 'Let's go then,' he said, picking up the car keys from the hall table. Slightly mollified, Audrey drew a woollen cape round her shoulders and with her head held high swept forward with the aplomb of a duchess about to make a grand entrance.

Susie Burchfield was tall and willowy and she reminded

Nicholas of a mermaid as she slithered forward to greet them in a long, tight, shimmering green dress. Her hair was long and blonde too, and she was for ever stroking it and tossing it to one side, and fiddling with its tendrils.

'Hel-*lo*!' Her voice was low and husky, her full lips scarlet and glossy. 'You must be Audrey and Nicholas Bevan. I'm *so* glad you could come tonight. Have a glass of champagne. Come and meet everyone.' She extended pale arms and tossed her hair over one shoulder and then the other, revelling in the knowledge that she was the most beautiful woman in the place.

Audrey and Nicholas found themselves in a smothering room of grey velvet and pink satin, where groups lounged around on deep sofas or reclined on a white bearskin in front of the log fire.

Mesmerised by this exotic creature who had instantly made her feel like a provincial housewife, Audrey looked round and her expression became steadily more astonished. It wasn't just the vulgarity of the decor or the number of servants hovering around with trays of champagne, or even the booming rock music that emanated from another room, it was the guests themselves that were so strange to her conventional eyes. The girls, all years younger than herself, wore weird and very revealing clothes and exotic make-up. The men looked expensively grubby, some with long matted hair, others skinheads. Everyone, even the men, as she told Sophie later, wore several earrings in each ear, and occasionally a ring or a stud in the nose as well.

'This is Quentin,' Susie drooled, winding her arms round a small dynamic-looking man in his fifties, who had a shock of curly grey hair that framed Neanderthal features.

'Nice to see you. Glad you could come,' he said, shaking their hands. 'Make yourselves at home. Take a seat. Have a drink.'

Nicholas eyed Quentin's black leather trousers and waistcoat, worn over a flowered velvet shirt, with suspicion. Whatever Quentin Burchfield did for a living, it was far removed from the world of Nicholas Bevan.

'How do you like living in these parts?' Nicholas inquired politely. 'I'm afraid we're all rather country bumpkins.'

Audrey glared at him and then turned to Susie and Quentin with an ingratiating smile. 'Were you living in London before?'

Quentin spoke in short sharp sentences as he nursed a silver goblet filled with champagne. 'Yup. We lived in Maida Vale. We've still got a flat in town. The country's better for the children, though. That's why we moved.'

Audrey looked at Susie in amazement. She'd never seen anyone look less like a mother. Perhaps they were her stepchildren.

'How many have you got?' she inquired.

Susie flipped her hair over one shoulder with a languid Jerry Hall gesture. 'Four,' she purred. 'They're all under six. Two boys and two girls.'

For the second time in five minutes Audrey was made to feel inadequate.

'You've got kids too, haven't you? I've heard them,' Susie continued sweetly. 'Now you must come and meet our friends.' As she steered Audrey towards a group,

Nicholas asked Quentin what he did. Audrey strained to hear the answer.

'I manage a couple of groups,' their host replied casually. 'Lips and True Sensations. They're both doing well in the charts.'

Nicholas tried to look impressed. Then his nostrils twitched and he was reminded of the wilder days of his youth when he'd been at Edinburgh University. Unmistakable for its distinctive pungency and resembling cat pee came the drift of cannabis from the group Audrey was being introduced to.

Jean leaned forward to fill Alan's glass as they sat awaiting the chimes of Big Ben on the radio. It was their eighteenth New Year's Eve together and some dark premonition told her there wouldn't be many more. Alan was making a good recovery from his operation, but no one could confirm he was cured. With cancer, one could never be sure. The thought of his dying hung over Jean twenty-four hours a day like a black shadow, quenching the sunlight and filling her horizon with dread. Recently she'd even woken in the middle of the night and listened intently to make sure he was still breathing. Ridiculous, of course. There was no immediate deterioration in his condition. In fact, he was leading a fairly normal life, although he grew quickly tired.

'Made any good resolutions?' he asked, sipping the champagne.

'To continue to give up smoking,' she replied firmly. 'I think I've done very well, don't you?'

'From sixty a day to nothing is miraculous. The way

you were going, you were likely to be pushing up the daisies before me.'

Her heart skipped a beat. They didn't discuss death, at least not in a personal way. She couldn't bear to think of being left behind on her own. The thought of life without Alan was like being tipped into a terrifying black abyss without a safety net.

He was looking at his watch, thick and gold round his once powerful wrist. 'Not long to go,' he observed.

'And what good resolutions have you decided to make this year?' she asked, keeping the mood light.

'I shall double my usual intake of whisky, cut down on the soda water and prescribe myself at least one box of chocolates a week.' He raised his glass triumphantly.

Jean laughed, catching his good spirits. 'You'll get fat and debauched looking.'

'How divine.'

When the first chimes of Big Ben filled the room, it conjured up a thousand memories, going back over the past sixty-five years. It seemed to Jean to have been ringing out, marking special events and family anniversaries, since she'd been a child and her father had climbed in through the window as the 'first footer'.

'Happy New Year,' Alan whispered as the last chime died away. 'And may the best be yet to come.'

She told herself she had to be brave. 'I know it will, sweetheart.' She touched his glass with hers. 'We'll have a wonderful year and many more to follow.'

They sipped their champagne, eyes locked in tenderness. Then he kissed her again and she closed her eyes, praying her wishes would come true.

* * *

In the dignified quiet of her Eaton Place flat, Sophie and Tim drained their glasses, the emotional moment of midnight over. Neither spoke, Tim lost in a world of his own, Sophie sensitive to his mood, careful not to intrude on his thoughts.

'I suppose we'd better turn in for the night,' he said at last. 'Are you going to work tomorrow?'

Sophie nodded. 'I've given Frankie and Katie the day off because they were both going to parties in the country, but I thought I'd open up as usual.'

Tim looked interested. 'Can I help in any way? I'd really like to do something. You've been so kind, looking after me and letting me stay here.'

'It would be lovely to have your company,' she replied, trying not to sound too eager. 'But I don't suppose much will be going on.'

'That's OK. I can polish the odd bit of furniture, can't I? I'm even a dab hand at dusting if you'll trust me with a thirty-thousand-pound Chinese vase or whatever.' He was smiling with enthusiasm now, glad to have something to distract him.

'I tell you what you can do to help,' Sophie said thoughtfully. 'I need someone to sort out my accounts. It drives me crazy trying to do the books, and you're good at that sort of thing, aren't you?'

'As long as it's nothing too complicated,' he said with joking self-deprecation.

'Oh, that would be wonderful.' Sophie was genuinely grateful. 'You've probably saved my life.'

When they said goodnight, he gave her a big brotherly hug.

'Thanks again,' he said, almost embarrassed, 'for everything. You're a star.'

'That's OK, Tim,' she said, hugging him back. She watched as he turned and walked down the corridor to his room, moving with a natural athletic grace, his long legs striding out in an easy gait, his hands plunged casually into his trouser pockets. It was the back of his neck she found so endearingly vulnerable. There was something very boy-like about it with his hair cut short. Then she sighed. She couldn't go on like this; being so near him and yet so far was killing her. Maybe her mother was right; perhaps she shouldn't have invited him to stay without imposing a time limit. And yet she knew she couldn't bear to let him go either.

Alone in her bedroom, she tried to settle for the night, but it was impossible. Not thirty feet away, Tim lay on his own, lost to her, perhaps for ever, because he still worshipped the memory of Carolyn. How long, she wondered, did it take someone to get over the death of a spouse? She'd known people who had remarried within a year, and those who did had usually been the ones who had been the most happily married. But would Tim be like that? Or was he destined to spend the next few years steeped in grief, unable to come to terms with his loss?

The hands of her small bedside clock pointed to half past one. The New Year was already devouring each minute, carving its way through the present and turning it into the past. Burying her face into the pillow, she shut her eyes tightly and wondered if she ought to ask him to move out before she reached the point of no return. If she hadn't already.

* * *

Their faces floated smilingly around the walls, and the floor was so far away her feet never seemed to touch the ground. Then the faces multiplied and still grinning, swooped close, kissing her on the lips. Dozens of kisses; it seemed as if the whole world was kissing her. Audrey had never felt like this before. She vaguely remembered having her hands held tightly while everyone sang 'Auld Lang Syne' and the room had spun around her. Then she'd dropped back onto a sofa with people on either side, their arms and legs tangled with hers, laughing until the tears ran down their cheeks, shrieking with mirth but she couldn't recall why. What had been so funny? Not that it mattered. Nothing mattered except the sensations that were sweeping through her body now, making her insides quiver with longing, unleashing her hands so that they searched greedily, encountering with gasps of delight velvet soft skin encasing a steel shaft.

'Jesus, you're fantastic!' a male voice groaned in her ear. 'Take me inside you. Let me fill you up with my babies.'

Audrey barely heard the words, so enraptured was she by her find. Sliding onto the floor, she knelt and took the smooth silky organ into her mouth while the man held her head between his hands, gripping her hair with strong fingers over each ear. Then, withdrawing himself, he stood up, grabbed her round the waist, and pushed her down onto the vast mink-covered bed. Unresisting, Audrey allowed her panties to be wrenched off and she wound her arms round the man's neck as he thrust himself into her with a grunt.

She clung to him, her movements passionate, her cries shrill, excitement breaking out in scarlet patches across her now exposed breasts and on her neck.

'Yes!' the man roared. 'Oh, Christ, what a sweet tight pussy you've got. Oh, yes! I wanna fuck you all night. Fuck your tight little pussy until you're screaming for mercy. Oh, God! God! I'm coming ... I'm coming...! Fuck me, yes!'

Crazy with desire, Audrey moved her hips in rhythm, arching her back, pressing down as something hot and searing and exquisite started to grow, spread, become hotter and finally explode in an excruciatingly pleasurable sensation. The man had managed to keep going for those last few seconds, and then they were both gasping and panting as if they'd run a marathon, clinging stickily to each other, the sweat running in rivulets under their clothes.

Audrey didn't remember anything until much later. Somehow she was back down in the Burchfields' drawing room where the motley collection of guests still lolled about on sofas, and Nicholas was deep in conversation with someone who turned out to be Quentin Burchfield's accountant.

'Can I see you again?' she heard the man whisper in her ear. He thrust a flashy business card into her hand. 'I'll ring you. We must do this again. Christ, you're the greatest fuck I've had in years. You're quite a little raver, aren't you?'

Tucking the card very carefully into her purse, Audrey looked at him closely, seeing him properly for the first time. His face was long and thin, and his eyes were the sexiest, palest blue she'd ever seen. God! She swayed dizzily, and sat down rather suddenly on the arm of one of the sofas. She'd never felt so strange in her life. Or so happy. Or so excited. She hadn't even caught his name and some remnant of social etiquette now forbade her to look at his card, but *of course* she'd see him again. If Nicholas could have the dreadful Denise O'Brien, then she could certainly have someone too.

'Are you sure you're all right, Audrey?' Jean inquired, looking at her elder daughter quizzically. They were spending the weekend with Audrey, and while Alan rested upstairs after lunch and Nicholas took Amelia and Rebecca for a walk, they sat by the brightly blazing log fire in the drawing room, catching up on family news.

'There's nothing wrong with *me*,' Audrey said hurriedly. 'It's Sophie you should be worrying about.'

Jean raised finely arched eyebrows, knowing exactly what Audrey meant but deciding to stick up for Tim. 'Why?'

'She's gallivanting around London with Tim,' Audrey replied tartly. 'What does she think she's doing? Keeping that old boy friend of hers in a style to which he seems to be rapidly becoming accustomed to.'

'Tim's a heartbroken widower and I for one am glad if he and Sophie can give each other a little happiness,' Jean responded mildly. 'I can't think why you object, my dear. After all, we've known Tim for a very long time and Sophie was so sad when he went away.'

'The next thing will be she'll have him working in the shop,' Audrey said darkly, 'and he'll accept because then he will really have landed on his feet.'

'So what, dear?' Jean rearranged the sofa cushions more comfortably into the small of her back. 'Why do you grudge your sister every little pleasure she's ever had?'

'Little pleasure!' Audrey snorted contemptuously. 'She's been living on the fat of the land since she was twenty-one. She's had everything anyone could want, and now she's buying Tim, and that's the only reason he's hanging around.'

Jean's eyes narrowed. Audrey was so transparent, and never more so than when her own life wasn't coming up to scratch.

'How is everything between you and Nicholas?' she asked abruptly.

Audrey shrugged. 'Much the same, I suppose.'

'Is he still having an affair with his secretary?'

'I suppose so.'

'You *suppose* so? Don't you know? Don't you care?' She eyed Audrey incredulously. 'You sound as if you aren't even interested in whether he's having an affair or not.'

Audrey flung another log on the fire, and a shower of sparks gave a miniature firework display in the large grate. 'He can do what he likes,' she said coolly.

'Well, haven't you changed your tune,' her mother observed drily. Then she looked at Audrey searchingly. 'Would you by any chance be having an affair yourself?'

Audrey's blush was so acute, even her eyes reddened and seemed to brim as she hurriedly poked the fire, attacking the logs with the brass-handled fire iron. 'Don't be absurd!' she retorted, voice shaky.

'I'm not sure I'm being absurd at all. Who could blame you? Getting even is the best form of revenge there is, and if it makes you feel less resentful towards Nicholas then I think it's a very good idea.'

Audrey looked deeply shocked. 'How can you think like that, Mum? Two wrongs don't make a right.'

'And being a sanctimonious hypocrite is the worst of all,' Jean replied.

'But I . . .' Audrey burst into tears, her wet cheeks glistening in the firelight. 'I don't know what to do,' she sobbed, pressing a crumpled Kleenex to her mouth.

Jean's expression softened. 'In what way? Are you in love?'

'I don't think so . . . Oh, I don't know, I'm so confused.'

'So what's going on? Is he married too?'

'Yes, but that's not the point.' Audrey blew her nose and then sniffed loudly. They sat in silence, Jean knowing she would gain nothing by pressing her daughter too hard.

'I've never met anyone like him before,' Audrey whispered at last.

In spite of longing to know who this man was, Jean merely asked, 'How is he different?'

Audrey gazed into the fire. 'He's different in every way. He's . . . he's . . . Oh, sex is wonderful with him. I never knew it could be so good. It's never been like that with Nicholas, not even at the beginning.' She looked shamefacedly at her mother. 'I want to do it all the time with Troy. It's so fantastic. It's all I can think about.'

'Umm. Troy, eh? Who is he? Where did you meet him?'

'At a New Year's Eve party, given by some neighbours of ours,' Audrey replied dreamily.

'Does Nicholas suspect anything?' Jean felt in need of another cup of coffee. She reached for the coffee pot and helped herself.

'If he does he's given no indication, but then he's probably so wrapped up with Denise he doesn't care.'

'So what happens next? You're not going to dash off with this Troy fellow, are you? What about the children?' Jean was feeling deeply anxious now. She'd never seen Audrey in this dizzy mixed-up frame of mind before, and it could only bode ill.

'Of course I'm not going to leave Amelia and Rebecca,' Audrey replied scornfully. 'What do you take me for?'

'Someone I've never met before,' Jean replied promptly. 'It's all very well to play around like this if you keep your head screwed on, as I believe Nicholas has done with his secretary, but falling in love and being out of control is something else, Audrey. It's dangerous. For you all.'

'Troy *is* dangerous.' She made it sound like a great asset. 'He's like a drug, and all I long for is to be with him.' Then she closed her eyes and ran her tongue slowly along her bottom lip.

Jean felt embarrassed and awkward in the presence of such a blatant display of sexual desire. It was so unlike Audrey, too. She'd always been the prim one, fastidious even, certainly never given to making references to her sexual life. At times Jean had even wondered if she'd had a sex life after the girls were born. Once thing seemed certain, she was making up for lost time now.

'Well, you'd better be careful not to get caught,' Jean remarked matter-of-factly.

'There's no fear of that.' Audrey looked at her languidly through half-closed eyes. 'We meet in a secret place, known only to us,' she added in a whisper.

'Well, as long as you're careful . . .' Jean's voice trailed away, and she wished she didn't feel so depressed. A year ago Audrey had been supposedly happily married to Nicholas, Sophie was jetting around the world with Brock, and Alan had been in good health. How could so much change in such a short time?

'You won't tell Sophie, will you?' Audrey urged, breaking into her thoughts.

'As if I would.'

They sat in silence, on either side of the fire, and avoided looking at each other. Being locked in an intimate situation had never come easily to them and they were looking for a way out when they heard Nicholas returning with Amelia and Rebecca.

'Ah, there they are,' Jean exclaimed in relief, as if they'd been missing for hours.

Audrey had jumped to her feet, all brightness and good humour. 'Hello, darlings. Did you have a nice time?'

Nicholas looked nonplussed. 'We only went for a walk in the woods.'

'And Mummy! Mummy! D'you know what we found?' Rebecca asked eagerly as Audrey helped her off with her tartan-lined anorak.

'What?' Audrey asked absently.

'A sweet little hut,' Amelia cut in swiftly and with a triumphant smile.

Rebecca's face crumpled. 'I was going to tell Mummy!'

'Well, you were a slow coach, weren't you?' Amelia

responded with maddening smugness. 'Slow coach! Slow coach!'

'But you said I could tell Mummy!' Rebecca wailed loudly.

'Why don't you both tell Mummy, one at a time,' Nicholas suggested in his most reasonable voice.

'What's so special about this hut anyway?' Audrey demanded, suddenly cross. Jean, observing her closely, guessed at her daughter's sudden discomfort.

'It was like the house in that picture book, you know, Red Riding Hood, and it had a little door,' Amelia explained breathlessly.

'I was going to tell about the little door!' Rebecca screamed. She hung on to Audrey's skirt. 'It had a little door and we tried to open it—'

'But it was locked until a man came along and opened it with a big key,' Amelia added with a flourish. 'And Daddy knew him.'

'Yes. Daddy knew him,' said Rebecca, her expression crushed. 'I was going to tell Mummy that bit, too.'

'So who lives in the cottage? The witch with the big bad wolf?' Jean asked brightly.

'No,' said Nicholas, shrugging out of his sheepskin coat. 'Do you remember that chap we met at the Burchfields'?'

'There were dozens of men at the Burchfields' party,' Audrey replied crisply.

'The one you were dancing with quite a lot. He had a funny name. Greek or something. Anyway, he owns that part of the forest, up by Parson's Lane. There's a right of way running through it. That's how we came upon this funny little hut. Like something out of a fairy story,' Nicholas explained. He looked pink and healthy from being out in the open and he seemed to have enjoyed his walk with the children.

'How riveting,' Audrey said sarcastically, her cheeks flushed.

'And do you know what he uses it for?' Amelia asked eagerly.

Audrey seemed to look at her small daughter with distaste. 'So tell me,' she said coolly, avoiding Jean's eye.

'He makes music in there,' Amelia said importantly.

'Not quite, darling,' Nicholas corrected her gently. 'He writes lyrics for some pop band.' He turned to Audrey and Jean. 'Interesting chap. Troy something. That's his name. Says it's nice and quiet in the forest, and there's no phone or anything in this hut so he doesn't get disturbed.'

'Fascinating.'

Jean could hear the relief in Audrey's voice.

'You must remember who I mean, Aud,' Nicholas persisted. 'He was—'

'For goodness sake,' Audrey burst out. 'Why should I be interested in some man we met at a party?'

'I didn't say interested,' Nicholas responded swiftly. 'I said remember.'

PART FOUR

February

Nine

By the beginning of February, Sophie wondered how she'd ever managed the accounts on her own. Tim now accompanied her to Gloria Antica every morning and at his suggestion she'd bought a computer so that all the accounts could be stored on disk, and she could have a print-out whenever she wanted.

'It's fantastic,' she exclaimed the first time he produced a set of figures as if he was performing a conjuring trick.

'Watch this,' he told her, stabbing nonchalantly at the keyboard. 'You want to know how much profit you've made this month? How much VAT you owe? A list of your fixed expenses, including salaries, National Insurance and PAYE? Hey presto!' Tim pressed one more key and from out of the printer glided beautifully presented sheets of figures.

'It's amazing. It looks so professional, Tim.'

'So I should hope. I only happen to be an accountant, though a humble one.'

Laughingly, she rested her hands on his shoulders as she stood beside his chair, leaning forward to get a better look. Her cheek was only inches away from his and the warmth of his skin seemed to emanate from his body with a heady masculine redolence.

Her fingers tightened. Tim seemed so much better these days, almost like his old self in fact. He never responded to her gentle attempts at flirting though, and at times he seemed to regard her with puzzlement, as if he couldn't believe she was actually attempting to attract him. Then she'd back off, embarrassed and hurt by his obvious lack of interest.

'I think I'll have to give my accountants the sack,' she said half joking. Brock had told her they were the best, and as he'd invested heavily in Gloria Antica she supposed she ought to consult him first.

'Don't do that.' Tim spoke seriously. 'I'm only getting you set up with a straightforward system that you, or Frankie or Katie for that matter, can operate. I have to find myself a proper job soon, you know.' He leaned back against her for a moment, resting his head against her breast. The smell of his hair made her legs grow weak. She held her breath hoping he wouldn't move away too quickly.

'So you'd better start teaching us how to use this damned machine,' she said flippantly.

Tim turned to look at her. 'Frankie and Katie are already computer-friendly. Some of us have actually joined the twentieth century, you know,' he smiled.

Sophie released her grip on his shoulders. 'You don't say,' she shot back. 'So how come I had to show you how the microwave oven works?'

Tim rose, stretching. 'Woman's work, m'dear. You can't expect us chaps to know about that sort of thing.'

Sophie smiled up at him. She hadn't seen him in such good form since before Carolyn had died. He looked at her with those sexy eyes that always made her senses reel, and she had an almost irresistible urge to throw herself into his arms. Then he turned abruptly away and the moment of near intimacy was over.

'I'll file these print-outs for you, Sophie,' he said, all businesslike.

'Right. Yes. Thanks.' The anti-climax was unbearable. She left the little office and went into the showroom, just to get away from him for a few minutes. She found his physical presence overpowering at times, as if an electrical charge was being transmitted between them; only he didn't seem to notice. How much longer, she wondered, was she going be able to continue to be his friend only? How long does it take to get over the grief of losing someone you love? asked an inner voice, not for the first time. And the answer came back: who's to say he'll want you even when he does get over Carolyn's death?

February merged into March, and the first crocuses bloomed in Hyde Park in a riot of white and mauve and saffron yellow. The trees seemed spun with a gossamer veil of pale green, and there was a new brightness in the morning air. Tim was only going into the shop in the mornings now. In the afternoons he went for interviews, but it seemed without success. Sophie watched him closely, gauging his moods, doing what she could to keep him cheerful, cooking his favourite dishes in the evening, amazing herself by this uncharacteristic show of domesticity and patience. He responded with gratitude that she should be so caring, but that was all. If she stepped over the boundary of sisterly behaviour he shut her out and seemed to withdraw behind a barrier from where he watched her guardedly as if to protect himself. She would go into another room, nursing her hurt and frustration, telling herself the situation was crazy. It was time he returned to Wales and picked up the strands of his own life again instead of hovering so painfully on the edge of hers. But a few minutes later he would join her and make her laugh with his teasing. She'd relent and the battle was lost. She could not act rationally and sensibly while Tim was about. She was far too much in love with him for that.

At the end of March she gave a dinner party to celebrate her birthday.

'What is it? Your fifty-second birthday?' he quipped, coming into her bedroom that morning to bring her a cup of tea. He was wearing a Japanese-style cotton robe over his pyjamas, and in his other hand he carried a bunch of carnations which he plonked on her lap.

Sophie placed the mug of tea he'd brought on the bedside table and threw one of her pillows at his head. 'Do you mind?' She pretended to look indignant. 'I'll have you know I'm only thirty-four!'

'You'll be getting your old-age pension before you know it, ducks! I should have bought you a Zimmer frame as a present.' He sat on the side of her bed, crushing her feet, but she loved it. This was the first time he'd come into her bedroom in the morning and she couldn't think of a nicer way to start the day.

'I've got something for you,' he said, putting his hand in his pocket.

'What? As well as the flowers? Don't overdo it, will

you, Tim?' It was like being eighteen again, the way they joked with each other.

'Here.' He handed her a small square box, not unlike the one that had held the silver paperclip at Christmas. Inside lay a fine silver chain from which hung a tiny silver bear with arms and legs that moved and a head that could be turned from side to side.

'Oh, Tim!'

'Not quite up to what your ex-husband would give you, I'm afraid,' he said sadly.

She leaned forward, a sheen of tears in her eyes, and with all hesitancy gone she put her arms round his neck and pulled him close.

'This means more to me than all the jewels in the world,' she said. 'Thank you, sweetheart. I absolutely love it.' She hung on to him, never wanting this moment to be over. His cheek was hot against hers, and when he slid his arms round her, she closed her eyes, hardly daring to breathe in case he pulled away. But he didn't pull away. His grip tightened, she moved her head slightly and then her lips found his, and it was as if they'd never stopped being in love.

His kiss was deep and urgent and she could feel his arms holding her tightly. Slowly, with an inevitability that seemed predestined, they sank on to the pillows, and then Tim's hands started a loving search into all the valleys of her body, as if he was a blind man following the Braille on a familiar page. Clinging to him, Sophie felt herself experiencing a great awakening, as if she'd lain dormant, and only Tim's touch could bring her back to life. Her breasts swelled and grew tender, her insides seemed to blossom and ache and she pressed herself closer, wanting him to take her swiftly and carry her with him on a never-ending ride of pure pleasure. He was hers now, until the end of time, and she swore to make him happy for as long as they both lived.

Ten

It had never been like this with Brock. In the darkness of their bedroom in the Scalinata di Spagna in Rome, Sophie lay on her back while Tim slumbered beside her, marvelling at how right it felt being with him. There was such ease between them now, such total understanding that words were unnecessary, as their minds and bodies became attuned to each other in perfect mutual harmony. With Brock, especially after making love, there had been too much talk. He would want to know if she'd enjoyed the sex and if he had satisfied her and he wouldn't stop asking questions until she'd assured him that he was wonderful and their lovemaking was fabulous. With Tim, there was no need, and she began to feel that perhaps their meeting again was fate. And could it have been fate that killed Carolyn?

Sophie felt chilled by the thought, uneasy that perhaps this was all part of some grand design into which her personal destiny had been woven. Could she even have brought about Carolyn's sudden demise by wishing her out of Tim's life so that she could have him to herself again? The thought rose up to haunt her yet again. She told herself to stop being foolish. Carolyn had died because she'd stepped into the road from behind a parked van, and the driver of the oncoming car hadn't even seen her. Those were the facts. Tim had told her it was one of those freak accidents and that if anyone was to blame it was Caro herself.

Looking back now, Sophie realised that Tim had been on the brink of becoming her lover for some weeks, but she'd been over-anxious and had missed the signs. Maybe, she reflected, he had wanted to see how far he dared go without the spectre of Carolyn rising between them. Then, it seemed, he decided he was ready to commit himself and with an unbelievable feeling of euphoria, she had realised that her wildest dreams had come true.

That had been six weeks ago and in that time they had become so incredibly close that Sophie was sure it was just a matter of time before he asked her to marry him. At thirty-four she longed to start a family before it was too late, but all this she kept to herself. Tim must not be rushed or he might take fright and leave her again, as he had done all those years ago. They talked about the future in terms of work, though. He was determined to get a job, saying he could still do her accounts even if it meant putting in the odd evening and working for a few hours at the weekend.

'I've sponged on you for long enough,' he declared. 'I want to pay my way and share all the expenses.'

'You don't have to, Tim,' Sophie replied, admiring him for his independence but content to let things drift as they were. She was so happy these days, nothing could touch her. She was also very aware of the fact that thanks to Brock's generosity, she had a life style that few young men could keep up with.

'But I want to,' he said almost fiercely. 'It's only right that I should pay my way. Otherwise I'll lose my self-respect and you'll end up being resentful.'

She burst out laughing. 'I can't see that happening.'

He grinned. 'You're right. I'm more likely to go mad trying to teach you how the accounts should be done. You have a system peculiar to yourself and it's a nightmare to a trained accountant like myself.'

'I never was any good at maths,' she wailed.

'Tell me something I don't know.'

The idea of taking a trip to Rome had been his suggestion after he'd read an article in a magazine about shopping for antiques. Sophie was immediately enthusiastic. Brock had taken her to Rome many times, and they'd stayed at the Grand Hotel which was luxurious in an old-fashioned way, with cherubs painted on the ceiling of the reception area and festoons of carved fruit and flowers embellishing the walls. But now she wanted to see this greatest of all cities through Tim's eyes. That was why she'd chosen the Scalinata di Spagna. It was a comfortably converted eighteenth-century villa with a large terrace and a magnificent view over the city.

They flew from Heathrow to Fiumicino airport by Alitalia, landing in the early evening, and Sophie felt as excited as if she'd never been abroad before.

'Do you realise, Tim, that we've never been away together?'

He nodded. 'Not even on a day trip to Brighton. We had no money when we were young, and as far as I'm concerned nothing's changed.' He made the remark jokingly but she knew it hurt him that he couldn't keep up with her financially.

'Nothing's changed as far as I'm concerned either,' she countered swiftly. 'We're really both existing on the generosity of Brock. You've at least earned your own living for the past few years; I hadn't earned a farthing until I opened the shop.'

He grabbed her hand and squeezed it. 'You've been a kept woman all these years, haven't you?' he teased.

Sophie giggled. Tim had regained all his old sparkle and it thrilled her to see him so happy again.

Their room had a balcony overlooking the ancient courtyard in which were arranged wrought-iron chairs and little tables, and large carved stone urns brimming with majestic arum lilies and tall palms.

'Let's go down there and have some champagne,' Sophie suggested, longingly. 'It looks so ... so...' She struggled to find a word that would express her enchantment.

'So Italian?'

When she awoke the next morning, Tim was sitting in a chair by the window, absorbed in a travel guide to Rome. He looked rested and his expression was one of eager absorption.

Sophie stretched lazily, like a cat in the warmth of the sun. 'What are you doing, sweetheart?'

He looked up, eyes sparkling sexily. 'I'm planning our route for today.'

'You mean a list of the antique shops we want to go to?'

'Yes, but much more besides. This book is marvellous.

It lists all the main sights, like the Colosseum, the Sistine Chapel, the Pantheon – I'd love to look at the domed interior, and of course we must go to the greatest tourist attraction of all.'

Sophie grinned at his boyish enthusiasm. 'Which attraction is that?'

He burst into song, his rich baritone voice filling the room. 'Three coins in a fountain . . .'

'Oh, the Trevi fountain! It's beautiful.'

He read aloud. '"Built between 1732 and 1762." How the hell could it have taken so long?' He studied the guide book again. '"Designed by Nicols Salvi . . . it depicts Neptune, flanked by two Tritons, one with an unruly sea-horse and the other with a more docile creature." Blimey! These creatures symbolise the two contrasting moods of the sea.' He looked up, eyebrows raised comically. 'And there was I thinking it had been built in 1958 so that Anita Ekberg could jump around in the water for that film, *La Dolce Vita*.'

'I don't believe it!' Sophie laughed, leaning back against the pillows, her skin a glorious shade of gold against the white linen, the fine lawn of her nightdress revealing small rounded breasts.

His eyes twinkled. 'I believed in Father Christmas until I was eight. Actually I was quite relieved when I found out it was my father and not some strange old man coming into my room.'

'How sweet.' She looked adoringly at him. 'I bet you were an enchanting little boy.'

'I still am! You like to mother me, don't you, Sophie?'

Her smile was teasingly doubtful. 'Well . . .' She drew out the word tantalisingly. 'Sometimes. It makes a nice change to being constantly fathered as I was by Brock.'

He nodded and gave a wry smile. 'I can imagine. Now, let's get down to business. Let's work out a route we can take today so we'll be combining sightseeing with antique hunting.'

'There's plenty of time, Tim. We're here for several days. I'd like some breakfast, and I'd like something else, too, before we start out on this intellectual marathon.' She spoke wheedlingly.

Tim looked impassive. 'What else do you want?' he asked, deadpan.

Sophie threw a pillow at his head. 'Do I have to spell it out?'

That evening, after a hectic day buying antiques from the little shops in the Via Margutta and the Via dei Coronari, Sophie and Tim strolled down the Spanish Steps in the pale amber light of a Roman winter's evening, mingling with the crowds in the Via Condotti, admiring the domes and towers of this densely built medieval city with its grand Renaissance palazzos juxtaposed with busy pavement cafes exuding the fragrance of cappuccino, and divided by the limpid waters of the Tiber.

'It's really extraordinary to think that Julius Caesar walked these streets,' Sophie remarked.

'And Caligula and Virgil and Marcus Aurelius. It all happened here,' Tim added, nose buried in the guide book once more.

Sophie gently placed the flat of her hand on the mellow stone. 'I wish they'd made history more interesting at school, you know. We did a big project on Rome but I can hardly remember anything about it now. And when I came here with Brock, the only sights I saw were the insides of fashionable restaurants, and then he'd send me off to Fendi or Gucci or Giorgio Armani to buy myself a little something, and I was so damned lazy and spineless and *bored* that I agreed. God, was I bored! So bored, in fact, that I couldn't even get up the energy to go sightseeing by myself,' she added angrily, in self-disgust.

'It's always easiest to take the least line of resistance, you know,' Tim assured her. 'Don't be so hard on yourself. It's not much fun sightseeing on your own anyway, and if Brock didn't want to do it, then I can quite understand.'

They walked along the Via Poli in contented and companionable silence, looking appreciatively at the buildings and shops, each like an Aladdin's cave of treasures. Then they turned left and Sophie gasped. There, before them, in all its magnificent grandeur was the Piazza di Trevi with the famous fountain, its great white marble figures forming a backdrop to the dancing, shimmering jets of water that spouted into the air like strings of diamonds in the sunlight.

'Isn't it beautiful?' Sophie breathed. 'Every time I see it I'm filled with awe.'

Tim was leaning over, looking into the trembling green waters. Then he gave a long low whistle. 'Look at all that money. There must be millions of lire lying on the bottom.'

'And a lot of wishes, too,' Sophie pointed out. 'Come on, we must do it. Have you any small change?'

Tim hunted through his trouser pockets, eventually producing some coins. Picking out three, he handed them to Sophie before throwing in three himself.

'What are you wishing for?' she asked curiously.

'If I tell you, it won't happen and I really want this wish to come true,' he replied seriously.

Sophie closed her eyes and tossed her own coins into the water, hearing them go *plop* as they hit the surface before swirling down to join the others at the bottom. She had a wish too, and a great desire for it to be granted.

Frankie and Katie welcomed them back to the shop as if they'd been away for weeks. One look at Sophie's face told them the trip had been a success.

'So Rome was fun, was it?' Katie smiled.

'Yes,' Sophie replied smoothly. 'We picked up three Capodimonte snuff boxes, five exquisite figurines, one by Ricci, dated around seventeen fifty, I'd say, and a flawless cream Vezzi teapot with a design of dark red flowers and swags, with three matching cups and saucers and a sugar bowl, and *all* for a proverbial song. I can't wait to go back.'

'And for some more old china, too?' Frankie asked artlessly.

They were all laughing when Tim sauntered into the shop a few minutes later, casually elegant in pale trousers, a yellow cashmere sweater over an open-neck shirt, and a tweed jacket. Sophie felt a glow of pride. He looked handsome and sexy and she knew the girls thought the same.

'Hi, there,' he said jovially. 'How are the troops

this morning? When do I get my first cup of coffee?' His eyes swept intimately over Sophie, sending her pulse racing. It was only a few hours since he'd made love to her and it was as if she could still feel his thighs, his muscular arms, the flatness of his stomach against hers and she flushed with renewed desire.

'We're all rather busy, you might have to get your own,' she said perkily, daring to be cheeky, so confident did she feel this morning.

His serious expression did not disguise the twinkling wickedness in his eyes. 'Oh, I'm not used to doing it for myself,' he replied straight-faced.

'Too bad,' she said coolly. 'There's the VAT for this quarter to be worked out first.'

He smiled. 'I can wait. But not for too long.'

'Why don't you and Alan come to dinner?' Sophie suggested when Jean phoned the following week.

'That would be nice, darling.' But Jean sounded distracted and Sophie wondered if Alan was unwell again.

'What about Wednesday, Mum?'

'Yes. That would be fine.'

'Is everything all right? Is Alan OK?'

'He gets tired very quickly but I think he's all right,' Jean replied evasively.

'Then what's wrong?'

'I can surely phone you without something being wrong.'

Sophie knew her mother too well. 'Come on, Mum. What's the matter?'

'You won't let on to Audrey that I talked to you, will you? I did promise her that I wouldn't say anything but I'm so worried.'

'Of course I won't say anything. I hardly ever see her anyway. What's wrong?'

A moment later Sophie's jaw dropped open with amazement. 'Are you *sure*? Audrey? But she's never even been interested in sex! Who is this man?' It was early in the morning and she was in the kitchen getting breakfast for herself and Tim. As she spoke he looked up startled from eating his bowl of cereal and his expression was one of comic disbelief.

'Audrey?' he mouthed, wide-eyed.

Sophie nodded silently. With the portable phone held to her ear she continued to listen to Jean with growing amazement. 'His name's Troy? And he what? Writes lyrics in a hut in the woods where he also ... Oh, come on, Mum. Audrey's pulling your leg – although she never did have a sense of humour, did she? What? You think Nicholas suspects? Well, it would serve him right, wouldn't it? Why should he be able to play around but not Audrey?'

Tim continued to eat his breakfast while listening with obvious amusement. When Sophie came off the line he looked at her quizzically. 'What's sauce for the goose is sauce for the gander, eh? Is this the New Woman, Sophie? Sexual equality and all that? I'm not quite sure I approve, you know.'

Sophie's eyes widened and in their dark depths there were dangerous sparks. 'Oh, you don't, do you? Well, let me tell you something. If a husband cheats on his wife I don't see why she shouldn't cheat on him. There's only one thing I disapprove of and that's when the parents' behaviour affects the children.'

'I was only teasing,' he protested. 'Good luck to Audrey, I say.'

Sophie reached across the table and placed her hand on his. 'I didn't mean to snap. It's just that I'm worried about her. So is Mum. It's bound to affect Amelia and Rebecca if both Nicholas and Audrey are playing around.'

Tim looked thoughtful. 'Sounds like she's just discovered sex. Rather late in life, perhaps, but better late than never, I suppose.'

Sophie was frowning as she poured herself some more coffee. 'Nicholas will leave her if he finds out. He's that sort of a chauvinist. Maybe I should talk to her. Mum says she's besotted, though. Audrey of all people,' she added in disbelief. 'She was always so ... well, sort of squeamish.'

'Still waters and all that.'

'So it seems.'

Audrey herself phoned Sophie the following afternoon, as Sophie was writing letters in the back room of the shop. Tim looked up from the figures he was working on as soon as he heard who it was and he immediately began to whisper teasing remarks, knowing it would put Sophie off her stride.

'Ask her what it's like in the woods,' he mouthed. 'Ask her if she's changed her name by deed poll to Chatterley?'

'You what, Audrey?' Sophie asked. She was trying hard not to get the giggles but Tim was making it difficult. 'Sorry, I missed that, Audrey. You're going to a dance? Oh, is there a *chance*? Of your coming to stay for the night? Yes, of course you can stay. No. You won't need to go on the sofa because...'

Tim leaned forward, determined to get her attention. 'Tell Audrey that musicians are better at it than lyricists.'

Sophie clamped her hand over the mouthpiece of the phone. 'Shut up!' she hissed, making a face at him. Then she turned her back on him, still trying to stifle her laughter. 'Why won't you what, Audrey? Yes, I *am* paying attention, but this is a busy office, you know.' There was a pause and then she said, 'Because you can have the spare room, Audrey.' Then she turned back to look at Tim and winked. 'Of course Tim shares my room,' she continued coolly. 'It would be a pretty odd relationship if he didn't.'

When she came off the line a few minutes later, she sank into the chair opposite Tim. 'Oh, God. What will she think of me?' She was still laughing. 'You're a devil, Tim. How was I supposed to carry on a sensible conversation with you making remarks and pulling faces at me?'

'So when is she coming to stay?'

'Tomorrow night.'

Audrey arrived at the Eaton Place flat shortly after six o'clock, her arms full of parcels and her hair cut becomingly short in a feathery style.

'Princess Diana, eat your heart out!' Sophie teased when she opened the door. 'You do look good, Aud.'

Her sister looked offended. 'You needn't sound so

surprised,' she said huffily. 'God, my arms are breaking.' She deposited several large shopping bags on the hall floor. 'Can I dump these here?'

'Of course you can. Come and have a drink. What on earth have you been buying? You look exhausted.'

Audrey followed Sophie into the drawing room where Tim was opening a bottle of champagne. As always the elegance and richness of the room made her ache with jealousy and discontent. By comparison her own house was so plain. So ordinary.

'Oh, hello. What are you doing here?' she exclaimed ungraciously when she saw Tim.

He smiled expansively, coming forward with a brimming glass. 'Good to see you, Audrey.'

'Thanks.' She took the drink from him and then sat down carefully on the sofa, smoothing the skirt of her smart black suit as she did so. 'So, how is everything?' She looked from one to the other.

'Great,' Sophie replied. 'The shop's doing well and we're all fine.'

'And we had a fabulous trip to Rome,' Tim added.

Suddenly the atmosphere had become tense, the conversation stilted. It was obvious that Audrey didn't approve of Tim living with Sophie. Objection showed in every line of her pinched face and in the coolness of her manner.

'And what have you been doing with yourself?' Sophie asked. 'Our life is mostly work and no play, but what about you?'

'There's not much chance to play, with a house and a family to look after,' her sister replied sharply. 'I seem to spend my time chauffeuring the girls around the countryside. If it isn't school, it's tennis lessons, or swimming or riding, or there's some party they've been asked to.' She sighed as if she had all the cares of the world on her shoulders.

'But you're looking terrific,' Tim observed. 'No one would guess you were the mother of those two big girls.'

Audrey couldn't resist his charm completely. 'Thank you,' she said, before fixing her eyes on the carpet. Then they sipped their drinks in awkward silence, until Sophie rose with a purposeful air.

'Let me show you to your room, Aud, and then you can talk to me while I cook the supper.'

'All right.' Audrey shot Tim a slightly triumphant smile as if she'd won a contest for Sophie's attention and then she followed her sister into the hall.

'So what's really going on?' Sophie asked her in a low voice as she led the way to the spare room at the far end of the flat.

'Why should anything be going on?'

'Oh, come on. The new hair-do, all this shopping.' Sophie switched on the lights, revealing a room with a four-poster bed, decorated in the sort of expensive chintz Audrey would have given anything to have been able to afford. 'What does Nicholas think of the new you?'

'I've no idea and I really don't care.'

'Shouldn't you care? What about Amelia and Rebecca? You're not heading for a divorce, are you?' Sophie felt seriously worried. She'd never seen her sister like this; it was as if she was so far removed from reality she was on another planet.

'Maybe. Maybe not.' Audrey shrugged and slipped off the jacket of her suit, revealing a very pretty silk blouse beneath.

'Ummm. Stylish,' Sophie remarked approvingly.

'My friend, Patricia, helped me choose it. God, I owe so much money to American Express and Visa. Nicholas is going to go spare when he gets the bills, but why the hell shouldn't I get myself a few things?'

'I agree and you really needed some good clothes,' said Sophie sympathetically.

Audrey looked huffy again. 'My clothes weren't that bad.'

'For God's sake, Aud! Stop being so defensive. And stop jumping down my throat every time I open my mouth.'

'I'm not.' She looked around the room. 'Can I make a call in a minute?'

'Yes, of course you can. D'you want to check the girls are all right? Give them my love.'

'Yes. All right. Thanks.' She was obviously waiting for Sophie to leave the room.

'Right,' said Sophie, getting the message. 'I'll start cooking dinner.'

In the drawing room, Tim was watching television.

'If Audrey's phoning home, my aunt's the Queen of Sheba,' Sophie told him. 'This,' she continued heavily, 'is going to be a very long evening.'

'Shall I leave you alone? She obviously hates my being here. I can easily go to the pub.'

'Why should you, sweetheart?' Sophie slid her arms round his waist, inside his jacket. His body felt warm and muscular. She wished they were alone. 'We'll have a quick dinner and maybe an early night. I can always say we've got a lot on tomorrow.'

Tim kissed her gently on the lips. 'Poor old Audrey. I think just the two of you should spend a bit of time on your own. I'll leave you to it, and then we can go straight to bed when I return.'

Sophie kissed him back. 'Sounds good to me,' she whispered.

'Can I have another drink?' Audrey asked as Sophie mixed a green salad. She'd joined her in the kitchen after Tim had left the flat and she looked as if all her Christmases had arrived at once.

'Help yourself. You can pour me one too, please. How was everything at home? Are the girls OK?'

'What?' Audrey looked confused for a moment then she recovered herself. 'Oh, yes. They're fine.' There was a lengthy pause and Sophie deliberately didn't say anything to relieve the awkwardness. Audrey definitely had something on her mind and Sophie knew if she waited long enough it would all come spewing out. What Audrey did have to say caught her by surprise.

'You don't mind if I slip out after dinner for a while, do you?' She spoke with elaborate casualness.

'Where are you going?' Sophie asked in genuine surprise.

'I'm meeting a friend, that's all. Just for a quick drink.'

'Oh.' For some reason it was Sophie who felt guilty. Perhaps, she thought, it was because she really knew what was going on but had to pretend ignorance.

Audrey moved restlessly around the kitchen, glass in hand, a preoccupied expression on her face.

'So what's going on, Aud?' Sophie said at last.

'Nothing. Why should anything be going on?'

'Because I know you well enough to tell you're like a cat on a hot tin roof; or a hot cat on a tin roof.'

'Don't be disgusting.'

'Come off it, Aud. It stands out a mile that you're up to something. You're having an affair, aren't you?'

Audrey's face flamed so much her eyes watered. 'Mummy's been talking, hasn't she?' she asked furiously.

'She didn't have to.' It was true. Sophie would have spotted all the signs even if Jean had said nothing.

'Well, don't get judgmental with me!'

'For goodness sake, Audrey. It's up to you what you do. Good luck to you if you can get away with it, seeing how Nicholas has been carrying on. My only worry is that you might get hurt.'

Audrey shrugged, but her eyes were sparkling. 'Whether I do or not is beside the point. Troy is the most fantastic man. He's shown me a side of myself I never knew existed. It's heaven to be with him.'

'And I take it that's why you're spending the night in London.'

Audrey nodded.

'So why didn't you both book in to a hotel?'

'He's too well known. If the paparazzi found out, it would cause a real scandal in the pop world.'

'You weren't thinking of bringing him back here, were you?'

'We're meeting for a drink, like I said.' She looked shifty.

'And that is all it will have to be if you can't make other arrangements. I'm not being judgmental, Aud, but I don't want to get directly involved in your little fling. There are Amelia and Rebecca to consider, and there's Nicholas, too. It's entirely up to you what you do, but please keep me out of it.'

'You bitch!' Audrey exclaimed, stung. 'You sanctimonious bitch! Who are you to talk? You leave a husband old enough to be your father and then with his money keep a penniless young man in your bed. Don't you dare moralise to me about how one should behave.'

Sophie paled with anger but tried not to lose her temper. 'I'm not moralising, I'm merely saying leave me out of your plans. You had no right to presume you could sneak your lover into my home in the middle of the night, with instructions, no doubt, to creep out before I woke up.'

'But there's nothing wrong with your sleeping with Tim, I suppose.'

'I'm no longer married, Aud. I don't have children either. There's a world of difference between our circumstances.'

'Well, you can go stuff yourself for all I care,' Audrey stormed tearfully. 'Now Troy and I will *have* to go to a hotel and it will be all your fault if we get found out!'

PART FIVE

May

Eleven

'Lot 135. A fine pair of *famille rose* figures of hawks. Qianlong.' The auctioneer indicated the beautifully coloured china birds as they were placed on a velvet-covered table.

'Showing here, sir,' the porter announced loudly.

Sophie knew they had been estimated to reach between thirty and forty thousand pounds, and she desperately longed to buy them. One of her regular customers, an avid collector, would adore them. Porcelain made between 1736 and 1795, during the reign of Emperor Qianlong, was always popular, especially those pieces that were not overtly Oriental.

The atmosphere in the crowded showroom of Christie's was tense, and she knew she was up against heavy opposition from other dealers as well as private buyers.

'I'm starting the bidding at fifteen thousand pounds. Have I any bids for fifteen thousand?' The auctioneer's gaze swept across the room, sharp-eyed and alert. 'Thank you. Fifteen thousand.' He'd spotted someone at the back of the room making a covert bid. The ball had started rolling. The muscles of Sophie's stomach tightened. She wouldn't jump in yet. Better to wait and see what everyone else was doing. To start bidding now would only push up the price.

'Sixteen thousand ... seventeen ... eighteen ... nineteen thousand.' There was a momentary lull and then the bidding raced on again. 'Twenty thousand, twenty-two thousand ...'

Looking straight at the auctioneer, Sophie nodded almost imperceptibly but it was enough.

'Twenty-four ... against you at the back.'

Sophie nodded again.

'Twenty-six ... twenty-eight, thirty thousand. Thirty thousand pounds.' She nodded once more, feeling sick.

'Thirty-two thousand.'

There was a hushed silence. Would the bidding go on? It was with Sophie now. The auctioneer scanned the room again, searching for a nod or the gentle flick of a catalogue. Everyone seemed to have turned to rock. Sophie tried to breathe slowly and evenly, but her heart hammered in her rib cage.

'Any advance on thirty-two thousand? I have thirty-two thousand ...' He paused for what seemed like the longest moment she'd ever known. 'Thirty-two thousand,' he said loudly, and brought down his gavel with a sharp *click*.

It was over. The beautiful hawks were hers, and at thirty-two thousand, even with the buyer's premium, she would make a profit of at least ten thousand, probably fifteen.

'Lot 136. A Meissen octagonal dish ...'

Sophie wasn't listening. She slipped out of the room, flushed with delight. She'd got the one thing she'd wanted and now she could hardly wait to arrange the exquisite birds in the window of Gloria Antica.

When she got back to the shop she found Frankie was serving a well-known interior designer who was choosing a dessert service for one of his clients. Sophie greeted him, making sure he was being looked after before she went through to the back office where Tim was on the phone. In spite of the desk being piled high with papers he seemed laid back as he smiled at her warmly. Before him were neat piles of invoices, statements, petty cash slips and tax return forms which had arrived that morning.

'Hi,' he greeted her cheerfully as soon as he came off the line. 'I'm having a real clear-up. You won't know this office when I've finished.'

'What a ghastly job. I don't know how you can bear to do it. You've no idea how grateful I am.'

'Well, you can always show me later, can't you?' he whispered.

She flipped a paperclip at him, grinning. Life had never been such fun during the years she'd been deprived of his company. Every day was a joy now, full of laughter and light-heartedness. Her happiness, she knew, would be complete and absolute if he would only suggest they marry. Then she pushed the thought away. Why dwell on what was obviously not going to happen – right now, anyway? In front of her lay the morning's mail, still unopened. A moment later she gave an exclamation of dismay.

'Bloody hell!'

'What is it?' Tim asked.

She handed him a folder full of papers. 'It's from

Wiseman, Stroud and Halcrow. My accountants. Look what they're charging me! Nobody told me it would be so expensive to have them looking after my affairs. God! What a rip-off!'

Tim was studying the pages of figures as she spoke, and he was frowning. 'This is the firm Brock recommended, is it?'

'Yes. They look after all my money, do my tax, and they've been doing the shop accounts, based on my attempt at book-keeping, but they've charged *thousands*! Can that be right, Tim?' She looked shocked. This had been her first financial year on her own, and she felt completely out of her depth. She didn't even understand the figures. It was obvious she needed someone to look after her affairs, but surely not at this price?

'What do you think?' she asked anxiously. 'Is this justified? I mean I'm not ICI or some enormous corporation. Brock made over various shares to me, as well as some capital and property, and he did invest in this shop, but for an accountant surely that would be straightforward, wouldn't it?' It was awful to feel so helpless.

'It is all fairly straightforward,' Tim said slowly. 'What you're paying for is their name; they're a very smart firm, at a very fancy address. Berkeley Square, W1 – I ask you!'

'But what else can I do? Find a cheaper firm? Brock insisted I should have them because he knows how hopeless I am.'

'You're not hopeless at all,' Tim said with sudden tenderness. 'One either has a head for figures or one doesn't. You're artistic. That's where your talents lie. And you can afford their fee, can't you?'

'That's not the point. I feel like I'm being taken for a ride.' Sophie spoke fretfully.

'You know what's behind this, don't you? Brock still wants to keep tabs on you. Control what you're doing even from a distance. How friendly is he with these accountants? For all you know, he could be using them himself and employing them at the same time to report back to him about your affairs.'

'Oh no, surely not. Brock wouldn't do a thing like that.'

'You know him better than I do, sweetheart. But they always say you can learn more about a person from their accounts than any other way.'

'But that's spying. Brock would never stoop to anything so low. What would be the point? He was so generous when we split up and I know he'd never take back anything he's given me.'

'It probably makes him feel good to know exactly what you're doing with the money.' Tim sighed and then smiled at her affectionately. 'You're so sweet. And so trusting. You think the best of everyone, don't you?'

Sophie felt confused. Brock had never suggested there would be strings attached to his generosity. He was a very rich man who cared for her enough to want her to maintain the same standard of living she'd enjoyed when they'd been married. Could he really still be manipulating her from behind the scenes? Then she shook her head.

'You don't know Brock like I do, Tim. He's not

devious. I believe he just tried to organise everything so that I'd have no worries. It's up to me, in the long run, to do what I want to do, and for a start I'd like to ask Wiseman, Stroud and Halcrow what these charges are for.'

'They'll blind you with science; they'll justify every penny and you won't know whether to believe them or not because you don't know enough about accounting methods and how much work is involved. If you have a large portfolio they'll have to declare all your dividends; if you have money on deposit, there will be interest charges. There's the cost of running Eaton Place, La Madeleine, and this shop to take into accounts. Talking of which, it occurred to me that you'd probably do better to form a limited company as far as the shop's concerned because you'll be taxed at a lower rate and you can claim expenses—'

'Hang on a moment, Tim. You're going too fast. This is exactly why Brock suggested this firm look after my affairs. I only understand a fraction of what you're talking about,' said Sophie.

Tim looked thoughtful. 'Brock obviously still loves you. On the other hand it was always a controlling love, as if you were a possession. That's why you left him, isn't it? I believe he's motivated by his desire to go on controlling you now. It's the He-who-pays-the-piper syndrome. He knows you can't manage your financial affairs without help and this way he probably gets to know every time you buy a pair of tights.'

'Yes,' she said slowly, and she felt sad at the thought that she hadn't entirely escaped her former existence. Tim's remarks stung her, too. Was she really still a naïve child who couldn't manage without a father figure?

'I think I'll get rid of these accountants,' she said impulsively.

'You're an independent woman now,' Tim told her firmly. 'You can do exactly as you like. But it might be as well to find another firm to take over before you burn your boats and land yourself in a mess with no one at all to look after your affairs.'

She grinned at him in gratitude. He'd restored her confidence, and suddenly, in a wave of euphoria, she knew she could take control of her life. Why not? She wasn't stupid. She might not be numerate, but she could get someone who was to do her accounts. The most important thing was that she knew what she was doing when it came to antique porcelain; Gloria Antica was proving even more successful than she'd hoped. If she could continue to make a go of the shop she had no real problems.

'Tim,' she began, leaning forward in her chair and looking at him intently. 'I've had the most inspired idea.'

'I'm not taking on your accounts.' He wasn't smiling now.

'Now wait a moment.' She knew what his objections were going to be. Not mixing business with pleasure. Not being dependent on her. Getting himself a proper job so that he could earn himself a living. They'd talked this through before. 'You're a qualified chartered accountant, aren't you? Qualified before you went to Australia. In other words, you know what you're doing.'

He raised his eyebrows. 'So?' He sounded guarded.

'Why don't you start your own business, and I can be your first client? I can recommend you to a lot of people, too. Women on their own, like myself, who don't understand one end of a balance sheet from the other,' she said enthusiastically. 'It's a brilliant idea, Tim, and I can't think why I never thought of it before. With your knowledge and my contacts you could make a packet, especially if your charges are anything like Wiseman, Stroud and Halcrow's,' she added, laughing.

Tim remained serious looking, but she could see he was thinking about it.

'To start off, you could rent a small office somewhere with an assistant to help,' she continued encouragingly, 'and then you can expand as the business grows.'

'And what do you think Brock will say when he hears you've left the accountants he recommended and got in your old boy friend to look after your finances instead?'

'Tim,' she looked determined, 'I don't give a damn what Brock says. I'm not married to him any more and I can do as I like. It's time he realised I'm not a silly little girl who needs looking after. I can look after myself,' she said sturdily.

His face broke into a smile. 'I love you when you're like this, all assertive and independent,' he said fondly. Then he took a deep breath as if he was about to plunge into a deep pool. 'OK, Sophie. I'll do it. Actually the thought of having my own little company sounds rather fun.' He looked boyishly eager and her heart swelled with love for him. 'Do you really know people who could use my services?'

'You bet I do. And you could raise the money to get started by selling your house in Wales, couldn't you?'

There was a long pause and suddenly his face looked drawn and strained. She immediately regretted her remark. No doubt the memory of Carolyn was very much tied up with the house and while she felt jealous that his late wife still had the power to affect him, she realised she had been tactless.

'Better still,' she said breezily as if she hadn't noticed anything, 'get a bank loan and use the house as collateral, or I could guarantee a loan.'

Tim looked relieved and the colour came back into his cheeks. Then he laughed. 'It sounds as if you know more about business than you realise.'

'Well, of course I heard Brock talking; business was and is his life. Oh!' She clapped her hands. 'Won't he be amazed when he realises I'm taking complete control of my life?'

'And you can do it, sweetheart,' Tim warmly assured her.

She glanced at her wristwatch. 'Let's go out to lunch and celebrate.'

'What about work?'

'We *have* worked. I had a brilliant morning at Christie's sale, and you've decided on a new career. If that isn't a good enough excuse to celebrate I don't know what is!' She jumped to her feet, her dark eyes sparkling with happiness.

'OK. You're in charge,' Tim laughed.

Sophie laughed also, grabbing his hand and looking up into his face. 'I suppose I am,' she said wonderingly. 'And what a lovely feeling it is, too!'

Audrey was so relieved that her night at the Berkeley

Hotel with Troy had passed unnoticed by the tabloids that an element of recklessness had taken over. If she could meet Troy in London, and even pass whole nights with him without either of their families suspecting anything or the paparazzi noticing, then perhaps they could do it more often. She suggested this the next time they met in the little hut in the woods.

'It was so wonderful being able to stay the whole night with you, darling,' she whispered as they lay curled up on cushions on the floor. The hut was romantic and exciting, but nothing, she thought, compensated for a large soft bed. Especially if you could stay in it all night. 'Let's do it again soon. I can always say I'm staying with my sister, and it was OK for you to say you were in town on business, wasn't it?'

Troy looked up from unbuttoning her blouse. 'Rana's no fool. I got away with it last week, but it's hellishly risky.'

'Oh, Troy, in your job you're surely away from home a lot. What about when you tour?' Audrey had a desperate feeling that she might lose him if she didn't somehow consolidate her position.

'I'm hardly ever on my own, and Rana knows everyone in the group. I couldn't take you along with me, and I couldn't go on my own without them.' He nuzzled her breasts, driving her crazy. 'We'll just have to go on meeting in this little ol' hut and if you get a sore arse from the hard floor, then that's too damn bad.'

'Oh, I love it here,' Audrey said quickly. She struggled with the buckle of his trouser belt; in her eagerness she broke a nail. 'This is the cosiest, warmest, nicest little hidey-hole in the world.'

'No, this is,' he murmured, his hand in her crotch. For the next twenty minutes Audrey was transported to a world of rapturous sensations where her body took over, leaving her mind far behind in limbo, without thought, without conscience and without any fear of the consequences should they be caught. Nothing mattered except assuaging the feverish heat that consumed her loins and as flesh pounded flesh, and she heard a voice that couldn't possibly be her own cry out, 'Oh, God, yes! Fuck me ... fuck me, Troy, fuck me till I die,' she was unaware of someone knocking on the door of the hut.

Within two weeks, Sophie had left Wiseman, Stroud and Halcrow, and Tim had taken over her finances. They'd also started negotiating for a small office suite on the first floor of a building almost opposite Gloria Antica in Walton Street.

'It's perfect,' Sophie said with delight. 'We can still meet for lunch and pop across the road to see each other.' Tim had raised a bank loan, and as he still seemed edgy about using his cottage in Wales as collateral, Sophie was happy to be his guarantor. There was no point, she figured, in letting him do anything that would involve memories of Carolyn. Not at this stage anyway. In time he was going to have to face the fact that she was dead and that life had to go on, but Sophie hoped he would come to this realisation naturally and by himself. If they were ever going to get married, he'd have to come to terms with what had happened.

Meanwhile, the days passed in a flurry of excited

activity while Sophie awaited a reaction from Brock with trepidation. She hoped he wouldn't be hurt and upset as she moved further and further out of his life. Without Wiseman, Stroud and Halcrow, he would have no idea how she was handling her affairs, and the thought gave her a curiously free feeling; nevertheless she couldn't help being uneasy, like a child who has done something naughty.

When the phone rang late one night, a week later, she was certain it was Brock. To her surprise she found it was her stepfather.

'Alan! Are you all right?' she asked at once. He still tired very easily and there were times when she and her mother worried about him.

'I'm all right,' he said calmly. 'Your mother asked me to ring because she's worried.'

'Mum? What's she worried about?'

'You, actually. Can you drop in for a drink, on your own?'

'What is this, Alan? Why on my own?'

'It's something private we want to talk about.'

Sophie felt bewildered. 'Why can't you talk to me now?' She'd never known Alan sound so strange. 'Is it to do with Audrey? Oh, don't tell me she and Nicholas have had a final bust-up.'

'No, it's got nothing to do with Audrey. This isn't a heavy deal, Sophie. It's just that your mother and I would like a quiet word with you, and we think it would be better if we saw you on your own.'

'I can't manage tomorrow, Alan. Or the next day. There are big sales on this week and I'm after quite a few nice pieces. What about Friday lunchtime?'

'Friday would be fine. Here, at the flat? At noon?' He sounded insistent.

'Yes. Great. I'll see you then.' As she was saying goodbye Tim came out of the bathroom where he'd been having a shower.

'Who was that?' he asked.

'It was Alan. He and Mum want to talk to me about something – goodness knows what. He sounded most mysterious. I'm seeing them on Friday.'

'Don't you realise,' Alan pointed out after he'd poured Sophie a glass of white wine, 'that you've actually jumped out of the frying pan into the fire?'

They were sitting in the drawing room of their Kensington flat and both Jean and Alan were looking concerned.

Sophie stared at them blankly. 'What are you talking about?'

'We met Tim a few days ago, coming out of Harrods,' Alan said. 'He said he was setting himself up as a freelance accountant and that you were his first client.'

'Yes. He is. It's a great idea and he's found himself an office and I know I can get him lots of business—'

'There's nothing wrong with that,' Jean cut in. 'What worries Alan and me is the fact that he told us you'd got rid of your own accountants. The ones Brock suggested you use.'

Sophie looked stubborn. 'I'm fed up doing everything Brock says. We divorced over a year ago and I still feel dependent on him. I want to do my own thing.'

'But you're not doing your own thing. You've let Tim take control instead of Brock. To really do your own thing would mean refusing to take a penny from Brock. You always talked about your desire to be free, to do as you liked, and I respect that. But now, by putting your affairs into Tim's hands, you're back to square one. You might as well have stayed with Brock.'

'And at least he was rich,' Jean added, almost to herself.

'But I haven't let Tim take over.' She was appalled by what they were saying. She made her own decisions these days. Tim didn't tell her what to do; if anything it was the other way round. 'Tim hasn't made me do anything,' she protested hotly. 'Everything we've done has been my idea because I wanted it that way. If anything, I've been the controlling force.'

'There are more ways of killing a cat than choking it with butter,' Alan quoted enigmatically.

'What's that supposed to mean?'

'It means it's possible, though I'm not saying definite, that you're being manipulated without realising it. You've got to remember you're so used to someone else being in charge, you probably don't notice any more.'

Sophie looked at her stepfather aghast. Then she looked at Jean as if for an explanation, but her mother was watching her anxiously.

'Alan's right, you know, Sophie. We're really worried at the way he's insinuated himself into your life.'

'But Ma!' She was lost for words. 'What's going on? I've known Tim since I was seventeen! We'd probably have married if he hadn't gone away. I still hope we'll marry. I love him more than anyone else in the world. Why are you both saying these horrible things?' She was near to tears.

Jean's face softened. 'I know, love. That's one of the reasons we're so concerned. We don't want you to be hurt by him again.'

'But why should I be?' She felt genuinely bewildered. 'Tim only has my best interests at heart. In fact I think you're both being really horrid about him. Here he is, trying to get his life together after the death of his wife, and you're talking as if he was a fortune hunter.' Tears were streaming down her face as she scrabbled in her handbag for a tissue. 'He's suffered so much,' she said through her sobs, 'and I love him so much . . .'

Alan laid a gentle hand on her shoulder. 'Don't get so upset, my dear. Your mother and I are concerned for you, that's all. And we're worried at your allowing Tim to take control of your money. You are a very wealthy woman, you know. That's why Brock wanted you to go to a highly reputable firm of accountants.'

Sophie looked up sharply. 'Has Brock been talking to you?'

Alan looked surprised. 'No. I haven't seen or heard anything of him for over a year.'

As Sophie rode back to the shop in a taxi, shock and distress became replaced by anger. Her mother and Alan were as good as accusing Tim of embezzlement. What the hell did they think he was going to do with her money? Abscond with it? Marry her for it? A fierce feeling of protectiveness swept through her. She would show them! She would prove that Tim was utterly trustworthy, had her best interests at heart and would no more think of controlling her life than the man in the moon. He wasn't another Brock. He was of a different generation for a start, a generation that did not believe in men 'owning' women. A generation that abhorred the idea of the 'trophy wife'. And she was of that same generation.

Back at the shop, Frankie and Katie were rearranging the window display with a Coalport dinner service decorated with designs of hand-painted wildlife in shades of soft burnt umber.

'That looks pretty,' she commented.

Katie looked at her searchingly. 'Are you all right, Sophie? You're awfully pale.'

'I'm fine,' she replied quickly as she hurried into the little back room. Thankfully, Tim was out. She needed time to herself to clear her head and get her thoughts in order. How could Alan have come to the conclusion that she was letting Tim run her life?

'Hi, there.' It was Tim and he was in high spirits. 'How are you?'

'Alive,' Sophie replied, smiling wanly.

'As good as *that*?' He dropped into the chair on the opposite side of the desk and regarded her fondly. 'What's up?' he asked, more seriously.

'Nothing,' she said quickly, avoiding his gaze.

'Come on, Sophie. Spill it out. What did Jean and Alan have to say?'

She flushed uncomfortably. 'Oh, nothing really. They think I've bitten off more than I can chew with this shop and everything. That's all.'

She knew he didn't believe her. He was too perceptive to be fobbed off with such an unlikely story.

'And what else?' he asked.

'Oh, just family stuff,' she lied, trying to sound vague.

To her relief the phone rang and she seized the opportunity to grab it before Tim did. It was an American client who had been buying from her on a regular basis, inquiring if she had any more Meissen figurines in stock. Sophie spent as long as she could talking to him, hoping Tim would lose interest in questioning her, for how could she tell him that her mother and stepfather didn't trust him?

Audrey strolled through the woods at a leisurely pace, because she was early for her usual assignation with Troy. How she looked forward to these secret meetings. How wonderful it was to make love with him in the afternoons when normally she'd have been catching up on the ironing or working in the garden. What absolute heaven life was these days! Audrey couldn't recall a time when she'd been happier. She felt like running and even dancing now, so energised was she by the thought of seeing Troy in a few minutes. There was a breeze that tumbled her hair about her face and whipped at the scarf round her neck. She felt playful and idiotically young, and she started to hum a little tune.

So engrossed was she in fantasising she didn't hear the rustle of feet among fallen leaves or sense the presence of someone following her. Onwards she strode on light feet, humming brightly. Suddenly her arm was seized from behind and gripped tightly with fingers of iron. Startled, Audrey spun round in fear and found herself face to face with a woman she'd never seen before.

'What do you want?' she cried shrilly.

The face that looked back at her was smiling broadly;

it was an attractive face despite its lined, hard-living appearance. She must have been stunning when she was young, Audrey thought in that first moment.

'Don't you remember me? We met on New Year's Eve, at the Burchfields' party.' Her voice was brightly cheerful.

Audrey hesitated. The face was vaguely familiar but she couldn't be sure.

'I think you know my husband.' The woman's tone was less friendly now.

'Your husband?' A dreadful suspicion was growing in Audrey's mind.

'That's right. My husband is Troy Kessler. I'm Rana.'

A deep flush started at Audrey's neck and spread up her face. 'Oh. Oh, yes. Of course. I remember now. How stupid of me. How are you? That was a good party, wasn't it?' She knew she was babbling, that her hands were shaking and her legs were in danger of folding beneath her but she had to try and brazen this out. How much did this woman know? Keep cool, flashed through her mind. Don't panic. Deny everything and bluff your way out of this nightmare.

She attempted to keep her voice steady. 'The Burchfields do give such wonderful parties, don't they? We were very glad when they moved into the area. Do you live around here too?'

Rana's eyes were blue pools of hostility now, and her wrinkled mouth no longer smiled.

'You know the answer to that. I'm not a fool, you know. If you don't stop meeting Troy in secret I shall have no choice but to tell your husband what's going on.'

'Why don't you?' Audrey spoke wildly. 'Nicholas

wouldn't give a damn. My marriage is as good as over anyway.'

'But mine isn't, and I don't intend to lose Troy to a dreary little slag like you.'

Audrey drew in her breath sharply. No one had ever spoken to her like that. Incensed, she retaliated. 'At least I have youth on my side.'

Rana's hand had the sting of a wasp. Audrey reeled from the slap on her cheek. 'Go home, you little bitch!' Rana's voice was hoarse with rage. 'If I ever find you with my husband again you'll regret it.' Then she strode on, an eccentric figure in an ankle-length stockman's raincoat and a mane of frizzy gun-metal grey hair.

Audrey stood in shock, watching the receding figure head towards the hut where Troy would be waiting for her. A sob of frustration and misery bubbled up from her chest and a mascara-stained tear slid slowly down her cheek as she retraced her steps to her own house and her old life because she had a desperate feeling that she wouldn't be seeing Troy again.

Twelve

Sophie moved closer to Tim, feeling the warmth of his body next to hers. She loved these moments after they'd made love when they talked quietly, so completely at ease with each other it was almost as if they'd become one person.

'So when shall we get away for a few days to go to La Madeleine?' she murmured. 'We need a break, you know. We've both been working very hard.' Tim's freelance accountancy business had got off the ground with greater speed than either of them had expected, and she'd been very busy in the shop and going to auction sales.

'Maybe next month,' Tim replied sleepily.

'Not sooner?' she asked, disappointed. 'I'd hoped we could slip away next week. There are no important sales on, and we've no engagements.'

Tim put his arms round her, pulling her closer. 'But I've got a few people to see about doing their tax for them. This is not the best time, sweetheart. Why don't you go on your own?'

Sophie pulled back and looked into his face. 'What do you mean, go on my own? I'd never do that, Tim. We do everything together, don't we?'

He kissed her lightly on the tip of her nose. 'Of course we do, sweetheart. It was only a suggestion as you seemed so keen to go.'

'Not that keen,' she retorted.

'I really do have a lot of work on. I've only just started this business, and I think it will look bad if I skip off right now, don't you?'

Reluctantly, she nodded. 'Yes. You're right. We'll go later on. Perhaps...' Her voice trailed away uncertainly.

'Perhaps what?' Tim seemed relieved she'd abandoned the idea of going to France for the time being.

'Perhaps...' Some inner frustration made her speak rashly. 'Wouldn't it be perfect if we got married this summer and spent our honeymoon at La Madeleine?'

The silence that followed her remark was filled with reproach. Tim took his arms away and moved back to his side of the bed. His expression was filled with astonishment. 'What are you talking about?'

'Us,' she replied in a small voice. 'Us getting married one day. Isn't that what you want too?'

'What made you think we'd marry one day? I've never suggested it. I don't think I'll ever marry again. What's the point?'

Sophie felt diminished, as if she was a tiny person alone in a huge world. 'The point is we love each other,' she quavered. 'And I'd like to have a baby soon.'

Tim turned and looked at her anxiously. 'I'm sorry if you think I've led you to believe we were heading for the altar. I never meant to do that.'

Marriage hadn't crossed her mind at first. Just to be with him was enough. To make love with him was enough. But as someone said, the more you have, the more you want, and now she wanted marriage. And a baby. In fact, she wanted everything in her life to be shared with Tim.

'I thought it was what we both wanted – eventually,' she said lamely.

'Everyone would think I'd only married you for your money.'

'No, they wouldn't.'

'If what we have isn't enough for you—'

She remained silent.

'If you can't settle for what we've got, then I'll just have to go back to Wales.' As he spoke, he clambered out of bed. 'I'm getting myself a drink. D'you want anything?'

Her throat ached with unshed tears. 'Some water, please.'

As he walked out of the bedroom, she watched his naked back view, broad-shouldered, with long lean flanks and strong calf muscles, and she knew she could never bear to let him go. If she couldn't have the whole cake, would she settle for half? It was too soon to say. Maybe she'd pushed him too soon after Carolyn's death; perhaps in another six months he'd feel differently about remarrying.

'Here we are,' he announced with forced cheerfulness as he made his way back to the bed with two glasses and a bottle of Perrier. He avoided eye contact, she noticed, as he handed her one of the glasses. 'You gave me quite a shock there,' he said with a nervous laugh.

'I'm sorry I read the wrong signs,' Sophie replied quietly.

'The wrong signs? I'd say you lost the whole plot!' He kissed her briefly on her bare shoulder, all banter and beguilement again. 'Here comes the bride,' he sang, raising his glass to her. Sophie tried not to appear as hurt as she felt. She'd been serious. It seemed at that moment that Tim didn't know the meaning of the word.

After he'd fallen asleep, Sophie lay awake wondering what to do. Give it another six months? Or split up right away, before she was hurt more? Tim had broken her heart once before and she knew she was a fool to risk that happening again, but she loved him so much, the thought of losing him a second time was unthinkable.

At last she fell asleep, a troubled dream-laden slumber that caused her to wake at dawn feeling depressed and with a headache. She had become so dependent on Tim that the realisation that he didn't feel as committed to their relationship as she did disturbed her deeply. Of course they could go on living together, but it wouldn't be the same.

Carefully she slipped out of bed so as not to disturb Tim. In the bathroom adjoining their bedroom, she ran a hot bath and thought about Carolyn. Pretty, dainty, child-like Carolyn, with whom Tim had been besotted. Perhaps a part of him would be in love with her for ever. They shall grow not old as we that are left grow old... the famous poem echoed in her head. It was true. Carolyn was no longer around to grow fat and grey, or become wrinkled and boring; she would remain for ever fair and beautiful in his eyes and how could one compete with that?

After a long, hot and perfumed bath, Sophie felt

calmer. She was also determined to wait and see what happened. After all, six months was no time at all to recover from such a devastating trauma. She'd been foolhardy to mention marriage to Tim so soon. He was bound to feel that even for decency's sake he couldn't remarry yet. Resolving to be cheerful and not to mention marriage again, she wrapped a large towel round herself, like a sarong, and quietly opened the bathroom door. To her surprise Tim was sitting on the edge of the bed with his back to her, and he was whispering into the phone.

Instinctively Sophie froze, straining to hear what he was saying, puzzled that he should be talking to someone so early in the morning.

'There's no question of that so don't worry ... believe me, it's you I love. I just wanted you to know what's happening ... Oh yes ... yes ... of course ... take care, sweetheart ...'

Sophie couldn't move, couldn't speak. So that was why Tim didn't want to marry her. He was in love with someone else.

Frankie and Katie exchanged looks, wondering what had happened. Tim was tapping away at the keyboard of the computer, working on the accounts of Gloria Antica, but he was in a strange mood and there was no sign of Sophie.

'She's got a migraine,' he'd told them offhandedly as he swept through the showroom and into the office beyond. 'I don't think she'll be in today.'

'Do you think they've had a fight?' Katie whispered as she polished one of the display tables.

'I think something's wrong. Sophie always phones us herself even if she's unwell, doesn't she?'

'Perhaps I'll ring her when Tim leaves, just to make sure she's all right.'

Frankie looked thoughtful. 'And I wonder why he isn't in his own office. He doesn't usually come here until the late afternoon now he's got his own business.'

Katie sighed. 'Oh God, I do hope he's not going to mess Sophie about. It'll break her heart if anything goes wrong.'

'Tell me about it,' Frankie said gloomily. They were both fond of Sophie, as a boss and as a friend. She never asked them to do anything she wouldn't do herself, from cleaning the odd brass or silver trinket to sweeping the floor and, in spite of her wealth, she never showed off.

'Do you like Tim?' Katie asked, still whispering.

'I think he's great. Good looking, amusing, what more do you want?'

Katie gave the table a final rub. 'Too amusing, perhaps.'

'How can anyone be too amusing?'

'Flippant, then. Not serious.' She shrugged. 'I don't know, but I feel worried for Sophie's sake.'

'Oh!' Frankie suddenly put her hand over her mouth. 'I've just thought of something.'

Katie looked at her, blonde eyebrows raised questioningly.

'Do you think she's pregnant?' Frankie hissed. 'I suppose she could be. Maybe that's why Tim's in a bad mood.'

'Oh, my goodness!' They eyed each other with a mixture of excitement and dismay.

* * *

Sophie spent the day alone in her flat, trying to make herself believe what Tim had told her, but still so filled by doubt that there were moments when she thought she was going crazy. Feeling physically ill with shock and misery, she was certain he'd lied to her.

'Believe what you like,' he'd retorted angrily, 'but I was talking to my mother.'

'At six o'clock in the morning?' she demanded incredulously. 'And why in God's name should you have to reassure your mother that you love her?'

'You know how possessive my mother is. You know that's the main reason why I went to Australia. What's the matter with you, Sophie? You're not getting insanely possessive too, are you?'

Suddenly, he'd managed to turn everything round so that she felt as if it was she who had somehow betrayed him.

'I just don't like being made a fool of,' she snapped.

Tim gave an exaggerated sigh. 'Unlike your mother, mine works. She takes her first class at nine o'clock, having cleaned her house, done her shopping and everything else that has to be done. If I don't catch her first thing, she's gone for the day. Satisfied?'

Sophie didn't answer. She was far from satisfied but somehow Tim always managed to get the better of her in an argument. He took her lack of response to be acquiescence, and muttering something about having a shower as he was now already up, he banged out of the bedroom, slamming the door behind him.

Going to the kitchen, she put on the coffee, but somehow the light had gone out of the day. Depression swamped her and Alan's words came back to her with unnerving clarity: 'You've jumped out of the frying pan into the fire . . . you've let Tim take control . . . you might as well have stayed with Brock.'

For a moment Sophie felt quite faint as she realised Alan could be right. She'd handed every part of her life to Tim on a platter: her home, her shop, the management of her finances and herself. Now she felt trapped. Yet again. And scared, too. She'd heard him talking to someone and she was sure as hell it wasn't his mother. So who was he having an affair with?

'We must be able to tell how much profit we made last month,' Sophie protested, looking at the computer screen in frustration. 'This is ridiculous.'

Frankie tapped with expert fingers at the keyboard. 'It's got to be here somewhere, I just can't find where Tim's filed it. I'll try some of the other menus.'

Sophie watched as a mass of figures appeared. 'What are those?'

There was a long pause. 'I've no idea,' Frankie admitted worriedly. 'I'll have to get Tim to show me how he's programmed the accounts. It's probably me just being stupid, but I don't know what he's done.'

Sophie turned to Katie who was unpacking some china she'd bought at auction the previous week. 'Did Tim tell you how this works?'

Katie shook her sleek blonde head. 'I haven't a clue, I'm afraid. Frankie's the one with the know-how.'

'Yes,' Frankie spoke with agitation now. 'He did explain how it all worked to me, but now I can't seem to find anything I want. Ah! Wait a minute.' She leaned forward scanning the screen anxiously. 'Shit. No, that's not right. I've no idea what these figures are. They don't make any sense to me. I'm sorry, Sophie. We'll have to get Tim to explain it again. It looked so simple when he showed me. I should be able to summon up our purchase figures, our sales figures, the relevant VAT, our outgoings, everything—'

'Hang on a second,' Sophie cut in. 'I bet I know what's happened. He does my personal affairs as well. Maybe that's what you're looking at instead of the shop accounts.'

Frankie's face was screwed up as if she'd had a sudden pain. 'I don't think so,' she said slowly. 'God, I wish I knew how to work this damn thing.'

'But you do,' Katie observed. 'You've taken a course, haven't you?'

'Yes, but it doesn't seem to have done me much good in this case,' she replied drily. She looked up at Sophie who was still standing beside her. 'Is Tim coming in later on today?'

'Yes. He said he'd pop in this afternoon.'

'Well, thank God for that. I'll write down his instructions so this doesn't happen again.'

Sophie smiled. 'That's OK, Frankie. Don't worry about it. I should really learn to work the machine myself. Perhaps I should go on a course too.'

Tim breezed in shortly after three o'clock, looking pleased with himself.

'I've got another client,' he told Sophie triumphantly. 'That makes four altogether. Not a bad start.' He kissed her lightly on the lips before seating himself at the desk.

'We need you here, Tim,' Frankie wailed before

Sophie had time to say anything. 'I've had a disastrous morning because I can't find anything to do with Gloria Antica on the computer.'

Tim grinned. 'Are we being the helpless little woman today, Frankie?' he teased. 'Let me show you.'

His fingers flew at the keyboard like a concert pianist while he gazed complacently at the screen. Suddenly he burst out laughing.

'What is it?' Sophie asked.

'Sorry, girls. My fault,' he chortled. Flipping through the smart briefcase Sophie had given him to mark the start of his new business, he pulled out a thin square disk. This he exchanged with the one already in the computer.

'I'm not surprised you couldn't make head or tail of anything. I was using this machine to do the accounts of your friend, John Clifford, yesterday. Somehow I left his disk, programmed to do his accounts, in your machine while I put your disk in my briefcase.' He grinned up at Sophie. 'Sorry, sweetheart.'

She looked relieved. 'So it wasn't just us being stupid?' For a dreadful moment back there she'd had a terrible suspicion that maybe . . . but no! She chided herself for getting paranoid.

'Can you go through everything with Frankie again,' she said with a touch of insistence. 'Just to make sure.'

'Make sure of what?' Tim looked surprised. 'Frankie knows exactly how to do it. The problem this morning was that she was into the wrong program.'

'Maybe you should show me too. I feel I should be able to see at a glance how much, for example, we've made in the last week.'

His smile seemed to fade and he spoke with the patience of someone talking to a child.

'I thought the whole point of the exercise, Sophie, was that you didn't want to be burdened with the accounts on a day-to-day basis. I thought all you wanted was to be given a monthly print-out of a balance sheet which I would explain to you, in simple language, if required.' The sarcasm in his voice made her flush angrily.

'Maybe if you were more efficient we'd all be able to keep track of the figures without a problem,' she said sharply and turned on her heel and strode out of the office into the showroom. How dare he talk to me like that, she fumed in silent fury as she stared through the window into the street beyond. A couple were admiring the window display, the woman pointing eagerly at a small Bow figurine of a young man in yellow breeches playing a flute, but Sophie barely saw them. Something was dreadfully wrong, and yet she couldn't put her finger on it. Tim's phone conversation, the wrong disk in the computer – it added up to nothing and yet she felt it was somehow linked.

'How much is that adorable little figure?'

Sophie started. The couple had entered the shop and she hadn't even noticed. Flipping over the tiny price tag, she told them.

The woman looked pleadingly at the man, and he nodded to Sophie.

'Right. We'll have it. My wife's not going to give me a moment's peace otherwise,' he added with an indulgent smile.

As Sophie made out the bill she wished with all her heart that she was better at figures; that she'd got some control and some understanding of the financial side of her business as well as her private affairs – and that she'd kept on Wiseman, Stroud and Halcrow.

It took Audrey several weeks to accept the fact that Troy was gone from her life. As she'd suspected after meeting his wife in the forest that day, he never contacted her again. Many were the times she tried to get hold of him, both at home and at the London recording studios, but someone else always answered, forcing her to hang up, weeping with frustration. Then she opened the *Daily Mail* one day, and there was a picture of him with Rana beaming broadly by his side, bound for Los Angeles.

'That's where it's all happening,' he was reported as saying. 'Rana and I are looking forward to a new life.'

'I bet,' Audrey seethed, jealousy and hurt making her feel quite unhinged for the next few days. She found herself screaming abuse at Nicholas and yelling at the children, and then she put away all her fancy clothes, certain she'd never need them again. It simply wasn't fair, she told herself. Just as she'd discovered there was more to life than she'd realised, it was all snatched away from her and she was left on her own once again. Well, she grudgingly admitted, not quite so much on her own these days. For some reason that she didn't entirely welcome, Nicholas had taken to coming home much earlier, so that for the first time in ages he was there for dinner at the normal time. Once, Audrey would have been delighted but since she'd met Troy, she preferred to get Amelia and Rebecca off to bed early so that she could sit and listen to the group Lips singing Troy's lyrics, while she daydreamed about him.

Susie Burchfield next door told her that Troy was fed up with England and everyone in it and that was why he'd gone away. Audrey wept when she heard that. Had she counted for nothing in Troy's life? It seemed poor consolation that Nicholas was now at home and getting under her feet all the time.

Frankie's face was ashen. 'Can I have a word with you?' she murmured discreetly when Sophie arrived at the shop the next morning. Katie had her back to them, dusting a display of vases, pretending not to have heard.

'What is it?' Sophie asked, involuntarily whispering also.

'I've done something awful,' Frankie confessed. 'I hardly know how to tell you.'

'Let's go into the office and make some coffee.'

'OK.' Frankie led the way, and Sophie could see she was very nervous. Her hands shook, rattling the cups and nearly spilling the milk as she made the coffee.

'Let me assure you, here and now, Frankie, that we're fully insured. If you've broken something, it is not the end of the world,' Sophie said maternally as she took her seat at the desk.

Frankie's smile was wan and she looked more uncomfortable than ever. 'I haven't broken anything, Sophie. It's not that.'

'Then what is it?'

'I . . . er . . . I . . . did some more work on the computer, after you'd all gone home last night.'

Sophie looked at her in surprise. 'That was very good of you but was it necessary? I thought Tim had the whole thing under control – assuming the right disk was in the computer,' she added.

'That's the point.'

Sophie frowned. 'I don't understand. It's all straightforward, isn't it? Tim explained everything to you, didn't he?'

'Yes. He did. I was worried about one or two things, though,' Frankie continued, speaking carefully. 'I wanted to satisfy myself that I'd grasped the system.'

'And had you?'

Frankie leaned forward, elbows on the desk as she looked directly into Sophie's eyes. 'Yes. I had. Something's terribly wrong, Sophie.'

Sophie paled, alarmed. 'What do you mean? We're losing money? God, I thought we were doing so well.'

'It's not that.' Then she looked down at her neat tanned hands and the gold signet ring on her little finger as if she couldn't face Sophie's questioning expression.

'After you and Tim and Katie had left, I went through all the shop accounts for the past three months. And I was only able to do that because,' she took a deep breath and her voice became almost harsh, 'because I'd pinched the disk containing the program for your accounts out of Tim's briefcase without him seeing.'

'I don't understand.'

'After he'd finished demonstrating to us why we couldn't make head or tail of the figures because we had the wrong disk in the machine, I noticed him replacing our disk in his briefcase again.'

Sophie felt cold and sick. She knew instantly what Frankie was getting at. 'And if you hadn't done that, you'd have got his other client's figures again, like you did yesterday.'

'Exactly.'

It seemed to Sophie a very long time before she was able to find the words that were needed to discover what Frankie had found, and in those moments her fears rose up and threatened to suffocate her.

'And what did you find?' she asked at last.

Frankie spoke rapidly now, as if she wanted to get the whole business over with. 'I spent hours comparing the figures on the computer print-out with the bank statements that arrived yesterday. Then I took the liberty of phoning the bank this morning. I know I should have waited for you to—'

'You did the right thing. Tim explained everything to you and you're the one to handle the accounts in his absence.'

'I don't think he ever intended to be absent.' Frankie spoke candidly now. 'I hid the bank statements yesterday too because he usually takes them away in his briefcase.'

Sophie spoke with rapid urgency. 'How long has this been going on? Why did you do this? What was the discrepancy between the figures on the computer and the bank statement?' She rattled off the questions with the sharpness of a machine gun, a note of controlled panic in every syllable.

'I've had a funny feeling about the accounts for a while now, but I couldn't be sure. I didn't want to accuse anyone of anything until I was certain.' She looked almost apologetically at Sophie, knowing every word was like a painful blow. 'The bottom line is that the figures on the computer print-out don't tally with the amounts in the bank statements. Maybe there's a perfectly reasonable explanation but I don't know what it is. And I feel dreadfully sneaky for pinching the disk from Tim's case and for doing all this checking,' she added miserably.

Sophie sat in silence, gazing into space, outwardly still but inwardly in a turmoil.

'Maybe I'm mistaken,' Frankie said in distress. 'Maybe I just don't understand Tim's methods although I did work in the accounts department of Christie's for a while.'

'You did the right thing,' Sophie said soberly. 'Now it's up to me to sort out this mess.'

Thirteen

'I think it's a good idea that you're taking a trip. Then you can't be asked awkward questions, can you?' Mr Turnbull, Sophie's bank manager, remarked. 'Meanwhile, we'll monitor all payments and withdrawals, while Wiseman, Stroud and Halcrow find out what's been going on. And you can rest assured Mr Calthorpe will be totally unaware of our surveillance of your financial affairs.'

'I feel dreadful about this,' Sophie said, looking washed out and strained. 'I should never have got rid of my accountants, but as my friend is a chartered accountant I thought it would be a good idea. I hate going behind his back, but I'm so worried I don't know what else to do.' She knew it was pointless to question Tim herself; her knowledge of finance was so sketchy he could tie her up in knots in seconds. The atmosphere between them had anyway become strained as she struggled to come to grips with the situation and she was finding it very difficult to communicate with him. He was defensive and irritable and every time she said anything, about their relationship, the shop, or her finances, he accused her of trying to pick a quarrel and he'd look at her like a little boy who has been wrongly accused of pinching chocolates. While a part of her was moved by his performance, a larger part of her resisted because she now realised it was a performance. She'd also come to realise something else. For the first time in her life she was not letting her emotions get the better of her.

'If you need to get hold of me,' she told Mr Turnbull, 'I'll be staying with friends in South Africa. They've been inviting me over for ages, so this seems a good time to go. I'll give you their phone number in case you want to contact me urgently. You can always leave a message as I've told them what's happening. I know I can count on their discretion,' she added.

'As, of course, you can count on ours,' he replied, smiling. Mrs Sophie Duval was not only a valued client but also a very beautiful young woman, and he admired her. In his private opinion the best thing she'd ever done was getting away from the powerful and controlling personality of Brock Duval. Now he could only stifle his fears that her present liaison with Tim Calthorpe hadn't cost her too much.

Audrey looked disconsolately at her mother. 'Nice for some,' she grumbled. 'What on earth does Sophie need to go to South Africa for?'

Jean's face was smooth and bland and if she did have her suspicions, planted in her mind by Alan, she was not going to admit anything.

'Sophie has known Jennifer and Peter Cornish for years, even before she married Brock. Don't you remember, she and Jennifer became friends when they were at secretarial college together? They've been longing for her to stay with them for ages and I think the break will do her good.'

'How long is she going for? I could do with a holiday myself. The last few months haven't been much fun.'

'Then why don't you have one, darling? I think it's a very good idea. You and Nicholas should go away on your own.'

Audrey looked startled. 'On our own?' She sounded horrified.

'Why not? It's what you need now that...' Jean hesitated. Audrey had admitted some weeks previously that Troy had gone to the States. It was still a sore point and Jean skirted round it as tactfully as she could.

'What about the children?' Audrey demanded. 'And where would we go?'

Jean clicked her tongue impatiently. 'Don't be so hopeless, dear. Alan and I can move into your house while you're away and look after Amelia and Rebecca. And as to where you should go, what about the Greek islands? Or Sardinia? Or even the south of France? I'm sure Sophie would lend you La Madeleine.'

'I don't want to go back there. I have too many unhappy memories of last summer.' Audrey shook her head dolefully. 'That's when I realised Nicholas was having an affair with that dreadful woman.'

'Which is why you and Nicholas should get away. If I were you, Aud, I'd get some travel brochures, buy myself a sexy bikini, and then I'd go away with him and fuck him until he can hardly stand.'

'*Mummy*!' Audrey looked deeply shocked. 'How can you talk like that? For goodness sake!' She'd actually turned deep red.

Jean threw back her head and laughed. 'You're as stuffy as your late father,' she chortled. 'Loosen up, Aud. Give Nicholas such a good time he'll never forget it. That is if you want to put the zip back into your marriage.'

Audrey remained silent, slouched in thought. 'I suppose Sophie will marry Tim one of these days.'

'That's entirely up to her,' Jean replied brightly. 'Another cup of tea, dear?'

Sophie arrived at Terminal 4 at Heathrow late the following afternoon, to check in for her flight to South Africa. Wearing comfortable cream cotton slacks and a shirt and blazer, she willed herself to concentrate on the holiday ahead. Somehow she had to push to the back of her mind her worries and her hurt over Tim. This time it wasn't a case of a young girl being abandoned by her boy friend; this time fraudulence and deception and embezzlement might be involved. And something much, much worse.

To her surprise, he'd taken her trip with equanimity, assuring her he understood her need for a break. He promised to keep an eye on everything, with the assistance of Frankie and Katie. Sophie found it impossible to tell whether he was sorry she was going or not. He was full of banter as usual, making her laugh in spite of her anxiety but there was also something inscrutable about him and that was what frightened her.

The airline clerk handed her a boarding pass, breaking into her thoughts.

'The first-class lounge is opposite Gate Ten,' she told Sophie, 'and your flight will be leaving on time.'

As Sophie made her way down the long concourse which seemed to stretch almost as far as the eye could see, she stopped to buy newspapers, magazines and a paperback novel. Then, in duty free, she bought a bottle of her favourite Issey Miyake perfume, and a litre of gin as a house present for Jennifer and Peter.

The next hour passed swiftly and Sophie felt there was something unreal about this whole trip as she looked around the low-ceilinged VIP lounge, with its sofas and chairs upholstered in muted shades of blue and arranged to form what the designers referred to as 'conversation groups'. Dumping her things on one end of a sofa in a quiet corner, she strolled over to the buffet. Here, bottles of every imaginable liquor, as well as mixers and freshly squeezed orange juice were laid out so passengers could help themselves. There was also coffee, tea, sandwiches, cakes, a large variety of biscuits, and an even larger choice of canapés.

'And it's all free!' she heard an elderly woman whisper to her companion who replied with a chuckle, 'Let's get stuck in then, love. This is what first class is all about.'

Sophie smiled to herself as she poured a cup of coffee and put a couple of biscuits on a small plate. Thanks to Brock, she'd never travelled any other way, but she still appreciated the comforts and privileges that went with it.

Settling herself with the newspapers while she waited for her flight call, she tried to immerse herself in the news of the day but it was impossible. She couldn't get Tim out of her mind. Before she left she'd been tempted to confess her deepest fears to Alan, but in his delicate state of health she felt it was unfair. Of course Brock would have been the right person to consult; in his position he'd be able to winkle out the truth about Tim's activities without difficulty, but she couldn't go to Brock. Pride forbade it. This was a situation she had to handle herself, with just the help of professional accountants. But what of her other dreadful suspicion? Who did she dare talk to about that? Peter and Jennifer seemed the only answer. They'd be impartial, they lived a long way away from England and she could trust them implicitly. Surely they'd be able to advise her. And perhaps tell her her fears were unfounded.

At last the flight was called. She boarded the plane and was ushered to her front row seat by smiling stewards where she allowed herself to be pampered with down pillows, cashmere rugs and vintage champagne, but a consuming wave of depression swept over her. Suddenly, she realised that by the time she returned to England, all would be disclosed and she'd know whether she had a future with Tim or not.

Jennifer greeted Sophie with shrieks of joy, hugging her tightly and saying repeatedly, 'I can't believe you're here at last! How many years has it been? Oh, Sophie, it's so good to see you again.'

Peter's greeting was more restrained but no less welcoming. Immediately, Sophie felt better. She was among old friends who would be able to advise her dispassionately which was something her family were unable to do, and she knew their advice would be sound. Meanwhile there was a lot of catching up to do.

'I'm dying to see your new house and hear all your news,' she said with enthusiasm as they drove through Cape Town, with its elegant buildings and tree-lined streets. 'Do you love living here? Oh, you must! It's so beautiful.'

'It's sheer heaven, especially where we live at Camps Bay,' Peter replied, smiling. He was a tall, rangy man, deeply tanned and with eyes that Sophie thought looked like the colour of the sea.

'Don't tell her about it. Let it be a surprise,' Jennifer cut in quickly.

'How far outside Cape Town are you?' Sophie asked.

'About ten minutes away.'

'Is that all?' There was a shade of disappointment in her voice. She'd been looking forward to getting away from city life.

'That's all, but just you wait and see,' Jennifer replied mysteriously. Then she looked at Sophie more closely. 'You're looking very thin,' she observed. 'How do you do it?'

'Probably because I no longer eat in hotels all the time as I did when I was married to Brock,' she replied laughing. 'I'm into home cooking these days.'

Jennifer, who was plump and lively, her smooth skin tanned to a satiny shade of bronze, threw up her hands in mock dismay. 'God, home cooking is my undoing. Especially as Peter likes everything that's fatty, sugary or covered in chocolate,' she giggled.

'I like that,' he exclaimed with a good-natured grin. 'Who's the one that bakes cakes every day? And makes puddings? And likes eggs and bacon for breakfast?'

Jennifer's fat chuckle was infectious. 'Well, why not? Anyway, Sophie, who are you cooking for? A mouse?'

Sidestepping the question, Sophie gazed through the car window. On their right was a magnificent beach, the silvery sand stretching for miles. Beyond it the sea lay like a giant sapphire, glittering in the morning sunlight. 'Oh, how beautiful,' she said, awestruck. Beaches in Europe were never so vast, so perfect, or so free of people. 'What's this place?'

Without answering, Peter suddenly swung the car left, up a wide paved drive, and into the shelter of tall palm trees. He came to a stop in front of a two-storey white house, part colonial, but with a Spanish influence. Dazzling white arches led into the ground-floor rooms, and a balustraded terrace encircled the first floor, from where there was an uninterrupted view of the sea.

Sophie gasped, stunned. 'You live *here*?'

Jennifer giggled delightedly. 'A bit of all right, isn't it?' she said. 'Ten minutes from the best shops in the world, including dress designers, though you wouldn't think it to look at me, and then here we are, on the edge of the world.'

'It's fantastic.' Sophie got out of the car and stepped on to the lawn where flowers grew in profusion and the air was a heady mixture of the scent of frangipani and ozone. 'Why did Brock and I never come here? It's paradise!'

'Isn't it just?' Peter agreed, carrying her cases into the house. 'Jen and I wouldn't live anywhere else now.'

'We've another surprise for you,' Jennifer announced, linking her arm through Sophie's. 'We're having a baby in October, and we'd like you to be godmother.'

'That's the best news in the world.' Sophie hugged her friend. She knew they'd been trying for a baby for several years and her delight for them was unreserved.

In high spirits, they entered the house, with its light, spacious rooms which Jennifer had decorated with cool clear colours and comfortable furniture. Already Sophie felt the strain of the past ten days slipping away, leaving her feeling refreshed and invigorated as the affection of her friends wrapped itself round her like a protective cocoon.

'I expect you'd like a bath and a sleep, wouldn't you? That flight from London can be a killer.'

'I'm fine,' Sophie insisted. 'I certainly don't want to go to bed. I want to see all over your house, hear all your news. Do you realise this is the first holiday I've ever had without someone in tow? I've never been away on my own before.'

Jennifer nodded. 'You were always with Brock, weren't you? And before that, do you remember that boy friend you had? Tim something. The one who went off to Australia.' Before Sophie had time to respond, Jennifer went on, 'Such an extraordinary thing, I met someone last year who knew him in Australia. Apparently he was nearly deported. I'm not sure what he did, but he left an awful stink behind. There was quite a scandal. Lucky it ended between you when it did, or God knows where you'd be today!'

'Where do you want to go?' Nicholas asked, trying to

keep the astonishment out of his voice. Audrey, who hated 'abroad', preferring instead to go to Cornwall every year, had just suggested they go away, on their own, to a 'tropical place'.

She shrugged. 'What about Corfu?'

'Hardly tropical,' he commented, polishing his spectacles. 'Now Bermuda is tropical. Or Jamaica.'

'They're very far away.'

'Tropical is far away, from the vantage point of Newbury.'

'Well, not necessarily tropical then. Hot. And sunny. With a nice beach.'

'Corfu would do very nicely then,' he said carefully, 'if we stay near Palaiokastritza. There's a nice beach there.'

'How do you know?'

'We went there when I was a boy, on a family holiday.'

'It'll have changed.' Audrey made it sound as if it was his fault. 'I expect it will be full of German tourists now.'

'I don't think there's much scope for the laying out of beach towels in Palaiokastritza.' His tone was dry. 'It's not that sort of place.'

'What beach towels?' she demanded. 'What are you talking about?'

Nicholas sighed inwardly. Maybe Cornwall would be a safer bet after all.

'Mummy says Sardinia is nice,' she continued doggedly.

Nicholas nodded, mostly to himself. He had the measure of it now. Audrey didn't particularly care where she went as long as it was 'hot'. This whole holiday idea was Jean's. Just like her to suggest an expensive trip as a remedy for a shaky marriage. Well, he supposed he'd had his fun with Denise, who had now left for lusher pastures and richer beds. Audrey had never had any fun. He didn't think she knew how. To make up to her for all the burnt dinners and lonely hours, he supposed he'd better push out the boat and give her a good time. She was, after all, a good if complaining wife, and an excellent mother.

'Sardinia is supposed to be sensational,' he agreed, putting his spectacles on again and looking at her cheerfully. 'Shall I fix it up then? The best hotel on the Costa Smeralda?'

'Do you think we can leave Amelia and Rebecca for as long as ten days?'

'No problem. They'll be at school all day, and if your mother and Alan are here, they can look after them perfectly well in the evenings and at the weekends.'

'All right.' She still sounded cautious, and it occurred to Nicholas that in her whole life Audrey had only ever dipped her toes gingerly into the sea of life – unlike Denise who plunged in with glorious abandon and let the current take her wherever it was going. Poor Audrey, he reflected. She'd never known the sheer thrill of risking all, of taking a chance, of living dangerously. Well, the least he could do was give her a nice holiday in a nice hotel, with a bit of sun and sand and . . . well, she wasn't really into the sex stakes, but he supposed he'd be able to give her a bit of a thrill. Perhaps.

Sophie lay in the bath with her eyes closed and her mind in turmoil. She'd been so startled by Jennifer's remark about Tim that she'd been unable to say anything for a moment, and by that time her friend was off on another verbal tangent and the opportunity had passed. So what had he done in Australia that was so dreadful? It could be anything. She was torn between wanting to know and dreading to find out.

Feeling suddenly sick with exhaustion after her night flight, she climbed out of the bath and wrapped herself in a white terry towelling sheet. Jennifer had said lunch would be on the terrace in an hour's time. Sophie padded on bare feet into her adjoining bedroom which had an incredible view of the ocean, and flopped on to the bed. Although she didn't fall asleep, the quietness and the strong sea air gradually restored her energy, making her feel more relaxed. As soon as she went downstairs, she would ask Jennifer to tell her exactly what she'd heard.

They sat at a long white painted table, under the shade of a cream awning. Jennifer emerged from the house with a large platter of grilled prawns and a dish of savoury rice which she placed beside bowls of avocado salad and crusty bread.

'Why am I suddenly starving?' Sophie said as she sniffed appreciatively. 'Jennifer, that looks good enough to eat!'

Peter had poured planter's punch into tall green goblets, and now as he took his seat he raised his glass to Sophie.

'Welcome to the Cape,' he toasted her warmly. 'Jen and I have been waiting a long time for this moment.'

'Yes, welcome, love,' Jennifer echoed, raising her glass. 'I can't tell you how good it is to have you here.'

'It's more wonderful to be here than you'll ever know,' Sophie replied, suddenly emotional from tiredness and strain. 'If I hadn't got away from London when I did, I think I'd have cracked up.' She took a gulp of her drink and felt its zinging fruitiness hit her stomach.

'You are all right, aren't you?' Jennifer asked in sudden concern. 'You don't regret leaving Brock?'

Sophie shook her head, recovering herself. 'Not at all. No, it's not Brock. It's to do with the business,' she added vaguely. She wanted to hear about Tim in Australia before she told them anything.

They could sense she wasn't ready to talk yet, so the conversation became general and soon Sophie was relaxed and laughing, her troubles momentarily pushed to the back of her mind. In all her travels, she'd never come across a place as stunningly beautiful as this, and her gaze was repeatedly drawn to where Table Mountain, swathed in the hazy veil of the noonday sun, formed a backdrop to the glittering white buildings of the city.

'I don't suppose you ever go away on holiday, do you?' Sophie observed. 'What would be the need? You've got it all here.' She turned to look at the view behind their house where the Twelve Apostles rose thousands of feet high, great rocky mountains sculpted by nature over millions of years to form a protective ridge between land and sea.

'You're right,' Peter agreed. 'Occasionally we miss city life and long for a few days in London or Paris, but on the whole everything's here. Especially the great climate.'

'Let's have coffee by the pool,' said Jennifer, jumping to her feet. 'And if you want to snooze, Sophie, just say.'

And as they lounged on comfortable garden seats watching the ever-changing blues and greens of the sea as it unravelled with lacy surges up the beach, Sophie spoke at last.

'Tell me what you heard about Tim in Australia, Jennifer.'

Her friend looked surprised. 'It was very vague. I can't remember much of the details. I just thought it was a coincidence that this woman had known him. Why do you ask?'

Sophie evaded the question. 'Can you remember what she said? Was she a friend of his?'

Both Peter and Jennifer looked at Sophie inquiringly.

Jennifer spoke. 'Something happened, I'm not exactly certain what, but she did say a girl had died and it was Tim's fault. She said he was involved in several dodgy deals, too. That's when she remarked you'd had a lucky escape.'

Sophie stared at her, and an icy shiver crawled down her spine.

'I remember something else, too. He vanished from the scene a few days later. There was a rumour he'd flown to Hong Kong.'

'That's right,' Sophie said, without thinking.

Jennifer suddenly sat up straight. 'How did you know that?'

Sophie swung her feet to the ground and sat up also, so that she faced them.

'He came back into my life last summer,' she said simply.

Then she told them all that had happened, leaving nothing out. She even told them she suspected him of having an affair, which was something she'd seen no reason to mention to the bank manager.

'It's my own fault,' she concluded gloomily. 'I broke all the rules, like never do business with friends. I also let my heart rule my head. What maddens me is just as I thought I'd taken control of my life, I realise I've done nothing of the kind. I'm as much in Tim's power, though in a different way, as I was in Brock's. But at least Brock was faithful to me. It's hurt me more to realise Tim's found someone else than it has to acknowledge the fact he may be embezzling my money.'

'Does Brock know about this?' Peter asked, concerned.

'No, but he soon will,' Sophie replied grimly. 'Apart from everything else, I feel such a fool. How could I have let myself be taken in? He'd already let me down years ago, and I should have realised, no matter what explanations he gave me, that people don't change. He's got "shit" printed all the way through him like Brighton rock. Oh, when I met him again in the south of France it was so wonderful, even though he was married and I never thought we'd be able to get together. It was almost as if we'd never been apart. Like an idiot I fell in love with him all over again,' she added in a small sad voice.

'I'm so sorry, love,' Jennifer said sympathetically. 'Perhaps the money side isn't as bad as you think. Maybe you've nipped the situation in the bud. Maybe Tim hasn't had time to defraud you.'

'From what you say it looks as if he'll walk right into a trap if he tries anything on now,' Peter remarked. 'But why have you left him living in your flat? If he's having an affair, mightn't he bring back his—'

Jennifer silenced him with a look as she saw the pain in Sophie's eyes.

'Everything I've told you is supposition and suspicion on my part,' Sophie explained. 'I haven't got a shred of proof. I don't understand the computer, and I've never had a head for figures. Maybe he's on the level. Maybe he really was talking to his mother and not a girl friend on the phone. Perhaps he isn't embezzling a penny, and Frankie is mistaken about him swapping the computer disk. Who knows? One thing is certain, though. I couldn't possibly accuse him without having my facts straight, and the only way to do that was to involve the bank and my previous firm of accountants to check everything without Tim realising. As to him staying in the flat, my cleaner goes in every day, arriving before breakfast, and I don't think even he would import a girl friend under those circumstances.'

'What was his wife like?' Jennifer asked. 'Did you get on with her?'

Sophie didn't reply but looked down at her slim hands, the nails long, white-tipped and elegant.

'Her accident must have shaken you up,' Peter observed gently. 'It was a dreadful thing to have happened.'

At last Sophie spoke. 'I don't think it was an accident.'

Jennifer clapped her hand over her mouth and gave a little shriek. 'Sophie! What do you mean? You don't think she threw herself into the path of an oncoming car, do you?'

'Or that Tim pushed her?' Peter said, horrified.

Sophie shook her head. 'I don't think she was killed in an accident at all,' she said slowly. 'I think she was murdered to get her out of the way.'

Audrey and Nicholas arrived in Sardinia in the early evening. They were met at the airport by a car which swept them through rocky hills carpeted in sweet-smelling wild flowers and shrubs to Porto Cervo.

'There's not much to see,' Audrey remarked, looking out of the car window.

'It's the coastline of the island that's special,' Nicholas told her. 'The Costa Smeralda is famed for its beaches.'

Audrey remained silent, wondering if she was going to like the place. It looked very dull and deserted to her, and she was glad now they hadn't brought the children because it didn't look as if there was anything to do.

Suddenly the car turned a corner in the winding road and Nicholas exclaimed, 'Look at that!'

Ahead of them, built among the rocks along the edge of the sandy beach, was a series of low white buildings with curved archways and windows and deep pink thick-tiled roofs. The style was rustically Sardinian but the surrounding lawns were lush, and exotic flowers bloomed in abundance.

'Oh!' said Audrey, brightening.

'Looks OK, doesn't it?' Nicholas felt relieved. He'd spent a fortune on this holiday and now it seemed as if it was going to be all right.

Within moments of arriving, they found themselves being guided from the heat of the driveway into a cool white reception area with archways leading off it. It was like being in the centre of a giant honeycomb. Low blue and yellow sofas were arranged around coffee tables, but before Audrey had time to take it all in, they'd registered and were being shown into a large airy room, with a big bed, simple but comfortable local furniture, and French windows that led on to a balcony overlooking the Mediterranean.

'Oh!' she said again, her expression stunned. Then she walked on to the balcony. There was a little private lawn just below their window, where lavender and rosemary bushes drugged the air with their perfume, and beyond, the beach. The sand was pink and white, and the sea pale emerald. Audrey's eyes filled with tears, and unsure whether she was crying for the loss of Troy or gratitude to Nicholas for bringing her to such a beautiful place, she gave a little sob.

'Are you all right?' Nicholas asked nervously. 'Is there anything I can get you?'

'I'm absolutely fine,' she replied shakily but she was smiling.

'Then let's get unpacked, have a shower, and then go to the bar for a drink.'

'Good idea.'

Nicholas hid his surprise. It was the first time for years she'd considered anything he'd said was a good idea.

Later, in the bar that opened on to the garden, they had a bottle of champagne before going to the dining room where more wide archways maintained the honeycomb feeling. Sky-blue tablecloths and scarlet chairs and flowers on all the tables gave the restaurant a festive air. They were shown to one of several raised tables, set into an alcove. 'This table,' they were told, 'is where

Princess Alexandra and Angus Ogilvy always sit when they stay here.' Audrey's pleasure was complete.

Nicholas didn't want to push his luck, but after dinner, when they'd had coffee on the lantern-lit terrace, he said, 'Shall we have an early night?'

Audrey looked towards the sea, black and mysterious now. 'I'd like to walk along the beach,' she said, 'in bare feet.'

Fourteen

'This is the most awful thing I've ever heard!' Jennifer said, appalled. 'You mean you think Tim killed his wife so he could take up with you again, because of your money?'

Sophie leaned back, suddenly weary. It was evening now and they were sitting in the living room, after dinner. They'd talked of little else all afternoon, and then Jennifer had insisted they all have a bracing walk along the water's edge to clear their heads.

'I just can't believe it,' she kept saying as the sand scrunched under their shoes and the breeze whipped at their hair. 'It's too dreadful for words.' An hour later, they returned home for dinner and now, over cups of coffee, Sophie longed for bed, but they kept asking her questions.

'So you really think he murdered Carolyn?'

'I'm certain he did,' Sophie replied. 'I know it sounds farfetched and wildly melodramatic, but nothing surprises me about Tim these days. And now that you've told me about a girl dying in Australia, and dodgy deals, I'm more convinced than ever.'

Jennifer spoke gently. 'But why didn't you go to the

police? And why have you let him remain in your flat while you're away?'

'I've told you. I've no proof, no evidence.'

'I think you've got enough to go on,' said Peter. 'You say you couldn't find any mention of his wife's death in back copies of *The Times* or *Telegraph*, although he'd told you it was announced in those papers. You contacted the police and the hospitals in Cardiff and could find no one who'd ever heard of Carolyn Calthorpe or had a record of any such accident.'

'That's right,' Sophie said. 'And then I went up to St Catherine's House. That was when I discovered there was no death certificate either.'

'Well , as I said, I think you've got enough to go on for the police at least to make inquiries. In fact, you must tell all this to the police. How do you know your own life's not in danger? If Tim were to get hold of all your money, who knows what he might not do?'

'Oh, God.' For the first time, Sophie felt fear. Up to now it was as if everything was happening to someone else; she'd had a sense of unreality about the whole situation because it seemed too melodramatic. She'd also considered herself safe while she remained Tim's meal ticket. Now, Jennifer and Peter's consternation brought home the possibility that she, too, could be in danger.

'Don't you think you should stay with us until you hear from your bank and the accountants?' Jennifer suggested.

'I don't like to stay away from the shop for long. There are several good sales coming up, including one at Sotheby's that I must go to.'

Peter looked at her. 'Afraid of missing a bargain? I wouldn't have thought it mattered now that you're so well established.'

Sophie shook her head. 'One is never established enough to risk losing a bargain to a rival. Besides, half the thrill of having the shop is the excitement of bidding at auctions and discovering treasures in out-of-the way places. It's better than gambling,' she added, smiling for the first time. 'It really gets the adrenaline going.'

'But how long will it take before it can be proved Tim's been embezzling?'

'I don't think it will take that long.'

'Well, while you're here we should make a point of turning this into a real holiday for you,' Jennifer resolved.

'And we should talk about other things,' Peter added, 'or we'll go round and round in circles and you'll get demented by the whole ghastly business.'

'You must tell us what you'd like to do,' Jennifer continued energetically. 'Going up Table Mountain in the cable car and driving along the coastal road is a must. We'll take you to the Cape of Good Hope, too, and another day we'll drive you to Paarl which is the most exquisitely manicured town in the world. It's part of the winelands, beyond Stellenbosch.' She leaned forward and impulsively grabbed Sophie's hand. 'Oh, it's *so* good to have you here, love. Do stay as long as you can.'

'Yes,' Peter interjected. 'You've got to sample the full range of Jen's South African cooking. She's learned how to stew Karoo lamb, with garlic and peaches, and wait until you try her roasted springbok and ostrich.'

'I've eaten most things around the world because Brock is an adventurous gourmand, including raw fish in Japan and sheep's eyes in Abu Dhabi, but I've never eaten ostrich or springbok,' Sophie laughed.

'They're rather like chicken only with a richer flavour,' Jennifer remarked airily. 'What I've never done is crocodile tail. If you like lobster you'll like crocodile.'

'I can't wait. Is it true that South African cuisine is a mixture of Dutch, English, German and Malay?'

'I say,' Peter looked impressed, 'you have done your homework. Yes, it's true. It's evolved over the last three hundred years. Jen's got it down to a fine art.'

'I rather like cooking too these days. Tim and I hardly ever go to restaurants...' Her voice trailed off as she remembered how she'd taught herself to cook in the last few months, making dishes she knew would appeal to him and having such fun experimenting with new recipes. Those days, and they'd passed so swiftly, were already gone and it was a painful realisation. Jennifer saw the sadness in her face.

'Nothing lasts for ever, love,' she said understandingly. 'Not the good days or the bad ones either. You'll find happiness again.'

Sophie turned to her in anguish, tears suddenly brimming in her dark eyes. 'But it's a nightmare right now,' she said, brushing them away.

'Yes. It is.' Jennifer's tone was motherly although she was the same age as Sophie. 'The sooner you get the whole mess sorted out, the better. Then you can wipe the slate clean and start again.'

'You're right, of course,' Sophie replied. She'd thought

she'd wiped the slate clean when she left Brock. She'd intended to create a new life then, a life in which she had complete control. But once again she'd fallen for a man who wanted to dominate every aspect of her life, only this time the motive was self-interest not possessive love.

Audrey emerged from the bathroom looking pink and scrubbed in her white cotton Marks and Spencer nightdress. Nicholas was sitting on the bed, reading the hotel brochure.

'Do you feel like a spot of water-skiing?' he asked without looking up. 'It says here there's also skin diving, sailing, all with qualified instructors, and there's golf and tennis.'

Audrey sat down on the bed beside him and looked over his shoulder at the typical pictures of couples eating and drinking, dancing in the discotheque and diving into the pool.

'It all looks great fun, but for the next few days I'd be quite happy lying on the beach or by the pool,' she remarked. Then she stretched a pale hand and arm before her. 'I want to get a tan. I look disgustingly white.'

Nicholas folded up the brochure. 'That's fine by me, but you will tell me if there's anything special you want to do, won't you?' He took off his glasses and folding them put them on the bedside table. Audrey was silent for a moment and then with a tentative gesture she laid her hand on his bare arm.

'All right, pet?' he murmured.

She nodded, avoiding looking at him.

'This is like a new start, isn't it?' he said, laying his large hand over hers.

Audrey nodded again 'But will we be able to . . . ?' Her voice faded.

'Yes. We will,' Nicholas replied sturdily. Then he put his arms round her and held her close. In response she slipped her arms round his neck, pressing her cheek to his, her body suddenly awakened by the memory of her time with Troy. He had taught her how to enjoy her body and how to revel in sex. For the first time in her life she'd been shown how to reach orgasm; how to prolong foreplay until she felt sick with desire, how to give pleasure to a man, and bring him to a climax. Now, it was as if her body was a delicate instrument which, skilfully tuned and handled, could soar to heights of acute pleasure. Turning her head, she kissed Nicholas with such passion he found himself immediately aroused. Then she slipped her leg between his, pressing her thigh against his groin, so that he gasped, partly in surprise but also at the speed with which he'd achieved an erection.

There was no need to ask her, as he usually did, whether she felt like having sex or not. With skilful hands she was undressing him, stroking him, kissing his chest and his belly and his penis, while all the time undulating her hips slowly against him. His astonishment gave way to desire for her, and that in itself was astonishing. Audrey, to whom sex had been a duty she could well have done without, was now rampaging all over his responding body, driving him crazy with her mouth and her deft little hands. She sat astride him now and he wondered what had happened to the missionary position.

'Oh, Aud!' he groaned, as she eased herself up and down using her internal muscles with skill. 'Oh, God, Aud!' He had to try and control himself and not come too quickly, he thought. It was also time he took the initiative. With a movement that owed much of its skill to frequent practice with Denise, he rolled over so that Audrey was underneath him and then he proceeded to exercise all his own accomplished ability to bring pleasure to her.

Afterwards they lay entwined, breathless and exhausted but most of all astounded. Neither spoke. For a moment Nicholas had wondered if she'd been to bed with someone else! How on earth had she acquired such expertise? Audrey, of all people. Audrey, who usually rushed to the bathroom to douche herself after sex but was now reaching for him once more. Audrey who had even been known to glance at her wristwatch right in the middle!

'That was wonderful, wasn't it?' he heard her say in a husky voice.

'It was bloody marvellous!' Nicholas replied, awestruck.

She was snuggling close to him again, her legs wound round one of his, her hand stroking him with tenderness. He had to ask her. He'd never rest content until he knew how she'd become such an expert and also what had happened to cause her libido to jump from zero to top gear.

'Aud, how did you learn all this stuff?'

Audrey looked coy. 'What do you mean, Nicholas?'

He raised himself on the bed into a sitting position and looked at her with interest. 'Well, you know, all that stuff ... you seem ... that is ...' For some reason he couldn't fathom he was the one who was getting embarrassed by this conversation and not Audrey. 'You seemed to enjoy it, just now. I wondered what had happened.'

'Women's magazines are always full of articles on ... you know. I read somewhere that everyone's responsible for their own orgasm.'

He turned startled blue eyes on her. 'Really? I've never heard that.'

'I think it's true though, don't you?' He noticed she wasn't looking at him but was examining her red painted nails with close scrutiny.

'Well, I suppose it's possible.' He sounded doubtful. 'On the other hand, aren't people supposed to give each other pleasure?'

'Oh, yes. Certainly.' She thought about Troy and the exquisite pleasure he'd given her. 'It has to be mutual.' Her cheeks were flushed and she was pushing back the quick of her nail as if her life depended on it.

'Absolutely,' he agreed. 'Oh, yes.' There was an awkward silence, then he reached for her hand, bringing it up to his face so that he could kiss the scarlet-tipped fingers. 'If it was as good for you as it was for me, shall we ...?'

In answer, Audrey slid her arms round his neck and pressed herself against him, her face buried in his neck.

'Oh, yes, Nicholas. Yes. I want you. I want you now,' she whispered, her breath hot against his ear.

* * *

Sophie slept fitfully, in spite of her tiredness. In her mind she kept going over everything Tim had said about Carolyn's accident, but it hadn't actually amounted to much. At the time she'd put his reticence down to an unwillingness to talk because it hurt too much, but now she realised it might be because he had so much to hide. What had he told the people in the Welsh village where they lived? And his mother in York? Had he perhaps said Carolyn had left him? Or had he said they'd both gone to work in London? No one would question that – except of course the bank where Carolyn worked. Stupidly, she'd forgotten to find out which bank she had actually worked for. A phone call to them might yield some very interesting information.

She got out of bed and went out on to her bedroom balcony to watch the dawn. It was chilly with a fresh breeze blowing in from the sea, but breathing the cool salty air into her lungs, she immediately felt better. Soon, Table Mountain became visible against a rich blue sky, rising majestically above Cape Town, and along the shore and stretching among the palm trees inland a band of morning mist hung like gauze in the air.

Sophie stretched her arms above her head, and then on impulse slipped into her swimsuit. Grabbing a towel, she crept downstairs so as not to awaken Jennifer and Peter, and let herself out of the front door. A minute later, she was racing across the pale golden stretch of sand and plunging into the sea, gasping with joy at the impact of cold water and the heady feeling of being free. For ten minutes she swam briskly as the sun rose higher and the mist began to lift. Then wrapping the towel round herself, she jogged back to the house, surprising Jennifer who was in the kitchen brewing a pot of coffee.

'Well! And aren't you the early one,' she greeted Sophie. 'I'm most impressed. I thought you'd have grown soft, living in London.'

Sophie laughed. 'You forget I spend a lot of time at La Madeleine where I swim several times a day. Oh, that was so good, Jen. I feel marvellous.'

'Did you sleep well?' As she talked she was putting guavas, mangos, pawpaws and bananas onto a shallow basket, ready to be carried out to the veranda where Peter was already opening out the large cream sunshade.

'I hardly slept at all,' Sophie admitted, 'but I feel fine. The trouble is I can't stop thinking about Tim. I feel so betrayed, Jen. You've no idea how much I still love him. Actually it's as if I've been in love with him since I was seventeen. How could he have done this to me?' She sounded bewildered.

'Because he's a swine, my darling,' Jennifer replied succinctly. 'An out-and-out bastard. Now, before you get pneumonia, why don't you have a hot bath and get dressed, and by the time you come down, breakfast will be ready.'

Sophie grinned. 'I can just see you as a mother, you know, Jen. You're going to love it, aren't you, clucking around all your little ones?'

Jennifer patted her still-flat stomach. 'I can hardly wait. I hope I end up with at least four.'

'I don't!' said Peter, coming into the kitchen. 'Two's

enough for me – unless I suddenly and unexpectedly become a millionaire.'

Jennifer playfully flipped the corner of a tea towel at him. 'Well, you're going to, aren't you, sweetheart? That's why I married you.'

Laughing at their good-natured banter, Sophie hurried upstairs again. It was good to be with straightforward, contented and happy people. A dose of Audrey with her endless complaining or a spell with her mother who still worried about Alan's health was not what she needed right now.

She was relaxing in the bath when Jennifer knocked on the door.

'There's a call for you, Sophie. Brock's on the line, from New York, and he sounds agitated.'

Sophie sat up suddenly, creating a surge of water that nearly spilled over the end of the bath.

'What?' she said in horror. 'Brock? Oh, God, now the proverbial shit's going to hit the fan!' Rushing out of the bath, she flung a towel round herself and opened the door.

'What did he say, Jen? Does he know what's happened?'

'He didn't say. He just said he'd been trying to get hold of you and the girls at Gloria Antica had told him you were staying with us. He said he needed to talk to you urgently.'

Sophie clutched her towel tighter. 'Oh, God, what am I going to say?' She plumped herself on the bed, and grabbed the phone. 'Hi, Brock!' She sounded a great deal more confident than she felt. 'How are you?'

His voice was dangerously quiet and calm. 'Can you tell me what's going on, Sophie?'

'What do you mean?' She knew she sounded like a defensive schoolgirl.

'Why did you get rid of the accountants I appointed to look after your affairs? And why, may I ask, did you let Tim Calthorpe, of all people, take over the handling of your finances?'

'Brock, he's a qualified chartered accountant,' she protested.

'I'm sure he is.'

'So? What's the problem?' Sophie longed to say many things but was unable to. She longed to say, 'It's my money so I can do as I like,' but Brock had invested his money in Gloria Antica and she felt beholden to him. She wished she could say, 'Mind your own business,' but if it hadn't been for Brock's generous settlement, she would be a pauper. She remembered the time, not so long ago, when Tim had told her Brock had wanted her to use his accountants as a way of still keeping some control over her. And of always knowing what she was doing.

'I've been talking to Wiseman, Stroud and Halcrow—'

'Why, Brock?' she burst out, unable to stop herself. 'Why do you need to concern yourself now we're no longer together? Honestly, you make me feel like a child who can't even be trusted with a piggy-bank!' Her face was flushed with anger, and Jennifer, sitting on the dressing-table stool, watching her, grinned in amusement.

'Actually, they phoned me,' Brock replied icily. 'You surely don't think I've got time to chase up all your little transactions when I'm handling hundreds of millions every day of the week.'

Sophie felt smaller than ever but she was determined to brazen it out. 'So why are they bothering you when you're so busy?'

'Apparently you've reappointed them, in conjunction with the bank, to look into your affairs because you suspect your boy friend of embezzlement. This is very serious, Sophie. If it's as bad as that, why haven't you called in the Fraud Squad?'

Sophie spoke carefully. 'I don't know that it is as bad as that,' she pointed out. 'That's why I've asked Wiseman, Stroud and Halcrow to look into my affairs.'

She heard Brock sigh. 'You should never have dropped them in the first place, and to replace them with your lover is about as unprofessional as you can get. If you weren't happy with Wiseman, why didn't you talk to me before you acted so rashly?'

Sophie's hand shook as she held the receiver to her ear. 'I'll tell you why!' Her voice was shrill. 'I didn't tell you because I'm sick to death of the way you treat me. I'm not a child, Brock. I won't be controlled by you as if you were my father. Will you please let me get on with my own life, without interference, without you breathing down my neck, without you poking into my affairs all the time, and without you treating me as if I was thick.' Then she slammed the phone down and looked across at Jennifer whose eyes were wide with amazement. 'I've really done it now, haven't I?' Sophie said in a small voice. She was shaking all over, appalled at her own ferocity and yet triumphant at having stood up to Brock.

'Poor old Brock,' Jennifer said lightly, but she was still grinning. 'Not that it will do him any harm.'

Sophie fell back against the pillows, exhausted by her outburst. 'I've never talked to anyone like that.'

'It's very therapeutic to lose your temper occasionally.'

'With Brock?' Sophie raised her eyebrows. 'Oh, Jen, why is he so maddening? He always rubs me up the wrong way. It's almost as if he's spoiling for a fight, and of course I rise like a salmon to the bait, every single time. He knows it makes me wild to be talked down to.'

'Maybe it's as well that he knows you have suspicions about Tim's honesty. Think how much worse it would be if you knew nothing and he'd been the one who had to tell you what was going on.'

'Don't! It doesn't bear thinking about. Oh, God, what a bitch I am. Was I very nasty to him, Jen?'

'You weren't exactly sweetness and light,' Jennifer laughed.

'D'you know my trouble?'

'Tell me.'

'I actually resent Brock's money, you know. In my heart of hearts I hate the fact that everything I have and everything I do is thanks to Brock. That's why I almost hate him at times. I know I should be grateful, but instead of gratitude I feel ... I feel stifled, owned, imprisoned.'

'In a gilded cage? Any more clichés?' Jennifer had her head thrown back she was laughing so much. Sophie dissolved into giggles.

'Oh, hell, Jen. What am I going to do?'

'Get on some clothes and come down and have breakfast. I'm starving even if you're not.'

Sophie looked serious again. 'I wonder if I should phone the accountants to see how they're getting on.'

'I doubt if they'll be able to tell you anything yet. I'd leave it for a few more days if I were you. Do they know where you are?'

'Yes. Everyone knows where I am.'

'Will Tim be ringing you?'

'There's no reason why he shouldn't. I don't think he suspects anything. In fact, he should phone me, in the normal course of events. We're supposed to be missing each other.'

'And are you?' Jennifer looked at her penetratingly.

Sophie hung her head sadly. 'Yes.'

'Very much?'

She nodded. 'Yes. I thought, when we started living together that I'd got it right this time. We're so compatible. That's why this situation is so terrible, why it's tearing me to pieces.'

'It's the first love syndrome, too, isn't it? Oh, Sophie love, I'm sorry. You deserve someone really nice.'

Sophie made a rueful face. 'I was married to someone really nice, too nice for me, perhaps. Maybe I need a bit of a bastard to make me tick.'

'What? You? One of London's prime movers and shakers?'

'More like one of London's tremblers,' Sophie replied.

Jennifer rose to her feet. 'Now get dressed, for goodness sake, or it will be time for lunch.'

'I wonder what Tim's doing right now?'

'Better not to know, probably,' Jennifer replied.

* * *

'Good morning, girls!' Tim greeted Frankie and Katie with his usual bonhomie as he sailed into the shop. 'How's everything?' He cast a proprietary glance around the shelves and table tops as if checking the stock.

'Great.'

'Fine.' They spoke in unison.

'Good, good. I can't stay long because I'm popping up to York to see my mother.'

'Will you be away long?' Katie asked.

'No, only about a week. I'll be back before Sophie returns. Have you heard from her, by the way?' He seated himself at the desk in the back office and switched on the computer.

They shook their heads, one so shining blonde, the other raven.

'What are you doing in York,' Katie asked, 'apart from visiting your mother?'

'Isn't that enough?' Tim boomed. 'Seeing the old mater is enough for most people.'

When he'd gone, the shop became quiet and peaceful again.

'He's great fun, isn't he?' Katie remarked.

'But quite exhausting in a way, don't you think?' Frankie said.

'I suppose so.'

'You once said you didn't think he was in love with Sophie and would never leave his wife for her,' Frankie said. 'Do you still think that, now that he's free to love her?'

Katie looked troubled. 'I'm not sure. It's not that long since his wife died. I expect he still misses her, though he certainly puts on a brave show in public.'

* * *

Although used to travelling extensively, Sophie couldn't remember enjoying herself as much anywhere else in the world as she did in South Africa. During the next few days, Jennifer and Peter, who had taken time off work, took her out in the car to show her the wide and peaceful expanse of False Bay, the grand and elegant Cape Dutch homesteads of Constantia set in lush grounds, and the impressive parliament building in the centre of Cape Town. Sophie was impressed by the white gabled houses and the colonial style of the Mount Nelson Hotel, but it was the magnificence of the mountainous countryside that enchanted her. They showed her the red flowering gum trees growing at the foot of Table Mountain, the silver trees of the many varieties of the protea family, shimmering in the heat, the purple and white orchids that grew wild, and the stately arum lilies that bloomed by the roadside. Then they took her to dinner at the famous seafood restaurant, Trawlers, set in a nineteenth-century pavilion, and to the Round House which stood under tall trees near the beach.

'It's all unbelievably glamorous,' Sophie exclaimed. 'And so clean. Buildings painted white like this would be grey in ten minutes in London.'

'It's the sea air,' Peter explained. 'And of course the climate. It's a perfect place to bring up children.' He stopped the car and they sat gazing out to sea, at Kalk Bay.

'Why don't you buy yourself a house here?' Jennifer asked. 'You could always let it for a few months every year, and it would be a sound investment now there's such a surge of hope running through the country.'

'I love the idea,' Sophie replied, 'but it might just be one house too many. I'd never want to sell La Madeleine and that's where I go as often as I can. I love that villa so much. It's as if I've left a part of my soul there and I only feel a complete person when I go back. I'd love you both to come and stay one day.'

'Is it anything like this?' Jennifer flung out her arm, encompassing the unspoilt coastline, the rocks sculpted smooth into fascinating shapes, while the wild baboons hopped on the wall that was built along the sea road, hoping for scraps of food from passing motorists.

Sophie replied unhesitatingly. 'It's nothing like this. It's pastoral and gentle, and very, very peaceful. And very French. Old men, watched by women in black, always black, play *boules* on the sandy village square, and the smell of Gauloise and coffee permeates the air wherever you go. There's much more energy in the atmosphere here. Much more get-up-and-go.'

Peter let in the clutch. 'Shall we go on to Sunrise Beach, Jen?' He glanced in the windscreen mirror, caught her gaze, and smilingly held it. 'We might see some local colour, and the shrimp fishermen.'

'Is that all right with you, Sophie?' she asked.

'Everything's all right with me. Didn't I say I was having the best time ever? I never want this holiday to end.'

They were sitting in the garden having drinks before dinner when the phone rang. Jennifer carried on talking to Sophie while Peter went indoors to answer it.

'I must introduce you to the most fantastic dress designer who's opened a new couture salon in the best part of Cape Town,' she said. 'His clothes are—' She broke off suddenly and looked up at her husband. 'Peter, what is it?' Sophie looked at him too. His expression was grave and he addressed her, not Jennifer.

'It's a call for you, from England,' he said.

Sophie's heart felt as if it was plunging down to her stomach and for a moment she felt quite sick. A hundred thoughts raced through her brain. Was it her accountants confirming that Tim had stolen money from her? Would they recommend that she press charges? Had Tim already been arrested?

Her hand flew to her mouth. 'Who is it, Peter?'

'It's your mother.'

'My mother?' Relief left her angry with herself for being so nervy. She really must stop jumping to conclusions. The trouble was, Tim was in her thoughts night and day and she was more upset about what was happening than she'd admit even to herself. She hurried into the cool square hall to take the call.

'Mum? Hello, how are you?' she asked brightly.

She could tell at once that Jean was in tears. She was almost incoherent and she thought she heard her mother say something about 'Audrey has to pay'.

'Mum. What's wrong? Has something happened to Audrey?'

'No, no. I said I'm sorry to worry you but Audrey is away.'

'I didn't know she was going away. Where is she?'

Jean blew her nose and Sophie could hear her voice catch in a sob.

'It doesn't matter, Sophie. Alan's very ill again. He's in Newbury General Hospital.'

'Oh, God! But why Newbury? Why aren't you in London?'

'We've been staying in Audrey's house, looking after Amelia and Rebecca. They're in Sardinia. I've been trying to get hold of them but they've been on some excursion. Alan collapsed last night and I'm terribly worried about him. The doctors have put him in intensive care but they won't say if...' Her voice broke and she was unable to continue.

'I'll come back right away,' Sophie said immediately. 'Oh, poor Mum, it must be terrible for you. And you've got the children as well. Don't worry, I'll—'

'No, Sophie. I don't want you to come back. Don't shorten your break, whatever you do. I just wanted you to know, in case, you know...'

'Of course I'm coming back,' Sophie replied stoutly. 'I can't bear to think of you on your own at a time like this. I'll be with you tomorrow.'

'Oh, but Sophie, truly, I didn't mean you to—'

'Not another word, Mum. Give my love to Alan, and I'll drive straight from Heathrow to Newbury. I'll call you again to let you know exactly when I'm arriving.'

Peter, hovering in the doorway, guessed from what he'd overheard what was happening. When Sophie hung up, both her friends were watching her anxiously.

'Is he bad?' Jennifer asked at once.

Sophie shrugged her shoulders helplessly. 'It's hard to

tell. He made a good recovery from the operation last year, and I'm not sure whether this is a recurrence of the cancer or something else.'

Smoothly and efficiently, Peter phoned the airline, found there was an evening plane leaving for Johannesburg where she could change flights for London.

'I'm so distressed you have to dash back like this,' Jennifer said sadly. 'Your poor mother. She must be dreadfully upset.'

Sophie, throwing her things into her suitcase, nodded worriedly. 'She'll be lost without Alan if anything happens to him.'

'Don't even think of it,' Jennifer commanded her. 'That way lies a nervous breakdown.'

They both got in the car to drive her to the airport, and before Sophie entered the terminal she gave a last wistful look up at Table Mountain in the distance.

'You're coming back,' Jennifer said fiercely as she hugged her goodbye.

Sophie returned her hug, feeling closer to her friend than she felt to her own sister.

'Try keeping me away. I want to see that baby of yours.'

'That's a date. We can't have the christening without the chief godmother.'

'Take care, Sophie,' Peter said earnestly, kissing her on the cheek. 'Good luck with everything, including Tim.'

'Yes.' Jennifer kissed her warmly. 'Lots and lots of luck, my darling. And you'll keep us posted, won't you? Tell us how Alan is. And what's happening with Tim.'

'I promise.' Sophie gave a wobbly laugh.

'And don't let the bastard get you down!' Jennifer called after her, while Peter grinned and waved.

As Sophie waited in the departure lounge, she watched the sun setting in bands of crimson and molten gold merging into turquoise and gentian violet. It was the most dramatically beautiful sunset she'd ever seen, rivalling even those in the Caribbean, but it left her feeling strangely depressed. As the riot of colour finally faded to dark purple and grey, it was as if her hopes for the future had faded too. Her joy at rediscovering her love for Tim had gone, replaced now by a dreadful sense of betrayal and fear. She thought he'd loved her, while all the time it was possible he'd been planning to kill her.

There was no change in Alan's condition when she arrived at Newbury General Hospital. Jean, sitting by his bedside holding his hand, had not left him since he'd been admitted and she looked grey with exhaustion and strain.

'Mum, go home and get some sleep,' Sophie said immediately. 'You'll collapse if you go on like this.'

Jean's eyes filled with tears but she was too tired to wipe them away. She took Sophie's arm and led her away, so they could talk.

'I'm so scared,' she whispered when they were out of earshot of Alan who was sleeping.

'What do the doctors say?'

'They're afraid the cancer may have spread. They're doing tests but we don't know the result yet. What shall I do if anything happens to him?' Her voice broke in a sob.

Sophie gripped her mother's hand. 'Don't even think like that. They can do so much these days with all the new types of chemotherapy. It may not even be cancer.'

They sat on two chairs in the centre of the large ward, watching Alan while they talked in low voices. All around them male patients lay in their beds, some to recover, others to die. All had a look of hope on their faces, however ill they were, and Sophie found this heartbreaking.

'If only he'd gone to a doctor when he first realised something was wrong,' Jean said. 'Do you know, the wife of another patient told me there are over ten thousand deaths a year from prostate cancer because it's not caught in time.'

Sophie felt a sense of dread spread through her like an icy chill. She remembered how he'd been unwell when they'd all stayed at La Madeleine last summer. If only ... She sighed. The tragedies of the world began with 'if only' and regrets were useless now.

'They're giving him diamorphine. He was in such terrible pain when he first collapsed. I was terrified, Sophie. He was crying out in agony. I thought he was going to die.' Jean blew her nose and took a deep breath in an effort to control her emotions.

Sophie looked over to where Alan lay, his face as white as his beard, his skin waxy and transparent looking. For a moment she wondered if he was dead and not asleep. But then she saw the slight movement of his chest as he breathed in, and she felt weak with relief.

'Mum, have you got hold of Audrey and Nicholas?'

'Yes. They returned from Sardinia this morning, thank goodness. I was a bit worried leaving Amelia and Rebecca in the care of the cleaning woman, but what else could I do? I felt very bad at disrupting your and Audrey's holidays but I was so desperate about Alan.'

'You did the right thing, Mum. I'd never have forgiven you if you hadn't called me, and I'm sure Audrey feels the same.' Privately, Sophie wasn't so sure about Audrey who was notoriously selfish, and so she was surprised at Jean's next words.

'Audrey was wonderful about it. I think something's happened between her and Nicholas. I can't remember when she last sounded so happy and contented.' For a moment Jean brightened. 'Wouldn't it be wonderful if their marriage was working again?'

Sophie nodded. 'Perhaps he's got rid of his secretary.'

'She said they'd had a wonderful time and she really sounded as if she meant it.' Jean gave a faint smile. 'Nicholas must have been paying her special attention or something.'

'Let's hope.' Sophie raised her eyes to the ceiling. 'Listen, Mum. I'm just going to phone the shop to tell them I'm back.' As she spoke, she took her mobile phone out of her shoulder bag. 'Is there somewhere private I can go?'

'There's a rest room along the corridor.'

'Right. I shan't be long. And then I want you to go back to Audrey's house and have a rest. I can stay here.'

Jean shot her a grateful look. 'As long as he has one of us with him...' Her voice trailed off and her lips trembled.

'Of course.' Sophie laid a reassuring hand on Jean's shoulder.

The rest room smelled of stale cigarette smoke mingled with disinfectant. Sophie sat down on a black plastic chair and punched out the number. Katie answered at the first ring.

'Sophie!' she squealed in delight. 'I wondered if you'd ring. Are you having a blissful time? Is Cape Town wonderful?'

Sophie quickly explained the position. 'I don't know how long I'll be down here. It depends on whether we can transfer Alan to London where his own doctor is. How is everything in the shop?'

'Fine. No problems. Frankie made a big hit yesterday with a customer. He came in for that pretty Sèvres bowl we had in the window.'

'The blue one with the picture of sailing boats painted on one side?'

'Yes, that one. But he went off with that twenty-eight-piece Meissen dinner service you bought in Chester.'

Sophie's heart leapt. She'd paid a very high price for the 1850 china, and she'd been worrying she would be stuck with it. 'That's fantastic! And he didn't quibble over the price?' She'd put on a healthy mark-up in spite of her fears that only a millionaire would be interested.

'He paid with a platinum American Express card, which Frankie did a check on, and it's all fine.'

'Thank God for that. Can I have a word with Tim, if he's there?'

'He's away, Sophie. He went up to York four days ago.'

Sophie felt a frisson of apprehension. 'Did he say why?'

'He said he was going to see his mother.'

'Did he leave his number?'

'No. I'm sorry, you weren't expected yet, and he said he'd be back before you returned.' Katie sounded anxious, afraid she'd done the wrong thing.

Sophie spoke lightly. 'Not to worry. I'll wait until he comes back to catch up with him. And if you need me, you can get me on the mobile.' After she'd switched off, she glanced at her wristwatch. It was half past three. Now was as good a time as any to phone Ellis Wiseman and ask if he had anything to report.

'Good afternoon. Wiseman, Stroud and Halcrow. How can I help you?' asked the voice of the receptionist who sounded like a programmed robot.

As soon as Sophie was connected she came straight to the point. 'Have you discovered any irregularities in my accounts so far?'

There was what seemed like a long pause before Ellis Wiseman answered. 'We are in the process of going through everything,' he said at last. 'The position is, we have so far spotted lack of funds, nearly three million pounds in fact – '

Sophie gasped aloud, her head reeling.

' – in certain accounts. On the other hand, there appears to be more money than we would have expected to find in other accounts. You see, the gross amount transferred from . . .' Ellis droned on and Sophie stopped listening. The more she was told, when it came to accounts, the less she understood, and then she became irritated because she didn't understand. In ten minutes she'd have a headache and be totally confused. It was as if a shutter came down on all comprehension with regard to figures and she cursed herself for not being numerate.

'When will you be able to tell me exactly how much money may have been embezzled?' she asked.

Ellis Wiseman paused and sounded almost hurt. 'Well, as I was saying—'

'Please I can hear all the details later. I just want to know the bottom line.'

'It's too soon to tell, Mrs Duval.'

Wondering why he couldn't have said that right at the beginning, Sophie said goodbye and switched off. Then she went back to sit with Alan while her mother went home. Later, she'd get Mrs Calthorpe's phone number in York from directory inquiries, and if that failed, it should be easy to get the number of the school where she worked. But why had Tim gone to see his mother without telling her before she left for South Africa? Was it possible he'd realised he was under suspicion? Then an even worse thought crossed her mind. Tim had run away once before, to Australia, because he'd professed to feeling 'caged in' by his mother. Had he run away again? And this time with three million pounds of her money?

Sophie sat with Alan all afternoon, trying to read the newspapers but the words became blurred as tiredness and lack of concentration overcame her. From time to time a nurse came to check his drip, but when Sophie asked how he was doing, she was told she'd have to ask the doctor. Alan remained in a deep sleep, never moving, barely breathing, impervious to the activity of the busy ward around him. With a sense of foreboding Sophie wondered what Jean would do if he died.

It was six o'clock when Sophie looked up and saw a woman she only half recognised entering the ward. She was tanned and stylish looking in a smart red linen skirt and white shirt, and she was striding confidently in their direction.

'Audrey!' Sophie croaked, feeling dirty, crumpled and washed-out by comparison. 'I needn't ask if you've had a good holiday.'

Audrey kissed her on both cheeks and, pulling up a chair, sat down beside her. She glanced at Alan with concern but nothing could hide the radiance in her face.

'I've had a wonderful time,' she agreed, smiling. 'How is Alan? Has there been any change?'

Sophie shook her head, still trying to come to terms with the change in her sister. Gone was the droopy martyred look, the sulky mouth, the disappointed expression in the eyes. 'The nurse won't tell me anything.'

'You look terrible, Sophie. Why don't you go back to my house and have a bath and a rest? You were flying all night, I presume. By the way, do you mind sharing the spare room with Mum? I imagine you want to hang around until ... until ...' Alan stirred, moving his head slightly. Sophie and Audrey watched him closely. Then he seemed to give a big sigh, before resuming his shallow breathing.

'Until he's better,' Audrey finished, wondering if Alan could hear her.

'Thanks, Aud. I may have to commute, though. A lot's

happening in the shop at the moment and I may have to attend to some urgent business.' Sophie didn't want to talk about Tim. Not until she knew where she stood.

'But isn't this more important? To be here with Mum?'

'Don't worry, I'll be here mainly, but I may have to dash up to town for a few meetings,' she replied evasively.

'How is Tim?'

'I don't know. I've got to try and get hold of him.'

Audrey looked at her in astonishment. 'Wasn't he in South Africa with you?'

'I went on my own. I wanted to spend time with Jennifer and Peter Cornish.'

'Surely you could have taken Tim too?'

'I could have done but I didn't,' Sophie replied. Then to bring the conversation to an end, she rose. 'I'll be off then, and thanks for saying I can stay with you. Is Mum coming here later?'

'I expect so. She was asleep when I left and I didn't want to disturb her.'

'By the way, how was Sardinia?'

Audrey closed her eyes for a moment. 'Absolute heaven,' she replied, softly. 'Quite wonderful.'

'Good.' Sophie repressed a smile. She'd never seen her sister look so dreamy and satisfied. Jean was right. It looked as if Audrey's marriage was on course again. As long as no one ever told Nicholas about a rangy sex-mad pop lyricist called Troy.

Early the next morning, Sophie set about getting hold of Tim's mother's phone number in York. Jean was back by Alan's bedside again and Audrey had gone with her.

Nicholas was at work and the girls at school. With the house to herself, Sophie got through to directory inquiries.

'I'm afraid there's no listing for Calthorpe in the York area,' she was told.

'Perhaps the number's ex-directory.'

'We'd still have it listed.'

'Yes. Of course. Thank you.' Sophie hung up, trying to remember the name of the school where Mrs Calthorpe worked. She was sure Tim had told her what it was called – his mother had been teaching there for at least twenty-five years. She decided to phone directory inquiries again. This time she asked for the phone numbers of all the schools in York.

'I'm sorry, I can't remember the name but I do know it's near the centre of the town,' she explained to the operator.

There was the Thornton Comprehensive, the York Minster Primary School, Crockley Hill Public School, Moor End Grange—

'That's it!' Sophie said. 'I remember now. Moor End Grange.' She jotted down the number, feeling triumphant. A minute later she was asking to speak to the bursar.

'Good morning. How can I help you?' He sounded charming and amiable.

'I'm sorry to bother you but I'm trying to get hold of Mrs Calthorpe, Mrs Angela Calthorpe, and as I can't find her home number, I wondered if you'd be kind enough to—'

'Angela Calthorpe?' He sounded stunned. 'Are you a relative?'

Sophie knew something was wrong. 'No. No, I'm an old friend, I know her son very well. He's staying with her at the moment but she doesn't seem to be on the phone,' she gabbled.

His voice was so dry it seemed to crackle. 'That is hardly surprising.'

'Oh? Why?'

'Well, I'm sorry to have to tell you,' he hesitated before continuing, 'Mrs Angela Calthorpe hasn't worked here for many years.'

'Oh?'

'I'm afraid she died about eleven or twelve years ago.'

Who could she turn to? Sophie walked round and round her sister's kitchen, drinking coffee and wondering what to do now. Nothing about Tim seemed to be as it appeared. Why had he lied about his mother? She even remembered him telling her that Angela Calthorpe had attended Carolyn's funeral. And then what had he done with Carolyn? And had he gone off with three million?

'Oh, my God,' Sophie groaned, sitting down suddenly at the kitchen table. Of course, that was it. He'd taken the opportunity, while she was in Cape Town, of absconding from the country, telling Frankie and Katie that he was going to visit his mother in York, giving himself at least a week in which to cover his tracks. 'Oh, Christ, what have I done, letting him into my life?' Three million pounds. Probably already salted away in some offshore company. And where was he now?

Fifteen

'The line is busy,' the telephone operator assured Sophie.

'Are you sure? It's been giving the engaged signal for ages. Are you certain there isn't a fault on the line?'

'We've checked it, madam. There are people talking. It's definitely in use.'

Sophie thanked the operator and hung up. So it looked as if Tim had gone to his cottage in Wales. But why did he say he was going to York? Neither Frankie nor Katie would have thought it odd his returning to his own home for a few days.

Next she phoned her bank manager, Mr Turnbull.

'I'm very glad you're back in England, Mrs Duval,' he told her. 'Mr Tim Calthorpe tried to cash a very large cheque when you went away, saying you had asked him to pay an antique dealer, in cash, for some china you'd agreed to buy.'

'How large?'

'Just over three hundred thousand pounds.'

'*What?*' Sophie was stunned. 'What did you do?'

'I told him that I couldn't sanction that amount without your written permission and he then said that you had sanctioned his signing company cheques for Gloria Antica in your absence – which of course you did some time ago – but I pointed out that was for small amounts and mostly to pay the overheads of the shop.'

'Quite,' said Sophie faintly, wondering what on earth had induced her to do anything so stupid. But of course she had trusted Tim implicitly then. 'So what was his reaction?'

'He said he quite understood, and not to worry, and you could settle this amount when you returned.'

'He did, did he?' Sophie spoke quietly but inside she was seething with rage. What kind of fool did Tim think she was? 'Thank you, Mr Turnbull. With any luck it won't be long before we have Tim Calthorpe tied up in such knots he won't be able to move. Meanwhile, I'm going to go and pay him a little visit.'

'Is that wise, Mrs Duval?' He sounded alarmed.

'I'm not sure, to be honest,' Sophie replied. 'But it's time I had a talk with him.'

Her last phone call of the morning was to the shop. It was time too, to tell Frankie and Katie what was going on.

There was little change in Alan's condition overnight. He still lay, heavily sedated with diamorphine, in a state of semi-conciousness. Jean, intent on remaining by his bedside, waved aside Sophie's apologies that she was having to attend to a crisis in the business.

'I promise I'll be back this evening, Mum,' she said as she stood at the foot of Alan's bed. 'I wouldn't leave you like this if it wasn't important.'

'My darling girl, don't worry,' Jean assured her.

'There's nothing you can do. We've got to wait for the results of yesterday's tests. Personally I think he looks a little better, don't you?'

Sophie looked at the still grey face of her stepfather, and wondered what she could say to assure her mother it was so.

'The more sleep he gets the better,' she said at last. 'Sleep is the best healer of all, both physically and mentally.'

Jean nodded. Audrey caught Sophie's eye, sisters in a conspiracy to keep up their mother's spirits.

'His blood pressure and temperature were normal this morning and that's a good sign,' Audrey remarked.

'And he had a restful night,' Jean added.

They all nodded in agreement. Who was bluffing whom? And could Alan hear their words of encouragement?

'I'll be off then,' Sophie said, kissing her mother.

'Don't worry about us,' Audrey said, and Sophie realised that for once she was being neither sarcastic nor longsuffering. 'I've arranged for the girls to be picked up from school and taken back to tea by some friends of theirs.'

'I'll be back this evening,' Sophie promised.

She'd parked her car opposite the hospital. The tank was full and she was ready to go. Providing the traffic wasn't heavy, she should arrive at her destination by mid-afternoon.

Frankie and Katie gazed at each other in a state of shock.

'And to think he may have murdered his wife.' Katie

had to sit down, she felt so shaken. 'Why hasn't Sophie reported it to the police?'

'Because there's more to it than that,' Frankie said. 'There's the missing money and everything. God it's unbelievable. She was so in love with him, too. I think she wanted to marry him, and now . . .' Frankie shook her head.

'I wonder how it will all end.' Katie felt sorrowful at the hurt, above all else, that Sophie must be feeling. 'I hope she gets her money back but nothing's going to make up for what Tim's done to her. What an act he's been putting on all these months, and there we were, feeling so sorry for the poor young widower. Did she tell you, on the phone just now, when she is going to tell the police?'

'As soon as she gets confirmation from the accountants and the bank. She said that if she rushes off to the police now and the whole thing has been a ghastly misunderstanding, Tim could sue her for defamation of character,' Frankie explained.

'I suppose she wants to tell him face to face what she thinks of him,' Katie said thoughtfully. 'I can't begin to imagine what she must be going through. I think it's very brave of her, don't you?'

'But very satisfying, you must admit,' Frankie replied. 'I'd give anything to be a fly on the wall. God, he'll get a shock when he sees her, won't he?'

'Yes. He thinks she's still in Cape Town.' Katie crossed her fingers. 'Here's to Sophie. I hope she wipes the floor with him.'

'Why don't you go home, Audrey?' Jean said as they sat

by Alan's bed. 'There's no need for you to stay here too, my dear. I'll be all right.'

'Don't worry, Mum. I'm fine. Everything's under control, and Mrs Bates is looking after the house. You can't sit here on your own, it's far too depressing.'

'No, really. It's quite peaceful actually.' Jean gazed at her husband, holding his hand. 'I have a feeling he's going to get better. I've prayed so hard, he has to get better. God couldn't let anything happen as cruel as allowing Alan to die.'

Audrey said nothing. The chance of Alan recovering looked impossible to her. He'd lost a lot of weight and was being permanently sedated for the pain. If he recovers, she thought, it will be a miracle.

'Pray for him too,' Jean begged. 'You've no idea how the power of prayers can help.'

Audrey gave a small, embarrassed smile. She hadn't been to church, apart from at Christmas and going to friends' weddings, since she'd left school. 'I don't suppose God will listen to me,' she said lightly.

'He listens to everyone,' Jean said firmly. 'Even sinners.'

Audrey averted her face, thinking of Troy. Yesterday she'd heard from him again. He'd phoned in the morning when he knew Nicholas would have left for work and the children for school.

'I can't talk now,' Audrey had whispered nervously. 'My mother and sister are staying – my stepfather's very ill and it's chaos here.'

'I'm flying back next week. Got some business for the band to attend to. Rehearsals and all that. Let's meet. Usual place? Around three in the afternoon on

Wednesday?' Troy spoke with the casual assurance of someone who thinks they will never be turned down.

Memories of molten afternoons flashed through her mind: hot breath, hungry lips, hands that explored with feverish delight, deep probing, deeper plunging, cries of ecstasy, heat, and a pulsing river that filled her to overflowing...

'All right,' she heard herself say. 'Wednesday.'

'What are you thinking about, Audrey?' her mother was asking.

She blushed crimson and came back to the present with a start. 'Oh, nothing, really.' She busied herself smoothing the cotton cellular blanket that covered Alan's feet.

'I always say,' Jean continued smoothly as if she hadn't noticed her daughter's discomfort, 'what the eye doesn't see the heart doesn't grieve over. It's not so much what you do, it's not hurting other people that's important.'

Audrey looked at Jean out of the corner of her eye. Had her mother guessed she'd heard from Troy again? It was said mothers always had a special intuition when it came to their children, and yes, she always knew when Amelia or Rebecca had done something naughty or were lying.

'And confessing what one has done is the silliest thing of all,' Jean was saying. 'It's merely pushing the burden of guilt from your own shoulders on to someone else's.'

Audrey remained silent, fussing over Alan's blanket, silently amazed that her mother never seemed to miss a trick. But what about next Wednesday? Would she meet Troy? Just one more time?

* * *

Sophie found the house without any difficulty but it was not what she expected. 'Tyn-y-coed' suggested a picturesque cottage set in an old-fashioned garden; in fact Tim had described the place as a romantic hideaway which they'd been lucky to find. Number 23 Llantrisant Road, however, turned out to be one of many grey terraced houses, its only claim to cosiness being the wooden sign on the gate, bearing the fancy name. Otherwise it was a bleak, grey block of a small house in a road that stank of poverty and depression. She sat for several minutes in the car, adjusting her thoughts to this newest development. Not that she was greatly surprised. This was just another example of Tim's lying. The only thing that was true about the house was that it was fifteen minutes drive from the centre of Cardiff.

Sitting in the car on the opposite side of the road, she looked over at the black front door and the windows like small, dark, watchful eyes. Had he killed Carolyn in the house? And how? A fight would have been heard by their neighbours; so would a shot. Was he staying there now with his new girl friend? That was a possibility she hadn't thought of when she'd started on this trip. There was nothing for it but to get out of the car, walk up that mean garden path and knock on that forbiddingly shut black front door.

It took enormous effort even to get out of the car. Her legs felt heavy with dread and her heart was beating so violently she felt she was being suffocated. She hadn't even planned what she was going to say, and now here she was, about to ring the bell and face Tim.

There was no reply at first and for a wild moment she

hoped he was out. Then the door opened with a confident flourish as if a welcome guest was expected. A moment later she was looking into the startled face of Carolyn.

Sixteen

They stared at each other in stunned silence. Carolyn's small, child-like face was ashen and her eyes were huge with terror. Waif-like, in a skimpy cotton dress with tiny shoulder straps such as she'd worn at La Madeleine, she stood as if immobilised, like a petrified rabbit in the glare of headlights.

'I thought you were dead!' Sophie blurted out before she could stop herself.

Carolyn didn't answer but stepped forward on to the front doorstep to look up and down the street, as if to see if there was anyone about. Then she withdrew into the small hallway again and spoke.

'Why are you here? We thought you were still in South Africa.'

'Perhaps it was just as well I came back early,' Sophie replied, regaining her composure. 'Are you going to ask me in or do we have to talk on the doorstep?'

'You can't stay long.' Carolyn's voice was shrill. 'Tim will be back soon. What do you want?' She backed away a couple of steps, still barring Sophie from entering the house.

'As it's Tim I want to see I think I'd better wait.' Sophie felt cool and confident. Now she knew Tim was no more than a cheap confidence trickster, she was no longer afraid. In fact, she was inwardly kicking herself for her melodramatic suspicions.

'I don't know what Tim will do if he finds you here,' Carolyn quavered in a high-pitched voice.

'Well, it will be interesting to find out, won't it?' Sophie gently pushed past the petite figure and entered a cramped living room filled with cheap sixties furniture, the three-piece suite covered in crudely patterned cretonne. It was so different from Tim's taste that she looked around, surprised. But then, did she know what Tim's taste really was? He'd loved everything about her own elegant flat and he'd seemed to fit in perfectly but perhaps, like a chameleon, he was able to adapt to any setting in which he found himself.

Without waiting to be asked, Sophie seated herself in one of the armchairs. 'I suppose you know Tim told me you were dead?'

Carolyn didn't reply.

'And I've no doubt you're aware I have a lot of questions to ask him about my accounts which he's been handling.'

Still no reply. Carolyn stood in the living-room doorway watching as a cat will watch a tin of sardines being opened. There was a look of excitement mingled with avarice on her little face, and then she slid the tip of her pink tongue daintily along her bottom lip. When she spoke in a harsh voice it was quite a shock.

'You're so bloody rich, why should you care?'

'As it happens I care a great deal. Some of the money actually belongs to my ex-husband, but I expect you know that. Have you been here, in hiding, all this time?' In spite of her cool exterior, Sophie felt incandescent with rage. How dare Tim and Carolyn connive to steal her money, and in such a diabolical way? She could see it all now. Tim, on his frequent trips to London, job-hunting, takes her out to lunch, acting the old friend until he is sure she not only trusts him but has fallen in love with him again. Then comes the big drama of Carolyn's 'death', and in no time the heartbroken widower has wormed his way into her flat – still on a platonic basis though, driving her crazy with frustration, which no doubt he was well aware of. Finally, he makes love to her, and in the euphoric aftermath she hands over to him all her finances to look after because he says her ex-husband is using her accountants and she can't be bothered to do anything else. No wonder he flipped when she suggested marriage! All the time his wife was secreted in this horrid little terraced house. When he'd embezzled enough for them to live on for the rest of their lives they would no doubt have absconded to a country from which they could not be extradited, never to be heard of again.

'What are you going to do?' The momentary look of greed on Carolyn's face had been replaced by fear again.

'That will be up to the police when I bring charges of fraudulence and embezzlement.'

Suddenly, Carolyn burst into sobs and collapsed on to the sofa.

'Oh, God! Oh, no! You don't know what it'll mean,' she wept, covering her face with her hands and rocking backwards and forwards. 'You don't know the real Tim.

He's capable of anything. He's ... he's a psychopath. If this goes wrong, after all his scheming, he'll kill me. And if he finds you've been here today neither of us is safe. Don't you understand? He's a desperate man. The minute he heard you were rich and divorced he started planning my "accident" and "death", his moving up to London and keeping me hidden here ... He sees it as our big break to make money. If you bring in the police he really will go berserk. Go! For Christ's sake, go! He could come back at any time now.'

Sophie looked at her closely. Carolyn wasn't acting. The tears were real and so was the fear.

'And was having an affair with me all part of your grand scheme?' Sophie said angrily. 'Did you both sit here, working out ways to lure me into a trap? To rob me of millions of pounds? To encourage me to fall in love with him because I thought he was a widower? God, you must have taken me for a fool.'

'Tim planned everything. Not me. I didn't want him to have anything to do with you.'

'Why not?' Sophie demanded. 'Didn't you also see it as a chance to make a fast buck and to hell with my feelings?'

Carolyn didn't reply but started sobbing again.

'Why do you stay with him, for God's sake, if you're afraid of him?' Sophie asked more gently.

'I did something ... years ago ... and Tim knows about it. He's threatened to expose me if I ever leave him. He's all I've got.' She was shaking all over, her fist rammed against her open mouth as if to suppress a scream, her breath caught in a spasm of acute distress.

Sophie was lost for words in the face of such agony.

She'd never seen anyone lose control like this. If Tim had turned Carolyn into this gibbering wreck, then this was the action of a man she didn't know. But the implications were clear. This was not the right way to handle the situation. She was apparently dealing with a psycho on the one hand and a hysteric on the other.

Rising, she walked past the huddled figure sitting on the sofa to the door. For a moment she felt a pang of sympathy for Carolyn, a woman who hadn't the strength to leave Tim and face the consequences, a woman who seemed to be ruled by fear, despair and the prospect of being alone.

'What are you going to do?' Carolyn asked in a hoarse voice as she let herself out.

Sophie paused for only a second. 'What do you think I'm going to do?' she replied.

As she drove back to Newbury, the image of Carolyn, stuck in that poky little house, filled Sophie's mind. Had she really stayed there, alone, day after day and night after night, waiting for Tim to pull off the big one? Had she imagined them sleeping together? Sharing a life together? And was it Carolyn Tim had been talking to on the phone when she'd walked into their bedroom that morning? It seemed incredible and outrageous that a man could think up such a scheme and get his wife to agree to it. But then what sort of a woman would agree to let her husband embark on an affair, with the sole intention of embezzling money from the victim? To Sophie, the answer was clear. Carolyn was ruled by terror.

* * *

Sophie drove straight to Audrey's house before going to the hospital. She wanted to make several urgent telephone calls. To her surprise she found her mother and Audrey in the kitchen. They both looked as if they'd been crying.

There was no need to ask what had happened. Her heart took a painful dive as she rushed to Jean's side.

'Oh, Mum! Oh, I'm so sorry...' What would her mother do without the man she loved above everybody else? Sophie's eyes filled with tears. She'd loved Alan, too. He'd always been like a father to her and the realisation that he'd gone was hard to accept.

'I'm so, so sorry,' she said again. 'I know how much you loved Alan.'

Audrey was looking at her strangely. 'It's not Alan.'

'What?' Sophie looked from her mother to her sister in confusion. They were watching her and their expressions were a mixture of sympathy and concern. 'What's happened?'

'I'm afraid it is bad news, darling,' Jean explained, taking her hand. 'It's Brock. He's had a major heart attack, in New York.'

Sophie felt as if all the breath had been squeezed out of her body.

'Brock?' It was the last thing she expected. He always kept himself in good shape, he'd never had a day's illness in all the years of their marriage. 'I must go to him,' she said immediately.

'Darling...' Her mother spoke gently, forcing Sophie to look at her. 'I'm afraid he's dead, sweetheart. His lawyer has been trying to get hold of you and they finally phoned here, half an hour ago. We'd just come back from the hospital for a rest because Alan's sister turned up and he's much better. He's going to be all right. He had kidney stones but he's on the mend.'

Sophie was only half listening. She registered that her stepfather was going to be all right and for that she felt thankful, but the pain and shock of hearing about Brock made her senses reel. How could Brock have died? she thought wildly. Brock, who always had such a grip on life, who was always in control of everyone and everything, who had loved her so much he'd let her go.

'I don't believe it,' she said, looking at her mother who was watching her with tenderness. 'Not Brock!'

'I'm afraid so, darling. I know this is hard on you. You still cared for him, didn't you? One can't just blot out all the years you had together; they existed, they'll always exist and be a part of you and so they should.'

Sophie covered her face with her hands and sank on to a kitchen chair. Shock and grief tore through her, devastating her, making her feel like a child who'd been abandoned. For all her show of independence which she'd wanted so badly and had struggled so hard to gain when she'd left Brock, she now felt alone, vulnerable, and utterly bereft.

'What am I going to do without him?' she wept, knowing she was contradicting everything she'd said in the last few years. 'Oh, Brock ... Brock...' Then she looked up at Jean and Audrey in anguish, the tears streaming down her cheeks, her mouth trembling. 'The last time we spoke ... it was on the phone ... we quarrelled,' she sobbed. 'I never got to talk to him again. I never got to say goodbye.'

When Jean left to go back and sit with Alan in hospital, Sophie tried to gather her wits as she sat by the phone in Audrey's kitchen with her Filofax open on the table in front of her.

'Shall I get you a stiff drink?' Audrey offered. 'You look done in.'

'I'd love some coffee, Aud. God, what a terrible day this has been. Now I must get on to British Airways and book a flight to New York.'

'You're going to Brock's funeral?' Her sister looked astonished.

'Of course. I couldn't not go, Audrey.'

'I thought you were so wrapped up in Tim you wouldn't feel so bad about Brock,' Audrey commented.

'Oh, God, Tim,' Sophie groaned. 'That reminds me I must phone the bank and the accountants.'

Audrey looked intrigued. 'What's going on with Tim? I was expecting the sound of wedding bells any day now.'

'You're more likely to hear the clang of prison gates,' Sophie replied grimly. Then she told Audrey what had happened, including her encounter with Carolyn earlier that day.

'Why did you keep all this to yourself until now?' Audrey exclaimed when Sophie had finished. 'The situation is a nightmare.'

'But not as bad as my original suspicions when I thought he'd murdered Carolyn. I was really letting my imagination get the better of me then.'

'So what happens now?'

'As soon as we have the evidence, I'll bring charges. The quicker that bastard is locked away the better,' she added bitterly. Then she called Ellis Wiseman and Mr Turnbull.

'Well?' Audrey hovered as Sophie finally put down the phone. She didn't want to miss a minute of the drama.

'I'm going to ring my lawyer. We've now got all the evidence we need to bring charges. It looks as if Tim's helped himself to three million pounds. The only problem is, we don't know what he's done with it. I bet it's in an offshore company or a Swiss numbered account by now.' Then she stopped and leaning her arms on the table, rested her head on them. 'Oh, I need Brock so badly right now. He'd have known how to handle all this. Although, of course, I'd never have got into this mess if he'd been around in the first place,' she added sadly.

'Do you wish you'd stayed with him?'

'No.' Sophie sounded sure. 'The marriage was over and it wouldn't have been fair to him if I'd hung in there any longer.'

'I bet you would have stayed if you'd known he only had a couple of years to live.'

Sophie's brow puckered in distress. 'If we could see into the future, Aud, we'd do a lot of things differently.'

She booked herself on a flight to New York, leaving early the next morning. A call to Brock's sister confirmed the time and the place of the funeral, in two days' time.

'Where will you be staying, Sophie?' Rose Duval-Hamilton asked. She had a duplex on Park Avenue complete with live-in servants but she had no intention of inviting her ex-sister-in-law to stay. Rose had never forgiven her for leaving Brock after he'd been so good to her.

'Oh, I'm all fixed up,' Sophie lied. She decided to book into a hotel where she'd never stayed before, where there'd be no reminders of Brock and where no one would know or care who she was. 'I'll call you when I arrive, Rose,' she added. It was strange to be part of Brock's family, and yet no longer a part. Rose would give her a bad time, and so might some of the others, but she was going regardless because in the end this was what she knew Brock would have wanted.

'Do you mind if I make one more call, Aud?' she asked her sister. 'I promise I'll pay your phone bill when it comes in, but the battery on my mobile has gone dead.'

'Go ahead. Don't worry about it. At least Nicholas won't be able to say it's me running up huge bills,' she replied good-naturedly.

Sophie looked at her closely. 'You're happy again, aren't you?'

Audrey looked embarrassed but she was smiling. 'Yes, everything is OK between Nicholas and me. Better than before I . . .' She broke off, turned scarlet and busied herself at the kitchen sink.

'Better than before what?'

'Oh, nothing, really. Just better.'

Sophie didn't pursue it. She knew her sister hated talking about her personal life. 'I'm so glad, Aud. You certainly look good these days. It's wonderful what happiness can do for the skin,' she added lightly. As she spoke, she dialled Jennifer and Peter's number in Cape Town. They'd asked her to keep them posted about Tim. Now she had the bad news about Brock to tell them as well.

PART SIX

June

Seventeen

Sophie booked into the Dorset Hotel on 54th Street and Fifth Avenue, on the advice of Nicholas.

'I think you'll like it, it's nice and old fashioned and very English,' he told her. 'I always stay there when I'm in New York on business.'

It was mid-afternoon when she arrived in the city, to find a heat haze shimmered off the skyscrapers, chrome car fenders flashing blindingly, and the air still and humid and so heavily laden with grit it parched the throat and tightened the chest. Within seconds of stepping out of the air-conditioned limousine, Sophie felt sticky and grubby, and all she wanted after the long flight was a cool shower and a change of clothes.

Several messages were awaiting her arrival. One was from Ellis Wiseman, asking her to return his call urgently. Another was from Brock's sister Rose, inviting her for drinks that evening. Then there was a reassuring message from Jean, saying Alan was better and they were both thinking of her. Sitting on the bed, she phoned her accountants first.

'Ellis? This is Sophie speaking. What's the news?'

'I just wanted you to know everything is now in the hands of the police. We expect someone from the Fraud

Squad to arrest Tim Calthorpe this afternoon,' he told her briskly, in a voice rich with satisfaction.

'At his house in Wales?' she asked, picturing the scene. Carolyn would be distraught but she had the feeling Tim would put on his devil-may-care act and be so charmingly reasonable they'd wonder if they'd got the right man. Nevertheless, she felt sick at the tragedy of it all. It seemed such a waste of an otherwise delightful and talented person, the man she had loved and still loved, the one person who had filled her horizon in both her youth and her maturity. What in God's name had made Tim like this? Why had he lied about everything, including the death of his mother?

'I'll keep you informed,' Ellis was saying. 'How long are you going to be in New York?'

'Three days at the most,' Sophie replied succinctly, remembering Rose. Not for a moment did she think they were going to make this trip easy for her.

When she phoned Rose a few minutes later, she found her businesslike and direct.

'I thought we ought to meet, Sophie, so I can tell you about the arrangements for Brock's funeral.'

'Fine,' Sophie replied, suddenly feeling very emotional. Brock's funeral. It didn't seem possible. She couldn't believe those gentle dark eyes would never look at her again, or his large strong hand hold hers. Here, in New York, Brock's home town, the situation was all the more poignant. She half expected him to phone her any minute now, or walk into her suite, telling her his plans for the rest of the day. Now he'd never do that again.

'Come round at six o'clock,' Rose commanded. 'I'm going out to dinner and I don't want to run late.'

'OK, Rose.' No, how are you feeling? I expect this has hit you hard, in spite of everything. No, come for supper, you won't want to be alone.

Well, what had she expected? The same regard she'd received when she'd been married to Brock?

Sophie arrived at Rose's expensively elegant duplex on the dot of six. The uniformed doorman ushered her into the lift, and when she arrived on the third floor she stepped straight into Rose's marble hall where a crystal chandelier threw a million rainbow droplets of light on the ivory silk walls, and the scent of roses filled the air with their heady perfume. Rose only had roses in her home. They were her signature, along with the decor which ranged in colour from dusky rose to the palest shade of pink. Not for the first time when visiting the apartment, Sophie felt she'd stepped into a box of pink fondants.

'Ah, there you are, Sophie,' Rose greeted her when the maid showed her into the large over-furnished drawing room.

Rose looked like a black pipe cleaner, in a chenille dress with long sleeves, her dark hair cut short, her face deathly pale. Her only jewellery was a diamond ring the size of a postage stamp and diamond stud earrings.

'Hello, Rose.' They kissed politely.

'Would you like a drink?' There was a heavy silver tray on a side table, holding a variety of decanters, each with a dinky little silver label hanging round its neck, identifying the contents.

'Thank you. I'd like a vodka and tonic, please.' How Brock had hated those twee labels! Sophie suppressed a smile when she remembered how he'd changed them all around once, while Rose had been out of the room. 'Now she'll be pouring out tumblers of sherry thinking it's whisky, and gin thinking it's vodka, and God knows what will happen when she gives people brandy thinking it's Martini!' he'd whispered mischievously. Sophie remembered that evening so well. The room had been bathed in the reddish gold of evening sunlight. As she watched Rose get her drink now, she could almost feel Brock beside her.

'There you are.' In the American tradition, she also handed Sophie a dainty little napkin.

'Thank you.' Sadness and loss swept over Sophie. There was no one in her life right now. Brock had gone. And so had Tim.

'I'm sure you'll understand that we only want family flowers on the casket,' Rose was saying. 'Of course if you want to send a wreath you're very welcome and we'll put it with everyone else's.'

It was the most hurtful remark Rose could have made and inwardly Sophie flinched. The implications were clear. She was no longer a member of the Duval family, although she still bore the name, and Rose was determined to make her feel as much of an outsider as she could.

'I don't agree with that,' Sophie said coolly, determined not to show her vulnerability. 'I may be Brock's ex-wife but I know what he would have liked. We remained on excellent terms, you know,' except the last time you talked to him, said a voice in her head and she momentarily wavered, digging her nails into the palm of her hand. God, Rose is a bitch, she thought, and

Brock's voice said in her head, she always was, my darling. Sophie took a long sip of her drink to steady herself and looked defiantly at Rose. 'What arrangements have you made so far? I know Brock left detailed instructions in his will,' she said, her chin held high. Rose's white face became even whiter, and she looked at Sophie with undisguised dislike.

'You'll know then that you've already received everything you're getting,' she replied acidly. 'Brock has left his estate to his two sons and myself.'

'Naturally.'

'The service is being held at Our Lady of Peace Church, on Sixty-third Street and Second Avenue, at eleven o'clock tomorrow morning. After the internment I am holding a reception here. I don't know whether you want to come . . .' Rose left the sentence hanging.

Sophie let it hang. 'Brock wanted his ashes to be scattered out to sea, off the coast at Southampton, didn't he? He loved Long Island so much.' She thought back with nostalgia to the many weekends when New York had been hot and airless as it was now and they'd taken a short internal flight there, arriving half an hour later at a spot he'd called 'Paradise'. He'd always planned to buy a house in Southampton, but somehow there had never seemed to be the time. Sophie swallowed the lump in her throat. This was all much more painful than she'd expected. Funny how death enhanced memories and added lustre to the departed. She drained her glass and prepared to leave. After tomorrow she need have no more dealings with the Duval family. With her head held high and a brave smile on her face, she bid Rose goodbye. But as ever Rose had to have the last word.

'Of course Brock died of a broken heart,' she said matter-of-factly as she walked with Sophie into the hall. 'He never got over your leaving him like that. He was devastated.'

Sophie looked at her for a long moment, taking in the disagreeable lines on the older woman's face. Rose was only happy when she was making other people miserable.

'Brock understood,' she said quietly, but the painful thought lurked that maybe Rose was right.

Audrey spent Wednesday morning in a state of indecision about everything, beginning by not being able to make up her mind whether to have tea or coffee for breakfast, to wondering what she should wear this afternoon. That is, if she went to meet Troy. A part of her wanted to and a part of her knew it was crazy. Everything was going so well with Nicholas that she felt she must be out of her mind even to contemplate seeing Troy again. On the other hand, would it do any harm? But where was his wife? He hadn't mentioned her on the phone. Had she come to England too? Supposing she decided to prowl around the wood as she'd done that last time? Audrey went cold at the memory. No. She definitely wouldn't go. It wasn't worth it.

She tidied the girls' bedrooms, loaded the washing machine, put fresh flowers in the drawing room and did some ironing. And all the time she ached with longing to meet Troy. Would they really be discovered if she went? Just for one last time? But what if Nicholas found out? The pros and cons shuttled back and forth in her head, until she thought she would scream. She got as far as going up to her bedroom to change into her new summer dress when the phone rang.

Oh God, don't let it be Troy cancelling our meeting, she thought in panic, grabbing the receiver.

It wasn't Troy. It was the school, telling her Rebecca had been violently sick and could she come right away to collect her.

As Audrey got into the car to drive to the school, she was surprised to find that she felt greatly relieved, in spite of her initial disappointment. Fate had stepped in to prevent her making what would probably have been a fatal mistake and she was actually thankful. She switched on the car radio. A pop group were pounding out a loud number, and the lead singer was yelling something about 'Don't give way to temptation, baby, don't give way to a lie'.

When the school matron handed Rebecca over to her mother, she wondered why Audrey Bevan seemed to be laughing to herself about something.

'Tim Calthorpe was arrested two days ago,' Ellis Wiseman told Sophie when she phoned him on her return to England. 'He's been charged with embezzlement and fraud, but he's been released on police bail, pending his trial, which probably won't be held until October.'

'Oh my God, so he's on the loose?' Sophie exclaimed. 'What about his wife?'

'She's been charged too, for aiding and abetting.'

'Poor little thing.' Sophie shook her head. 'She must be terrified. I'm really sorry for her. I feel she's as much a victim as I am. What do we do now?'

'Collect every bit of evidence we can to give to the prosecution.'

'And do we know what's he's done with my three million pounds?'

Ellis Wiseman sighed heavily. 'It's my bet he's salted it all away in some foreign account, probably in Switzerland where it's going to be very difficult to trace. The police want to ask you a few questions too.'

When Sophie met Detective Inspector Warren Parsons, one of the chiefs of the Scotland Yard Fraud Squad, she found he was a middle-aged man of great charm, whom she liked immediately. Wearing an ordinary grey suit, with a blue shirt and a navy blue tie, he sat with her in the back office of Gloria Antica, questioning her about her finances. She'd warned him right at the beginning that it was her lack of understanding of accounts that had led her to hand over everything to Tim in the first place.

'I have a real problem, it's like a blockage,' she explained. 'And now it's become a phobia.'

'No one can be an expert at everything,' he said, smiling sympathetically, 'and your talents obviously lie in the world of antiques. Your greatest mistake, if I may say so, was getting rid of your accountants and putting Tim Calthorpe in charge of everything, including your foreign investments.'

'Tell me about it,' Sophie replied gloomily. 'It was a mad thing to do, I realise that now. But, well, Tim was very persuasive. I thought I was doing the right thing. I completely trusted him, you see, and thinking he was a widower, I was sure we'd get married one of these days.' She averted her face so he wouldn't see the pain in her eyes. 'It's his wife, Carolyn, that I'm so sorry for. I met her when I went to Wales to see Tim,' she continued. 'She seems to be absolutely terrified of him. Apparently she was involved in some scandal a few years ago. I don't know what happened, she didn't say, but Tim has been blackmailing her ever since, threatening to expose what she did if she ever left him.'

'He sounds a real charmer.' The detective put down his cup and saucer and looked at her searchingly. 'What else do you know about him? You first met him nearly fifteen years ago, didn't you? It would be a great help if you could tell me who his friends were then, and who he knows now. We're very anxious to compile a dossier on all his contacts.'

'Now that you come to mention it, the only friends I know of are a couple who are friends of mine, Ginny and Jonathan Howard. They live most of the year in Monte Carlo. Tim and his wife were staying with them when we met up again.'

'You don't think it's odd that he had no other friends? Did he never meet a chum for a drink? Or mention people he might know in Wales?'

Sophie looked thoughtful. 'No, he didn't. I suppose that is odd, but it never struck me before because, well, we were so wrapped up in each other, we didn't seem to need other people around.'

'He wasn't sociable, then?'

'He got on with everyone he met, and as Frankie and Katie will agree, he was so charming everyone liked him. I'm sure he could have had friends if he'd wanted them.'

'Do you think his wife was possessive? Maybe she

didn't encourage people to become friends,' Parsons suggested.

Sophie looked at him. 'She doesn't seem to have objected to him having an affair with me in order to get money,' she replied with asperity. 'I don't know who I feel the most betrayed by. Tim for leading me up the garden path or Carolyn for letting him. Have you been able to find out why he left Australia in a hurry? I gather a girl died.'

'Really? That's news to me, no one told me that.' Parsons reached in his back pocket for his notebook. 'When was this?'

'I think it was nine or ten years ago. Friends of mine were told by friends of theirs, so it's all second-hand, but apparently he went to Hong Kong and that's where he met Jonathan Howard.'

'Was he married at that time?'

'He told me he met Carolyn when he came to England a couple of years ago, but of course he must have been lying.'

'Is there anything else that might be of importance?'

Sophie sat with her hands in her lap, trying to recall anything that might be significant but all she could think of was the months Tim had spent living with her and loving her, when everything had seemed so right between them and the future had looked so full of promise.

'I can't think of anything,' she said bleakly. 'This is like a terrible nightmare, and it seems to be going on and on. I just wish to God it would end.'

Parsons closed his notebook and rose. 'I can understand how you're feeling.' He shook her hand warmly and firmly and Sophie liked the strength of his clasp. 'We'll keep in close touch, Mrs Duval. And be careful.'

She looked surprised. 'In what way? It's too late to close the barn door now.'

'You told me Carolyn Calthorpe said her husband was a psychopath. She might have been deliberately trying to frighten you off to prevent you from bringing charges, but it is something you should remember. It's a serious accusation to make about anyone, but if she's right – well, like I said, just be careful.'

While Sophie was preparing a salad for her supper that evening, the phone rang. When she picked it up, there was a moment's silence, then a click and the caller hung up. A few minutes later her mobile phone rang. Thinking it must be Jean or Audrey trying to get through, she pulled out the aerial, switched on and gaily said, 'Hello!' Once again there was silence, then a click as the caller hung up. Feeling vaguely uneasy, she made sure the front door of her flat was locked and had the chain on, and that the French windows leading on to her front balcony were also locked. Watching television as she sat curled up on the sofa with her supper tray, she tried to put the calls to the back of her mind.

At nine o'clock, an hour after the first calls, exactly the same thing happened again. And at ten o'clock. And at midnight. By one in the morning, when the silent caller phoned for the sixth time, she had become seriously frightened.

Eighteen

'I'd get out of England if I were you,' Jean said when Sophie told her what was happening. 'The man's obviously a nutter. You can't possibly stay in that flat by yourself.'

'But I've just been away,' Sophie replied.

'Attending Brock's funeral in New York is hardly going away, darling,' her mother pointed out.

'I was in South Africa before that; I can't keep running.'

'Then why don't you stay with Audrey?'

'No, Mum. I don't want to do that. I'll be OK.'

'I hope you've got the operator intercepting all your telephone calls?'

'The police have a permanent tap on the lines, hoping to trace whoever it is. Of course, we can't be sure it's Tim. It might be some crank.'

'Who has got hold of both your mobile number and your home one? That doesn't sound likely. Have you had any anonymous calls in the shop?' Jean added in a worried voice.

'Not so far. If it is Tim, he'd know I wouldn't be nervous if it happened when I'm with Frankie and Katie.'

'It's happened two nights running now, has it?'

'Yes. I've hardly slept at all.'

Jean spoke sympathetically. 'I'd offer to come and stay to keep you company, but I'm taking Alan back to London tomorrow and I know he just wants to get home.'

'Mum, don't worry. I'll be fine. Maybe tonight I'll take the phone off the hook and switch off my mobile.'

But when the time came, she didn't. If the police ordered all her calls to be intercepted, she reflected, it would only hinder their efforts if she disconnected the instruments.

The calls started earlier on the third night, making her instantly feel besieged. First one phone rang, and then the other one started, but when she answered there was a short pause before the caller hung up. She switched on the TV set, turning up the volume, and the same thing happened again. By the time she'd washed her hair and had a leisurely bath, both phones had rung alternately another half a dozen times. She made an omelette, opened a bottle of wine, and tried to read the newspapers, and still the phones rang and still the caller hung up. Then she laid out her clothes for the next day, checked her diary for tomorrow's appointments, turned down her bed and hoped to God the calls would stop.

It was now eleven o'clock. If this went on all night, she knew she'd go crazy. This gross intrusion into her home was a kind of rape. The walls seemed to have eyes, the atmosphere was threatening. She sat on the edge of her bed and stared at the two instruments, knowing the police would have been unable to trace the calls because the caller had only remained connected for ten seconds at the most. What in God's name was Tim trying to do to her? What did he hope to gain? Sleep was impossible and anyway she felt too jangled. She tried to read a book but her concentration was shot to pieces, as the calls continued. Then, some time after four o'clock, they stopped. After an evening of torment the shrilling noise ceased and the flat was quiet for the first time in nearly nine hours.

The silence was suddenly terrifying. Sophie felt that while her phones were ringing she knew where Tim was – by the side of another phone somewhere. But now the ringing had stopped she had no idea where he might be. Outside, standing on the pavement, looking up at her windows? Hovering in the communal hall downstairs, having been let in by one of her neighbours? Right outside her flat even? She'd had the locks changed but it gave her small comfort. No one who was sane would play these tricks, unless of course he hoped he could make her drop the charges against him by making her life unbearable.

Sophie went to work as usual the next morning, carrying her briefcase and a shoulder bag. Anyone seeing her, in a neat pale grey suit and matching shoes, would think she was a well-to-do business woman on her way to a meeting. There was just one difference today. Inside her briefcase was her passport.

'Katie, Frankie, can you come into the office for a moment? I want to have a quick word with you both,' she said as soon as she arrived.

Frankie looked horrified and Katie's large blue eyes filled with tears as Sophie told them what was happening.

'You must be a nervous wreck,' Frankie said. 'I thought you looked a bit tired yesterday. Oh, you poor thing. What are you going to do now?'

Sophie sat at her desk looking much more confident than she felt. 'I want you to go to the bank and cash a cheque. And Katie, can you phone for a car, please? I want to leave here in about twenty minutes.'

'OK. Where are you going?'

'Heathrow.'

They looked at her, surprised. Katie was the first to speak.

'Where are you flying to? Back to your friends in Cape Town?'

Sophie shook her head. 'No one is to know where I am, so keep it a secret, but I'm going to La Madeleine. I spoke to the detective who's handling the case this morning, and in view of everything, he says I must go away. He says Tim is probably trying to wage a war of nerves, so I'll get too scared to go on with the case. If anyone asks for me, and that includes my sister who's a real old gossip, say you don't know where I am. Say I'm driving around various country sales looking for china and you're not sure when I'll be back. OK?'

The girls nodded. 'What happens if Tim comes here?'

'I don't think there's any likelihood of that. He's out on police bail but I don't think even he would have the gall to turn up here.' Sophie glanced at her gold wristwatch, a twenty-fifth birthday present from Brock. 'I'm really sorry to do this to you,' she continued. 'Will you be all right? Here's the name of the detective, and the accountants and the bank, but I don't think you'll need them.'

Feeling calmer now that she'd made the decision to leave London, she wrote a cheque and an accompanying note to the bank.

'I'll leave you with lots of petty cash, in case of emergencies,' she told Frankie.

'Terrific,' she grinned. 'Katie and I can have smoked salmon and champagne for lunch every day.'

'With beluga caviar to start,' Katie declared.

For a moment the atmosphere was like it had been at the beginning when Gloria Antica had first opened. It only needed Tim's lively banter to complete the scene. Sophie laughed but her stomach seemed to be in the grip of a nauseous ache and her mirth sounded false in her ears.

At La Madeleine, the phone rang at lunchtime. When Hortense answered, a woman's voice asked if Mrs Duval was staying at the villa. In halting English Hortense replied that Madame was expected later that day.

Hortense had prepared the villa for Sophie and within hours of her arrival the atmosphere at La Madeleine seemed to protect her from the outside world and cocoon her in comfort. Her bed was a snowy nest of white linen and lace, there were flowers in every room, and on the marble-topped table on the terrace there was a basket of fruit and a pot of fresh coffee.

'This is perfect, Hortense,' said Sophie sinking down on to one of the sunbeds.

Hortense nodded gravely. 'We are sorry to hear about Mr Duval. Such a shock. He not old. You miss him, Madame.' It was a statement not a question.

'It hasn't really sunk in yet,' Sophie said with honesty, 'but as you say, it was a terrible shock.'

'You not look well, Madame.'

'I'm very tired.'

'My cooking make you feel better.'

'I'm sure it will.' Sophie smiled politely, wanting to be alone.

'Henri, he clean the pool yesterday,' Hortense continued. 'Everything ready for you. You have guests to stay, Madame?'

'Not this summer,' Sophie replied. It was exactly twelve months since Ginny and Jonathan Howard had brought Tim and Carolyn to lunch at La Madeleine. How she wished that day had never been.

During the next few days, as Sophie relaxed with books and her favourite music, the nightmare began to recede. In the mornings she swam and walked to the village for the English newspapers and fresh bread, and in the afternoons she sunbathed and had a siesta, and swam a little again. And all the while Hortense prepared delicious Provençale luncheons and suppers, not letting Sophie wash up even a cup. Best of all, the phone never rang.

Slowly, the dark shadows under Sophie's eyes faded, and a spring returned to her step. Day by day she was trying to put the past behind her and come to terms with all that had happened, but it wasn't easy. The death of Brock still affected her deeply; it was unbelievable that he was no longer around, especially here where she had so many memories of their time together. As for Tim, she no longer knew what she felt, so overwhelmed was she by how he had used her – and how willingly she'd let herself be used. Perhaps, she reflected, that was what angered her more than anything. Now she was going to have to face life without either of them.

The evenings had always been the best time at La Madeleine, when the perfumed mountains of Grasse, backed by the moonlit Alps, formed a backdrop to the garden so that it resembled a romantic stage set. Sophie liked to walk in it before she went to bed, her bare arms cooled by the silent breezes that gently stirred in the spinney of wych-elms and whispered in the thicket of tall bamboos which screened the pool area from the house. At night the garden became a magic place where the mimosa trees filled the air with their sweet aroma, the lime trees cast long shadows, and floodlit spots revealed the papyrus plants, with heads that looked like the spokes of tiny umbrellas, and gossamer cobwebs which hung with fragile threads between the branches of the rosemary bushes.

Henri was strolling through the olive grove, enjoying his last Gitane of the day, for Hortense would not allow him to smoke indoors. Suddenly piercing screams split the silent night. Again and again the cries filled the air, stabbing the darkness with fearful intensity. Henri started running towards the garden, in time to see a figure dart back into the thicket of bamboos. Then, as he neared the pool, he saw a sight that nearly made him collapse with horror. A woman's body lay slumped by the floodlit pool, blood pouring from her head, dripping over the side, staining the water with wisps of a darker shade.

Nineteen

'Are you sure you weren't spotted?' Carolyn's pale blue eyes swept watchfully over Tim as he sat slumped on the cretonne-covered sofa.

'There was no one about,' he replied dully.

'You left the car some distance from the villa?'

His face twisted into a grimace of fatigue and fear. He looked as if he was at the end of his tether. 'Of course. What do you think I am? A fool?'

Carolyn didn't answer. She licked her bottom lip with the tip of her tongue. She'd been jealous when Tim had seemed to enjoy his planned 'affair' with his old girl friend but her revenge had been sweet when it came to terrorising Sophie with her barrage of silent calls.

'That's the end of her, then.' She spoke almost gloatingly. Today her child-like fragility was tempered by an excitability that made Tim more nervous than ever. Her grip on reality could be tenuous but today she seemed to be charged with an inner turbulence and a recklessness that made her behaviour unpredictable. Twisting her thin hands in her lap, she turned to look at him with glittering eyes. 'All we have to do now is get away from here. Your forged passport worked OK when you went to France, didn't it?'

He nodded. 'That might have been because I chose to go by ferry. I'm sure passport control is much tighter when you fly.'

'Why do you always make such heavy weather of everything?' she stormed. 'All we have to do now is get away from this hellhole and fly to Rio with our new passports. Then we transfer the money and bingo! We're set for life!' Carolyn managed to make it sound as easy as a shopping trip to Marks and Spencer.

Tim dropped his head into his hands, overcome with exhaustion and apprehension. The trip on the car ferry to Calais, the long drive down through France to Grasse, the hours of waiting in the thick dark shrubbery overlooking the garden of La Madeleine, until the moment when Sophie had strolled out of the villa alone and had walked down the terrace steps to the pool . . . He closed his eyes tightly when he remembered that moment, the feeling of nausea when the iron bar he was holding had cracked down on her skull ... and then the nightmare journey back to Wales and a woman who had the power to make him do anything she wanted because—

'Don't tell me you loved her,' Carolyn broke into his thoughts. Her voice was harsh, scoffing. 'If you did, you were a fool. You knew from the very beginning what was going to happen.'

Tim didn't answer because Carolyn was right. He had indeed known from the beginning how it was going to be and he'd had no option but to go along with Carolyn's plan; and no option except bitterly to regret what had happened all those years ago in Australia.

* * *

She was warm and sweet and responsive as she lay in his arms and looked up at him with her dark velvety eyes.

'I love you, Tim,' she whispered as she returned his kiss. He knew she loved him and in this moment of rapturous intimacy he loved her too; loved her more than he'd ever loved anyone, loved her mind and her soul, loved her face and her slim body, loved every part of her until the end of time. He ran his hands through the mass of dark silky hair that lay spread on the pillow, and whispered her name.

'Sophie, my love, Sophie...' Her smile was sad, and she was turning away from him. Tim held her closer, never wanting to let her go, thrusting himself against her with fierce longing.

'Sophie, don't leave me!'

Something sharp dug into his ribs, pushed roughly against him, and a shrill voice echoed in his ears. 'Tim! Tim, wake up! What the hell do you think you're doing?'

Startled, he opened his eyes and found Carolyn glaring at him as she turned on the bedside light.

'You *did* love her,' she said accusingly. 'You were dreaming about her.'

He rolled away as far as he could and shut his eyes again, wanting to recapture the last flickering vestiges of his dream before it vanished completely. Oh God, he had loved Sophie, loved her from the beginning, but the hold Carolyn had over him because of what had happened in Australia had forced him to destroy everything. The past, the present, and the future. Sophie was dead and now he was rich. Soon he would be safe in some far-off place. He and Carolyn, his tormentor, bound together by secrets that were so dark his soul was for ever damned and his heart broken with regret.

When the phone rang the next morning in the hallway of the small terraced Welsh house, Carolyn answered it. They didn't have many calls because they'd made no friends among their neighbours in Llantrisant Road but from time to time her elderly mother and father phoned from Dublin, where they lived. Carolyn was an only child, born when her mother was over forty, and they worried about her, which annoyed Carolyn. What was there to worry about? Just because she'd had a bit of a breakdown when she'd been fifteen . . . She snatched up the receiver impatiently.

'Hello?'

It wasn't her mother. A woman whose voice she didn't recognise was jabbering away in French and she couldn't understand a word, except 'Monsieur Tim'. Carolyn frowned.

'Tim is not here,' she shouted slowly and clearly.

'Tim there,' the woman insisted. 'I speak to him.'

'What's going on?' Tim asked nervously, appearing in the kitchen doorway. 'Who is it?'

Carolyn shook her head, indicating he should be quiet.

'Tim not here,' she repeated loudly.

A flood of agitated French reached Tim's ears from the receiver in Carolyn's hand, but seeing he was about to take it from her, she slammed it back on its cradle.

'Are you mad?' she shouted. 'It was someone from France. What the fuck could they have wanted? Why should they ring here?' Carolyn stormed past him into the kitchen and switched on the electric kettle with an angry gesture. 'Christ! Supposing you were seen?'

Tim was sweating, his face ashen. 'No one could have recognised me. I arrived in the dark and I left in the dark. For God's sake, I even had on a balaclava helmet and my number plates hidden.'

Carolyn shrugged. 'The sooner we get out of here the better.'

'But why should . . . did it sound like long-distance or a local call?' His hands were shaking now.

'I don't know. I thought it was my mother fussing over me as usual.' She slammed two mugs down on the kitchen table and slung a teabag into one of them. 'God, I hope you haven't screwed up as usual. This is our one chance. Our only hope of being really rich, of living a life of comfort . . .' Her voice trailed off, edging on hysteria. She slopped some of the boiling water from the kettle onto the table and swore.

'It's *got* to work,' she screeched.

The phone rang again. Tim jumped nervously, but Carolyn stood stock still.

'Don't answer it,' she said.

It continued to ring, its shrill note piercing the silence of the small hallway. After several minutes, Tim closed his eyes, unable to bear the tension any longer. At that moment it stopped as abruptly as it had started.

'Thank God,' he breathed.

Carolyn was resolute. 'We must leave tonight. Meanwhile, take the phone off the hook,' she commanded. 'I can't think why Sophie didn't do that when I was making all those calls to her.' She laughed, a brittle high-pitched sound. 'It shows you what a fool she was.'

Tim stood uncertainly as if he couldn't make up his mind what to do.

'Just take the phone off the hook and leave it. For God's sake, what's the matter with you? Whoever is phoning us will soon get bored if they keep getting the engaged signal.'

Tim clenched his teeth, desperate to know who was phoning, certain it would set his mind at rest because no one could have known of his secret mission to La Madeleine. It must surely be just a coincidence that the caller was French.

'Take it off the hook and leave it!' Carolyn was screaming at him. 'What the fuck's the matter with you? Christ! I have to do everything round here.' She tried to push past him to get into the hall but at that moment it started ringing again.

He never knew what impelled him to pick up the receiver and say, 'Hello?'

Carolyn gasped in horror and stood quite still, watching his face drain of colour as he started to shake.

'Yes, Hortense,' he said. His French was almost fluent and he had no trouble in understanding the hysterical-sounding stream of words that was issuing from the phone. Then he exclaimed, '*Merde! Oh, mon Dieu! Oh, mon Dieu!*'

To watch him was like seeing an inflatable figure slowly subsiding. He gripped the telephone table, his knees buckling, his body slumped forward in an attitude of despair.

'What is it?' Carolyn hissed. Tim ignored her, his whole attention focused on what Hortense was saying. At last he spoke in a hoarse voice.

'*Oui. Je comprend. D'accord.*' When he replaced the receiver he looked as if he might collapse.

'What is it?' Carolyn repeated fearfully.

'We're wiped out.' Tim staggered back into the kitchen and sat down heavily, resting his head on his arms, on the table.

'What do you mean?'

'Hortense knows everything.'

'But—'

'She was at an upstairs window.'

'She *saw* you kill Sophie?'

Tim nodded, unable to speak. He felt as if his guts were going to fall out and his heart stop. 'She knows everything.'

'What do you mean, everything?' Carolyn's voice was harsh.

'Sophie had told her I'd embezzled three mill.'

'She discussed it with ... with her *servant*?' Carolyn asked, shocked.

'Oh, Jesus. What are we going to do now?' With an effort he stood up and took an unopened bottle of vodka out of the cupboard.

'That isn't going to help,' she said icily.

He didn't reply. Grabbing a tumbler from the draining board, he poured himself a large shot of the alcohol, which he then drank, neat, and in one gulp. For a moment he looked as if he was having a painful spasm, but then he took a deep breath and straightened up.

Carolyn spoke again. 'What happens now?'

'I'm going to have to go back to the villa.'

'What? Are you crazy? Have you lost it completely?' She was becoming hysterical again.

'Listen.' He sat down again and refilled his glass. 'I can strike a deal with Hortense. I know I can.'

'What sort of deal is a French peasant like that going to listen to? We must leave for Rio tonight, or first thing in the morning.'

'*Listen*,' Tim said again. 'Hortense and her husband are trying to blackmail me. They haven't so far told anyone what's happened. Henri has apparently buried Sophie's body in the olive grove. Hortense said on the phone just now that she'll never tell anyone what happened two nights ago providing I give her and her husband the three mill.'

'How do you know you can trust her?'

'I believe I can. They're greedy, the French. Remember her, when we had lunch at the villa, last year? Slinking around the place in black, watching us all? She's already an accomplice to murder because she and her husband have covered up what happened. I'll tell her she can only have half the money, and if she demands more I'll threaten to report *her* to the French police and prove she was an accessory to the crime.'

Carolyn bit her lip and twisted her hands in her lap. 'So she hasn't told Sophie's family what's happened?'

'She says she hasn't told anyone.' While he'd been talking he'd finished the second half-tumbler of vodka and was pouring himself a third. He was calmer now. More in control. He knew exactly what he should do.

'You're crazy!' Carolyn suddenly burst out in fury. 'Forget Hortense! If we leave now we'll be out of the country and it won't matter what the hell Hortense tells anyone. She's as guilty as you are if her husband's buried Sophie's body. Why are you letting some French cleaning woman tell you what to do? Jesus, we've spent *months* getting to this point. Months of planning and hard work and scheming—'

'You've done nothing,' Tim retorted, 'except sit here, nice and cosy, while I did everything.' He thought about Sophie, in bed, and knew he wasn't being fair, but what loyalty did he owe Carolyn? She was no better than Hortense, holding him to ransom because she knew what had happened in Australia, threatening him with exposure unless he stayed with her, provided for her – more and more and on and on it went.

Suddenly, he felt sickened by the whole business. He swallowed his drink and rose unsteadily.

'I'm going to go and see Hortense and settle this business with her. I don't want to spend the rest of my life looking over my shoulder for *two* shadows.'

'But once we get to Rio and transfer the money we'll be safe, don't you see?' She had become excitable again. 'Safe and rich. Think about it, Tim. At last we'll have everything we ever wanted.'

Tim walked out of the kitchen, taking the bottle of vodka with him. Then he went upstairs to pack.

It was late afternoon when Tim awoke, stiff and cold, wondering for a moment where he was. Then he looked around the small low-ceilinged bedroom of the terraced house and everything came back to him in a rush of regret and fear. By his side lay the empty vodka bottle. Slowly he sat up, trying to gather his thoughts together, wondering woozily what he was supposed to be doing. He'd come upstairs to pack ... Jesus! He sprang to his feet, head thundering, throat dry as gravel.

It was then he noticed that the room was in a terrible mess, clothes flung around all over the place and drawers pulled open. The large suitcase they kept behind the door was missing. It didn't take a genius to work out that Carolyn had packed her things and gone.

Tim wasn't sure whether he was relieved or angry. In one way it would be a Godsend if she was out of his life for ever; on the other hand, while she was around he could keep an eye on her. The trouble was, Carolyn was so unpredictable. Wild as a stray bullet, she could vacillate between loyalty and treachery in seconds. Her unstable personality was capable of great sweetness as well as ruthless cunning, depending on how she felt at any given moment. He'd never felt safe since she'd witnessed the dreadful incident in Australia eleven years ago and he knew he never would. At times she clung to him, needy and wanting reassurance, and then in a moment she could turn and threaten to expose him unless she got her own way. Worst of all, he knew that if anything happened to her, her solicitor had enough evidence, in a sealed envelope, to send him to prison for life.

Hungover and befuddled, it took him a while to collect his thoughts. His forged passport was on the dressing table, hers was not. Slowly he gathered together some shirts, a couple of pairs of trousers, his navy blue blazer, and an armful of socks and underpants. He'd travel light. There'd be plenty of opportunity to buy a new wardrobe when he reached Rio.

As he shambled down the stairs with his holdall half an hour later, the phone rang again.

He picked it up warily. 'Yes?'

'Monsieur Calthorpe?'

Tim listened, sick at heart, as Hortense jabbered away, demanding to know when he was arriving. Why wasn't he already en route? Didn't he realise she would call the police if he didn't come soon? On and on she went, repeating everything she'd said that morning but in more volatile terms.

Suddenly he lost his temper. That high-pitched harangue was getting on his already frayed nerves.

'OK! OK!' he yelled into the mouthpiece. 'I'll be with you tomorrow, you greedy bitch!'

Carolyn had taken the car. Cursing, he realised he'd have to get a bus into the centre of Cardiff. Then he'd take a train to London, and another one to Heathrow, and then catch a flight to Nice where he'd have to hire a car to get to La Madeleine. Could he get away with it for a second time? He wasn't even supposed to leave Cardiff, according to the conditions of his bail. He gritted his teeth and mentally cursed Hortense. Why should he succumb to extortion? Carolyn had talked blithely about flying to Rio; it sounded so easy, so why didn't he just ignore the demands of the housekeeper of La Madeleine and go? Once in Rio his worries would be over and he'd be richer by three million pounds. It would be the most sensible thing to do, so why, in spite of everything, did he feel compelled to go back to the villa? Something about returning to the scene of the crime? A morbid urge once more to see the spot where he had crept up on Sophie and brought the iron bar crashing down on her head? Or was it a desire to get Hortense off his back because this was one secret too many?

Tim shook his head. Picking up the holdall, he started walking in the direction of the bus stop, telling himself he needn't make up his mind until he got to Heathrow.

Twenty

'Hortense says Sophie's not at La Madeleine,' Frankie said worriedly. 'I don't understand it. Where else could she be? She definitely said she was going there, didn't she?'

Katie, who was dusting a blue and white Chinese vase worth over three thousand pounds, replaced it carefully in the window and then straightening up looked at Frankie.

'Maybe she's out. What exactly did Hortense say?'

'"Madame Duval not here." I did ask her if Sophie was merely out of the house but my French is so bad I don't think she understood. Then I asked her when Sophie would be back, but she just kept saying she wasn't there,' Frankie replied.

'So what are we going to do?'

'What can we do? All I can do is leave a message to ring Brock's sister in New York. Otherwise we'll just have to wait until she returns. There's not much she can do about it anyway, is there?'

Katie looked thoughtful. 'Sophie's going to be terribly shocked, though. Brock was supposed to be worth millions. To think he went bankrupt a few days before he died!'

'It won't affect Sophie financially, though, will it?'

'I don't think so, except he did back this shop.'

'God! I'd forgotten that.'

Katie, not trusting herself to pick up another valuable piece of porcelain for the moment, sat down on a small brocade-covered chair which had the price tag pinned to one of the arms.

'I wonder if the shock of going bankrupt brought on his heart attack.'

'Could be. His sister didn't say.'

Frankie raised her clearly defined eyebrows. 'Shit! I hope this doesn't mean Sophie will have to close down Gloria Antica.' She looked around the elegant shop with its beautiful antique wares and knew that she'd miss working here.

'She may have to if Tim really has defrauded her of three million pounds,' Katie said. 'And maybe some of her alimony was tied up with Brock's fortune. This could really affect her badly.'

'I think it's vital we get hold of her as soon as possible.' Frankie looked worried. 'Why don't we phone her mother? She might know where she is.'

'You don't suppose she changed her mind and flew to Cape Town after all, do you?'

Frankie shrugged. 'God knows. What shall we say if Brock's sister phones again? It sounds so inefficient to say we don't know where the hell she is.'

'Say what you said before. That Sophie is on a buying trip and as she's touring around, it's difficult to locate her.'

Frankie went back into the office behind the showroom and wished she didn't have such a heavy sense of foreboding.

* * *

The hired Fiat rattled along the dusty French roads under the relentlessly hot sun, throwing up a cloud of fine yellow grit in its wake. Tim, at the wheel, wiped the sweat from his face with a grubby handkerchief, and then leaned forward a fraction to let the air get to his sticky back. Heat and hunger combined with taut nerves made him feel slightly sick. He'd spent the night on a hard bench at Heathrow because he'd missed the last plane to Nice, and he hadn't had a proper meal for days.

Soon he'd be arriving at La Madeleine and he was suddenly filled with deep apprehension. Supposing this was a trick? Supposing Hortense had already tipped off the French police and they were waiting for him up at the villa? Worst of all, he realised with a gut-wrenching pang, the memory of that night, less than a week ago, was going to unnerve him completely when he saw the pool area.

Jesus Christ, he said under his breath, how the fuck did I ever get into this mess? Because I listened to Carolyn's hare-brained scheme. Because I knew I could still attract Sophie. Because she was lonely and vulnerable. It hadn't been as simple as that, though, had it? Sophie had made it plain that she wasn't going to get involved with a married man. That was when Caro solved the problem by dreaming up the idea of an 'accident' in which she died.

Henri was standing outside the villa when Tim brought the car to a standstill. Surly-faced and arms akimbo, he stood like a sentinel, watchful and silent.

Tim clambered out of the car, a crumpled figure,

flushed and sweating, his legs weak with tiredness and fear. Somehow he managed to put on a show of bravado.

'Hortense is expecting me. And I'd like a drink.' He spoke in French, his chin raised arrogantly. *'J'ai soif.'*

Henri shrugged and led the way round the back of La Madeleine to the terrace. It was deserted. Henri indicated a chair by the marble-topped table and Tim sank into it, glad of the chance to sit down. Then Henri stomped off, returning a couple of minutes later with a carafe of water and a glass.

In silence, Tim poured himself a drink, and quaffed it down thirstily. He would have preferred something stronger.

'Ou est Hortense?' he demanded.

'Elle arrivant toute de suite,' Henri replied shortly.

Thank God for that, Tim thought, pouring himself another glass of water. Then he noticed that although the gardener moved away, he remained where he could keep watch.

Tim braced himself to look in the direction of the pool. By daylight it looked surprisingly ordinary, the honey-coloured stones dry in the heat, the water a brilliant aquamarine. What had he expected? Crimson stains? Pink water? He sipped his drink and wondered how long it would be before Hortense appeared, slinking on silent feet like a black shadow. He looked at his watch. It was four o'clock and Henri's face was like a mask of moulded leather, his eyes expressionless.

The cicadas chirruped in the bamboo thicket, the sun scorched the grass and cracked the clay soil, bees hovered by the lavender bushes and the minutes ticked by with maddening slowness. Where the hell was Hortense? The suspense was draining away the last shreds of his confidence, and any moment now he knew he'd leap to his feet, dash round to the car and make off down the drive like a projectile from a cannon.

When, at last, he heard footsteps coming from the other end of the villa, he spun round. Then he nearly collapsed with shock. It was not Hortense in dense black, with her sallow skin and scraped-back black hair. It was Sophie, a tanned, radiant figure in a sapphire-blue sarong, her dark hair swinging loosely around her shoulders.

'Sophie!' Stunned, he looked at her, met the cool gaze of her velvet brown eyes, wondered what in God's name was going on. Had he only injured her? But Christ, he'd been there, he'd seen her fall, blood gushing from her head, body inert as she lay by the side of the pool.

'Hello, Tim,' she said quietly. With a graceful movement she sat down opposite him.

'What . . . what are you doing?' he croaked.

'What do you think I'm doing?'

He glanced nervously at Henri. He was still standing there, as if his feet were rooted in the soil.

'What's going on, Sophie?' he asked, appalled.

'You know what's going on.'

'But Hortense said—'

'You've no idea what Hortense said because you've never spoken to her in your life.' Sophie's tone was icy.

'But she phoned me twice!' Tim blustered, defensively. 'She told me—'

'I phoned you twice.'

'You? But she spoke—'

'Perfect French? So do I, as it happens.'

He reached for his glass, saw both it and the carafe were empty and then looked at Sophie with his little-boy pleading expression.

'Sophie, can I have something to drink, please?'

She nodded to Henri and he shambled off towards the kitchen with the empty carafe.

Tim leaned forward, arms resting on the table, his face a sickly grey. 'Stop playing games with me, sweetheart,' he said desperately.

'I'm not playing games and stop calling me sweetheart.' Her voice rose, suffused with anger. 'You tried to kill me, you've defrauded me of three million pounds, you've lied to me about *everything* and you've used me mercilessly. Once, a long time ago, we loved each other – at least I thought we did, but maybe that was all an illusion too. Maybe you've used me, off and on, all my life.'

Henri silently placed the refilled carafe on the table and took up his post a few feet away.

'You don't understand,' Tim blustered.

'I understand perfectly. I want my money back. Every penny of the three million pounds you stole. If you won't return it, I shall call the police and tell them what happened here last week.'

Tim looked at her, eyes dazed. 'But nothing happened here last week. You're OK,' he blurted out. Instantly he regretted the remark.

'Oh, yes. I'm OK. But Hortense isn't.'

'What?' he said, aghast. He suddenly felt cold, and his heart was like a heavy stone falling from his chest down into his gut.

'You thought it was me the other night, didn't you?'

Tim stared at her, unable to move or speak.

'I watched the whole thing from an upstairs window,' Sophie went on.

'But . . . but it *was* you,' Tim stuttered. 'I know it was. I can even remember what you were wearing, for God's sake!'

'You mean what Hortense was wearing.' Sophie was in complete control now, holding all the cards in the pack. As Tim looked at her across the table, he saw a very different woman to the one who had been his lover for the past six months. Sophie knew exactly what she was doing, and it showed in the positive look in her dark eyes, and the confident way she spoke. Gone for ever was the malleable girl who would so easily put her trust in a man and allow him to control her.

Tim started to panic. He uttered a strangled oath. 'I don't believe this.'

'It's quite simple, Tim.' Sophie was solemn. 'I frequently give Hortense some of my cast-offs. On that particular night, she'd actually decided to wear something I'd given her. We both have dark hair, and we're the same size. In the dim lighting of the garden at night, I can see how you mistook her for me.'

'And all the time I thought . . .' Tim dropped his head into his hands. Then as if struck by a sudden thought, he looked up and turned to stare at Henri. 'So it was

Hortense he buried in the olive grove,' he whispered. God, how the old gardener must hate him. He averted his gaze quickly, unable to look at Henri again.

'Shall we get down to business?' Sophie interrupted his thoughts. 'I believe you've placed the money in a Swiss bank account.' It was a wild guess. Her accountants had no way of knowing what he'd actually done with the three million pounds, and neither had her bank. It hit the mark; Tim's body jerked involuntarily with shock. She noticed there was a bluish tinge to his lips now, and his neck was glistening with sweat. He did not deny it. He just sat there and looked at her with anguished eyes.

Sophie waited, saying nothing. This was her moment of triumph, but she felt none; her sense of betrayal left no room for triumph.

Reaching into the shoulder bag that was slung over the back of her chair, she withdrew her mobile phone and handed it to Tim. Her gaze was calm and level. 'Phone your bank in Switzerland and transfer the money to Coutts in Sloane Street. Here is the number of my account.' She placed a Gloria Antica business card, on which she'd written the number, in front of him.

'I'll have to get my briefcase from the car. I . . . I don't remember the Geneva phone number.' He was sullen now, angry with himself for coming here. What the fuck did he think he was doing? Why in God's name had he come here in the first place? He knew the answer only too well. After eleven years of being blackmailed by Carolyn, he couldn't bear the idea of having Hortense on his back as well. And all because . . .

'Henri will fetch your briefcase,' Sophie was saying. 'I suppose you remember the code word for your own account.'

Tim shot her a haunted glance. 'How did you know about code words?'

She shrugged her slim tanned shoulders expressively. 'Everyone knows about Swiss bank account code words.' Then she paused for a moment. 'Brock's dead, you know.' She hadn't meant to mention it but somehow it slipped out.

'I didn't know. Sudden, was it?'

She nodded. 'Very sudden.'

They sat in silence while Henri fetched the briefcase, the hot still afternoon, heavy with the mingled perfumes of lavender and roses, enclosing them in a cloak of torpor.

Tim needed to be reassured. 'If I do this, you won't tell the police about,' his voice dropped to a hoarse whisper, 'about Hortense?'

Sophie seemed to look straight through him and he couldn't tell what she was thinking. At that moment, Henri plonked the briefcase on the table with a surly grunt.

'Did you hear me, Sophie?'

'I'm not deaf.'

'Can I have your assurance then?'

'You know me well enough not to need it.'

'Even so . . .' He was like a disgruntled boy.

Sophie snapped. 'For God's sake, Tim! Get on with it and get out of here! I never want to have anything to do with you again. You're rotten. Through and through. What Carolyn has had to put up with is beyond understanding.'

'You don't know anything about Carolyn,' he said, flushing angrily. 'You don't know how she's been—'

'I know enough to realise that she's terrified of you, and that you've been blackmailing her ever since—'

Tim threw back his head and gave a harsh guffaw. 'That's rich. My God, she did do a number on you, didn't she? And you actually believed all that crap about my having a hold over her because of something that happened in Australia all those years ago.' He made a grimace. 'Christ, that's ironic.'

'By the way, how did you know I was here? It was supposed to be a secret.'

'Caro phoned, on the off chance. Hortense told her you were expected. Caro had planned to scare you with more silent calls.'

Sophie rose impatiently. 'Well, let's get on with it. Ring your bank, and as soon as I have confirmation from London that Coutts have received the money, you can go.'

She stood over him while he made the call, heard him use his account code word, which was 'Jupiter', listened as he asked for the money in his account to be transferred to her Coutts account in London. Then he turned to her. 'They're ringing me back. What's your number here? I don't remember it.'

Sophie told him, adding, 'Tell them to get a move on.'

When he'd ended the call, he leaned back in his chair, looking utterly defeated. 'You should have your money within the hour,' he told her. 'Though God knows what I'm going to do now.'

'You'll go back to your wretched wife and no doubt

think up another confidence trick to play on your rich friends.' Sophie suddenly felt weary, drained of energy and sick at heart.

Tim remained silent. He was not going to further humiliate himself by telling her that Carolyn had left him. Instead he shrugged, wanting to leave this place as much as she wanted him to go. It had all been a crazy idea anyway.

The mobile phone suddenly rang, a shrill sound on this quiet afternoon. Tim jumped, then reached out to grab it.

'Hello? Yes, yes, this is Tim Calthorpe speaking.'

Sophie watched him closely, wondering why he was suddenly sitting upright, a shocked expression on his face.

'What?' he suddenly gasped. '*What?*'

Sophie felt herself grow tense. Something had gone seriously wrong.

'The fucking bitch!' Tim was yelling. 'The mother-fucking little slag! I'll kill her for this!' He slammed the phone down on the table where it hit the marble with a loud crack. Then he jumped up and started pacing two and fro on the terrace. 'I'll get her for this! It was *her* idea I bump you off! It was *her* idea I pursue you in the first place! The whole fucking scheme was hers from first to last, and now she's run off with all the money, leaving me to face the fucking music!' He was scarlet in the face with rage, his eyes bloodshot as if he was crying.

Watching him, Sophie realised this was no act, Tim was speaking the truth. For a moment she was too astonished to speak. Then it dawned on her that if Tim had lost the money, then so had she.

Tim was slumped in a chair now, his head buried in his hands. 'Oh, Jesus Christ, what a fucking mess,' he moaned.

'Did you have a joint bank account?'

He nodded, his eyes tightly shut as if he was in pain. 'Caro insisted on it in case something happened to one of us.'

'Then surely your Swiss bank can tell you where the money's been transferred to?'

'They're looking into it now. We'd planned to go to Rio. She may be there by now, where she'll be safe.' He dropped his hands to his sides and raised his face skywards. 'Why the fuck did I listen to her?'

'It was never your money, Tim. You're no worse off than you were this time last year.'

'When I came here to see you again,' he added in a flat voice.

'Yes.'

'But I am worse off than I was a year ago because now I've got a murder on my hands as well. Thanks to Caro,' he added bitterly.

'Isn't it time you took some responsibility for your actions? Why are you blaming Carolyn for every damn thing? You always blame other people for your actions, Tim. You even said it was your mother's fault that you left England to live in Australia because she was suffocating you, or some such rubbish,' she said angrily. 'And why did you tell me your mother came to stay with you when Carolyn supposedly had the fatal accident? I found out your mother died years ago.'

He flushed guiltily. 'I was afraid if you thought I was

alone you'd come rushing down to Cardiff to comfort me or something.'

How well he knows me, Sophie reflected. Aloud, she said, 'Your life is just one big lie, isn't it? When is the Swiss bank phoning back?'

'As soon as they have the information. In the meantime I suppose you're going to call the police and have me arrested.'

'Still thinking of yourself. You don't seem in the least concerned that you attacked and killed an innocent woman. And what about Henri? They'd been married for over twenty years, you know. You did the most terrible thing.'

Tim avoided looking at her. 'I know.'

'And it was supposed to be me.'

He remained silent, shoulders hunched, eyes staring at the paved terrace beneath his feet, shrunken and pathetic. He was hardly recognisable as the man she had twice fallen in love with. When he spoke his voice had the deadly calm tones of the condemned man. 'You might as well call the police. Have me arrested for the murder of Hortense. There's nothing I can do to stop you now.'

She was about to reply when the phone rang. They both reached for it, but Tim grabbed it first.

'Yes. It's me speaking.'

Sophie watched him as he talked to the Swiss bank, his face filled with anguish, his full-lipped mouth drooping, and it seemed as if everything that had attracted her to him in the past now repulsed her. He really was weak. If it was true that Carolyn had some hold over him, then he should have faced it, head on, years ago. Tim was a man who would always save his own skin, no matter how much he hurt other people. At last he put the phone down.

'Well, that's that,' he said.

'What's happened?'

'The money has been transferred to another bank and they refuse to tell me which one.'

Sophie rose, her face drawn. 'I'm going to call the police.' She turned to Henri who was still standing on the terrace. In fluent, rapid French she asked him to stay with Tim and keep an eye on him.

Henri grabbed a pitchfork that was leaning against the wall of the villa and stood, legs apart, blocking the way to the drive.

Tim hadn't the heart to try and escape. His capitulation was total. Defeated, he sat slumped and inert, awaiting his fate. For him, the struggle to get rich was over.

The police arrived twenty minutes later. Tim had sat alone, under the watchful eye of Henri, until he heard a car coming up the drive at the front of the villa. Nervously, he took a sip of water and wondered where they'd take him. He knew nothing about French law, and although he understood the language, he was going to be at a disadvantage in a French court. He didn't even know, he realised in panic, whether there was capital punishment in France.

As the two gendarmes came striding on to the terrace, he saw they were accompanied by Sophie who was talking to them earnestly, gesticulating like a Frenchwoman.

Tim rose shakily, leaning on the table with both hands to support himself.

'Monsieur Timothy Calthorpe?' The policeman who spoke had a Hitler moustache and a rotund body, so that his uniform strained at the buttons.

Tim nodded, dumbly, staring in the direction of the swimming pool. The memory of the night he'd killed Hortense flashed vividly through his mind. There had been no moon and the garden spotlights, picking out cascades of roses and creating mysterious shady parts, played tricks on the eyes. He could have sworn it was Sophie he had seen the other night, standing by the pool, bending over to pick up a cushion, walking away from where he hid in the shrubbery, her hair tied back with a ribbon, her flowered skirt swishing around her ankles. Tim blinked. Blinked again, and whipped off his sunglasses. Sophie was walking down the side of the pool now. Picking up the sun-lounger cushions, strolling away from him on bare feet, her floral skirt swishing...

'What the...?' Was he going mad? Having a nervous breakdown? Sophie was standing beside him with the policemen, and she was watching him intently.

'That's what you saw the other night, isn't it?' she asked.

'Yes! But...'

The figure turned round and walked slowly towards them, the sallow face thin and angry looking, the eyes narrowed in hatred.

'You mistook Hortense for me,' Sophie said. 'It's lucky she's alive. She was concussed and had to have several stitches in her head.'

Tim's hand flew to cover his mouth. He watched, mesmerised, as Hortense came slowly up the terrace steps towards them. From the front she didn't look remotely like Sophie, but the back view ... Tim sank back into the chair, this fresh shock making him feel physically ill.

'They're escorting you to Nice airport where you will be put on a plane for England,' he heard Sophie say. 'You'll be met at Heathrow by the English police. You're in big trouble, Tim, for breaking bail. I think you'll be kept in prison this time, until you come up for trial.'

As he was led away, Sophie walked down to the pool, unable to bear the sight of his stooping figure and haggard face. It took her several minutes after he'd been driven away to regain her composure and collect her thoughts. Then she walked slowly back into the villa, wondering if the three million pounds Carolyn had absconded with would ever be traced.

The polished red tiles of the living-room floor were cool under her bare feet and as she sank on to one of the white sofas, she suddenly thought of Brock. What had made her think of him at this moment? The stolen money? The departure of Tim, of whom he'd undoubtedly been jealous? Dear Brock, she thought, with your kind face and broad shoulders to lean on. I miss you. Not as a husband or a lover, but as my friend. Strangely, now that he was dead, she felt much closer to him than when he'd been alive. Was that because the dead were beyond reproach?

Half an hour later the phone rang. It was Frankie, with the news that Brock had been bankrupt when he died.

Twenty-One

'What could have happened?' Jean looked at Sophie in amazement. 'It's hard to believe that a clever man like Brock could lose all his money.'

'It was caused by the collapse of Thornton-Collins, the investment company. They looked after Brock's personal fortune,' Sophie replied grimly. She'd arrived in London from France that morning, and one of the first things she'd done was drop in to see her mother and Alan and tell them what had happened.

'Poor Brock,' she continued. 'He'd worked so hard all his life and now it's all gone. Including the money he gave me when we split. I feel terrible about that. I must have been mad to hand everything over to Tim.' She dropped her head into her hands.

'What are you going to do?' Jean asked anxiously as she busied herself putting on the kettle to make coffee. Unhooking two gaily painted mugs from the pine dresser, she plonked them on the kitchen table.

'Instant all right for you? It's quicker.'

'Fine,' Sophie replied absently. She was thinking about the moment when Brock had heard he'd been wiped out. Had he received a letter, impersonally typed, spelling out the disaster? Or a fax explaining that the catastrophic collapse of the yen was the cause? Or had someone phoned him? The fact that he had suffered this shock while alone hurt her more than anything.

'So what are you going to do?' Jean asked again.

Sophie came out of her reverie with a start. 'Do? In what way?'

Jean sat down and pushed the bowl of sugar towards her. 'For a start, you've lost a fortune. Three million pounds! God, don't you feel like killing Tim? When are you ever going to have that sort of money again? Brock also invested in Gloria Antica, didn't he? What happens if his executors want his money returned to what's left of his estate? For all you know, he may have left debts. You might have to sell the shop. And what about your flat and La Madeleine? Will you be able to afford to keep them on?'

Sophie sighed impatiently. 'Mum, I don't know. So much has happened. I'm so shocked I can't even think straight. It's too soon to make plans. I have to find out what the accountants say first. Maybe I haven't lost three million. Interpol are doing their damnedest to trace Carolyn, and if they find her, they'll hopefully recover my money too.' She sipped her steaming coffee gingerly. 'I still can't believe it,' she added, sounding dazed. 'What with Brock's death and Tim's betrayal, I feel utterly, totally gutted. I can't focus my mind on anything right now.'

Jean reached across the kitchen table and laid her hand on Sophie's. 'You can be comforted by one thing, though, darling. You know now that no matter what that bitch Rose Duval-Hamilton says, you weren't to blame for Brock's death.'

'True. Mum, do you suppose, if Brock hadn't died, he'd have come to me for financial help?' Sophie looked in anguish at her mother, and Jean was reminded of her as a little girl when those dark velvet eyes would gaze at her and will her to give the answer she wanted to hear.

'I think he probably would have done, love. Why do you ask?'

Sophie's eyes brimmed and she gave a loud sniff. 'Because I hope he would have turned to me. I hope he wouldn't have been too proud, or too independent. He was so good to me. Everything I have is thanks to Brock. So if he was in difficulties, I'd like to think he'd have let me help.' Her voice broke on a sob.

Jean squeezed her hand. 'I'm certain he'd have turned to you,' she said, though secretly she doubted it. Brock, she felt, would have been too proud to turn to anyone, but what was the good of saying so? Sophie had enough to cope with as it was, without getting upset over what might have been.

'I tell you one thing,' Sophie announced more cheerfully as she blew her nose on a piece of paper kitchen roll.

Jean raised her eyebrows. 'What?'

'This whole saga about Brock and his money has certainly put my feelings towards Tim into perspective.'

'What do you feel about him now?'

'Nothing. I feel nothing. He's just a jumped-up little con artist whose only claim to fame is that he's sexy and funny.'

'And weak,' Jean pointed out.

'Terribly weak,' Sophie agreed.

'I'd like to know why his wife was blackmailing him.

It must have been over something very serious if he was prepared to murder you rather than be exposed.'

'I told you she'd given me a completely different version of their relationship, didn't I? God, she had me fooled.'

'But you believe Tim? Not her?'

'I believe Tim because I know him so well. I'm convinced he was telling the truth.'

Jean said nothing. Sophie hadn't seen through all the lies Tim had spun her for the previous six months, so why should she be so sure he was to be believed now? 'No doubt the trial will reveal everything,' she observed tactfully. 'They sound like they deserve one another.'

Sophie rose, her coffee hardly touched. In the last few days she'd lost her appetite. 'I'm going to the shop now,' she said wearily. 'Somehow I've got to pull myself together and get on. I'd better see my bank manager too.'

'Oh, this is awful, darling. I wish there was something we could do to help,' Jean said, distressed.

Sophie kissed her mother's cheek; it was soft and scented, like a peach. 'Mum, don't worry. You and Alan just take care of yourselves.'

Sophie sensed the tense atmosphere as soon as she entered Gloria Antica. Both Frankie and Katie looked pale and worried as they emerged from the back office to greet her.

'What's happening?' Frankie asked almost immediately.

Sophie looked at them both, realising they were aware of the seriousness of the situation.

'The first thing is, don't panic,' she said in a calm voice. 'I shan't know how bad it is until I've had a full report from the bank and the solicitors. That might take days if not weeks but I intend to do everything possible to keep this shop going. Maybe I'll be able to recover the money Tim took, and if that's the case, we're laughing.'

They both nodded in understanding.

'The stock we've got is worth several hundred thousand pounds,' Sophie continued. 'If the worst comes to the worst, I'll put some of the most valuable pieces in auction. I won't make such a big profit, but at least it will raise some capital. But let's not get in a state. The situation may not be as bad as we think.'

'Business hasn't been very good in the last few weeks,' Katie said mournfully. 'We've only sold two pieces this week.'

'Business is never good at this time of year, and come August we probably won't sell a thing. This is a rather seasonal business, you know. Apart from tourists, most of our clients are abroad by now,' said Sophie. 'We're unlikely to get busy again before mid-September. January and part of February will also be quiet.'

'So we're carrying on as usual?' Frankie asked in a relieved voice.

'Absolutely,' Sophie replied robustly, sounding more confident than she felt. 'Now, let's have a cup of coffee and then get some work done.' She pointed to a Sèvres dinner service displayed in a glass-fronted cabinet. 'Why don't we put that in the window? And take out those vases and the coffee service? They could go on that shelf. We need fresh flowers, too.' She seized the arrangement of white peonies, roses, delphiniums and lilies and carried it towards the office. 'These are definitely past their sell-by date. Frankie, when you get the flowers, could you buy some chocolate biscuits as well. Help yourself to the petty cash box.' In a matter of moments she'd turned the atmosphere around and the girls were soon back to their usual cheerful selves.

When Sophie finally locked up for the night, she felt very stressed. It had been a strain keeping Frankie and Katie's morale high all day, and it hadn't helped that there'd been no customers either. She hailed a taxi for the short journey to Eaton Place, knowing she should walk as she usually did to get some exercise, but feeling too tired tonight. All she wanted was a hot scented bath, a light supper and then bed. The strain of the last few weeks was beginning to get to her. Not knowing what lay ahead was the worst part of all.

As she let herself into the communal hall which was all white marble and mirror and glass, she saw a stack of mail on the console table. It was all for her. Grabbing it with an inward sigh, because she knew it was going to take an hour to go through it, she climbed the grey-carpeted stairs to her flat, flipping through the envelopes as she went.

'Oh! There you are!' she heard a familiar voice call out.

Sophie looked up, and there was Audrey sitting on the top step. She was grinning.

'What are you doing here?' Sophie asked in astonishment.

'I had to come up to London today and so I thought I'd drop in to see you before I go home.' Audrey rose as she spoke, and Sophie noticed she was wearing an elegant taupe silk skirt with a matching thigh-length jacket.

They kissed briefly and then Sophie unlocked her apartment door and led the way inside.

'You're looking amazing, Aud. I like your outfit. Have you been having a shopping spree?'

'No. Not today. I went to see Mum and Alan. It's amazing the recovery he's made, isn't it? I really thought he was going to fall off the perch the other day.'

Sophie nodded. 'So did I.'

'I dread to think what Mum would have done if he had died.'

'It doesn't bear thinking about,' Sophie agreed. 'Would you like a drink?'

Audrey seemed to hesitate for a moment, then she said, 'Can I have a very weak vodka and tonic, please. Really weak, Sophie, with masses of tonic water.'

Sophie's eyebrows shot up. 'Really? Since when have you practically gone on the wagon?' She opened the drinks cupboard which was set into the bottom half of the bookcase and reached for two crystal tumblers.

'I haven't gone on the wagon entirely,' Audrey replied casually. 'I'm just trying to live a healthier life.' She took off her jacket and settled down in one of the large armchairs. 'What's this about Brock being bankrupt when he died?'

'Poor Brock.' Sophie, pouring out their drinks, shook her head, her expression troubled. 'He must have got the most tremendous shock. I can't bear to think of him alone, in the New York apartment, when it happened.'

'Do you know what went wrong?'

'An investment company he was involved in went

bust, and took him and several other people with them.'

They sat in silence for a moment, then Sophie said, 'Let's talk about something more cheerful. How are the girls?'

'In terrific form. So is Nicholas.' Audrey crossed her legs and smiled complacently.

Sophie frowned, puzzled. 'What's going on, Aud?'

'I don't know what you mean,' she replied, trying to keep a straight face, but not succeeding. 'Why should anything be going on?'

'Because,' her sister informed her bluntly, 'for once you're not complaining and grumbling about everything.'

Instead of getting angry, Audrey burst out laughing.

'For heavens sake, what is it?' Suddenly Sophie looked dismayed. 'Oh, God, Aud. You're not about to leave Nicholas, are you?'

'No, of course I'm not. Don't be silly.'

'Then why are you looking so happy?'

'Because I'm pregnant again.'

'You're...? Oh, that's great news, Aud. Is Nicholas pleased?'

'He's over the moon. We're hoping for a boy this time. Amelia and Rebecca are thrilled too.' Audrey smiled happily. 'And we're going to move, away from...' Her face flushed. 'Away from the area we're in and find a bigger house on the other side of Newbury. The new baby's giving us the opportunity to ... sort of ... well, start again.'

'I'm so glad,' Sophie said warmly, going over to give Audrey a hug. 'So that's why you wanted a weak drink.'

'Exactly. Oh, I'm so happy, Soph! Everything's worked

out wonderfully well. Denise is off the scene, and I'm . . . well, I'm back with Nicholas again, and everything's great between us.'

'You don't mind about Denise?' Sophie asked curiously. Brock had been so utterly faithful to her, she couldn't imagine what it must be like to have a husband who cheated.

'I would have been,' Audrey said slowly, 'if I hadn't had an affair myself. That sort of took away the resentment I felt. It made me understand Nicholas's position, too. And it taught me *everything* about sex. I feel like a different woman,' she added shyly.

'I'm really glad for you. When is—'

The front door bell rang.

'Oh, hell, who can that be?' Sophie rose and went into the hall of her flat and spoke into the entry-phone. 'Yes? Who is that?'

'A delivery for Mrs Duval.'

Sophie frowned, and turning to Audrey who had followed her into the hall, whispered, 'It's someone delivering something.'

'At this hour?' Audrey looked at her wristwatch. 'It's nearly eight o'clock.'

Sophie spoke into the mouthpiece again. 'What are you delivering?'

'Flowers. For Mrs Duval. They should go into water. I don't want to leave them here on the doorstep.'

Sophie shrugged. 'OK. Bring them up, please. First floor.'

Audrey looked intrigued. 'Who's sending you flowers? Have you got a new admirer?'

Sophie's laugh was mirthless. 'I sincerely hope not.'

She opened the door and waited. Footsteps came running up the stairs and a small slim figure carrying a large leather shoulder bag hurtled past her into the hall. Hostile blue eyes glared at her and a small white face pushed itself so close to hers she could feel the hot breath on her cheek.

'Have you got the bastard here?'

'Carolyn!'

Audrey, standing in the drawing-room doorway, gave a little scream. Sophie quickly pulled herself together. It was obvious that Carolyn was both hysterical and deranged; she reminded Sophie of a horse about to bolt. With three million pounds at stake, she'd need careful handling.

'What a surprise, Carolyn,' Sophie said gently. 'My sister and I are having a drink. Will you join us?'

Audrey's jaw dropped. 'What the—'

Sophie silenced her with a glance.

Carolyn barged past Audrey without saying a word and strode into the drawing room. 'Where is the bugger? I know you're hiding him here.' She looked around as if she expected Tim to materialise from behind a piece of furniture.

Sophie eyed her cautiously. She was wearing filthy jeans and a man's striped shirt. Her blonde hair looked as if it hadn't been washed for weeks and it hung about her pinched little face in greasy tendrils. Whatever had held her vaguely together in the past had now snapped completely.

'Let me get you a drink.' Sophie tried to speak soothingly, although her hands had started to shake. 'Tim isn't here,' she added.

'Don't lie to me,' Carolyn rasped.

Sophie poured a glass of mineral water and handed it to Carolyn while Audrey edged her way nervously round the room.

'You can search the flat if you like. He's not here.'

'Then you know where he is!' She took the glass but remained standing, her feet wide apart, her chin jutting. 'He went too far,' she continued. 'He wasn't supposed to sodding fall in love with you.'

Sophie looked genuinely surprised. 'He didn't. It was all an act, which you planned. You know that, Carolyn. He never loved me. You were both after my money.'

Carolyn's eyes narrowed, became glittering blue slits, full of sly cunning. 'We were going to live in Rio. A new start. It was all planned. But then he fucking did the dirty on me.' She gulped the water, almost pouring it down her throat. 'I'll get him yet, though.' She wagged her head, knowingly. 'He's afraid of me. Afraid of what I'll tell.'

'But you can still go to Rio,' Sophie said carefully.

Carolyn spun on her, suddenly enraged. 'How the fuck can I go now?'

'You don't need Tim. You've got the money. Forget him. Go on your own.'

'And leave him here so you and he can go on being lovers? You'd like that, wouldn't you?'

'I hope I never see him again as long as I live,' Sophie said coldly. 'You're welcome to him.'

'I don't want Tim!' she suddenly screeched. 'I want the *money*! Don't you understand, you stupid bitch?'

'You said you came here looking for Tim.'

Carolyn shook her head, her face contorted. She was

so angry she could barely speak. 'I came here looking for Tim because he's run off with all the money,' she spluttered. 'Why can't you understand?'

The silence in the room was almost palpable. Audrey drew her breath in sharply. Sophie stared in bewilderment.

'But *you* took the money out of the Swiss account,' she said.

A dazed, almost puzzled, expression crossed Carolyn's face, but then the crafty look returned. 'You're lying!' she screamed, hurling her glass at Sophie. It exploded in a shower of water and crystal on the wall behind her head. Audrey grabbed the phone in alarm but Sophie rushed over and took it from her.

'No, Aud,' she said firmly.

'But—'

'It's OK. I'll handle this. Why don't you go home? There's nothing you can do.'

'I'm not leaving you alone with...' Audrey paused uncertainly.

'It's all right. I know what I'm doing. Go on. Go home.'

Audrey shook her head and slid into one of the armchairs. 'I'd rather stay.'

Sophie, who had never taken her eyes off Carolyn, went over to where she still stood, gazing at the patch of damp on the silk wallpaper with a blank expression.

'Why don't we sit down, Carolyn, and talk this over,' she said soothingly. She took her thin arm, protruding like a white stick from the shirt sleeve, and led her to the sofa. She sat down beside her, watchful for another outburst of violence. 'Tim is in prison, Carolyn,' she said gently. 'He's awaiting trial. I know he hasn't got the money. I was with him when he phoned the bank in Switzerland and they told him it had already been withdrawn. He thinks you took it.'

'He took it,' she insisted, starting to cry. 'He took the money we were going to run away with and he's left me with nothing. Nothing. He's here, with you, isn't he? You're lying to me.' She was weeping bitterly now, but they were the tears of a five-year-old child, helpless, hopeless, filled with despair, inconsolable.

Sophie put her arm round Carolyn's shoulders. 'Give Duncan Edwards a ring,' she mouthed to Audrey who nodded in understanding. Duncan Edwards was the family doctor who looked after Jean and Alan as well as Sophie. 'Get him to come round now.'

Audrey hurried out of the room to make the call from Sophie's bedroom.

Carolyn did not notice. 'You're lying ... lying,' she kept sobbing. 'He's taken the money ... and ... and he's going to stay with you.'

Nothing Sophie could say would make her believe otherwise. Only one question remained. If Carolyn hadn't withdrawn the three million pounds, and Tim hadn't either, who had?

'I've given her a sedative. She'll sleep for a few hours but she must be admitted to a clinic without delay. She's very disturbed,' Dr Edwards told Sophie. He drew out his mobile phone from his back pocket. 'I'll make arrangements right away to get her into the psychiatric ward of the Grange. Do you know anything about her medical history?'

Sophie shook her head. 'I hardly know her. I've only met her twice before; the first time I thought she was fine, the second time I believed her when she told me her husband victimised her. Tonight, though, she was violent and aggressive and altogether different.' She looked down at Carolyn who was lying on her side on the spare room bed, still and pale, knocked out by the injection she'd been given.

'I'd like to ask you a few questions,' he said when he came off the phone, having also arranged for an ambulance to collect Carolyn. 'She was too distressed to tell me much; but I gather she thinks her husband has run off with you and has taken the money that was supposed to be hers. It all sounds rather improbable,' he added, smiling. Duncan Edwards had known Sophie, both as her general practitioner and as a friend, since she'd been fifteen, and he had a high regard for her.

'It's a long story,' Sophie warned him as she led the way back to the drawing room where Audrey was on the phone to Nicholas, explaining why she was still in town. 'Sit down and let me get you a drink.'

He settled himself at one end of the dark green velvet sofa. 'So tell me, Sophie, who exactly is this Carolyn Calthorpe?'

Briefly, Sophie outlined what had happened since Tim and Carolyn had driven over for lunch at La Madeleine the previous year.

The doctor regarded her quizzically. 'Are you quite sure she's the mad one?' he asked when he heard how Tim had mourned Carolyn's 'death' in an 'accident'.

'The whole thing is bizarre,' Sophie agreed. 'At first I was convinced it was him; I even thought at one point he'd murdered Carolyn. But then I talked to her. I could see she was hysterical but I thought she probably had cause. She told me Tim threatened to expose her for something she'd done in Australia if she didn't do as he said. She told me he was a psychopath. She seemed to be living in fear of him. But then, when I saw him in France the other day, he told me everything had been *her* idea, and it was Carolyn who was blackmailing him about what had happened in Australia. I think that part's true. Friends of mine told me he had to leave in a hurry.'

'What an extraordinary story. I remember Tim, of course, from when you were going out with him in your teens.'

Sophie gave a hint of a smile. 'Thank you for not saying when I was "young",' she said. Then a shadow passed over her face. 'I wish to God I'd never met up with him again.'

'You've been through a lot in the past year,' he said, looking at her with concern. Once again he was the doctor on duty, showing solicitude for a patient. 'How are you bearing up? Are you sleeping?'

'I'm OK,' Sophie replied, 'though I'll be glad when this year comes to an end.'

'You'll be all the stronger for it in the long run,' he remarked in his quiet, reassuring voice. 'They say steel has to go through fire to become strong and it's the same with us human beings.'

'Things haven't turned out as I'd planned,' she said, her eyes full of regret.

Dr Edwards raised bushy grey eyebrows. 'My dear, they very rarely do,' he admonished gently.

'I know, but I do so want to start a family and be in control of my life again.'

'But you are in control of your life. You've opened your shop. Made a success of it.'

'But I allowed myself to be taken over by Tim. I wonder if I'm the sort of person who actually attracts controlling men.'

Audrey, who had remained silent, suddenly spoke. 'Perhaps, in loving a man, a woman automatically relinquishes her own power. Without realising it, she actually wants the man to be in control.'

Sophie looked at her in silent surprise.

'You could be right,' Dr Edwards said.

'But you don't like doing everything Nicholas wants you to do, do you?' Sophie asked. 'Most of the time you get your own way.'

'I do, over all the small issues,' Audrey agreed cheerfully, 'but I like the security of knowing he's really in charge. When it comes to the big things, I let him make all the decisions. After all, he's the one who's responsible for keeping a roof over our heads.'

Sophie grinned. 'I think that's what is known as having your cake and eating it.'

'It suits me and I think it suits most women,' Audrey protested.

Dr Edwards nodded in agreement. 'On the whole women like being looked after, to a certain extent. I know my wife does.'

'Men are bound to be in control,' Audrey went on. '"He who pays the piper calls the tune,"' she asserted, adding, 'Brock decided everything because he was paying.'

'Are you saying that being in love takes away a

woman's need to be in control?' Dr Edwards asked. There was nothing he enjoyed more than a lively discussion.

Audrey hesitated, unsure of herself now. 'I don't think so.'

'Well, it damn well took away my need,' said Sophie robustly, 'and now I'm paying the price.'

Twenty-Two

The walls were white. The ceiling was white. Even the bedspread was white. She was in a blank world of nothingness and that's where she longed to remain. Pretend nothing was wrong. Pretend it wasn't really her lying in a high narrow bed. Pretend to be somebody else. Just as she used to do when ... Carolyn's mind instantly veered away from what had happened. But every time she managed to forget, along came one of the doctors or whatever these shrinks called themselves, and they started probing, digging, insisting there were things she wanted to talk about. But she didn't want to talk. Why couldn't they understand that? She didn't want to talk about anything.

Carolyn turned on to her side and shut her eyes tightly. Their probing was so painful. Why couldn't they leave her alone? It was over and done with and she'd probably never see Tim again. Once he knew the truth about Australia, he'd never forgive her. Again her mind spun off, refusing to accept what had happened – happened to her, not to him as she'd pretended.

She opened her eyes, wishing she could sleep. Her lies about what had happened in Australia had never bothered her before, so why couldn't she forget them now? It was all the fault of these damned shrinks. If only they hadn't asked her about Tim. Hadn't asked where he was, what he was doing, why she wasn't with him, whether they were happily married. On and on they went until she wanted to die, wished she could die, cried so much she thought she would drown in her tears. Then they gave her an injection and she knew no more. But their questioning had unsettled her, unlocked something in her head and released something she was now having difficulty putting back, shutting away again.

She was damned if she was going to tell them it was her who had ... There! She'd nearly let it out! If that ever happened, her hold over Tim would be finished. He thought he'd killed that woman when his car ran her down on the outskirts of Sydney as they were returning from a party. It had been so easy to let him think that. He'd been drunk and he'd been smoking dope that night. She'd slipped out of the driving seat in the pitch dark and by the time the police and the ambulance arrived, he was propped behind the steering wheel, unconscious from the blow to the head he'd received. They never questioned who had been driving.

Three days later when he regained consciousness, she told him they had to flee the country before he was charged with manslaughter. They'd flown to Hong Kong, although Tim was far from well. Started a new life. Met Jonathan Howard who gave Tim a job. And all the time Tim believed he was responsible for killing the woman.

Carolyn rolled on to her back and stared up at the white ceiling. It had also been necessary to pretend she had 'evidence' that would prove his guilt, which she warned him she would use unless he did as she wanted. The best card of all, though, she kept up her sleeve, refusing him the one request which would have made his position safe. A wife cannot give evidence against her husband. Every time Tim asked her to marry him, she refused. While they remained unmarried, she was safe. Tim would look after her, provide for her, see that she had everything she wanted. Once married, he could have left her at any time.

'Let's pretend, though, for social reasons,' Carolyn said as they settled into a flat in Hong Kong.

Pretend ... pretend ... Carolyn squeezed her eyes tightly shut but the pictures in her brain wouldn't go away. They hurt her eyes like an old flickering movie, and the sense of panic was rising again, making her pulse race, her heart pound, her body turn ice-cold. She knew she couldn't go on, couldn't keep on pretending ... as she'd started to do when she'd been fifteen ... couldn't bear another moment of this agony that was tearing her apart and had been killing her slowly ever since...

Suddenly she felt quite calm. It was obvious what she must do, and now the decision was made she felt an enormous sense of relief. Slowly she climbed out of bed. The corridor outside her room was deserted although she could hear one of the hospital cleaners talking to a nurse in the dispensary room. At the end was a door marked FIRE EXIT. Swiftly and with purpose, Carolyn made her way towards it.

'If you're going to maintain Gloria Antica, I'm afraid other things are going to have to go, Mrs Duval,' Mr

Turnbull told her with a mixture of gravity and sympathy.

'I was afraid of that,' Sophie replied. They'd heard from the executors of Brock's will that, as she'd feared, he'd left debts to be paid. All his assets, which included his New York apartment and the money he'd invested in the shop, would be required to pay off his creditors. She looked at the bank manager and her tone was positive. 'For a start the flat can be sold. I don't need a million-and-a-half-pound apartment in the best part of London.'

For a brief second she thought of the beautiful rooms with their French windows and high ceilings, so cool in summer with a breeze coming in from the balcony, so inviting in winter with fireplaces to sit by. She felt a pang of regret. She'd been so happy in Eaton Place and it was unlikely she'd ever have so grand a home again.

'Perhaps I'd better sell La Madeleine as well,' she added grimly.

Mr Turnbull looked distressed. 'How much capital do you need to keep your shop going?'

For the next half-hour they talked figures. If the money Brock had invested in Gloria Antica had to be paid back to his estate, it would be necessary to sell both properties. That would allow her to buy a smaller flat in Kensington and keep the shop going, including paying Katie and Frankie's salaries.

'That's it then,' Sophie said, putting her papers back in her briefcase. 'I'll put the flat in the hands of Hobart Slater, and I'll ask their advice about La Madeleine.'

'This is very disappointing for you,' he said sadly.

Sophie looked at him levelly. He seemed almost more

upset about selling the properties than she was. 'It's not really disappointing, Mr Turnbull. When I asked Brock for a divorce, I was prepared to leave with practically nothing. I mean, why should he give me money and places to live when I was actually walking out on him? I think it's grossly unfair to leave someone and expect to take half of everything with you. I was astonished that he was so generous.'

'But La Madeleine was his wedding present to you, wasn't it?' he pointed out.

'Yes, but I still think it was good of him to let me keep it when we parted.'

As Sophie walked back to the shop she realised to her surprise that she wasn't as upset at letting La Madeleine go as she thought she would be. She'd always loved the place; loved the stones that were so hot they scorched the soles of your feet and the sky that was such a solid blue it dazzled, loved the sunlight on frangipani, the leisurely luncheons with warm apricots, cool green grapes and ripe cheese that melted and spread across the carved wooden cheeseboard like liquid ivory. Best of all were the long balmy nights when the stillness was broken only by the shrilling of the cicadas. It had been so wonderful, once. But now it was overcast by dark shadows and bitter memories. The sooner she sold it, the better.

The old gentleman always walked his dog along the leafy tree-lined road at the same time every afternoon. His route never varied. On leaving the semi-detached where he'd lived for forty years, he turned left and then at the bottom of his street he turned right, and there it was, Magnolia Avenue. There were no magnolia trees; as far as he knew there never had been. Plane trees lined the route, their densely growing leaves covered with a film of grime, their trunks dappled with the constant shedding of bark.

'Come on, Rutland,' the elderly man said gently to his old dog, tugging at the lead. The terrier sniffed along the bottom of a low brick wall before automatically raising his back leg. The old man walked slowly on.

Suddenly, a swishing, rustling noise above his head made him stop and look up. There was the sound of snapping branches. Something was hurtling down through the tree in his direction. A second later a body swooshed headlong through the leaves and landed with a sickening crunching thud at his feet.

Rutland yelped with fear, cowering back, straining on his lead to get away. The old man stared, immobilised with horror at the sight of the young woman who lay sprawled on the pavement, arms and legs awry, blue eyes staring sightlessly, fair hair wispy round the child-like face.

The headline on page three of the *Daily Express* said it all. Sophie read it as she sat in her office drinking the first cup of coffee of the day, and for some dreadful reason it seemed a predictable and fitting end to a tormented soul.

'...Carolyn Reece, aged twenty-nine, committed suicide when she jumped from the roof of the Grange, a mental hospital in Wimbledon where she had been a patient for the past month.'

'Oh, my God,' Sophie said slowly. 'I wonder how Tim's

going to feel.' There was a photograph of Carolyn when she'd been seventeen, an exquisitely pretty girl in a summer dress but with wide blank eyes and a twisted little smile.

Carolyn's father, Sean Reece, was quoted from his home in Ireland, as saying: 'Caro never recovered, emotionally, from being raped when she was fifteen. It left her depressed and unbalanced although she did receive counselling at the time.'

Sophie read on, only giving a gasp of surprise when she got to the last paragraph. 'Listen to this,' she exclaimed to Frankie and Katie who were hovering in shocked amazement as she read out bits of the story to them. 'They weren't married! They were never married. I don't believe it.' She shook her head, stunned. 'All that ... and they weren't even married.'

'What was he playing at?' Katie asked.

'It wasn't Tim, it was Carolyn. She was the schemer who plotted everything in that mad little head of hers. Twisted and warped she was, but now we know why. The trouble was, Tim is weak and she had him running scared. For her sake it would have been better if he'd stood up to her and seen that she received treatment instead of thinking of himself all the time.'

'That's quite sad,' Frankie said. 'Her parents must feel awful.'

'So must Tim,' Katie pointed out.

'Do you think you'll get the missing money back now?' Frankie asked.

Sophie shrugged. 'I don't see how this will make any difference. Tim hasn't got the money and I believed Carolyn when she said she hadn't either.'

Frankie looked at Sophie sympathetically. 'You'd have been able to stay in your flat and keep La Madeleine if that money hadn't been stolen, wouldn't you?'

'Too late now,' Sophie was resigned, 'they're both under offer and I think the sales will go through. I've found a flat near my mother, in Scardale Villas. I've made up my mind and there's no turning back now.'

'What about Tim?' Katie asked. 'What's going to happen to him?'

'He'll be charged with attempted murder, grievous bodily harm, embezzlement and fraud,' Sophie replied succinctly. 'I expect he'll be in prison for the next few years and I'm just thankful he's out of my life.' She didn't mean to sound hard, but she still felt shattered by the way Tim had used her. 'The important thing is,' she continued, 'Gloria Antica is safe and so are your positions. I've got great plans for the future and the first thing I'm going to do is take on a public relations company to get us into all the art journals. We must also take a stand at the Grosvenor House Antique Fair.'

She leaned back in her chair and picked up the newspaper again. The face of Carolyn gazed back at her from under the dramatic headline and Sophie couldn't help feeling sorrow for the victim who had turned persecutor. Raped at fifteen, she'd had to become a control freak in order to survive. Being in control had meant she'd never be hurt again. Until, on a grey afternoon in July, the hurt had become self-inflicted.

A week later her bank manager Mr Turnbull phoned her.

'Hello, Mr Turnbull,' she said, 'how is everything going?'

'I have some news for you, Mrs Duval.' Sophie could tell by his voice that something was up. She braced herself for bad news.

'A most extraordinary thing has happened,' he began, 'and it's only just come to light.'

Sophie, about to leave for work, put down her brief-case and handbag. 'What's happened?'

'It appears someone tipped off Brock Duval about Tim Calthorpe's activities. This was before you'd actually reappointed your accountants to look after your affairs, when you began to have your own suspicions.'

'And?'

'With the multitude of contacts Mr Duval had in the banking world, he was able to trace where the money was going after it was stolen from your US dollar account. Something that most people would be quite unable to do. He managed to trace the three million pounds to the numbered account set up by Tim Calthorpe in Switzerland.'

She frowned, perplexed. 'So he knew what Tim had done with it?'

'Exactly.' Mr Turnbull seemed to pause for dramatic effect. 'It was Brock who withdrew the money.'

'No!' She gripped the phone to her ear and her heart raced. 'No!' she repeated.

'The manager of that Zurich bank broke every rule in the book when he let Brock know what the code word was. Of course Brock explained the money had been stolen from you.'

She'd always known Brock was immensely powerful

but this made her catch her breath. 'So where is it now?' she asked excitedly, and then immediately realised her hopes were foolish. Brock had died bankrupt. Her money would have gone down with his.

Mr Turnbull was still talking and she only heard the last word: '. . .Hamburg.'

'What was that?'

'Brock put your three million pounds in a deposit account in your name, and that's where it is now, in Hamburg,' Mr Turnbull repeated.

Sophie closed her eyes. 'I haven't lost it, then?' She didn't dare believe it.

'You haven't lost it,' Mr Turnbull confirmed. 'Does it come in time to save your flat and your villa?'

It had come in time. Just. She now had all the money Brock had originally given her, but she immediately decided she would use it for her business. If she was really going to start again, it would be better to get rid of the trappings of the past.

When she'd told Mr Turnbull she was still going to sell, she added, 'Why didn't Brock tell me what he'd done?'

'Maybe he had his reasons. Perhaps he wanted you to find out for yourself what Tim Calthorpe was like,' Mr Turnbull carefully suggested.

Sophie's eyes widened. It was a shrewd remark and it surprised her. She'd always thought the bank manager judged people in terms of pound signs rather than personality, and collateral rather than compassion.

'You may be right,' she replied slowly.

'Brock wouldn't have known he was going to die, so I imagine he planned to tell you what he'd done as soon as you discovered the extent of Tim Calthorpe's fraudulence.'

So Brock was thinking of me right up to the end, Sophie reflected silently. Protecting me, watching out for me, seeing that I was all right. 'Thank you, Brock,' she said under her breath. For a moment her eyes brimmed with tears. Brock had been the absolute opposite to Tim. One had given, the other had taken. One was devoted, the other selfish beyond belief. One had been strong, the other weak.

'Thank you for ringing me up to tell me, Mr Turnbull,' she said shakily, glad that she was at home so that he couldn't see how emotional she felt.

Walking slowly to the shop, deep in thought at the sudden change of fortune that had befallen her, Sophie realised for the first time that she was really on her own now. No Brock in the background to turn to. No Tim to ask advice from. She had the responsibility of managing her shop and the three million pounds that she would use to invest in stock, and she had Katie and Frankie to think about. They'd shown amazing loyalty to her over the past few months, and they'd run the shop during her absences with efficiency and flair. Now it was up to her to make sure she didn't fail.

She didn't recognise him at first, standing on the pavement outside Gloria Antica, looking up and down the street as if he was waiting for someone. She drew nearer, and looking into the pale face with the skin stretched tightly over his features, she realised with a profound shock that it was Tim.

He spoke first, while she gazed at him with something like horror.

'Hello, Sophie.' His voice was low, strained. His shoulders sagged and he'd lost weight.

'What are you doing here?' She couldn't help sounding alarmed. Had he escaped from prison? Was he on the run? Did he expect her to give him sanctuary?

Tim looked around, helplessly, like someone who has lost his way and can't find the return route. 'Can we go somewhere? I want to talk to you,' he said diffidently.

Sophie saw a hint of the little-boy look that she knew so well.

'How dare you come here!' she exploded, enraged. 'I have *nothing* to say to you.'

He didn't move, but continued to stand there, dejected and apologetic looking. 'It's all right, Sophie. I'm out on bail. My trial doesn't come up for months yet. I'm on my way back to Wales but I wanted to see you first.'

She blinked. 'Bail?' She wasn't sure whether to believe him or not. Who would bail him? He had no family and Carolyn was dead.

Tim nodded. 'Ginny and Jonathan Howard have bailed me.'

If he'd said the man in the moon, Sophie could not have been more surprised. 'In God's name, why should they do that?' she asked bluntly.

He looked around, conscious of people pushing past them on the narrow pavement. 'Please, Sophie. Couldn't we go inside? Just for a few moments?'

She pushed open the door of Gloria Antica. 'OK. But only for a couple of minutes.' Stony-faced, she led the way into the shop, to be confronted by Frankie and Katie. They were looking beyond her, at Tim, with fascinated interest.

'We'll only be a couple of minutes,' Sophie remarked, striding towards the back office. 'If we have any customers, I don't want to be disturbed.' She raised her wing-shaped eyebrows at them and they nodded in silent understanding.

Sophie sat at the desk in the chair that Tim had used when he'd been doing her accounts. He lowered himself, as if movement was an effort, into the opposite chair.

'So?' she began. 'What the hell are you doing here?'

Tim looked pained and she realised in that moment that his conceit was so colossal he'd imagined he'd be able to get under her skin again if he played his cards right.

'As I said, the Howards have bailed me out. When they heard about Caro, they flew over here immediately,' he explained.

'To console the grieving widower? That's twice in six months. Except you aren't a widower because you never married.'

'Oh, please, Sophie. You've no idea what I've been through.' Tim closed his eyes as if suffering from inner agony.

'What *you've* been through?' Her mouth fell open at his audacity.

'I don't mean since I was arrested. I mean since I first met Caro in Australia.' Then he described the car accident in Sydney and how for all these years Carolyn had made him believe he'd been driving at the time.

'I thought I'd killed the girl!' he exclaimed, and the wet glistening in his eyes was not feigned. 'Imagine! All these years I've been living with that nightmare, plus the added fear that at any time Caro might expose me if I didn't do as she said.' He dropped his head into his hands and when he spoke again, his voice was choked. 'Caro blackmailed me at every level. She pressured me night and day to do everything she wanted.'

'And you expect me to feel sorry for you?' Sophie demanded. 'Listen, Tim. Carolyn was very sick. The kindest thing, if you hadn't been so concerned with saving your own skin, would have been to help her get psychiatric treatment, years ago. She was demented! Why did no one do anything about it?'

'At times she seemed fine.' His tone was sullen now. 'When we had lunch with you, that first time, at La Madeleine, she was OK.'

Sophie thought back, remembering how Carolyn had played with her young nieces, almost like a child herself.

'Didn't Ginny and Jonathan realise she was ill?'

Tim raised his flushed, tear-stained face. 'No. They thought she was manipulative. Neurotic. They told me last week that they'd always felt sorry for me. They thought we were married, of course.' He sighed deeply. 'That girl has ruined my life.'

'And of course you've never done anything to be ashamed of,' Sophie said sarcastically.

'I don't expect you to forgive me, just like that,' he said earnestly.

'You're dead right.'

He looked at her wretchedly, his eyes red-rimmed. 'I know I've treated you terribly badly . . .'

'Terribly badly?' she echoed incredulously. 'Isn't that a bit of an understatement for attempted murder?'

'I know. I know.' Tim shook his head. 'I should never have listened to Caro.'

Sophie suddenly felt quite sickened by the snivelling self-pity of this wreck of a man who sat slumped before her. 'Get out of here, Tim,' she said, rising. 'Ginny and Jonathan may feel sorry for you, but I think you deserve everything a court of law can throw at you.'

'You've become awfully hard, Sophie,' he said pathetically. 'But I want you to know that everything I said earlier this year about loving you is true. Has always been true. The greatest mistake of my life was ever leaving you in the first place. God, that was a terrible mistake.' Tim paused, looking up at her as she stood behind her desk. 'In spite of everything, when this nightmare is over, really over, do you think...' He was pleading now, his eyes sweeping longingly over her body, exerting his sexuality. 'Have we a chance, darling?'

Sophie burst out laughing, and he drew back, as if stung. 'Dream on, Tim!' she exclaimed. 'What do you take me for?' Then she grew serious. She leaned forward, her hands on the desk, supporting her weight. 'You're about as low as they come,' she said scathingly. 'I can't think of anyone as debased as you. Now get out of here, and never, ever, come near me again.'

'But—'

'Get out, Tim,' her eyes sparkled angrily, 'or I'll call the police.'

Tim turned away, defeat written on every line of his face. 'I know how to make you happy. You loved me ... once,' he added.

A cold hand squeezed her heart. Had *he* ever loved

her? She straightened her shoulders. 'It's over, Tim.' She paused. 'But wouldn't you have been happy if I'd said yes and you realised I'd got back the money you stole from me.'

'You . . . ?' He turned grey, his mouth hanging open stupidly, his eyes blank.

'Yes,' she said pleasantly. 'Isn't that nice? Now goodbye, Tim. You know the way out.'

'I was horrified when I saw him, standing there, outside the entrance.' Sophie was having dinner with Jean and Alan. 'Can you believe the sheer gall of the man?'

Jean smiled, glad to see Sophie so much more settled in her mind than she'd been during the past few months.

'I bet he was shocked when you told him you'd recovered the money,' she remarked.

'Gutted,' Sophie replied with a pleased grin.

'Well, that about wraps everything up, doesn't it?' Alan observed with satisfaction. 'I don't think we'll be hearing from Tim Calthorpe again, except at his trial, of course.'

'What I don't understand,' Sophie said, 'is who tipped off Brock? I know he didn't like Tim but he had no reason to think he was going to embezzle my money.'

'I told him,' Alan said quietly.

'You?' Sophie looked stunned. 'But when we talked, you said you hadn't seen Brock for over a year.'

'Quite right. At that point it was true, but as you wouldn't listen to my words of warning I got hold of Brock and told him of my suspicions. Just as well, wasn't it?' He looked supremely self-satisfied.

Sophie gazed at her stepfather, dumbfounded.

Jean burst out laughing. 'He's a wily old fox, isn't he?' she chortled.

'Alan, be my chief business adviser,' Sophie said, half jokingly.

He looked at her with affection. 'You've come such a long way in the past couple of years, you don't need anyone, Sophie. You're truly in control of your life now.'